Please return on or before the latest date above.
You can renew online at *www.kent.gov.uk/libs*
or by telephone 08458 247 200

LOVE AFFAIRS FOR GROWN-UPS

LOVE AFFAIRS
FOR GROWN-UPS

Debby Holt

WINDSOR
PARAGON

First published 2009
by Simon & Schuster
This Large Print edition published 2009
by BBC Audiobooks Ltd
by arrangement with
Simon & Schuster UK Ltd

Hardcover ISBN: 978 1 408 42791 0
Softcover   ISBN: 978 1 408 42792 7

British Library Cataloguing in Publication Data available

Printed and bound in Great Britain by
CPI Antony Rowe, Chippenham, Wiltshire

This book is dedicated to the memory of my gloriously peculiar father, Keith Erskine, and my long-suffering but very loving mother, Audrey Erskine.

Many thanks to Philip Addis of Great Western Wine for being so generous with his time and knowledge and to my husband, David, for correcting all my mistakes about the world of law. My son, James, gave me an inspirational day out and I am as always indebted to my agent, Teresa Chris, and my editor at Simon & Schuster, Kate Lyall Grant. Final thanks to my actress daughter, Rosie, for help in all things Dramatic: go, light up the world, Rosie!

CHAPTER ONE

A Difficult Introduction

Cornelius stood on the deck and watched the white cliffs of Dover slowly recede into insignificant dots. He was not in a good mood. In fact, he was in a very bad mood and it was all Douglas's fault.

Douglas had been working for Cornelius for three years now and possessed many sterling qualities. He was an excellent office manager. He was bright, ambitious and quick to learn. He liked people; he liked to *help* people. He was friendly and sociable and full of enthusiasm. On the minus side, he never *stopped* being full of enthusiasm. Working with Douglas was like being in a room with a 150-watt light bulb. And because Douglas was sociable and liked people, he didn't understand anyone who wasn't sociable and who didn't like people.

Consequently, Douglas was impregnably convinced that Cornelius would *love* to meet Douglas's wife's solicitor friend on the SpeedFerry out to Boulogne. He was convinced that Cornelius would *love* to give a lift to the unknown woman and share an enclosed space with her all the way down to Montelimar. Douglas thought it was a harmonious coincidence that Cornelius and the solicitor woman were both travelling to the same destination. And, even better, Douglas said, they could travel home together again as well.

Cornelius had tried to make his feelings clear.

1

He had raised a variety of genuine objections. He wasn't sure which part of August he would be spending in France; he was an erratic driver; he was not very good at making conversation; he might decide to stop off for a night in Troyes. And furthermore, he would *not* be able to bring the woman home since he was only going to be in France for a week.

Most people would have understood that what Cornelius was *trying* to say was that he would rather fill his stomach with McDonald's beef burgers than give Douglas's wife's friend a lift. Not Douglas. Douglas assumed that everyone was as friendly and as eager to perform charitable acts as Douglas. In the face of such *niceness*, Cornelius found it difficult to explain that he *wasn't* very nice. He was reduced to throwing up objections which Douglas swatted with the same lethal success that he applied to errant wasps. The solicitor woman was happy to travel in whichever part of August suited Cornelius. The solicitor woman was apparently no stranger to erratic driving since she was teaching her son to drive. The solicitor woman was charming company who would entertain Cornelius all the way down to Montelimar. The solicitor woman would be very happy to spend the night in Troyes since she had always wanted to see its famous medieval architecture. And finally, Cornelius *would* be able to give the solicitor woman a lift back because she only wanted to stay a week in France anyway.

What Cornelius wanted to say was that he would rather sit through five party political broadcasts than give a lift to an unknown solicitor. What Cornelius wanted to say was that he didn't like to

2

share his car with people he *did* know, much less with some stranger who would probably talk like a hyperactive monkey. What he *did* say, faced with Douglas's implacable good nature, was that while he would be able to give the woman a lift, she should be warned that he would no longer be staying overnight in Troyes itself but would instead book a simple bed and breakfast in a small and primitive hamlet some twenty kilometres away.

Douglas reported back that the solicitor woman thought the hamlet sounded fascinating. Cornelius hated her already.

When he drove his car onto the boat, he contemplated the tempting idea of failing to find her. His conscience, always unpredictable, would not let him pursue this train of thought. More to the point, the SpeedFerry was far too small and intimate to guarantee the success of such a possibility. The woman had sent him an email in which she told him that she would have a large blue-and-white-striped canvas bag and she would wear a red rose fixed to her jacket lapel. The red rose carried with it a terrifying connotation of romantic assignations. For a terrible moment, Cornelius wondered if Douglas had been trying to play Cupid, but he knew that Douglas was far too straightforward to descend to subterfuge.

Glumly, Cornelius left the deck and wandered into the TV room where parents with glazed eyes sat watching appalling cartoons with their screeching offspring. He walked on, past the Duty Free shop and up the stairs. His eyes scanned the bar where passengers were already scoffing croissants and Danish pastries. Did they not *know* that they would soon be landing in a country that overflowed with the freshest of baguettes, the creamiest of cheeses and the best fruit and vegetable stalls in the world? He checked the tables and chairs down the left side of the boat and began to feel almost hopeful. Then he turned to the right side.

A woman was sitting at the back. She had no companion. She held a book in her hands but was gazing out of the window. It had to be her. On the table in front of her was a large blue and white canvas bag. Attached to the top buttonhole of her denim jacket was a generous red rose. He saw her take a mobile from her bag and as she checked it, he studied her surreptitiously.

From what he could see, she was short and reasonably slim. He guessed she was in her early forties. The pink and white top she wore under her jacket clashed with the orangey redness of the rose. She looked like she dressed for comfort rather than for fashion. She had soft, brown, shoulder-length hair and a wispy fringe that was far too long. Twice he saw her push it back from her face. She put down the mobile, looked up and caught his eye. He tried to hide behind the women in front of him but they were too short. Escape was impossible. He squared his shoulders and moved forward towards her.

*   *   *

Katrina hadn't even wanted to go to France. When she thought about it, her relationship with her sibling was punctuated by the numerous occasions on which she had agreed to do something which almost immediately she had regretted. These

4

moments would be followed by long periods of self-loathing in which she would promise herself that she would never again be talked into doing something she had not wanted to do. She would be calm, she would be rational, she would give herself time to develop a measured response. And the phone would ring and ten minutes later she would be hitting her head with a cushion, furious with her lemming-like behaviour in the face of her sister's supremely confident assurance that Katty would always think everything she suggested was brilliant.

There was the occasion twelve years earlier when her sister had decided to have a party to celebrate the fact that she was changing her name from Margaret to Rose ('I've met this wonderful man,' she told Katrina. 'Three of my friends have used him. He's amazingly perceptive. He told Henrietta to change her middle name from Anne to May and she's never looked back. She organized the tennis club ball last month. Anyway, he says Margaret has had a hold over me for far too long. He says I am definitely a Rose.') She insisted that the party could not go ahead without Katrina and though Katrina knew very well that it could, she still found herself travelling down to Salisbury with her children. Once there, she was given a lukewarm cup of coffee before being dispatched to Longleat with her sister's children as well as her own, so that Margaret, or rather Rose, could concentrate on getting her nails and her hair done.

Katrina drove her charges round the Safari Park and it was while they were in the lion and tiger enclosure that twelve-year-old Cam vomited over her companions in the back of the car. Katrina was unable to turn round and drive back. Nor could

5

she open the windows, let alone the doors, since there were countless posters telling her to keep them firmly shut. By the time they got to the Exit gate, there wasn't a child in the car who wasn't threatening to throw up.

The most infuriating point about that entire weekend had been the fact that Katrina had *known* she would have a terrible time. Her supine response to Rose's suggestions flew in the face of a lifetime's experience. And yet she never learnt.

Just a few months ago, Rose, in mourning for her husband who had died quite unexpectedly last summer, made one of her more exacting requests. She rang Katrina and came to the point immediately. 'I want you to have our cat,' she said. 'You know how Roger adored him. Every time I see that little furry face, it reminds me of Roger and I start crying all over again. Omo has to go. You will have him, won't you, Katty?'

Katrina did, even though she didn't like cats, even though Omo was possibly the nastiest and smelliest feline that had ever stalked the planet. Omo had immediately taken possession of Katrina's favourite armchair and had hissed furiously when she tried to remove him. Katrina had retaliated by marching to her study and sitting at her desk, from which she took out some paper and a pen. Then she sat down and made a list of all the things she had done for her sister that she had not wanted to do. The idea behind this labour-intensive operation was to make sure she had a tangible warning she could whip out whenever the need arose.

The list was long and infinitely depressing. It included some of the more notorious dares with which the young Margaret had challenged the even younger Katrina, the most memorable being the suggestion that Katrina should emulate Tarzan's exploits in their grandmother's garden, resulting in a two-week stay in hospital. Then there was the terrible afternoon when thirteen-year-old Katrina had let her sister cut her hair before an all-important party. It left her looking like evil Uncle Andrew in *The Magician's Nephew*. Margaret said it made her look mad and zany and fun. Katrina knew it simply made her look mad.

So when Rose rang, in April, to invite Katrina to spend some of her precious six weeks' annual leave in France, Katrina reached for the list and clutched it as if it were a bulb of garlic in the presence of a vampire. Unfortunately, Rose was, as she reminded Katrina, at her most vulnerable. 'I still can't believe Roger has died,' she said. 'I keep expecting him to walk in and surprise me. I'm trying so hard to make a new start and it isn't easy after twenty-seven years of marriage. Anyway, I've bought a house in France—'

'You've bought a house in France!' Katrina exclaimed. 'I thought you were moving up to London next month? You've only just bought the flat in Kensington! You're not planning to move abroad, are you?'

'Of course I'm not,' Rose said. 'I've bought it as an investment. I shall let it out for holidays. I've done a wonderful brochure. I'll send it to you. And it will also be a bolt hole for me and the kids. Katty, you'll love it, it's in the Drôme region—all lovely mountains and vast plains. It's got a huge courtyard with a perfect olive tree in the middle and there's a swimming pool and table-tennis.

7

We're going out for the month of August and I want you to come. I'd love to invite your two but Sam and Cam are both bringing their partners of the moment and there isn't the room. You will come, won't you?'

Katrina gripped her list and swallowed. 'That's very sweet of you but there's no way I can take a month off work and—'

Rose interrupted her impatiently. 'Surely you can manage two weeks at least?'

'Not really,' said Katrina, staring at her list, 'I mean, there are the children to think of and . . .'

'They're hardly children any more,' Rose said. 'Susie's in her last year at university, for heaven's sake! Were you planning to go on holiday with them? What are you doing?'

'Nothing *as such*,' Katrina conceded. 'Ollie's starting work with a car-hiring company as soon as his A Levels are over and Susie's spending most of August in Edinburgh with her boyfriend. But I thought I'd take one or two weeks off and catch up on the garden. It looks like a jungle at the moment.'

'That sounds very dull! And what will you do if it rains? Come to France! Come and swim in our pool! Get a suntan! Oh, Katty, do come. It's just going to be me and the kids and their partners. It's virtually my first holiday without Roger and I shall be the sole adult there in the presence of two pairs of very horny young lovers . . . Please come!' There was a pause and Katrina heard Rose give a forlorn sniff. 'I really do need some support at the moment.'

It was the sniff that did it. Katrina said that it *would* be fun to see the new house. She agreed that

Ollie was quite capable of looking after himself for a fortnight. She agreed it would be lovely to spend some quality time with her niece and nephew. She agreed it would do her good to get away.

It was only after she rang off that Katrina remembered that Rose had, in fact, had three holidays since Roger's death: a trip with her children to Corsica after the funeral, a week with one of her friends in Paris in the autumn and a restorative fortnight in the Caribbean in January.

Katrina went through to the sitting room, picked up a cushion from the sofa and hit herself on the head with it. She could see Omo, from the comfort of his armchair, staring at her. She could have sworn he sniggered.

The next day, at work, Katrina snapped at the blameless trainee solicitor with whom she currently shared her office. This was unfair. Carol, an energetic young woman with big teeth and a puppy-like enthusiasm, had been quite in order to ask her about the seminar on communication skills that afternoon and Katrina apologized at once, explaining that she had just agreed to go on holiday to France in August.

'Oh, I see,' said Carol, who clearly didn't see at all.

'I know,' Katrina admitted ruefully. 'I'm very lucky and I sound horribly ungrateful, don't I? It's only that, to be perfectly frank, I'd far rather stay at home for a fortnight. And there's the journey. It's right down in the south of France in Montelimar and my sister's expecting me to drive there and French roads terrify me. I keep forgetting I should be on the right side. It's almost as difficult as teaching my son to drive.'

9

'Is it *very* difficult to teach your son to drive?'

Katrina pushed her hair back from her forehead. 'You see those wrinkles? I swear I didn't have them before I let Ollie drive me around.'

'Well, anyway,' said Carol, trying to be helpful, 'Montelimar isn't nearly as far as you think. It's more in the middle of France than the south.'

'It's still far too far away,' Katrina said. 'France is a very big country.'

Carol laughed and went out, which surprised Katrina because, in the short time she had known her, she had discovered that Carol never abandoned a problem without finding a solution to it. Carol would have made a brilliant agony aunt: *Dear Disappointed, I am sorry you did not get the promotion you have been working for throughout the last ten years but you must try to move on. Have you thought about switching careers? England is very short of vicars at the moment.* Actually, Carol would be a very irritating agony aunt.

Three days later Carol came into the office with a smug smile on her face. 'I've sorted it,' she said.

Katrina eyed her warily over her glasses. 'You've sorted what?'

'Your holiday! As soon as you said Montelimar, it rang a bell and then when I got home and told my husband about it, he reminded me. Douglas's boss is going to Montelimar in August!'

'Is he?' asked Katrina absently. She had just read an email asking for feedback on the seminar on communication skills and was wondering what she could say. Unfortunately, she had fallen asleep while the lecturer was giving extremely long examples of how to calm a difficult client by repeating back to him everything he had said.

10

'Yes, he is,' said Carol, 'and Douglas has asked him if he could give you a lift down there and he said he'd be delighted. He'll give you a lift back as well.'

Katrina took off her glasses to direct an appalled glance at her trainee. 'That's very nice of your husband but he shouldn't have gone to so much trouble. And I certainly can't ask someone I don't know to give me a lift all the way to—'

'He wants to help you!' Carol crowed. 'End of story!'

Katrina stared at her trainee solicitor. She wanted to say that she would rather risk the dangers of driving on the wrong side than have to make polite conversation with Douglas's boss all the way down to Montelimar. Carol was smiling happily at her.

'Look,' Katrina said, 'it's very kind of you and your husband and his boss but—'

'There's only one problem,' Carol conceded. 'He's only going for a week and I know you were planning to go for a fortnight.'

Katrina hesitated. Could she really turn down such a perfect excuse to halve her holiday with her sister? She smiled at Carol. 'A week would suit me very well.'

'I'm sure you'll get on,' Carol said. 'Douglas thinks he's very nice though he also says he's rather odd. And he has a very peculiar name . . .'

*   *   *

So now, thanks to Carol, she was sitting on the ferry or the catamaran or whatever it was, determinedly staring out at the sea and very definitely not looking for a rather odd man. If she failed to find him, she could get a train down to Montelimar and get Rose to meet her at the station.

Her mobile made a noise and Katrina reached into her bag. She pulled it out and was intent on reading the message when she suddenly felt conscious of being watched. She glanced up and caught the eye of an extraordinary-looking man who was standing behind two generously proportioned ladies of uncertain age. If she didn't know better she would think he was trying to hide from her. She could have sworn he deliberately ducked his head a few moments ago. She saw him glance at her bag and wondered if he were Douglas's boss. He wore green corduroy trousers, a grey shirt and a battered-looking black velvet jacket. He was very tall and very thin and his limbs looked as if they had been stuck to his frame at the last moment. He had a tousled mass of rust-coloured curls and an aquiline nose on which perched a pair of large, dark-framed spectacles. She reckoned he was older than her: probably in his late forties or early fifties. His appearance was strangely familiar, yet she was sure she'd never seen him before. Flustered and unsure whether to hail him or not, she turned back to her phone.

*   *   *

Cornelius saw her look down at her mobile again and wondered if she really was the solicitor woman. After all, she probably wasn't the only woman to own a blue-and-white-striped canvas

12

bag. He approached her uncertainly. He could see she possessed a superb complexion. Her skin was almost translucent. He gave a small cough and said diffidently, 'Excuse me.' He coughed again. 'My name is Cornelius Hedge and I think I'm supposed . . .'

The woman looked up at him and promptly burst into tears.

CHAPTER TWO

A Display of Emotional Incontinence

Cornelius stared at her in horror and suppressed a craven urge to turn on his heels and run. The woman was *really* crying: heaving shoulders, a succession of rasping sobs that sounded like an automatic rifle going off, tears coursing down her cheeks. It was awful, he had no idea what to do. He reached into his jacket pocket, pulled out a handkerchief and held it out. 'I'm so sorry,' he stammered. 'I thought you . . . I wasn't sure . . . I didn't mean to startle you . . . I'll go . . .'

The woman shook her head violently. She had covered her mouth with one hand and accepted the handkerchief with the other.

Cornelius could sense a swell of interest from passengers across the aisle. A quick glance confirmed that a woman with pink-framed glasses and orange lipstick was staring at him quite ferociously. Hastily, he returned his full attention to the crying woman. 'Would you like some coffee?' he asked desperately. 'Shall I get you some strong, black coffee, or tea? Would you prefer tea?'

The woman nodded gratefully but continued to keep her hand clamped to her mouth. This was just as well since, despite the hand clamp, a strangulated sob managed to escape. The woman was like a pressure cooker, primed to explode, and Cornelius made a hasty escape to the refreshment bar. There was a long queue, for which he was grateful. He had no idea whether she wanted tea or coffee, so he decided he would order both. He kept his eyes fixed on the pastries, which now seemed rather enticing—funny how stress always made him hungry. Silently, he cursed Douglas.

When he returned to the woman, she was holding her book in front of her. She sat, rigid and stiff. Cornelius had a sudden recollection of a film he'd once enjoyed called *Clash of the Titans*; there had been a rather good scene where dozens of cracks suddenly spread across the statue of the goddess Hera until it fell to the ground with a terrible crash. He hoped the same sort of thing wouldn't happen to the woman. Her eyes were red and puffy but at least she'd stopped crying and her cheeks were no longer wet.

He put the tray he was carrying on the table in front of her. 'I thought you might be hungry,' he said, 'so I bought a couple of pastries.'

'That's very kind but I had a sandwich when I got on the boat.' She put down her book and, fixing him with anxious eyes, waited until he had sat down opposite her. 'I must apologize,' she said. 'What a terrible thing to do to you. You must be wondering who on earth you've been landed with.'

'Yes,' said Cornelius, 'I did rather . . . I mean, I

14

don't know that I—'

'Can we start again, please?' The woman extended a hand. 'I'm Katrina Latham.'

Cornelius moved the tray and shook hands. 'And I'm Cornelius Hedge. Do you take sugar? I forgot to bring some over. I've got you a choice of drinks. This is tea and that's coffee.'

'I don't take sugar.' Katrina helped herself to the tea. 'Thank you. This is perfect.'

Cornelius tried to think of something to say, something that would divert her from attempting to explain why she'd been crying, because if she *did* try to explain why she'd been crying, she would inevitably start crying all over again. 'Is your book interesting?' he asked. 'What's it about?'

She put her cup down and swallowed hard and, for a ghastly moment, Cornelius thought she was going to start the sobbing again. 'It's a biography of Mary Shelley,' she said. 'She's one of my heroines.'

'Really? How fascinating.' He would have liked to ask her why but he saw her take an abrupt sip of her tea. She blinked furiously and he surmised that for some reason Mary Shelley was not a safe topic of conversation.

The woman swallowed once more. 'Are *you* reading anything at the moment?' she asked with a pretty impressive assumption of interest.

'I am indeed,' Cornelius said. He pulled from his jacket pocket a dog-eared paperback. '*Hegemony or Survival* by Noam Chomsky. It is the most brilliant book. Everyone should read it. It is a *total* book, if you know what I mean.'

Katrina moved her cup to one side and rested her arms on the table. 'No, I don't.' She gave a

15

small sigh; it sounded like a car tyre losing air. 'What *do* you mean?'

'It's a particular sort of book.' Cornelius spoke with a nervous enthusiasm, propelled by a keen desire to convince the woman he had already forgotten her extraordinary behaviour. 'It makes one see everything in a totally different way. Basically, Chomsky's thesis is that given the choice of hegemony over the world or survival of the species, American governments have always gone for hegemony. It's very interesting.' He couldn't help noticing that the woman with pink-framed glasses was listening to him. Perhaps she too was a fan of Chomsky. 'He makes a distinction between American *people*, whose energy and enthusiasm he admires, and American presidents, whose collective arrogance appals him. He doesn't have a good word to say about any of the presidents.'

'Does he have any gossip about them?' Katrina asked.

'*Gossip?*' Cornelius repeated. 'No, he doesn't have gossip. He's not that sort of man.'

'What a pity,' Katrina said. 'You can learn so much from all the little personal stories.'

Cornelius raised his eyebrows. 'Can you? I'm not sure I agree.'

'I've always felt this about history textbooks,' Katrina said. 'They tell you all about political trends and movements and laws and wars and forget that the people who start them are just like us: they're influenced by headaches and love affairs and misunderstandings. Shall I give you an example?'

'Please do.' Despite himself, Cornelius was interested. He was also, somewhat grudgingly,

16

impressed by the woman's determined attempt to ignore the fact that she had been on the verge of hysteria a few minutes earlier.

Katrina took another sip of her tea. She continued to sit bolt upright, like someone who was being interviewed for a job she knew was beyond her capabilities. 'For the first few years of his reign,' she said, 'Louis the Sixteenth had a minor sexual abnormality that made his erections painful. Consequently, he got in the habit of getting rid of his frustrations on the hunting ground. As a result, he spent too little time finding out how discontented his people were, and as a result: bingo! The French Revolution happened.'

'That is very intriguing,' Cornelius allowed. 'But I can't help thinking the causes of the French Revolution might be a little more complex.'

'Of course they are. I'm simply saying that one man's sexual malfunction played a part in it. The personal is always important. I was watching a documentary about the Middle East a few weeks ago and Madeleine Albright described how President Arafat had once stalked out of a meeting and climbed into his car. She said she ran after it and as it tried to get away she beat upon the windows and made it stop. Now, I think that story says more about her character than any number of academic assessments. And, by the way, she was wearing high heels.'

'She must have run very fast if she caught up with a moving car.'

'Perhaps it was trying to turn round. Or perhaps it was going very slowly.' Katrina picked up her cup and drank her tea, sip after sip, like a child drinking her medicine. Her brief attempt at

17

animated conversation appeared to have exhausted her, which was a pity since he had hoped to hear more about the Madeleine Albright interview. Cornelius helped himself to the black coffee.

Katrina cleared her throat. 'I think I'll go and freshen up. And then I might get a little fresh air. I'll make sure I'm back here before the boat docks. It gets in at midday, doesn't it?' She stood up and hoisted her bag onto her shoulder. 'Thank you for the tea. I will see you in a little while.'

'Yes, indeed,' Cornelius said. He waited until she had left and then he rearranged his limbs, stretching his long legs out under the table. He was interested in that story about Louis XVI. It illustrated his belief that physical health played a dominant part in the history of one's life. He looked out of the window and wondered what had upset the solicitor woman so much. She was obviously deeply embarrassed about her violent display of emotion. He sincerely hoped she wouldn't repeat it. He sighed, picked up one of the Danish pastries and began to eat it.

*   *   *

Katrina fled to the Ladies and locked herself in a cubicle where she could weep in peace. It was clear that the poor man with the funny name thought she was completely crazy. She had burbled away in order to stop herself from crying any more but why had she had to burble about the failings of a man's penis, for heaven's sake? Even if it was a French king's penis. No wonder the man had looked at her with such horror.

18

She was hopeless. How could a name on a text message reduce her to this shrivelling body of incontinent emotion? How, after so many years, could Lewis still have the power to hurt her? It was so *sad* and *pathetic* and *feeble* and *wet*.

*   *   *

Katrina met Lewis Maltraver the day after her twenty-fifth birthday. She was acting for a television company which wanted to buy the warehouse it had been renting for the last few years. She had arranged to meet the client at the warehouse itself and when she arrived he gave her a tantalizingly brief tour of the place. She had glimpses of television cameras, colourful costumes, gesticulating people talking very loudly. It all seemed terribly exciting and Katrina, who had been quite satisfied with her appearance when she had set out, now felt that her trim grey suit was staid and dull. The best part of the tour was the last room she was taken to.

She couldn't believe it. There in the flesh in front of her were her favourite soap-opera stars from the *Medical Alert* series: sexy Dr Rubin, terrifying Mr Garside, who was possibly the most unpleasant consultant in the world, capable Sister Green, Alf, the cheery hospital porter who nursed a secret love for Sister Green, and, currently crying her eyes out, Dr Rubin's on/off girlfriend, Angelica.

She watched Dr Rubin go up to Angelica and slap her. Angelica stopped crying at once. Dr Rubin clenched his fists and spoke in a voice that trembled with repressed rage. 'I've had it with you, Angelica,' he said. 'I'm tired. I want you out of my

19

life. I can't be what you want me to be. I'm . . .' Dr Rubin stopped and gave a long, shuddering sigh. He looked so sad that Katrina felt a lump rise to the back of her throat. 'I'm tired,' he said, 'I am so, so tired.'

Angelica put out a faltering hand. 'But I love you!' she cried.

'You have sucked me dry!' Dr Rubin shouted. 'You have . . .' He stopped suddenly and grinned broadly. 'I am sorry,' he said, 'but there is no way I can broadcast to the nation that Angelica has sucked me dry.'

The client coughed nervously by the door and said perhaps they should move on. Reluctantly, Katrina followed him out but not before she had taken one last look at gorgeous Dr Rubin and not before, miracle of miracles, he had glanced across the room and smiled at *her*.

After her meeting, the client invited her to have lunch with him in the canteen. They were standing in the queue when Dr Rubin himself came up. 'Tom,' he said to the client, 'Gary wants to see you.'

'I can't,' said the client. 'I'm having lunch with my solicitor.'

'I'll have lunch with her if you like,' said Dr Rubin. 'Gary needs to see you now.'

The client looked anxiously at Katrina. 'I'm so sorry,' he said. 'I'd better see what Gary wants. I think we've sorted everything out. Do you mind if Lewis here looks after you instead of me?'

Katrina smiled. 'I'm sure I can manage.'

Lewis was a little smaller than he looked on television but his eyes were just as warm and rich and sympathetic and had an engaging twinkle that made him look as if he was permanently on the edge of laughter. Afterwards, she couldn't remember much of what they talked about. He was very pleased that she watched *Medical Alert* every week and he talked about some of the people on the show. What she did remember was that he kept his eyes on her all the time and that he made her, for the first time in her life, feel she was beautiful and beguiling.

Never had she left a canteen more reluctantly. But she had a meeting to go to and she was already late. She stood up and told him how much she had enjoyed herself. He asked if he could take her to dinner on Friday. She didn't hesitate.

He picked her up and drove her to a pub overlooking the Thames. She drank too much ('I'm driving,' he insisted. 'You have to drink for both of us.') and listened to the stories of backstage gossip with rapt attention and increasingly less concern about concealing the extent of her infatuation. Over coffee he took her hand and put his face close to her own. 'Do you want to know what I want to do?'

Katrina had a pretty good idea and there would be a time when she would cringe at the memory of her response. 'Tell me,' she whispered.

'I want to take you home,' he said. 'I want to go to your bedroom with you and I want to take your clothes off. I want to put my tongue in your mouth, I want to put your breasts in my mouth and most of all I want to taste you and feel you and love you. Shall we go?'

Katrina was a solicitor who specialized in commercial property law. She had successfully seen off office Lotharios and she prided herself on being able to distinguish between genuine feeling and phoney seduction lines. She had been one of the few girls at university to see through the divinely beautiful Greg Haynes and was the only girl not to be surprised to discover that he kept an intimate chart of his sexual successes. And yet, despite this impressive track record, she responded to Lewis's outrageously explicit proposition with a shameless and indeed breathless affirmative.

When she woke the next morning, she remembered the nocturnal activity of a few hours earlier and experienced a tremor of desire. She felt his hand stroke her thigh and knew she had to make love to him again.

Which was a pity since her daughter came in at that precise moment and demanded to know who was in bed with her.

'I'm a friend of your mother,' Lewis said, removing his hand from Katrina's thigh. 'How do you do?'

Susie giggled and asked him if he'd like her to show him her polar bear. Lewis said he would love to see it and the little girl ran out of the room.

Lewis cast a quizzical glance at Katrina. 'You didn't tell me you had offspring,' he said.

'Does it matter?' she asked.

'Of course it does,' Lewis said. 'A few minutes ago, I was hoping to make love to you again and now –' he paused as Susie rushed back in with her bear and climbed onto the bed—'I am going to be introduced to a bear.'

He left after breakfast, assuring Katrina that he would ring the next day.

He didn't. By Wednesday, Katrina had stopped jumping every time the phone rang. She didn't tell

22

anyone about him. She was ashamed that she had behaved like the worst sort of star-struck fan. He probably slept with a different woman every night.

Then, late on Saturday evening, he came to see her. Katrina, who had just had a shower, tightened her dressing-gown belt and asked him what he wanted. He told her he had tried to stay away but he couldn't. He said he had a bottle of Barolo with him and would she at least have a glass of wine. She said she would.

He told her the publicity people had said that the main reason for the popularity of *Medical Alert* was the sexual chemistry between Dr Rubin and Angelica. In order to foster this, they liked the public to think that Lewis Maltraver and Penny Darlington were romantically involved in real life. He and Penny had promised not to flaunt any private relationships with other people. 'From the moment I saw you,' Lewis said, 'I was nuts about you but I knew I should leave you alone. I can offer you nothing. If we had a relationship, we'd have to keep it secret. You don't deserve that.'

'In that case,' Katrina said, 'why are you here now?'

Lewis thrust his fingers through his luxuriant brown locks. 'I've tried to keep away,' he said, 'I really have tried.'

'If you'd tried all that hard,' Katrina said tartly, 'you wouldn't be sitting here telling me.'

He smiled suddenly. 'My teachers always said I had no self-discipline.' He had a lovely smile. She let him pour her another glass of Barolo and he watched her take a sip. 'Look at you,' he said. 'Your hair is damp, you're wearing the frumpiest dressing gown I've ever seen, you're sitting primly

23

on the edge of your sofa like a child and you have not the first idea how sexy you are.'

This, Katrina thought, was very true but she had little time to recognize his perspicacity since he had joined her on the sofa and was kissing her passionately while untying her dressing-gown belt. She didn't want to give in to him, she wanted him to know how unhappy he had made her, but it was difficult to be severe when his right hand had expertly located the green light between her legs and his tongue was exploring her mouth in a manner that made her feel she was melting.

There was no doubt about it. Sex with Lewis was incredible. Sex with her husband had been regular and efficient. His attitude to love-making had been like his attitude to food. He appreciated it but he didn't want to spend too long on it. Lewis was a true gourmet. He liked to take his time, he liked to try different things and, for him, anticipation was almost as important as consummation. Katrina was utterly in thrall to him.

Six weeks later, he came to supper and told her it was over. Katrina had prepared a special meal: cream of Stilton soup, trout with caper sauce and lashings of spinach, and a fresh fruit salad. He told her he cared for her deeply but his career had to come first and he couldn't combine his job and a relationship. After he had gone, she went round the kitchen blowing out all the candles she had lit such a short time earlier.

At home, she played Patsy Cline's 'Crazy' night after night. It was how she felt. She *was* crazy for crying and she *was* crazy for loving him.

Then one evening, while sitting in bed with the *Evening Standard,* she saw a photograph of a

24

smiling bride, with the caption: *Angelica Marries Her Very Own Doctor.* Underneath, a few lines stated that Penny Darlington from *Medical Alert* had married her boyfriend, Dr Peter Woodstock, at St Andrew's Church in Kingwood, Surrey. Lewis Maltraver, the journalist had added a little coyly, arrived at the wedding hand in hand with another member of the *Medical Alert* cast, prompting speculation that Dr Rubin and Sister Green clearly enjoyed playing doctors and nurses.

Katrina never heard from Lewis again. In the months that followed, she felt like a drug addict trying to get clean. Some weeks she managed not to watch *Medical Alert* and, when she did succumb, she stared at the screen with a mixture of longing and loathing, a cast-iron recipe for a sleepless night. Five years later, when *Medical Alert* came off the air, she was both relieved and dismayed. One thing was for sure. She would never date an actor again.

CHAPTER THREE

The Mad Woman of Boulogne

As they drove off the ferry, Cornelius suggested a quick lunch in Boulogne. They parked and settled on a pavement café opposite an ancient stone church, in a cobbled square off the Grande Rue. Cornelius left Katrina to choose a table while he plunged into the café to order lunch.

When he came back, armed with wine and water, Katrina was sitting with her chin resting on her hand, gazing at a group of boys vying for the attention of two magnificently insouciant girls in matching sunglasses. Katrina was wearing sunglasses too and Cornelius hoped that she had adopted them because of the sun and not to hide the fact that she had been crying again. Casting an apprehensive glance at her, he set a glass and a small stoneware jug in front of her and sat down. 'I've got you a small pichet of house red,' he said.

'Aren't you having any?' she asked.

'I'll stick with water,' Cornelius said. 'I have a long drive.'

Katrina poured herself a drink and raised the glass. 'Well, then,' she said, 'cheers!'

'That rose on your jacket,' Cornelius said, 'looks remarkably fresh.'

'That's because it's not real. Carol—the wife of your friend Douglas—gave it to me. The red rose in the lapel idea was hers. She said I needed something to mark myself out. I thought it was all rather tacky . . . like one of those ghastly blind dates when you both hold copies of the *Communist Manifesto* and wear flowers in your buttonhole.'

'Have you ever been on a blind date?' Cornelius asked.

'Only once,' Katrina said. 'Once was enough.' She took off her glasses and began cleaning them with a tissue.

'Was it so terrible?'

'Depending on one's point of view, it was either a brilliant success or an absolute disaster. I ended up marrying the man.' For a moment her eyes met those of Cornelius and then she looked away.

'Well,' said Cornelius, 'well . . .'

Now she was looking at him again. 'Cornelius,'

26

she said, 'I want to say something . . .'

Oh, God, he thought, she's going to tell me why she was crying and then she's going to start crying *all over again*! He had to do something. He pushed back his chair and leapt to his feet. 'I'm terribly sorry,' he said, 'I've just remembered something. Would you mind very much if I left you for a few minutes? I would like to buy some local cheese for my friends while I'm in Boulogne. I won't be long. Will you be all right on your own?'

'Of course,' Katrina said. 'It's a beautiful day and I'm sitting on a pavement in France with a glass of wine in my hand! Take as long as you want. I'm very happy.'

He wished she hadn't been so accommodating. He raised an awkward arm and strode off. He felt irritated with her for making him feel guilty and for making him dream up some spurious excuse. He didn't even know if there *were* any cheeses peculiar to this area. He had simply panicked. He could have told her that he had a very positive lack of interest in any aspect of her private life, but in his experience women seemed to regard this as insulting. Escape seemed the only answer.

He found an excellent delicatessen in Rue Thiers and purchased a quite superb cheese of the Pays du Nord region called Cremet du Cap-Blanc Nez. This acquisition put him in such good humour that he felt he could cope with anything Katrina had to tell him. Food shops in France always put him in a good mood. Right now, for example, he was walking past strawberries that looked bigger and better than any in England and next to them were tomatoes shaped like small pumpkins, their skins so much richer in colour than those of their

27

anaemic, tasteless cousins across the channel.

Their lunch was on the table when he returned and he felt another twinge of guilt. 'You shouldn't have waited for me,' he reproached her. 'It will get cold.'

'The waiter brought it only a few moments ago,' Katrina assured him. 'Did you find some cheese?'

'I certainly did.' He passed it over. 'Have a smell.'

She did so. 'Lovely!' she pronounced. She passed it back. 'Cornelius, before you went, I wanted to tell you something.'

'You did?' asked Cornelius feebly. He took a piece of baguette and dipped it with great deliberation into his bowl of mussels.

'Yes,' said Katrina. 'I wanted to say that I insist on paying for this meal and for our dinner tonight. We'll also go halves on petrol. It's very kind of you to give me a lift but I insist on paying my way.'

She was not going to reveal her innermost turmoil. He was almost beginning to like her. 'You can pay for lunch,' he conceded handsomely, 'but you certainly won't pay for supper.' He was aware that he had lost her attention and followed, enquiringly, her line of vision.

'You see that girl walking towards us?' Katrina whispered fiercely. 'Don't say anything. Just watch.'

The young woman was slight and blonde and very well dressed. She wore a narrow charcoal skirt and a short-sleeved pink top that looked expensive. She carried two carrier bags that by their glossiness and stylish simplicity suggested their owner had recently patronized some of the more fashionable shops in the town. As a child,

Cornelius had loved an old book of fairy tales belonging to his mother. One of the illustrations showed fairies in a grotto. The girl, with her flyaway hair and her blank blue eyes, looked as if she had stepped straight out of that picture.

Cornelius waited until she had walked past them. 'She's very attractive,' he said politely.

'Shush!' Katrina commanded. 'Watch her.'

The young woman reached the end of the pavement. She stopped, turned, stamped one foot twice and then the other. Then she proceeded to walk back towards them. Her expression remained serious and intent. She looked neither to the right nor to the left. She walked past them and when she got to the edge of the Grande Rue she stopped, stamped her feet twice, one after the other, and turned again.

'I've been watching her,' Katrina said, 'ever since you went off. At first I thought she might be waiting for some friends but in that case she'd be looking out for them or checking her watch or talking on her mobile. But all she does is walk backwards and forwards, backwards and forwards, with this grave, determined expression on her face. And every time she gets to either end of the pavement she stamps her feet with such precision. She's young, she's beautiful, she obviously has money but I think . . . I really, really think . . . she must be mad.'

Cornelius blinked. 'Isn't that a rather premature judgement? There could be all sorts of reasons for her behaviour. She might have gum on her shoes. Or perhaps she has a spot on her foot and she can only ease the irritation by stamping it at regular intervals.'

29

Katrina tried to prise open one of her mussels before reluctantly discarding it. 'In that case,' she pointed out, 'she would have to have spots on *both* her feet, because she stamps them both, one after the other.'

'Perhaps,' Cornelius suggested, 'she's trying to discover how many times she can walk up and down and stamp her feet before she gets tired.'

Katrina raised her eyebrows. 'In that case, she is definitely mad. It's funny because you don't expect someone so young and so pretty to be completely bonkers. I mean, she looks quite normal.'

Cornelius poured some water into his glass and cast a surreptitious glance at the girl who was passing them again. 'The point is,' he said, 'that you think she's mad because she's doing something for which you have no obvious explanation. It seems to me that people are far too ready to dismiss as mad those individuals who choose to be different. Peculiar people are only peculiar until you know them.'

'Sometimes,' Katrina retorted, 'you only realize people are peculiar once you *do* know them.'

'Well,' said Cornelius, 'all I can say is that I know many people who are often described as crazy and they are not at all.'

'Really?' asked Katrina. 'Give me an example.'

'Well,' said Cornelius, frowning thoughtfully, 'I have a friend who's always wanted to be a robin. Whenever he's stressed, he goes into his garden and he spends half an hour being a robin.'

Katrina's chip remained suspended in her hand. 'I'm sorry?'

'He goes into the garden and he imagines himself into the state of mind of a robin and then he stays in that state of mind for half an hour. It does him no end of good.'

'Right,' said Katrina.

Her eyes were very expressive. Her eyes were laughing even before her mouth turned up at the corners. It was good to see her smiling. 'I have another friend,' he said. 'He spends his free time trying to be picked up by aliens.'

'How does he do that?'

'Oh, you know,' said Cornelius airily. 'He goes to the sorts of places that aliens might be interested in and walks around looking hopeful.'

'You have some very odd friends,' said Katrina.

'You might think James is the oddest of all. I'm spending the next week with him and his wife. He used to be an extremely successful merchant banker. He had a smart flat in Knightsbridge, he had a smart car and he took smart holidays. When he was thirty-seven, he fell in love with a French schoolteacher called Odile. He followed her out to France, gave up his job and took up painting.'

'Is he a good artist?'

'He is an appalling artist. He has never sold a painting in his life. Some people think Odile is mad because she thinks he's a genius. They live on Odile's income. He brings up their children, does the housework and the cooking and paints terrible paintings. A lot of people think he's mad.'

'I don't think that's mad,' Katrina said. 'I'd love to give up being a solicitor. I'd much rather spend my time painting bad pictures.'

'Why don't you?'

Katrina laughed. 'My daughter has just finished her degree and wants to be an actress which means I will probably have to support her indefinitely. My

31

son is going to university next year. I shall have to carry on working for a long time yet.'

'Doesn't their father help with money? I would have thought—' Cornelius stopped, momentarily paralysed by the terrifying thought that Katrina's weeping fit might have been caused by the very man he was now referring to. 'I'm sorry,' he said, looking at her uneasily, 'that was very rude of me. I was thinking aloud. It is none of my business, please forget I said anything!'

Fortunately, Katrina remained quite composed. 'I promise I'm not offended! My ex-husband can't afford to help. He has far too many other children. My sister always calls him the Serial Propagator. He left me before Ollie was born. He married again and had two more children. Then he abandoned them and took up with someone else. He left her when their child was four. Now he's on his fourth partner. She's pregnant with their second child so he'll probably leave *her* soon.'

'Oh, dear,' Cornelius said. 'He sounds a little careless.'

'Try irresponsible,' Katrina said. She took a sip of her wine. 'Tell me about the friends you're going to stay with. Do they live in Montelimar?'

'It's their nearest big town. They live in a little village called Cleon d'Andran. Are you staying in Montelimar?'

'No, it's near a place called Pont-de-Barret. If you drop me anywhere near Montelimar my sister will pick me up.'

'There's no need for that. Pont-de-Barret is only a little further on from Cleon d'Andran. I'll be happy to drop you at—'

'*Jul . . . eee!*' The frantic, anguished shout

32

stopped him in his tracks. Both Cornelius and Katrina turned and saw a lanky, unshaven man with shoulder-length black hair and a flimsy grey T-shirt and torn denim trousers running down the street towards them. He was flaying the air with his arms as if he was besieged by locusts.

For a moment, Cornelius wondered if the man had mistaken Katrina for someone else and then he saw that the blonde girl had halted her march and come to rest a few feet from their table. She stood absolutely still, like a guard at Buckingham Palace.

Now the young man ran across the road, with no regard to the traffic around him. When he reached the church, he paused to catch his breath before crying once again, '*Jul . . . eee!*'

It was as if that second shout destroyed some terrible enchantment. Quite suddenly the girl smiled and cried, '*Armand!*' before running into his arms like a little lost girl who's found her mother.

Cornelius looked at Katrina. She was smiling and her eyes had filled with tears. Cornelius couldn't blame her since he had a large lump in his throat and had to cough quite fiercely before it would go. 'You see?' he told Katrina. 'I told you she wasn't mad.'

*   *   *

When Katrina awoke, they were no longer on the motorway but were travelling along a tree-lined avenue with vast, flat fields that seemed to go on for ever. She yawned and struggled to sit up straight. 'I'm *so* sorry,' she said. 'How long have I been asleep?'

'A couple of hours.' Cornelius sounded unconcerned. 'We should be there soon.'

'I am *so* sorry,' Katrina repeated. 'I'm not used to drinking wine at lunch.'

'Don't apologize.' Cornelius swung right into a road that exchanged elegant plane trees for scruffy hedgerows. 'It's only now that I need some help. There's a map in the glove compartment. I've circled the village we're looking for. We came off the A26 at exit number thirty . . . Have you found it?'

Katrina reached into her bag for her glasses. She had never been very successful with maps. She could never quite work out what was right and what was left. At home, she only had to look at her London A to Z to feel slightly nauseous. Now, she opened out Cornelius's map and said in what she hoped was a confident voice, 'What road are we on now?'

'It should be the D8. Can you see it?'

Katrina frowned. She turned the map upside down and scrutinized it anxiously. After due consideration, she said judiciously, 'I think it *might* be a good idea if we stop for a moment.'

Cornelius braked and put on his hazard lights. 'Let's have a look,' he said. Katrina was worried that he would be able to see at once where they were and so reveal her ineptitude but he seemed to be as puzzled as she was.

A knock on his window made them both jump. Cornelius wound it down. A short, balding gentleman with small black eyes and a bulbous nose nodded politely. 'You are English,' he said. He was stating a fact, not asking a question.

'Yes,' said Cornelius, 'I'm afraid we are.'

'You are lost,' said the man. He was clearly a man of some prescience.

'I'm afraid we are,' agreed Cornelius. He reached over for the map and showed it to the good Samaritan. 'We're trying to get *there* and I know we're somewhere *here.*'

The man nodded again. 'I see you and I stop,' he said. 'I am the mayor! I know everywhere. You follow my car and I indicate the road you must take.'

'Thank you,' said Cornelius. 'You are very kind.'

The man gave a magnificently Gallic shrug. 'I am the mayor,' he said.

They watched him return to his car and pull out in front of them. 'How kind of him to stop,' Katrina said. 'That is so nice of him. I bet he's a brilliant mayor.'

Cornelius followed the mayor's car as it turned left at the T-junction. Their subsequent progress was slow since the mayor responded to every salutation from passers-by with a cheery wave and a booming comment. Finally, he stuck out his hand and pointed to the right with a dramatic flourish. Cornelius hooted his thanks and turned right into a narrow country lane.

'Well!' cried Katrina. 'What a lovely man! And everyone knows him! *That's* why I'd love to live in France! Name me one provincial town in England where the mayor is recognized by anybody! *That's* what's wonderful about France: people are proud of their own districts, they're proud of their mayors and they know who their mayors are. We've lost all that in England. Local governments have no power any more and we don't have pride

35

in our communities. Most of us don't even feel we're part of a community. I *wish* I lived in France.'

'Really?' asked Cornelius. 'Would that be your only reason for moving?'

'Why not? It's a jolly good reason. But I'd also move because the French appreciate beauty. No one in Britain ever plants trees along the roads. I like tree-lined avenues.'

'You'd get on very well with my friend James,' said Cornelius.

'Why?' asked Katrina suspiciously, sensing an insult.

'He loves tree-lined avenues too. He goes on and on about tree-lined avenues. He can talk about tree-lined avenues for hours. He's very odd.'

Katrina folded her arms. 'Your idea of "odd",' she told him, 'is very different from my idea of odd.'

Cornelius laughed. 'That is the precise point I was trying to make during lunch.'

Cornelius had a lovely smile. His face, normally so severe, looked completely different. Katrina felt absurdly pleased that she had made him smile.

'Aha!' said Cornelius. 'Here we are!' He turned into a large square and parked in front of a big house with white shutters and sand-coloured walls.

'Is this it?' Katrina asked. 'I thought we were staying in some rustic little hamlet?'

But Cornelius had already got out of the car and was striding towards the door. It was opened by an attractive woman with an hourglass figure and friendly eyes, who greeted them as effusively as was possible given that her language skills were obviously as great as Katrina's. Cornelius surprised both women by breaking into fluent French and engaging madame in polite interrogation. Finally, he turned to Katrina. 'Apparently, there's only one restaurant here and it closes early. Do you mind if we set out in twenty minutes?'

'Fine,' Katrina said. 'Knock on my door when you're ready.' She smiled and turned to the lady of the house. '*Merci, madame,*' she said, just to show that she *could* speak French.

Katrina's room was small and clean and cheerfully decorated in cream and apricot. As soon as she had shut the door, Katrina threw off her shoes, went to her bed and lay down. Within thirty seconds she was on her feet again. She was *not* going to think about Lewis tonight. She was not going to inflict any more scenes on poor Cornelius. She was going to try very hard to be an entertaining companion. Even if she had never felt less entertaining in her whole life. She went to the window, which looked out onto the square. At first glance, the village seemed to be deserted but she could hear laughter from the bar on the other side of the road.

Katrina turned away and went over to her hold-all. She hoped the restaurant was not too smart since all her clothes were in her suitcase in the boot of Cornelius's car. Never mind. She would not be deterred even if the place was full of chic French women. Tonight she was not going to let anyone or anything upset her.

She pulled out her wash bag and went through to the tiny bathroom. She stared at her reflection in the mirror and her mouth dropped. She looked horrific. The ravages of her epic weeping on the boat and her big sleep in the afternoon had

37

conspired to make her resemble a squashed tomato while her hair appeared to have received some electric-shock treatment. Katrina swallowed, checked her watch and prepared to execute a hasty damage-limitation exercise.

When Cornelius came to collect her, Katrina was relieved to find that he hadn't changed his clothes either. They walked across the square, past the bar and down a narrow street towards the restaurant.

Cornelius stopped outside a square, grey building with grimy blue shutters. Katrina followed him in and glanced round the small, spartan room. It had an arch in the middle through which could be seen a large dining room. To the left of the arch was a rickety table with three chairs that looked as if they might fall apart at any moment. The orange-painted walls were bare but for an opaque mirror at one end and an old, curling poster advertising some long-gone festival. The whole place smelt of defeat. Or perhaps of cabbage.

To the right of the arch was a bar behind which stood a bald-headed man with bags under his eyes and a dark, drooping moustache that looked utterly unreal. He was conducting a desultory conversation with the only customer, a scrawny-looking man in blue overalls. Both men stopped talking when they saw the visitors and sucked on their cigarettes at exactly the same moment.

Cornelius stepped forward. *'Bonsoir, monsieur,'* he said. *'Je voudrais dîner, s'il vous plaît . . .'*

The landlord sighed, turned away from Cornelius and called, 'Brigitte!'

Brigitte emerged from behind the arch. Katrina wondered if she'd been called after Brigitte Bardot. She didn't look like Brigitte Bardot. She

38

wore a grubby white apron and her hair was inexpertly tied back in a listless ponytail. She had protruding eyes which, together with the fact that she had lost teeth on either side of her mouth, gave her the appearance of a frightened rabbit. As she listened to Cornelius, her brow furrowed and then she launched into a long explanation that was accompanied by a variety of hand movements all of which seemed to indicate that a delicious supper was not on the way.

Cornelius replied in a soothing, placatory tone which resulted in another torrent of words from Brigitte and a grim shaking of the head from the landlord. Finally, Cornelius said, '*À bientôt.*' The woman nodded and scurried back through the arch. The landlord gave a short, unsmiling nod and lit another cigarette.

'Right,' Cornelius said, once they were outside on the pavement again. 'This is the situation. Brigitte and her husband don't usually cook beyond eight in the evening. I think most of their trade is at lunchtime. She suggests we go to the bar in the square for half an hour while she sees what she can put together for us. I have to warn you . . .' Cornelius looked at her apprehensively, 'the main course will be tongue.'

Katrina blinked but refused to be downhearted. 'Well,' she said bravely, 'that will be a new experience at any rate. Let's go and have a drink.'

The bar had an altogether jollier atmosphere. A young couple sat at a table with their small son. Two teenage boys were playing table football and accompanying every move with a lively commentary. At the bar itself sat a tall, handsome woman who was holding forth to the young barman and two elderly gentlemen.

'Remember,' Katrina said, 'I'm paying for this evening.'

'We can discuss that later,' Cornelius said. 'Let me get the drinks. Why don't you sit down?'

She watched him go to the bar and hail the barman. The woman immediately engaged him in animated conversation that included her thrusting her glass at him, along with much subsequent laughter from the company. At one point she turned and smiled at Katrina, who smiled back and wished she'd paid more attention to her language lessons at school.

Her attention was diverted by the small boy from the end table. He came up and pointed a silver pistol at her heart. '*Pan!*' he said, '*Pan! Pan!*'

Katrina duly pretended to be dead and the little boy crowed with pleasure before running back to his parents and shooting them too.

Cornelius came over with two champagne flutes and a slightly reddened complexion. 'They all insist that we try the local champagne,' he said. 'I hope you don't mind.'

Katrina laughed. 'Do I mind drinking champagne? That's like asking if I'd mind winning the lottery!'

'Well, I'm not sure I would like to win the lottery,' Cornelius retorted, taking a seat opposite her.

'Really? Why not?'

'I wouldn't mind getting half a million,' he conceded. 'Any more would be far too difficult. Either I'd have to turn to philanthropy, which would involve lots of meetings with people I don't know, or I'd have to justify my good fortune by transforming my life and that would cause a whole host of problems.'

'I'd be happy to have problems like that,' Katrina said. She was aware that her companion was giving her a rather strained smile. 'Is something wrong?' she asked.

'Katrina,' Cornelius whispered urgently, 'would you mind very much if I held your hand?'

Katrina stared at him impassively before putting her right hand on the table. Cornelius patted it for a few moments and gave another ghastly smile. Katrina's mouth twitched.

'I hope you don't mind,' Cornelius murmured, 'but I told that lady you were my wife.'

'I'm flattered,' Katrina said, 'but she probably assumed that anyway.'

Cornelius shook his head. 'No, no. She told me she *hoped* you were my sister. I think,' Cornelius paused to give an unhappy sigh, 'she has taken a liking to me. It seemed *safer* to tell her we were married.'

'Is she looking at us now?' Katrina asked.

Cornelius nodded and gave her hand another quick pat. 'I think,' he said earnestly, 'we should just keep talking as if nothing is happening.'

'Right,' said Katrina. She couldn't think of anything to say so she drank her champagne instead.

'Well, now,' Cornelius said, in the desperate tones of one who has never mastered the art of polite conversation, 'you must be looking forward to your holiday. You said you're staying with your sister?'

'That's right,' Katrina said. 'She's older than me but she looks much younger. She looks like

41

Catherine Zeta-Jones.'

'Ah!' For a moment Cornelius looked mystified and then his face cleared. 'Yes. I've heard of her.'

'I should think you have!' Katrina retorted. 'Really, you are a very peculiar man.' She eyed him curiously. 'Tell me, have you ever looked at *heat* magazine?'

Cornelius shook his head.

'When was the last time you went to the cinema?'

Cornelius stroked his chin thoughtfully. 'I like going to the cinema,' he said. 'I used to go a lot. I haven't been for some time. I don't know why.'

'Do you have a DVD player?'

'I'm afraid I don't.'

Katrina grinned. 'It's just as well we're not really married,' she said, 'because we have nothing in common at all. Whenever my daughter's at home, I read every page of her *heat* magazine. I regularly go to the cinema and one of the highlights of my life is when I treat myself to a new DVD.' She paused. 'Actually, that makes me sound very sad, doesn't it?' She took another sip of champagne and hoped Cornelius would contradict her. He didn't. Katrina gave a defensive laugh. 'This is why I hate talking about myself. One makes these statements and, as soon as they're said, they settle like concrete. I mean, I don't want you to think I spend my whole life living for celebrity gossip. I do have other interests.'

Cornelius shaded his eyes with his hand. 'Oh, dear,' he said.

Katrina, initially disconcerted by his response, soon realized that his remark was occasioned by the sudden arrival of the French woman at their side. The lady was holding a bottle of champagne.

42

'*Bonsoir, madame,*' she said. '*Vous aimez la champagne?*'

Katrina smiled enthusiastically. '*C'est magnifique!*' she said.

The lady replenished their glasses. '*Votre mari est tres beau,*' she declared. '*Il est beau comme un dieu.*'

'*Oui,*' Katrina responded with just as much conviction and a lot less comprehension. '*Vraiment magnifique!*'

The lady gave a raucous laugh, clapped Katrina on the back and returned to the bar. Katrina noticed that Cornelius had gone very red. Behind her she could hear the people at the bar laughing loudly.

Katrina leant forward. 'Did I say something funny?' she asked.

Cornelius hesitated. 'I think the lady's a little drunk,' he said consolingly.

Katrina looked at him suspiciously. 'What did she say to me?'

Cornelius took a sip of his drink. 'She said that . . .' He paused and shrugged his shoulders. 'I think she was just making a joke.'

Behind them there was more raucous laughter. 'Well, it was obviously very funny,' Katrina said. 'What was it she said?'

'She said,' Cornelius said in a voice that was devoid of any expression, 'that I was as handsome as a god.'

'Oh,' Katrina said. 'I see.'

'And you agreed,' Cornelius continued in the same flat tone, 'that I was truly magnificent.' He nodded politely. 'Very kind of you.'

Katrina looked at Cornelius and, for the second

time that day, a smile broke across his countenance. It really was a very nice smile.

CHAPTER FOUR

An Unforgettable Dinner

After bidding self-conscious farewells to the barman and his customers, Katrina and Cornelius made their way to Brigitte's restaurant. They were ushered past the bar and through the arch by the landlord, who waited for them to sit down before muttering a query in which Katrina happily recognized the word *'vin'*. Cornelius responded with a question to which monsieur made a laconic shrug and then mumbled a few names. Cornelius frowned, then smiled and spoke again. For the first time, monsieur looked almost pleased. He nodded, saying, *'C'est bon,'* before leaving them on their own.

They *were* on their own. There was no one else in the room. 'This is terrible,' Katrina murmured. 'Poor Brigitte was probably looking forward to putting her feet up and now we've wrecked her evening.'

Cornelius glanced at the sea of empty tables surrounding them. The size of the room did little to induce a sense of comfort. It was large and presumably there had once been a time when the white-painted walls were bright and clean. The floor had a beige lino covering which might once have looked good but more probably hadn't. A small vase with a sprig of fossilized lavender on a

44

table in the corner only emphasized the paucity of decoration everywhere else. There was a definite tang of boiled cabbage which had settled in the air like a recalcitrant cloud. 'Well,' he said, 'we can't leave now so the best we can do is appreciate what she gives us and look grateful.'

The landlord reappeared with bottles of water and wine. He opened the wine, poured a little out for Cornelius to try and, as soon as Cornelius nodded his satisfaction, filled both their glasses. Cornelius said something and monsieur waved his left hand, became suddenly animated and, after a quick waterfall of words, left them with a smile.

Katrina took a sip. 'It's good,' she said. 'What were you talking to him about?'

'I said I thought the wines in this area were excellent. He agreed.'

'I wish I could speak French like you,' Katrina said. 'You actually sound French, if you know what I mean. I could never sound like that.'

'You could if you had to on a regular basis,' Cornelius said. 'No one can speak a foreign language without practice.'

Katrina nodded. 'Of course, you sell wine. Carol says you're based in Dulwich. I suppose you come to France all the time. Carol says her husband loves working for you. She says you have these lovely mornings when you get everyone in your office to sample your wines and as a result Douglas won't let her buy cheap plonk any more.'

'I'm sure that's not true. There are many excellent wines on the market that are quite inexpensive.'

'Are you here on business now? Are you going to go round Montelimar, sniffing all the vines?'

45

'I don't go in for a lot of vine-sniffing and I don't sell wines from that region anyway. I'm simply visiting friends. And even if I did buy wines from there, I wouldn't go and check them out in August.'

'Oh,' said Katrina. 'What *do* you do in August?'

'Well, this year I've been selling the 2005 vintages. Very satisfactory. It was an excellent year, as good as 2000.'

From the kitchen came a sound of a saucepan lid crashing to the floor. Cornelius ignored it so Katrina did too. 'I must remember that,' she said. 'Where *do* you buy your wines from?'

Cornelius moved his long legs from under the table and let them stretch out to the side. 'I buy them from all over the world,' he said. 'There's a Chardonnay in Uruguay I particularly like. In France, I suppose I tend to concentrate on Bordeaux, Burgundy, the Rhone, Languedoc . . .'

'Do you go away a lot?'

'Not as much as I used to. In the early days, when I was building the business, I seemed to be living out of a suitcase. Now I only go to places and events I want to go to. I never miss the Union des Grands Grus tastings in Bordeaux in March. I always have a good time there.'

'I suppose you're one of those people who spit wine out instead of drinking it.'

'Only when I'm working. I don't intend to spit anything out this evening.'

The kitchen doors swung open and Brigitte appeared, bearing their first course on two big white plates. Brigitte looked frazzled and unhappy. Most of her hair had escaped from its ribbon. She launched into a long speech which appeared to be

46

a passionate apology for the food she was serving them. Cornelius responded soothingly and Katrina nodded in support and tried to look as if she understood everything he was saying.

'Actually,' she said to Cornelius as soon as Brigitte had departed, 'this looks great. I love couscous salad. Did you tell her how pleased we were to be here?'

'I did,' Cornelius said, 'and for an awful moment I thought she was going to burst into tears.' His eyes met hers involuntarily and then just as quickly slid away. Katrina bit her lip.

Both she and Cornelius turned their attention to their couscous salad and applied themselves to consuming it with exaggerated care and diligence. Finally, Cornelius coughed and made what Katrina recognized was a brave attempt to retrieve the situation. 'Do you often go on holiday with your sister?' he asked.

Katrina responded with a polite shake of her head. 'No,' she said, 'I hardly ever do. But her husband died a year ago and her children are coming out with their current partners and she said she'd be feeling rather lonely. So here I am.'

'That's very nice of you.'

'Not really.' Katrina finished the last of her couscous and poured herself some water. 'My children are doing their own things this summer and Rose is giving me a rent-free stay in a lovely house with a swimming pool. It's no great sacrifice.'

The kitchen doors opened again and Brigitte came through to collect their plates. '*Merci, madame*,' Katrina said enthusiastically, '*c'est magnifique*.' She was rewarded with a wan smile

47

before Brigitte disappeared again.

Her exit only emphasized the silence. Cornelius stared thoughtfully at the bottle of water. Katrina stared at the empty table on their right. She pushed back her fringe, squared her shoulders and looked steadily at Cornelius. 'This isn't working. I want to tell you why I was crying this morning.'

'Really,' said Cornelius, 'there is no need.'

'Really,' countered Katrina, 'there is. Neither of us can relax while you're thinking I'm some crazy, hysterical woman who's going to start making another scene any moment.'

'I assure you,' Cornelius said, 'I don't think you're some crazy, hysterical woman.'

Katrina smiled. 'Thank you,' she said, 'but you *are* worried I might start crying again. I don't blame you. In your shoes, I'd feel exactly the same. I promise you, I'm not in the habit of weeping copiously when I meet someone for the first time. Actually, I'm not in the habit of weeping copiously, full stop.'

'Right,' said Cornelius, 'I'm sure you're *not* and even if you *are*, I promise I don't need you to tell me anything—'

'I understand *that*,' Katrina said impatiently, 'but *I* need to tell *you*. And if I don't tell you, I am aware that we shall spend a very awkward evening together, let alone tomorrow when we're in the car. Do you see that?'

'Well, yes, I do see that.' Cornelius sighed. 'I only meant that . . .' He paused and gave a little shake of his head. 'I don't know what to say.'

'You don't need to say anything,' Katrina said. 'You only have to listen.' She finished her glass of wine and then waited while Cornelius refilled it.

48

'After my husband left me, I fell in love with an actor. Actually, you might remember him. He was Dr Rubin in *Medical Alert*. Did you ever see it?'

'No,' said Cornelius, 'I'm afraid I didn't.'

'Of course you didn't,' said Katrina. 'Well, it was jolly good. Anyway, I fell in love with him and I thought—very stupidly—that he fell in love with me. And then I discovered that he hadn't at all and we stopped seeing each other. It was all rather sad and I felt pretty foolish. As one would. I never told anyone about it.' Katrina swallowed hard and gripped her wine glass with both her hands. 'On the boat, just before you introduced yourself to me, I found out that he is currently staying at my sister's house in France and the reason he is staying there is because he's my sister's new boyfriend. She sent me a text. She thinks I'll be thrilled. She knew I used to watch *Medical Alert*. Everyone used to watch *Medical Alert*. Everyone except you.'

The kitchen doors banged open again and Brigitte reappeared. 'Ah!' said Cornelius with a ghastly attempt at enthusiasm. 'This will be the tongue!'

*   *   *

The tongue exceeded Katrina's expectations. It sat on the plate surrounded by a mountain of pale cabbage. It was extraordinary that such an anaemic-looking vegetable could exude such a powerful smell. The tongue looked like an old, flaccid phallus. When Katrina took her first bite, she was pretty sure it tasted like an old flaccid phallus. She swallowed hard and reached for the wine.

'You don't like it,' Cornelius said.

Katrina tried to think of a polite way to describe it. 'It's different,' she said.

'Eat some of the cabbage,' Cornelius suggested. 'You can leave the tongue.'

'If I leave the tongue,' Katrina said, 'Brigitte will be upset.'

'I'll eat your tongue.'

'You hate it too,' she said. 'I can manage it. If I keep drinking wine with it, I'll be fine.' She took another mouthful and then groped for her glass.

The landlord called out to them from the bar. *'Ça va bien?'*

Katrina nodded fervently while Cornelius picked up the bottle and asked for another.

The last time Katrina had eaten a meal as horrible as this was when she'd been at her first school and had been presented with semolina pudding. Then, she had coped by stuffing it into the pocket of her skirt, and the fact that she had had to spend the afternoon with a wet, semolina-infested thigh had been a small price to pay. This time there was no hiding place but at least she had wine, and by the time she finally finished her ordeal she had downed three full glasses. She and Cornelius put their empty plates to one side and regarded each other with the respect of two mountaineers who have finally conquered Everest.

Cornelius poured out yet another glass for them both. 'I think I can say,' he declared, 'that that was, without doubt, the most disgusting thing I have ever eaten and that,' he frowned thoughtfully, 'you are an exceptional woman for eating it.'

Katrina flushed with pride. 'Thank you,' she said,

adding graciously, 'And you are an exceptional man.'

'Thank you.' Cornelius cleared his throat. 'Before we leave the subject, I would like to tell you that the doctor man doesn't deserve you.'

'Well, he doesn't want me,' Katrina pointed out, 'so whether he deserves me or not is immaterial. And he isn't a doctor. He's an actor.'

'My wife,' Cornelius said, 'is an actress.'

'Is she?' Katrina was surprised. Fleetingly, she tried to picture Cornelius surrounded by over-expansive thespians. 'What's her name? Is she successful?'

'She's called Lucy Lambert. She's not as successful as she should be. She is an excellent actress but Lucy says it's all about looks for women. She is very attractive but most writers and directors seem to lose interest in women over twenty-five, however attractive they are.'

Katrina sighed. 'Lewis was very attractive.'

'When did you last see him?'

'Years and years ago. I doubt if he even remembers me.'

'Perhaps,' Cornelius suggested, 'he isn't attractive any more.'

Brigitte had joined them again in order to find out if they wanted cheese or fruit. After a brief consultation with Katrina, Cornelius opted for coffee. Katrina said she felt as if she would never be able to eat anything again. Cornelius agreed he felt unpleasantly full.

'The last time I felt like this,' he said, 'was when I was forced to eat some chocolate pudding by our geography teacher, Mr Rodler. It's funny. Even now, I have only to catch a glimpse of a chocolate

51

pudding and I feel nauseous.'

Katrina nodded. 'I'm like that about milk puddings. I know people are always saying children today are far too indulged and spoilt but personally I don't see that there's anything remotely commendable about forcing a child to eat something he doesn't want to. It's verging on cruelty.'

'It's not verging on cruelty,' Cornelius said, 'it quite definitely *is* cruelty. There was a boy in the year beneath me who couldn't eat baked beans. He wasn't being faddish, he *couldn't* eat baked beans. He tried to explain this to Mr Rodler and Mr Rodler virtually pushed them down his throat. We all felt like cheering when the poor boy immediately threw up over him. I always remember watching him being sick and then seeing a lone baked bean, denuded of tomato sauce, slowly emerge from his left nostril.'

Brigitte arrived with two cups of black coffee and offered her guests a small jug of milk, which was politely declined by both of them. Katrina waited until she had left them and then put her elbows on the table. 'I think your school sounds utterly vile,' she said.

Cornelius pushed out his lower lip and considered her judgement. 'I suppose it was,' he agreed, 'but at least it ensured that I have never stopped being grateful for being an adult.'

Katrina nodded. 'I must say I far prefer being grown-up. I never have understood people who say schooldays are the best days of our lives . . .' She paused as another crash came from the kitchen. 'We ought to leave,' she said. 'Poor Brigitte looks so tired and we're stopping her from going to bed.'

She saw Cornelius reach for his wallet and added quickly, 'I'm doing this, I absolutely insist.' She pushed back her seat, walked towards the kitchen and called out, *'Madame? Nous finishons! L'addition, s'il vous plaît?'*

Madame reappeared, wiping her hands on her apron and pulling a notebook from its pocket. Katrina returned to the table, picked up her handbag, opened her wallet and produced a wad of euros, saying brightly, *'J'ai include un tip. C'est tout pour vous et mucho merci!'* Then Cornelius reached into his pocket and pressed some more notes into Brigitte's hand.

Cornelius and Katrina saw with dismay that Brigitte's eyes were shiny with tears. She uttered a low *'Merci,'* went over to Katrina, kissed her on both cheeks and then did the same with Cornelius. After another heartfelt *'Merci,'* she called her husband and showed him the money and suddenly he was gripping their hands and murmuring, *'C'est trop! Oh, merci, merci beaucoup! Je vous souhaite tout le bonheur possible!'*

By the time they got outside, Katrina felt quite overwhelmed. She took one last look through the window. Monsieur and Brigitte were embracing each other.

'Cornelius,' Katrina said, 'you are a very nice man. You must have given them one hell of a tip.'

Cornelius looked a little sheepish. 'I enjoyed the evening,' he said. 'I enjoyed it very much.'

Katrina laughed. 'You're just relieved that I didn't start crying again.'

'I *was* relieved,' Cornelius admitted. For a few moments they walked on in amicable silence and then Cornelius spoke again. 'I am not very good at polite conversation. I have never known how to talk to strangers. But I didn't feel you were strange.'

They had reached the bar. With unspoken accord, they continued to walk up the left side of the square, thus avoiding the chance of being spotted by the inmates. As they reached their temporary home, Cornelius took out the key he had been given by madame and let them both in. All was quiet and they tiptoed up the stairs. Katrina stopped outside her room and thanked Cornelius for the evening. 'I have to tell you,' she said, 'that I wasn't looking forward to this evening either. But I also enjoyed myself.'

'I'm very glad,' Cornelius said. 'I told madame we'd have breakfast at eight. Is that too early for you?'

'Not at all.' Katrina took out her room key. As Cornelius turned towards his own room she called his name softly and he stopped to look enquiringly at her.

'I just wanted to say,' Katrina said, 'that I didn't find you strange either.'

CHAPTER FIVE

A Plan is Made

When Cornelius came down for breakfast the next morning, he found a table for two laden with fresh croissants, pains au chocolat, orange juice and a selection of jams. Madame bustled in and asked if she should bring in the coffee. Cornelius told her that was an excellent idea and assured her with more optimism than conviction that Katrina would be here at any moment.

In fact, Katrina appeared shortly after the coffee. Her complexion was wan and she held herself in a manner that suggested her body was made of finest bone china. She sat down carefully and bade Cornelius a pale good morning.

Cornelius offered her a croissant and she shook her head. 'They're very good,' he said. 'Are you sure you won't have one?'

'They look lovely,' Katrina agreed weakly, 'but I think I'll just have coffee.'

'Are you all right?' Cornelius asked. 'You look rather white.'

Katrina swallowed. 'It's entirely my own fault,' she said. 'I drank too much last night.'

'I don't think you can blame yourself,' Cornelius said judiciously. 'It was the only way you could eat the tongue. It really was quite revolting—'

'Cornelius,' Katrina said, 'do you mind if we don't talk about the tongue?'

'Of course. I'm sorry.' Cornelius poured her out some coffee. 'You can sleep in the car. You'll feel much better once you've had a good sleep.'

'I'm sure you're right.' Katrina took a sip of her drink. 'When do you think we'll get down to Montelimar?'

'If we don't stop for lunch,' Cornelius said, 'we should be there by mid-afternoon. It's a beautiful day.'

Katrina glanced at the sunlight pouring through the window and winced slightly. She had another sip of coffee. 'When do you want to leave here?'

'Well,' Cornelius looked at her doubtfully, 'I

55

thought about leaving in twenty minutes but we can leave later if you like. There's no hurry.'

'Twenty minutes will be fine.' Katrina swallowed. 'I think if you don't mind I'll go back to my room for a little while. I'll see you out by the car.' She rose slowly from her chair. Her head appeared to be locked into a particular position, like a puppet with too few strings.

Cornelius watched her leave the room. He helped himself to another croissant and resigned himself to a late departure.

*　　　*　　　*

He had underestimated Katrina. Looking even paler than she had done earlier, she appeared at the precise time she had said she would. Having ascertained that Cornelius had settled the bill with madame, she insisted on paying her share at once. Then, as if exhausted by such a sudden flurry of activity, she got into the car and sank back into the passenger seat.

Cornelius turned on the ignition. 'Don't talk,' he told Katrina. 'Shut your eyes. Go to sleep.'

'Thank you,' Katrina murmured and duly closed her eyes. Cornelius shot her a swift glance. Apart from a slight shimmer of perspiration on her forehead, she reminded him of one of those statues on stone coffins. He did not look at her again until he reached the motorway and then he was relieved to see from the regularity of her breathing that she was asleep.

There was no doubt about it. She was an impressive woman. Anyone who could force a plate of tongue and cabbage down her throat

56

without complaint was not the sort of person to habitually indulge in emotional excess. Her stoicism over breakfast was further proof. She must have been very much in love with the doctor man and Cornelius hoped she wouldn't discover she was still in love when she saw him again. He was not impressed by the sister's behaviour. If she'd asked Katrina to come and keep her company, it was not very thoughtful to tell her at the last minute that there would be a boyfriend there as well. The more Cornelius thought about it, the more it seemed to him that the sister and the doctor man were made for each other. He would have liked to pass on this thought to Katrina once she woke up but was not sure that she would appreciate it.

Cornelius shot another look at her. It was extraordinary that even though she was a relative stranger, he did not find her company either jarring or uncomfortable. This was a rare experience. He presumed it was because her initial hysterics had inevitably accelerated their relationship, making the usual stiff formality instantly redundant. More important, it was impossible not to warm to a woman who had so gamely completed what had to be the worst meal of all time.

She did not stir until some hours later when Cornelius brought the car to a stop. She opened first one eye, then the other and said, 'Are we here?'

'No,' said Cornelius. 'I left the motorway. I thought we'd stop for lunch. I could do with a break and it might do you good to get some food inside you. We're not far from Lyons. This is a town called Bellevue. I've been driving around and I spotted a brasserie at the end of the road. I think we should try it.'

Katrina nodded. 'Fine. I'm sorry I've been such a useless companion. I *do* feel better.'

'Good.' Cornelius got out of the car and stretched his arms. Katrina joined him on the pavement and took a few deep breaths. He was glad to see that she no longer resembled a stone statue.

*   *   *

When they walked through the door, Katrina did momentarily wonder if Cornelius might be trying to compile a list of the worst eating places in France. The room was dark and small. Once her eyes had adjusted to the gloom she could see that a good-looking man in a long white apron was cooking pizzas over a charcoal fire and that the tables were clean and covered with red and white gingham tablecloths. Further, although she had decided she would not eat anything, she allowed Cornelius to order for her. Still more surprisingly, when the waitress brought them their meal, she found that she was able to eat at least half her pizza. Her headache no longer felt as if it would tear her skull apart and the mineral water was cool and refreshing. She even felt able to talk again.

'Cornelius,' she said, 'how did you get your name? It's very unusual.'

Cornelius put his head to one side as if it had never occurred to him before. 'It was my mother's choice,' he said. 'I think perhaps she didn't like me. I was an unprepossessing baby.'

58

'That doesn't sound very likely. There's no such thing as an unprepossessing baby. Have you ever asked her?'

'There's not much point. She has always had a rather selective memory. I'm pretty sure it isn't a family name. I've never heard of any great-uncle Cornelius. Years ago I heard a record by Johnny Cash and that did make me think of another possibility. I remember being rather struck by it.'

'What was the record?' asked Katrina. 'I adore Johnny Cash.'

'It was "A Boy Named Sue". As soon as I heard it, I felt an affinity with the eponymous boy. It did occur to me that my mother might have called me Cornelius for the same reason that Sue's father called him Sue.'

'In order to toughen you up, you mean?'

'Possibly. It could have been worse. I knew a boy at school called Endymion.'

Katrina blinked. 'You're right,' she said. 'It could have been worse. Poor Endymion.'

'Katrina's a good name,' Cornelius mused. 'Very strong.'

'Thank you,' Katrina said. 'I like it. My sister *will* call me Katty.' She bit her lip and wished she hadn't brought up her sister. She felt as if she had conjured up a big, black cloud that slowly blotted out all sunlight. She wished she could walk out of the restaurant, find a railway station and make her way back to Greenwich. She wished a miracle could happen, she wished Cornelius's car would break down, she wished Cornelius would trip and break his leg in such a way that he would need her to drive him back to an English hospital. She wished that *she* would break her leg.

59

Cornelius did not trip over anything and neither did she and the car did not break down either. Katrina sat, gazing out of the window, devising ever more improbably composed and confident conversations with Lewis and Rose.

Cornelius had noticed that his companion's mood had darkened and he had guessed that she was contemplating the unwelcome reunion with her former lover. He didn't say anything, partly because it was none of his business and partly because it might only increase her anxiety. He did think of reminding her that after so many years the actor/doctor man might have lost his appeal but the fact that he had secured the affections of the Catherine Zeta-Jones woman did suggest that he hadn't. He checked his watch. They were now on the other side of Lyons. Another forty minutes and they'd be there.

They had left the motorway for the last time when Katrina spoke again. 'Cornelius,' she said, 'I want to ask a favour of you. It is a very big favour but it doesn't involve you having to *do* anything. It does involve you not mentioning your wife to my sister.'

'I had no intention of mentioning anything at all to your sister.'

'No,' Katrina agreed. She looked at him doubtfully. 'The thing is my sister is quite old-fashioned in some ways. She's always found it difficult to understand how a woman can be happy without a man. Certainly, she finds it impossible to understand that *I* can be happy without a man. I gave up trying to enlighten her a long time ago and I don't care at all any more that she feels sorry for me. But—and I know it's silly—I find that I *do*

60

mind the idea of Rose . . . *and Lewis* . . . feeling
sorry for me, both at the same time. I'm not sure I
can bear to spend a week with both of them being
kind to me. So, what I was wondering was whether
you would mind if I let them think that you and I
are possibly more than just acquaintances. I know
it's presumptuous . . .'

Cornelius shifted uncomfortably in his seat. 'No,
no, not at all. But I don't think I quite understand.'
He put a hand to the side of his forehead and
rubbed it nervously. 'You want us to pretend we're
having an affair?'

'No, no, I want them to think you're not married,
I want them to think we're having a perfectly
legitimate relationship. You wouldn't have to do
anything. I've worked it all out. Rose would
probably want to invite you to dinner at some time
but I shall say that you want to concentrate on
your friends, you want to be with them every
minute of the holiday.'

'I'm not sure I *do*,' said Cornelius. 'I'm quite sure
my friends don't want to spend every minute of the
holiday with me . . .'

'That doesn't matter. The point is I shall only say
that in order to spare you the need to come round
and be polite to Rose and Lewis.'

'I see. I would certainly like to avoid that.'

'I know, I know. Believe me, I wouldn't dream of
inflicting my family on you. All I want is that you
let me introduce you when we get to the house and
you avoid mentioning your wife if possible.'

Cornelius gave a sigh. 'The thing is,' he said, 'I
don't like telling lies.'

'Oh.' Katrina reddened. 'I see. Of course you
don't. I'm sorry, it was a crazy idea. It only

61

occurred to me because . . .' She stopped and turned her head away.

Cornelius looked at her enquiringly and then, as understanding dawned, returned his gaze to the windscreen. '. . . Because I pretended you were my wife in the bar last night. I did indeed tell a lie. I panicked. I shouldn't have done that.'

'No, I don't mean that. It doesn't matter, it was a silly idea. Please forget I said it.'

Cornelius glanced at Katrina. She sat stiffly, her face closed and tense. He said, 'If your sister were to ask me about my marital status—and I see no reason why she should do so—I could say that my wife is planning to divorce me.'

Katrina shook her head. 'That's very kind of you but you're right. There's no reason why you should have to tell lies for me.'

'That wouldn't be lying. My wife *is* planning to divorce me.'

'Oh.' Katrina looked confused. 'I'm so sorry.'

'I don't see why you should be,' Cornelius said. 'It isn't your fault. The only reason I mentioned it is that it does at least mean that you can legitimately be in—what was it you said?—a legitimate relationship with me.'

'Are you sure you don't mind?'

'No, I don't mind. We don't have to hold hands or anything, do we?'

'Absolutely not. In fact, you probably won't have to do anything at all. I might not even say anything. It's just nice to know that I can if I want to.'

'As a matter of interest,' Cornelius said, 'how long have we been seeing each other?'

'I'm not sure. I know I told Rose I was getting a

lift down with you but I can't remember what else I said. I think it might be safer if we met for the first time on the boat and discovered we had a mutual affinity for . . . for Johnny Cash. Rose knows I love country music.'

'I don't, though. The only record I like by Johnny Cash is the one about Sue. I don't know anything about country music.'

'Well, never mind, we can say we discovered a mutual affinity for . . .' Katrina tried to think of a mutual affinity and could come up with none. 'Never mind,' she said again. 'We can say we just got on together. That'll do. Cornelius, I am very grateful.'

'Not at all,' said Cornelius. 'Ah. We're coming into Cleon d'Andran now.'

Katrina was guiltily aware that she had paid little or no attention to her surroundings since she had climbed into the car this morning. Certainly, Cleon was worthy of attention. Katrina spotted a boulangerie, a pâtisserie, a small supermarket, a pretty café with tables and chairs outside and, most impressive of all, a church with a magnificent tower and bell.

Cornelius pointed to a house on the corner and said carelessly, 'That's where I'm staying.'

Katrina's eyes widened. 'This is your village. So we're nearly there.'

'I'm driving out now, towards Pont-de-Barret. Do you have directions?'

'Yes, yes, I have.' Katrina dived into her capacious shoulder bag and pulled out two photocopied sheets. 'I've got one for you as well. It has the phone number in case you need to ring me. I'll put it on the back seat for you.' Her mouth felt horribly dry all of a sudden. 'The house is not actually in Pont-de-Barret, it's a couple of kilometres before and it's a little way off the road. We have to look out for a stone farmhouse and a pair of big sky-blue gates.'

'Fine,' said Cornelius, 'we'll be there in no time.'

Katrina stared despairingly out of the window. On one side were fields with dying sunflowers that stood to attention like tired old soldiers. On the other were rows of short, bushy trees with small pretty leaves. In the distance, Katrina could see banks of mountains undulating gently along the horizon. Rose was right: the place was beautiful.

'See those trees?' Cornelius nodded to the vast orchard on his right. 'They are almond trees and further on you can see the lavender fields. I'm afraid you've come at the wrong time, you've just missed the flowering season. You can imagine what it's like when the sunflowers and the lavender are out. And the whole area smells so sweet. It's a pity you didn't come here a few weeks earlier.'

Katrina didn't say anything. It was a pity, she thought, that she'd come here at all.

They drove on in silence until Cornelius turned left towards Pont-de-Barret. 'You know,' he said carefully, 'you might take one look at this man and wonder why you were ever worried. It's been a long time.'

'I might,' Katrina said. She sat up straight, her hands clasped fiercely together. 'You must think I'm very stupid.' She craned her head forward and swallowed. 'Cornelius, I can see a stone house on the right. Drive slowly in case there are some blue gates.' Her eyes strained painfully and her hand gripped the dashboard. She gulped. 'I can see the blue gates. Cornelius, you will come in with me, won't you? You don't have to stay but you will come in with me?'

'I will.' Cornelius turned into the drive and parked the car outside the gates. 'We're here,' he said. 'Shall we go in?'

CHAPTER SIX

A Night of Passion

The gates opened onto a large, enclosed courtyard. On the left, an azure-coloured pool could be glimpsed through a series of tile-topped stone arches and on the right was the farmhouse, its shutters the same colour as the gates. The olive tree that Rose had mentioned stood shimmering in the afternoon sun and beside it was a long wooden table around which a number of collapsible chairs stood in some disarray, like drunken revellers at the end of a party.

A delighted 'Katty?' from the pool area could be heard; Rose ran towards them, resplendent in wrap-around sunglasses and a flame-coloured swimming costume, split to the navel, that clashed gloriously with her voluminous Titian tresses. It was hard to believe Rose would be fifty next year. It was even harder to believe she was a grieving widow. 'Katty,' she cried again and ran up to her sister, enveloping her in a lavish embrace, 'you are here!'

Katrina was horribly aware of her crumpled linen

trousers, her limp T-shirt and her paste-like flesh. 'Gosh,' she said feebly, 'you're so brown!'

'So will you be soon,' Rose assured her. She turned to Cornelius and bestowed a brilliant smile on him. 'And you are the kind man who brought my sister to me! Hello. I'm Rose.'

Cornelius put down Katrina's suitcase and shook Rose's hand. 'I'm Cornelius Hedge. How do you do?'

'Cornelius Hedge?' Rose clapped her hands. 'I'd die for a name like that! That is an amazing name! May I call you Corny?'

'No,' said Cornelius, 'you may not.'

'Well, *Cornelius*!' Rose laughed. 'I'm sure I don't blame you!'

And now, through the archway, like a long-awaited star taking his place on the stage, came Lewis.

His hair was shorter than she remembered. He was not bald. He was not fat. Years of probable decadence and debauchery had neither coarsened his features nor dulled his eyes. Like Rose, his skin was the colour of burnished bronze. Like Rose, he wore sunglasses. Unlike Rose, he wore black bathing shorts that revealed a taut and muscular and undeniably desirable body. He came towards them with the heart-stopping smile that Katrina remembered so well. She heard herself saying with admirable coolness, 'Hello, Lewis, how are you?'

She thought his smile faltered momentarily but it was difficult to be sure. She heard Rose say, 'I don't believe it! Do you know my gorgeous man, Katty?'

Katrina knew exactly what to say. She had practised it in her head many times in the last twenty-four hours. 'We met very briefly a long time ago. I doubt if Lewis remembers. I was doing some legal work for the television company that was responsible for the *Medical Alert* programme and I seem to remember we had lunch together in the canteen.'

'Of course I remember you,' Lewis said warmly, grasping her hands. 'You haven't changed a bit. How lovely to see you, Katrina.'

'How extraordinary that you've met each other,' said Rose. 'I feel quite shivery. I'm so glad, my darling, that you didn't try to snap my sister up. You might have been my brother-in-law and that would never have done!' She put her arms round Lewis's waist and smiled lovingly up at him.

For the first time in her life, Katrina was glad to hear the words. 'Aunty Katty!' Until four years ago, Cam and Sam had been happy to call their aunt 'Katrina'. Four years ago, they discovered irony and rechristened her 'Aunty Katty', which Katrina loathed. She had long ago given up trying to stop Rose from calling her Katty but to have the ghastly sobriquet used by Cam and Sam was excessively irritating. Worse still was the 'Aunty' that preceded it. It made her feel middle-aged, which, of course, to her constant surprise, she was.

Cam and Sam had obviously been swimming. They came towards their aunt with their partners trailing behind them. All of them were beautiful. Cam was a nubile blonde with a bow-shaped mouth and extravagantly long eyelashes. Her boyfriend had equally blond hair and his grey floral bathing shorts were a perfect complement to Cam's pink bikini. He and Cam were of precisely the same height, which only accentuated the

67

similarity between them.

Sam was much taller than his sister. He had short spiky hair enlivened by what looked like expensive highlights. The silver chain round his neck glowed against his golden skin. His girlfriend wore a green bikini that strained to contain her generous breasts and when she pushed her sunglasses back over her gleaming black hair she revealed a pair of exceptionally fine eyes. All four of them held themselves with the careless confidence of people who are used to being admired.

'Thank God, you're here, Aunty Katty.' Sam spoke in the exotic south London cadence peculiar to those who wish to conceal a privileged education. 'Mum and Lewis won't play any card games with us.'

'They're hopeless,' Cam agreed. 'They go to bed straight after supper.'

'Cam, you're such a liar,' Rose said with an indulgent smile. 'Now, children, come and meet Katty's friend. Cornelius, this is my daughter, Cam, her boyfriend, Francis, my son, Sam, and his girlfriend, Sassy.'

Katrina watched Cornelius murmur something unintelligible and knew it was time to rescue him. 'We mustn't keep you,' she told him, 'your friends will be wondering where you are.'

'Do you have far to go?' Lewis asked.

'Cleon d'Andran,' Cornelius said. 'Katrina's right. I really should go.'

'But you're only down the road!' Rose said. 'You must come to dinner! Or perhaps we could leave these young things to their own devices and meet you somewhere.' She rubbed Lewis's chest with her hand. 'Wouldn't that be fun, darling?'

68

'Terrific fun,' said Lewis.

Katrina was aware that Cornelius had planted a rigid hand on the small of her back. 'I'm afraid that isn't possible,' she said. 'Cornelius is going to have a very busy time. He's on a working holiday, really. He's a wine merchant and when he's not with his friends, he'll be out every day visiting vineyards and smelling grapes and things.'

'I'm sure he can get out for at least one evening,' said Rose. 'Can't you get out for at least one evening, Cornelius?'

'No,' said Katrina, 'he can't. He doesn't see his friends very often. And besides, their marriage is going through an extremely rocky patch at the moment and they're both looking to Cornelius to help them.' She took Cornelius's spare hand. 'I'll see you to the car,' she said.

Cornelius muttered a strangulated farewell. He and Katrina turned and walked to the gates, hand in hand.

As soon as the gates were closed, Katrina released him. 'I'm sorry I made up that stuff about your friends,' she whispered, 'but I know what Rose is like. If I hadn't said something she'd have been knocking on their door tomorrow morning.'

'I quite understand,' said Cornelius. 'I hope I looked . . . I wasn't sure what to do . . . The hand on your back . . .'

'Very good,' Katrina assured him, 'very convincing. Thank you so much. I am so sorry to have dragged you into all this. I know you must hate it and I promise I won't tell any more lies. And don't worry: you won't see me or anyone else here until it's time to go home!'

'That's quite all right.' Cornelius climbed into his

car and put on his seat belt. 'By the way,' he said, 'just so you know . . . I don't have any intention of visiting vineyards while I'm here and I certainly won't be smelling any grapes.'

'Oh, don't worry,' Katrina said. 'Rose and Lewis won't know that.'

'Right.' He shut his door and wound down the window. 'I hope the holiday goes well for you. Phone me if you have any problems. If you need anything . . .' He reached out and took a pen and notebook from the inside pocket of the passenger door. He scribbled down a number and gave it to Katrina.

'Thank you, I'm sure I'll be fine. You've been so kind. Whatever else happens, I've had a lovely holiday so far.' She stepped back from the car, watched him drive away and waved until she could no longer see him.

*   *   *

Cornelius watched Katrina grow smaller and smaller in his driving mirror. He didn't like leaving her. She looked so forlorn, as if she were bidding farewell to her only friend. He didn't like the idea of leaving her to the gang in the courtyard: the four personifications of arrogant Youth, the Lewis man who had clearly forgotten all about her, the Rose woman who did not in fact look anything like Catherine Zeta-Jones. He was aware he had not acquitted himself well in front of them. Glamorous and confident people always reduced him to a gibbering wreck, largely because he had no idea how it must feel to be glamorous and confident and therefore such people were as foreign to his

70

understanding as aliens. The only confident and glamorous people he had ever really known were his mother and his wife. He still didn't understand his mother, and as for Lucy . . . The first time he had met her he had been struck by incoherent love. Lucy told him later she had found his silence mysterious and intriguing, and by some miracle she had ended up loving him too. He had never understood why.

He remembered the last time he had seen her. Her beautiful eyes had been full of tears so that they had shone like pools in the sun. He gripped his steering wheel. He was not going to think about his wife while he was in France and there was not much point in worrying about Katrina either. Her problems were nothing to do with him.

*   *   *

There were several reasons why Katrina accepted a glass of Chardonnay at half past six that evening, thus breaking a newly minted resolution to avoid alcohol for the rest of the holiday.

On returning to the bosom of her family after waving goodbye to Cornelius—and feeling oddly bereft in so doing—she had had to endure a litany of teasing questions and innuendos from Cam *and* Sam *and* Rose about the nature of her relationship with him, none of which were amusing or interesting or based on any semblance of reality.

She had taken an instant liking to Sam's girlfriend, Sassy, who asked Katrina if she always had to put up with such Gestapo-like interrogation about her private life. Francis was a different matter. While he was undeniably easy on the eye,

71

his facial repertoire seemed to be limited to knowing smiles and lustful leers, the latter, admittedly, being directed exclusively in Cam's direction.

Having finally wearied of the subject of Cornelius, Rose had decided to take Katrina on a tour of the house. After praising the large sitting room and the grand wooden staircase at the back, Katrina was then shown through to the annex and invited to admire Rose's bedroom and en-suite bathroom. Katrina tried hard to avoid looking at the vast unmade bed but she could not fail to notice the various garments, masculine and feminine, strewn haphazardly around the floor. She was then taken back to the sitting room and up the wooden staircase where she found that her own bedroom, a small monastic cell, was sandwiched between those of the two pairs of young lovers. 'I hope they're not too noisy,' Rose said with a grin. 'We had to put you in here, it's the only single bedroom in the place.'

The final straw was when Rose announced that the four 'Young' were in charge of supper. 'You and I and Lewis will sit by the pool and have a drink and we'll tell you how we met. Isn't this *fun*?'

In answer, Katrina said yes, it certainly was, and in answer to Lewis's query, agreed that she would love a glass of wine. Then she sat back on her sun-lounger and tried to appreciate her surroundings, which were indeed delightful. Beyond the pool and the small stone wall, there was a long field with a stream at the bottom. Beyond that, gentle hills, decorated with elegant poplars and bushy almond trees, formed a gracious counterpoint to the cloudless blue sky.

Concentrating on the cloudless blue sky was infinitely preferable to concentrating on Lewis, who lay stretched out between the two sisters like a gorgeous piece of steak. Rose, for reasons that Katrina found perfectly comprehensible, could not stop touching him, stroking first his chest, then sitting forward and grasping his thigh. Lewis, for reasons that Katrina also found perfectly comprehensible, did not touch Rose. It was a sort of comfort that he did seem to feel a little uncomfortable about lying between a past and present lover.

'Tell me, Katty,' said Rose, 'how do you think I look?' There was a slight hint of reproof in her voice as she said, 'Everyone tells me I am positively glowing these days!'

'You look wonderful,' Katrina agreed.

Rose laughed and swung back her hair. 'It's love! I tell you, it's better than any beauty treatment! Do you want to hear how Lewis and I met?'

'I'm sure,' Lewis murmured, 'that Katrina isn't interested in any of that.'

With anyone else, Katrina would have wholeheartedly agreed. As it was, she fixed Lewis with a steely gaze and said she would *love* to hear every last detail.

'Well,' said Rose, tucking her tanned legs beneath her and settling back against a cushion, 'do you remember when I moved up to London?'

Katrina did indeed remember. She and Ollie had spent a whole weekend moving odd bits of furniture between one room and another while Rose tried to decide what looked best where.

'Well,' said Rose again, 'a few days after I finally settled in, I met the couple on the floor below and

I realized instantly that we were going to be huge friends. They just took me to their hearts and made me feel I'd known them for ever. Martha is an interior designer and she has found me the most exquisite curtains for my bedroom; dove-grey silk, Katty, totally divine. Anyway, Martha and her husband, Anthony—he's a QC, absolutely brilliant—insisted on throwing a party for me, which was ever so kind because there I was, a poor little widow, who didn't know a soul . . .'

'Rose, you know hordes of people in London,' Katrina said, 'not least your children, who live within a fifteen-minute radius of your flat.'

'I know and I love the fact that they're so near but I've never been the sort of mother to foist myself on my young. So I went to the drinks party and I met some wonderful, wonderful people, all of whom have become my dearest friends, and then Lewis walked in and—it was extraordinary. Martha said later she could almost *see* an electric current pass between us. We just looked at each other and he came over and we talked for a bit and then we got separated and I thought I would never see him again—it was so frustrating because everyone seemed to want to talk to me—and anyway, at last we were on our own and he made the most outrageously naughty proposition to me . . . you won't believe what he said . . .'

'Oh, I don't know,' said Katrina. 'I think I can imagine exactly what he said.'

'If that's true,' said Rose with a smirk, 'you will be horrified to hear that I agreed straight away! We made our excuses and went back to my flat and . . . I will leave the rest to your imagination!'

'That's very kind of you,' said Katrina.

'The funny thing *was*,' Rose mused, 'the next morning we were lying in bed and I had the strangest feeling that Roger had given me his blessing, that he had seen everything and was happy.'

Lewis shot her a startled glance. 'Good lord,' he said, 'I hope he hadn't.'

'So do I,' said Katrina. 'It would probably have given him another heart attack.'

'Don't be naughty, Katty,' Rose said equably. 'The thing is, I knew it was *right*. Does that sound silly? Lewis and I have been inseparable ever since. The children are delighted. They've been so worried about me and they adore Lewis. Don't look so modest, darling, you know they adore you!'

'I don't know about that,' said Lewis, 'but they're certainly a credit to you.'

'It all sounds very romantic,' Katrina said briskly. 'So tell me, Lewis, are you still acting?'

'Oh, yes,' Lewis said. 'I was in *The Bill* a few weeks ago and I had a part in *Casualty* in February.'

'Really?' Katrina brushed away a wasp from her trousers. 'What were you? A corpse?'

'I had quite a meaty role. I played a man who's trying to persuade his wife not to leave him. She says she no longer loves him and she leaves because she thinks she's in love with a younger man who works for her who actually is only interested in securing promotion. My character is left alone in the house and he's utterly distraught and he sits down with a bottle of whisky and gets drunk and falls asleep with a lighted cigarette in his hand . . .'

'And he goes up in flames?' Katrina concluded.

75

'So you *did* play a corpse!'

'It was actually very moving,' Lewis assured her. 'You had to see it to appreciate it.'

'The funny thing is,' Rose said, 'I *did* see that episode and I remember thinking how wonderful Lewis was! It's almost like it was fate. It's almost like I knew it was going to happen. I wonder if I'm a little psychic.' She laughed and uncurled her legs. 'I'd better go and check on the kitchen and make sure the children are cooking something that is actually edible.'

'Let me go,' said Katrina. 'I've done nothing since I arrived.'

'Absolutely not!' said Rose. 'Not on your first day here! You can cook tomorrow if you like. Lewis will keep you company, I won't be a minute.' She stood up and adjusted her bathing-costume straps. 'Now, Katty, I know how you disapprove of public displays of affection so look away while I give Lewis a kiss!'

'I shall go and admire the view,' Katrina said. She walked over to the wall, looked out on the wooded slopes and wondered how she was going to endure the next few days. A buzzard rose from the undergrowth and hovered soundlessly in the sky before plummeting dramatically back to earth. She wished her children were here. If they were here, they would be splashing noisily in the pool or suggesting an early evening walk up the hillside. She wished they were here.

She jumped when a voice beside her said, 'Katrina.' Lewis had joined her by the wall. He stood, staring intently at her. 'Are you all right? I couldn't believe it when I saw you. It must have been quite a shock for you. This is an odd situation, isn't it? I want you to know I had no idea that you were Rose's sister.'

Katrina gave a light smile. 'I'm sure you didn't,' she said. 'And even if Rose had told you she had a sister called Katrina Latham who lived in Greenwich, you still wouldn't have known who I was because I'm pretty sure you'd forgotten all about me.'

'I don't mind you being angry with me,' Lewis said gently. 'I'd be surprised if you weren't. I *do* mind you putting yourself down. Of course I didn't forget you. You've hardly changed at all. I recognized you at once. You forget I'm an actor. I didn't know how you wanted to play it. I didn't know if you wanted Rose to know that we knew each other. I didn't know if you'd even told Rose about us . . .'

'It's pretty obvious I hadn't,' Katrina said acidly. 'I think she'd have remembered something like that.'

'You know what I mean. I was following your lead. If I'd known you were her sister, I'd have refused Rose's invitation to come out here.'

'That makes two of us,' said Katrina. 'Anyway, I'm sure I'm very happy for you. It must be so nice for you not having to hide your love affairs from your adoring public any longer.'

'Katrina,' said Lewis, 'you may not believe me but I promise I'm speaking the truth: you have no idea how glad I am to have the opportunity to talk to you again.'

'Really?' Katrina raised her eyebrows. 'Are you going to tell me you've been racked with guilt for years and years? I do hope not.'

'Everyone behaves badly sometimes. I'm not

trying to defend myself here. I was young and irresponsible and selfish when I met you. I look back on that part of my life and wonder how I could have behaved with such jaw-dropping callousness. There aren't many things I'm ashamed of and you'd be surprised if you knew how often I have thought about you.'

Katrina gave a little nod of agreement. 'I'd be very surprised.'

'I can offer no defence. I can only tell you I was terrified of commitment and responsibility. I thought you were lovely but the idea of getting involved with someone who was a mother was . . . I couldn't cope. You were—you *are*—a lovely woman and my earnest hope is that you can understand how very sorry I am and how very much I would like to be your friend.' He took her hand in his and squeezed it lightly. 'Did I make you *very* unhappy?'

Katrina removed her hand. 'No,' she said. 'You made me very angry.'

'I'm sure I did,' Lewis said. 'I was a scumbag.' He gave a deep sigh. 'I can't bear to have you hate me.'

'I don't hate you. I don't like you very much, that's all.'

'I understand.' Lewis took off his sunglasses and put them on the wall. 'I'm getting in that pool,' he said, 'and I shan't rise to the surface until you tell me you forgive me.' He turned and jumped into the water.

Katrina watched him form a tight ball on the floor of the pool. She folded her arms and stared stonily down at him. The man was an idiot. No doubt he expected her to jump in after him and confess her undying love for him. She glanced across at the courtyard. She wished Rose would come out again. She looked back at Lewis. He was still crouched, foetus-like, at the bottom of the pool. Katrina gnawed at her bottom lip. Suppose he *didn't* come up? She opened her mouth and then shut it again. If he were to die down there, it would be entirely his own fault. She glanced again at the courtyard. This was ridiculous. Finally, she couldn't bear it any longer. She got down on her knees and slashed the water with her hands. 'Lewis,' she yelled. 'Come up at once!'

His face, alarmingly puce, appeared in a second. 'Tell me,' he gasped, 'tell me you forgive me. I shall go back down unless you forgive me.'

Despite herself, Katrina laughed. 'You're mad,' she said, 'you're utterly mad!'

She looked up and saw that her sister was standing on the other side of the pool. 'My darlings,' Rose exclaimed, 'what *are* you both doing?'

*   *   *

Supper was lively, if rather late owing to the fact that the cooks had disappeared from the kitchen for a while. Francis was clearly one of those people who needed to snort stuff up his nose in order to construct anything resembling a personality. Throughout the meal, he was increasingly loquacious, telling rambling stories which no one paid any attention to. Conversational topics ranged easily from the weather, to Rose's plans to set up as a garden consultant, to the latest make-up freebies that Cam had acquired through her job in the Beauty department of *Simply Fashion* and, finally, over coffee, to Lewis's forthcoming rehearsals for a new television serial.

'I think it could be good,' Lewis said. 'I have a great part. I'm an MP, very charming and charismatic...'

'Perfect type-casting,' Rose cooed.

'Thank you. I have a stunning wife, gorgeous children, even a couple of cute grandchildren. I seem to be an all-round Mr Nice Guy. And then, with each passing episode, we learn more and more terrible things about him and his family... incest, adultery, stuff like that.'

'Just like real life, then,' Sam said. 'Do you have the main part?'

'In theory,' Lewis said. 'Unfortunately, I die in the first episode.'

'I'm thinking of writing a novel about incest,' Francis said.

'How clever of you!' Rose said. 'Do you know anything about the subject?'

Francis nodded. 'I do, actually. When I was a kid I used to fancy my sister. Then she had her hair cut and I didn't.'

'That must have been a relief for her,' Katrina said.

Rose gave a loud yawn. 'I think I'm rather tired! Lewis, darling, shall we go to bed?'

'I do feel a little sleepy,' Lewis said, rising from his chair with a swiftness that suggested otherwise.

Rose came over to give her sister a scented kiss on the cheek. 'Katty, dear, have a good lie-in tomorrow. We usually have breakfast about ten. It's so marvellous to have you here!'

'Thank you,' Katrina said. 'Have a good night.'

Her eyes met those of Lewis and she gave him an extremely brief smile. 'Have a good night both of you.'

No sooner had the happy couple left than their absence was filled by the arrival of two enormous May bugs which, after circling the light, started making kamikaze assaults on the table. Sam leapt to his feet and made for the door, at the back of which rested an old green fishing net. Despite, rather than because of, the attempts of Francis to lure the insects to their doom, Sam eventually caught them and hurled them out into the night.

'Yuck!' said Sassy. 'Horrible things! What shall we do now?'

'Have some more wine,' said Sam, reaching for the bottle. 'Tell me, Aunty Katty, what do you think of Mother's new boyfriend?'

'Very charming,' Katrina said.

'Now, that,' Sam said, returning to his chair and taking the bottle from his sister, 'is the sort of remark you make when you can't think of anything nice to say.'

'Not at all,' Katrina retorted. 'He *is* charming. I don't know him well enough to pass any sound opinions on him. I don't go along with first impressions.'

Francis gave one of his silly laughs again. Katrina tried hard not to give him a sour look. Certainly, her first impressions about *him* had been right.

'I think he's lovely,' Cam said. 'I think Mother's very lucky.'

Katrina refused Sam's offer of the wine bottle and stood up. 'It's been a long day,' she said. 'I think I'll go to bed.'

'Would you like a quick game of cards first?' Sam

suggested.

'How about a game of strip poker?' Francis asked. 'Do you fancy playing strip poker, Aunty Katty?'

Hearing Francis call her 'Aunty Katty' was like hearing chalk being scraped the wrong way up a blackboard. Katrina tucked her chair under the table. 'First, Francis, I am not your aunt and, secondly, the thought of taking my clothes off in front of you is even less appealing to me than it is to you.' She smiled sweetly. 'Thank you all for a lovely dinner. I promise I'll play cards tomorrow. I will see you in the morning.'

As she climbed the stairs, she could hear Francis laughing yet again. He sounded like a seal. She couldn't begin to understand what Cam saw in him.

When she got into bed, she reached out for her biography of Mary Shelley. She was *not* going to think of Lewis and Rose. She read two pages before she realized she had not taken in a single word. She closed her eyes for a moment, went back to the beginning of the chapter and tried to concentrate on poor Mary, so young and so in love, so plagued by the unwelcome companionship of a vivacious stepsister whose sexually provocative attitude made her feel so dull. Katrina put the book down. It was all too depressing.

Katrina turned out the light and started counting sheep. After she'd watched the hundred and twenty-seventh jump over a wall, she gave up. She had no idea how she was going to get through the holiday. All sorts of mean, ugly, petty thoughts were sticking to her like molluscs on a rock. If she was absolutely honest, her extreme irritation with the four specimens of youthful beauty was inspired by jealousy. They were young and gorgeous and confident and she was not. As for Lewis, she didn't even want to begin to analyse her feelings for Lewis. And then there was her sister. It was pathetic, it was nasty, it was grotesque for a middle-aged woman to be jealous of her older, recently widowed sister. Yes, said a hateful voice inside her head, particularly since she's a wealthy widow who has never had to worry about work or bills or mortgages. For twenty-seven years, Rose had been cosseted and adored by a sweet man with oodles of money. And now, having been on her own for hardly any time at all, she was being cosseted and adored by Lewis.

Katrina turned to the left and then to the right. She hated this. She hated herself. She was back to being a snivelling adolescent who couldn't understand why she had spots on her chin when her sister had none. Rose hadn't stolen Lewis from her because Lewis had never belonged to her. He would never have wanted to stay with a not-wildly attractive solicitor who lived in a terribly untidy terraced house in Greenwich.

She switched on the light again and reached for her book. This time, she did indeed get immersed in the tangled affairs of Mary and her (probably justified) suspicion that her poet was sleeping with her stepsister. It was when Katrina finally reached the end of the chapter that she sat up quite suddenly. Mary's stepsister, so much livelier, sexier and naughtier than Mary, was called Jane. While living with Mary and Percy Shelley, she decided to change her name from Jane to Claire.

Mary had a wildly attractive stepsister who

changed her name to Claire. Katrina had a wildly attractive sister who changed her name to Rose! How extraordinary! No wonder Katrina felt so drawn to Mary. They were so alike. Except that Katrina was a solicitor while Mary was the writer of *Frankenstein*. And Katrina had been married to a sleazy serial propagator while Mary had been married to the most gifted poet of the nineteenth century.

Katrina shook her head angrily. What was wrong with her? Now she was jealous of a woman who had died over a hundred and fifty years ago! She was jealous of a woman who had watched three of her four babies die, who had suffered a horrendous miscarriage only three weeks before the drowning of her husband, who had spent the rest of her life in unremittingly dreary genteel poverty! How could she be jealous of Mary Shelley? This was what always happened when she couldn't sleep. She would start creating problems out of nothing, manufacturing miseries, embroidering crises, nurturing paranoia and self-pity.

She shut her book and switched off the light again. Then she lay down and waited for sleep to come. Eventually, she heard the voices of Sam and Sassie on the stairs, Sam's slow, laid-back drawl contrasting with Sassy's quick light tones. Katrina tried to imagine herself lying on a velvet blanket and falling, falling, falling into it. It was an infallible yoga trick she'd been told about years ago and it had never worked yet but there was always a first time.

She stiffened as she heard the bed springs from Sam's room start a rhythmic squeak. Great.

Katrina tried to concentrate on the velvet blanket but the more she tried to concentrate, the louder Sassy's cries were: 'Oh, Sam! Oh, Sam! Oh, Sam!' Katrina put her hands over her ears but by this time Sassy's sounds were almost operatic. 'Oh, Sam, you're amazing! Oh, Sam, it's such paradise!' And then Sam let out a huge sound like the roar of a train as it emerged from a tunnel.

Katrina started counting sheep again. By the time she got to one hundred and seventy she was beginning to feel sleepy. Then she heard Cam's voice: 'Oh, Francis, Francis, Francis, don't stop!'

Francis didn't stop. Francis went on and on and on. And on.

Katrina got out of bed, took off her nightdress, wrapped her towel round her and went out to the pool. She swam ten lengths and dried herself thoroughly before returning to bed. All was quiet. Katrina fell asleep at last and dreamt of the woman in Boulogne.

CHAPTER SEVEN

A Game of Backgammon

Katrina came down the next morning, dressed in her swimming costume and clutching her towel. As she had hoped and expected, the house was silent. She went out to the pool and dropped her towel on one of the loungers.

A few cicadas had clearly been partying in the night. They had fallen into the pool where they floated helplessly, their little legs floundering in the air. Katrina located a net and fished them out, gently tipping them onto the stone tiles. They lay there, gathering their legs and their thoughts. Did cicadas think? Had they realized some munificent being—Katrina Latham—had saved their lives? Or did they just think: we were *there* and now we are *here*, heigh-ho? Perhaps they didn't think at all. They were clearly survivors, they were already looking better.

Katrina stood up and went to the edge of the pool. She took a deep breath and slipped into the water. She was here to conduct an exorcism and she had the perfect conditions in which to do it: a seamless blue sky, a warm friendly sun and exhilaratingly cold but not unpleasantly freezing water. She lowered her head and swam slowly but purposefully up and down the pool, letting the nocturnal cacophony of childlike, nasty thoughts and resentments fall away. I am a mature and intelligent woman who is happy in her own skin, she told herself. I am cool, I am calm, I am content.

Raising her face for a gasp of air, she noticed a pair of feet by the side of the pool. The feet belonged to Lewis. She felt oddly affronted as if she had been caught in an act of intimacy. 'Hello,' she said, 'have you been here long?'

'Long enough to admire your energy,' Lewis said. 'This must be the first time since I've been here that anyone's been in the pool before eleven.'

'It's nice to have it to myself.'

'I'm off to Cleon to get the croissants. Why don't you come too?'

'Thanks,' Katrina said. 'I think I'll swim for a little longer.'

'I'll see you later, then.' Lewis put on his sunglasses and walked away. In his cream linen shorts and crisp white T-shirt he looked like someone who'd stepped out of a washing-powder advert. He turned to give her a wave and Katrina, bobbing about in the middle of the pool, gave him a slightly wobbly wave back.

She could swear she had detected a note of surprise, perhaps even of pique in his voice when she declined his offer to tag along. *Yah boo sucks, Mr Beautiful Buttocks, that'll show you!* What it was she had shown she was not sure. She was beginning to get tired and her fingers were becoming numb but she could not get out of the pool until she was certain Lewis had gone. She turned and did yet another length. I am a mature and intelligent woman, she told herself, who cannot get out of the pool in case my sister's boyfriend is still around.

She heard the sound of a car engine and gratefully heaved herself out of the water. Her fingers were so wrinkled she could hardly hold her towel. If she got pneumonia she would jolly well blame Lewis.

A hot shower improved her spirits, as did the sight of her reflection when she put on her new wrap-round sundress. She might be immature and impossibly un-cool but she still had a decent figure.

Unlike her sister—who had an outstanding one. When Katrina came downstairs, she found Rose making coffee in a diaphanous lilac skirt and a tiny pink vest. Her auburn hair was piled high on her head, revealing an elegant swan-like neck.

'Katty!' Rose said. 'Fancy me being up before

you! Did you sleep well?'

'Very,' lied Katrina. 'Actually, I *was* up before you. I've had a lovely swim.'

'Isn't this place just too beautiful? Really, I feel quite blessed!'

'I should think you do,' Katrina said. 'I was a little surprised to get your text on the boat. I thought I was coming out here to console a grieving widow. I suspect I'm quite surplus to requirements.'

Rose laughed. 'If I didn't know you better, I'd think you were quite put out to find I *wasn't* a grieving widow! You *are* happy for me, aren't you?'

'Yes, of course I am, it's just that—'

'Good, because I am quite *deliriously* in love! I've made the coffee, so we can eat as soon as Lewis comes back. Would you like some orange juice? Get us a couple of glasses from the tray and we'll sit outside. I don't want to miss a moment of the sun.'

They sat at the table in the courtyard, sipping their juice and watching a dusty green lizard traversing the tall wall behind the barbecue.

'He's amazing,' said Katrina. 'One moment he's still as a statue and then he shoots across the stones like he's powered by a jet-controlled engine!'

'I love the way they disappear through the holes in the wall. It must be wonderful to be so flexible. No wonder lizards don't need the gym.' Rose sat back in her chair and adopted a concerned, even sorrowful expression that made Katrina instantly apprehensive. 'I'm glad we're on our own at last,' she said. 'I want to talk to you. I know you're hiding something. Lewis and I were talking about you last night.'

Katrina swallowed. 'Were you?'

'We were. I told him I'd hate to be you.'

'Really? Thank you for sharing that with me.'

'Don't take offence, Katty, I meant it in the best possible way. I admire you so much. You've had to work so hard to bring up Ollie and Susie without any help from that awful ex-husband of yours, who seems to think he's on a God-given mission to spread his seed as widely as he can. And you live this nun-like life. I couldn't bear it! I told Lewis it makes me weep sometimes.'

'What did Lewis say?'

'He said it was a terrible waste.'

'How very nice of him.'

'He likes you very much, Katty. I'd love to see you as happy as I am. Which is why I want to talk about your friend Cornelius. I could see you didn't want to talk about him in front of the Young but you can tell *me*! Is there romance in the air?'

'Would you be happy if there was?' Katrina asked, playing for time.

'I'm sure he's very nice,' Rose said, 'if a little peculiar.'

'I don't see how you can think he's peculiar,' Katrina said hotly. 'You only met him for a few minutes.'

'You have to admit he was a little brusque when I asked if I could call him Corny.'

'How would you like to be called Corny?'

'I wouldn't mind. He didn't have to be so short with me.'

'He's not very good at small talk, that's all. He doesn't like it.'

'I'm sorry,' said Rose, 'but that is so self-

89

indulgent! Have you ever met anyone who *does* admit to liking it? We'd all love to have deep, meaningful discussions—don't look at me like that, I can do deep and meaningful as well as anyone—and also, of course, we all love cosy, confidential chats. Unfortunately, when you meet someone for the first time, you can't plunge straight into gossip or moral dilemmas, you have to start with small talk and it helps if you can do so with at least a modicum of common courtesy.'

'I don't think Cornelius meant to be rude. He was simply telling you he didn't like to be called Corny. He has very strong opinions about speaking the truth.'

'Very laudable, I'm sure,' said Rose without any conviction. 'I have to say that he's not my type but if *you* find it fun to be with him then I adore him already. Of course,' Rose paused to kick off her sandals, 'he is a little odd-looking. He looks like a scarecrow.'

'He does not!'

'He does, you know he does! I shouldn't think he's had a proper haircut in years! I'm not being rude. He looks like a very nice scarecrow. I'll tell you something else. He looks exactly like that ugly pop star you always liked: Jarvis Cocker!'

'Of course!' Katrina clapped her hands. 'I *knew* he reminded me of someone. Apart from his hair, he looks just like him!'

'Well, that explains everything,' Rose said. 'Now I understand why you like Cornelius! You *do* like him, don't you? What odd taste you have! Can I take it you're an item?'

Katrina shifted uncomfortably in her seat. 'We might be,' she said. 'We only met for the first time on the boat. My trainee at work is married to his office manager. When she told him I was coming out here, he got Cornelius to offer me a lift. It was very kind of him.'

'So,' said Rose, putting her hands together like an inquisitorial judge, 'you met on the boat. And then what? Was it like me and Lewis? Did you feel you'd met your soulmate? Did you look into his eyes and feel him mentally undress you? Did you feel an uncontrollable urge to kiss him?'

'Sort of,' Katrina said. She reached into her pocket. It was easier to tell lies with her sunglasses on.

'Was it love at first sight?' Rose demanded. 'Did you know at once that something was going to happen? Did Cornelius look surprised or shaken the first time he met you?'

'Yes,' said Katrina truthfully. 'He was definitely shaken. And surprised.'

'So then you got to France and you stayed the night en route. My next question is simple: one bed or two?'

Katrina was about to hotly deny that there had been any bed-hopping but the thought that Rose and Lewis had been solemnly bemoaning her celibacy goaded her into a more ambiguous answer. 'I am not going to discuss my sex life with you. And—'

'You slept together! Oh, Katty, I'm so happy for you! It is so frustrating that you won't let me ask him over. If his friends are arguing all the time, he might be very glad to spend a bit of time with some nice, happy people like us.'

'No, he won't,' Katrina said firmly. 'He's promised to devote the week to them.'

'Well, it's very annoying . . .' The gate clanged open behind them and Rose turned and held out her arms, 'Lewis, you're back! Come and give me a kiss!'

Lewis obligingly came over, deposited the bread and the croissants on the table and kissed Rose.

'Katrina and I have been having a lovely, girly talk,' said Rose.

'I'm sorry you had it without me,' Lewis said. 'I love girly talks.'

'It's all very exciting,' Rose said. 'Katrina's been telling me about her and Cornelius.'

Lewis raised an eyebrow and adopted a smile that he probably thought was playful but which Katrina interpreted as patronizing. 'Do I take it that love is in the air?' he asked.

Katrina stood up. 'You can take it any way you like,' she said. 'I'll go and get the coffee.'

*   *   *

After breakfast the three of them went on an expedition to the hypermarket. Katrina, sitting in the back like an awkward child, tried not to notice the way Rose kept stroking Lewis's thigh.

'We need to get some more booze,' said Rose, 'and olive oil and water and tomatoes and something for supper.'

'I'll cook tonight,' Katrina said. 'How about ratatouille and sautéed potatoes?'

'Let's have some chops as well,' said Lewis. 'I can cook them on the barbecue.'

'Don't you agree, Katty,' said Rose, 'that there's something terribly sexy about men doing a barbecue?'

Katrina folded her arms. 'I wouldn't know,' she said. 'I've never had much experience of barbecues.'

For some reason Lewis and Rose found this terribly funny. Katrina sat sourly in the back and consoled herself with the thought that she had only six days left before she went home.

She had to remind herself of that again later in the day. She had emerged after a swim to find Sam and Lewis playing backgammon on the little white table at the far side of the pool. It was funny to think that she had introduced this game to both of them. She had taught Sam when he was only ten and he had proved a quick pupil. Lewis had been less adept and had never managed to beat her. The thought occurred to her that her constant supremacy in this area might have been a small factor in his unwillingness to form a permanent attachment to her. One of Katrina's most besetting sins was her intense competitiveness where card and board games were concerned. She was probably the only mother who had never let her children win at anything. She had only to see a snakes and ladders board to feel the blood rise, along with a fierce determination to get to the final square before anyone else. So now she could not see the backgammon without saying casually to Sam, 'I'll play the winner.' Then she went to the sun-lounger, lay down, shut her eyes and waited for Sam to demolish Lewis.

A few minutes later she heard Sam call her. 'He beat me! Come and tear him apart, Aunty Katty!'

Katrina sat up immediately. 'No problem,' she said. She had a pleasurable rush of anticipation. It would be good to beat Lewis. She walked over and took Sam's place by the table.

'You haven't a chance of beating Aunty Katty,' Sam said. 'She's the master.'

'Really?' Lewis picked up the dice. 'Would you like to go first, Katrina?'

'That's all right, you throw.' Katrina pulled her chair closer to the table. For the first time this holiday she felt on superior ground to the man sitting opposite her and the feeling was sweet.

Lewis had improved. In the old days he would move his counters with little thought, interested only in bouncing his competitor. He was different now, ready to sacrifice instant gain in order to pursue eventual success. When she threw a double six and sent two of his counters back to his corner, she couldn't resist glancing up at him with a triumphant curl of her lip.

'Katrina,' he said, 'you have a very nasty streak. I would never have thought it.'

'First rule of backgammon,' Katrina said crisply, 'never underestimate your competitor's desire to win.'

'I can assure you,' Lewis said softly, 'I would *never* underestimate you.'

Perhaps it was the way he looked at her that led her to carelessly expose one of her counters. Katrina bit hard on her nails when he got her and scrutinized the board with painful concentration. She rolled the dice three times before she got free. Then she had a four and a three and bounced him but he got a two and a six and landed on another of her counters.

'First rule of backgammon,' he reminded her, 'never underestimate your competitor's desire to win.'

Katrina ground her teeth and rattled her dice as hard as she could, but once again luck was against her. Six goes later, Lewis had won.

Katrina was mortified. 'I can't believe it,' she said. 'I can't believe you beat me!'

Lewis gave a modest little shrug. 'I play a lot these days. I'm better than I used to be.'

'That's for sure,' Katrina said. 'And of course you were terribly lucky. That was a one-off. You do realize that, don't you?'

Lewis smiled sweetly. 'Far be it from me to suggest you are a sore loser,' he said. 'I can see it's quite hard for you to accept I can play this game rather well.'

'To hear you two talk,' Rose said, 'you'd think you've played together loads of times . . . Why, Katty, you've gone bright red!'

Cam looked up from her paperback. 'Why Aunty Katty, so you have! Are you nursing a guilty secret?'

Suddenly, everyone was looking at her. If she *hadn't* been nursing a guilty secret, she would have been able to laugh and everything would have been fine. She *should* have laughed: there was absolutely no need to do anything else and, if panic hadn't scrambled her brain, she would have done.

'Well,' she said with a rueful smile that concealed the fact that her mind was throwing up and rejecting possible explanations like a possessed ploughshare, 'it's all very embarrassing and I don't really want to talk about it.'

She should have known that this particular group of people would react to such a statement with all the sensitivity of a starving rhinoceros. While Cam and Sam and ghastly Francis and Rose insisted that she reveal all, Lewis reached for the suntan lotion and proceeded to pay grave and exclusive attention to his epidermis.

Katrina, having finally thought up something, gave in at last. 'You remember I mentioned I met Lewis many years ago? In those days he was a big television star so it was very exciting to talk to him. Anyway, for some reason, for a few weeks after that, I had a recurring dream about him in which we played backgammon together and in my dream, I always won.'

'Is that *all* you did?' asked Sam. 'You just played backgammon together?'

'That's all we did,' Katrina said. She could see she had disappointed her audience and added apologetically, 'I do love backgammon.'

'Actually,' said Cam, 'it's quite weird that you used to dream about Lewis. You must have felt very odd when you found out he was going to be here.'

'Oh, I did!' Katrina laughed. 'I told Cornelius about it on the boat and we both agreed it must be fate!' Really, she amazed herself, she had no idea she was such an inventive liar.

Rose came over to Lewis and put her arms round him. 'I'm not surprised you dreamt about this man,' she told Katrina. 'I would have done too. But in *my* dreams we'd have been playing a different game!'

'For God's sake, Mother!' Cam protested. 'Do you have to say things like that?'

Rose laughed and kissed Lewis's forehead. 'I'm going upstairs for a shower, darling. Are you going to join me?'

Lewis put an arm round her waist. 'Give me a few minutes and I'll be there. I'll give Katrina a chance to make her dream come true, first.'

'Just as long,' Rose smiled, 'as you come up soon and make *my* dream come true.'

'Mother!' Cam protested. 'Stop it!'

Rose laughed and walked towards the house. Katrina made a great play of setting out the counters and was glad she could concentrate on the game. This time she was more careful, only allowing herself to be momentarily distracted when Cam and Sam and their partners jumped into the pool and splashed her legs.

This time she won. She looked up and beamed at Lewis. 'That's better,' she said.

Lewis smiled at her. 'It's just like old times,' he murmured.

Katrina glanced fleetingly at the occupants of the swimming pool. 'I am trying very hard,' she said in a low, urgent voice, 'to forget about old times. And anyway, it's not at all like old times. For a start, we're a great deal older and you're in love with my sister.'

Lewis raised an enquiring eyebrow. 'And you're in love with Cornelius?'

Katrina shut the backgammon case. 'I think,' she said, 'it's time you went up to see Rose.'

CHAPTER EIGHT

A Difficult Lunch

'It's just like old times.'

Katrina did not sleep well that night. She kept replaying that comment of Lewis's. Why had he said that? What did he mean by it? Did he mean anything at all by it? Did he perhaps mean anything *unconsciously* by it? Given that he had behaved so disgracefully in old times, he had considerable nerve in referring to them in tones of such wistful nostalgia. The remark was doubly outrageous given that he had gone off to the annex straight afterwards where he had almost certainly, judging by the smug smile on Rose's face when she finally reappeared, indulged in activities of a strictly un-wistful nature.

There was something else that kept Katrina awake. Her relationship with Cornelius had developed at an alarming rate in the last twenty-four hours, progressing from a gently burgeoning friendship into a full-blown passionate love affair. It was only fair that Katrina should inform Cornelius of this development. She should never have told any lies in the first place, they were constantly threatening to spiral out of control, she should have simply told Rose that she had once had a relationship with Lewis, and that would have been that. Except it wouldn't, because Rose would have wanted to know why Katrina had never said anything about it at the time and the whole thing would have been horribly humiliating. Although

98

come to that, she thought glumly, her position here was pretty humiliating: Maiden Aunt Katty, who spent her nights dreaming about backgammon, surrounded on all sides by sexual athletes. At which point, as if on cue, Francis began one of his nocturnal marathons. Katrina gave a resigned sigh and put her pillow over her head.

She slept late the next morning and came down to find a funereal atmosphere round the breakfast table. This was because the sky was the colour of tarmac and the rain was falling with such ferocity that it looked like a divine hosepipe was aiming itself directly at the house.

After a long and agonized discussion about the possible causes of the transformation (global warming, Katrina's arrival), and the likely duration (one hour, one week, for ever), Rose decided that there was only one possible solution. 'We shall go out to lunch,' she said. 'We shall go to the restaurant near Cleon and have a nice, long, lazy meal.'

Katrina would have been quite happy to spend the day drinking coffee and reading her book. The problem with being a holiday guest, especially with being an unattached holiday guest, was that one was effectively neutered from doing what one really wanted to do. So once again Katrina found herself watching her sister stroke her ex-lover's leg as they drove through the rain. Katrina would have almost preferred to go in the other car with Cam and Sam and Sassy and Francis. Actually, that wasn't true: her dislike of Francis had now reached stratospheric proportions. She knew her antagonism was not wholly rational. There was nothing too terribly wrong with him apart from the fact that he was smug, vacuous, unintelligent and vain. Nevertheless, every time he opened his mouth, she could feel her nerve endings jangle.

Les Voyageurs was a jolly, sprawling place with a main concourse and a few ante-rooms; it was to one of these that their party was shown. Katrina sat at one end of the table while the others sat on either side of her. Katrina imagined them all playing footsie with their partners and tucked her own feet primly behind her chair legs.

She felt better when the first course arrived—a salmon mousse which was quite delicious—and she enjoyed hearing Sassy talk about her travails as a script editor, particularly her account of an apparently sweet-natured television star who had slapped a poor underling when her car received a parking ticket.

It was during the main course that things went wrong. It began quite innocently with Cam asking after Ollie and Susie.

'They're very well,' Katrina said. 'Ollie's working in an office at the moment. He's hoping to earn enough to go travelling with a friend next January. And then he'll be off to university.'

'Ollie,' Rose told Lewis, 'is three years younger than Susie but he looks older. He's tall, dark and drop-dead gorgeous and he has not got the first idea that he is an utter babe magnet!'

Sam gave an exaggerated wince. 'I think there should be a rule,' he said, 'that no one over twenty should describe anyone as a babe magnet.'

'I don't think *anyone* should describe *anyone else* as a babe magnet,' Cam said. She rested her elbows on the table and nodded encouragingly at

100

Katrina. 'So tell me about Susie. She's done her Finals. What's my lovely little cousin doing now?'

'She and her drama group are up in Edinburgh. They put on *Hamlet* in the spring and it did so well they decided to take it to the Festival. I was very impressed when I saw it. Susie was a great Ophelia and her Hamlet had fantastic stage presence.'

'We must introduce her to Lewis,' Rose said. 'He'll be able to give her all sorts of advice, won't you, darling?'

'I'd be delighted to be of any help I can,' Lewis said. 'Is she going to drama school?'

'She got through the first three auditions for RADA,' Katrina said, 'and then they turned her down. She's determined to try again. Susie never does things by halves. She is absolutely passionate about acting. The plan is for her to get a job and earn as much money as she can in the meantime.'

'Is she still going out with her stand-up comedian?' Cam asked. 'I'd love to meet him.'

'You'd like him,' Katrina assured her. 'He's very charming. He's just finished university, like Susie, but he's been earning money from his comedy all through his student years.'

'Susie,' Rose told Lewis, 'is a brown-haired beauty.'

'How funny,' Lewis said, 'I imagined her blonde.'

'I can't think why,' Rose said, 'unless you think all pretty girls are blonde.'

'You know very well,' Lewis countered, stroking Rose's hair, 'that I do not think that at all. I suppose I just assumed she'd have the same colour hair as her cousins.'

'Well, she was blonde when she was young,' Rose said. 'She was a funny little girl, she went

101

everywhere with this horrible old moth-eaten polar bear. Do you remember, Katty?'

Katrina did remember and, after a fleeting glance at Lewis, was pretty sure he did too. 'I'm sorry,' she gave an apologetic smile. 'I wasn't listening. I thought for a moment I could hear Cornelius in the other room. There's someone out there who sounds just like him.'

'There's no hope for you, Katty,' Rose said. 'It must be love!'

The diversionary tactic had worked. Lewis's unwise comment had been forgotten and instead, for the next few minutes, Katrina had to endure yet another family inquisition. She was aware that she had become an unwilling cabaret act to Cam and Sam and their friends. To them she was a sad, single lady who was completely at sea over her first love affair in years. Worse, she had painted herself into a position where she was duty bound to *play* the part of a sad, single lady who was completely at sea.

Things got worse as the meal progressed. Rose went off to the lavatory and came back, bursting with news. 'Katty, you'll never guess! You *did* hear Cornelius! He's in there with his friends and they all look very happy. They have two children with them who are absolutely adorable.'

'You didn't speak to them, did you?' Katrina asked.

'Well, of course I did. Did you expect me to ignore them? I said we ought to invite them for a meal or a drink. I told Cornelius we were very keen to get to know him better!'

'We certainly are,' said Cam. 'I want to know if his intentions are honourable towards—'

'I think,' Katrina said hastily, 'I'll just go and say hello. I won't be a moment.'

She went through to the main concourse. She spotted Cornelius at once. He was sitting between two little boys. He had made a hat out of his napkin and was offering it to the smaller child. Their parents—a bearded man with shoulder-length hair and a fine-boned woman with a loose chignon and a big smile—looked like people that Katrina would like to know.

She took a deep breath and walked up to them.

Cornelius stood up immediately. 'Katrina! This is James and this is Odile and these two are Luc and Pierre.'

'Hello . . . Hello . . . Hello,' Katrina said quickly. 'I'm so sorry to interrupt your meal, I just wanted to say . . . Cornelius, it's blatantly obvious that your friends are very happy together and so Rose is determined to have you all over and that would be disastrous because . . .' She paused and turned to James and Odile. 'I'm so sorry, this must all seem very confusing to you and it certainly does to me . . .' She turned back to Cornelius. 'The thing is, you and I are now very much in love and I'm really sorry but it just kept escalating and they all want to look at you and you would definitely loathe it and so of course you mustn't come over and I am so sorry but short of you getting your friends to stage a fight in the restaurant I can't think what you can do but I have to tell you if you *do* come over it will be excruciating.'

'I see,' said Cornelius, who clearly didn't. 'I see.' He glanced across at James who was, not surprisingly, regarding Katrina with a mixture of curiosity and bewilderment.

'Look,' said Katrina desperately, 'I'll tell them I forgot to ask you but I know my sister. She'll want to come over here and ask you herself. You're going to have to come over to us at some point and refuse Rose's invitation if she gives you one and she *will* give you one. If I tell Rose you're coming over to say hello, then she won't come over to invite you but . . . Anyway, see what you think . . . I'm so sorry . . . This love affair has got so out of control and I don't really know why . . .' She gave a hopeless shrug, said an anxious goodbye to Cornelius's companions and returned to the table from hell.

'Well?' Rose demanded. 'What did they say?'

Katrina sat down and reached for her wine glass. 'Oh,' she said airily, 'they were very nice. Cornelius introduced me to his friends.'

'Did you see what I was saying? Don't you think they looked jolly? I reckon they've had a grand reconciliation.'

'I don't know,' Katrina said. 'I didn't feel I could ask them.'

'Well, of course you couldn't,' Rose said, 'that would have been very silly. Did you invite them over to see us?'

'Yes,' said Katrina, 'but Cornelius didn't think it was a good idea.'

'Well, for goodness' sake, I'm only suggesting a drink or even a light meal—'

'But Cornelius is going to come and say hello to you all before they leave and so,' Katrina said, mentally apologizing to Cornelius, 'you can ask him yourself.'

'I shall do,' said Rose, raising her chin.

Katrina could see Cam and Sam exchange

glances and she knew exactly what they were thinking. Poor Aunty Katty was in love with a man who was so far from interested that he couldn't even bother to drive the three kilometres from Cleon to call on her. Katrina contemplated the idea of refilling her glass and getting mindlessly drunk, which would, of course, only confirm to her niece and nephew that she was the most pathetic member of the human race. She picked up her glass of water and felt a sudden wave of homesickness. She wished she was back in her own home with its small rectangular garden and the little pond that she and the children had made a few years ago. She drank some of her water and made herself concentrate on the present conversation, which had switched from the subject of Cornelius to plans for the next day. Sam was saying that he and Cam and Sassy and Francis were planning to drive down to the famous gorge of the Ardeche. 'We thought we'd go white-water rafting,' he said. 'We have to get there by half past ten so it means getting up early but—'

'You lot will never get up early,' said Rose. 'And if the weather's like this ...'

'Of course we won't go if the weather's like this,' Sam said. 'But as long as it's not raining—' He stopped and Katrina, following his gaze, saw that a rather nervous Cornelius and a considerably more relaxed James had come to their table.

Rose turned and beamed at them both. 'How lovely of you to come over!' she said. 'You must be Cornelius's friend from Cleon.'

'James Armitage,' said James, taking Rose's outstretched hand.

Rose batted her eyelashes at him. 'I was saying to

Katrina that I would love you all to come over and see us. You live so near and we've heard so much about Cornelius!'

Katrina, inwardly cringing, stared intensely at Cornelius, trying desperately to convey in her eyes her remorse, her culpability and her complete inability to have any control over anything. She watched Cornelius clear his throat. He looked every bit as unhappy as she was. He said feebly, 'I don't know what to say . . .'

'I'm afraid,' James said firmly, 'that you've caught us at a bad time. I'm sure you'll understand if I don't go into details. Cornelius is being a tower of strength but I know you'll appreciate why we're turning your kind invitation down.' He smiled directly at Katrina. 'I'm sure we'll be seeing *you* again . . . hopefully in happier circumstances.'

The man was brilliant! Katrina stood up and quite spontaneously kissed him on the cheek. 'Thank you,' she said with heartfelt gratitude. 'Thank you so much!'

'Well,' said Cornelius, 'we'd better get back.' He looked down at his shoes for a moment and then side-stepped James to give Katrina a very abrupt peck on the cheek. 'I'll see you soon,' he said. He cleared his throat. 'You look very nice in that . . . That dress is very . . . I'll see you soon.'

*   *   *

The next day the weather was still grey but at least it wasn't raining. Katrina came down at nine and was impressed by the fact that the white-water rafters had already dressed, bought croissants and eaten their fill. She waved them off and tidied the kitchen while wondering how she could avoid playing gooseberry for the day ahead. Before they had gone to bed last night, Rose had suggested that the three of them go to Montelimar. Apparently, there was a wonderfully romantic restaurant there that Katty would just adore.

The thought of being in a romantic restaurant with Lewis and Rose made Katrina's skin crawl. She put on some more coffee and sounded out various excuses in her head: a sudden migraine, an even more sudden recollection that she had to work on some important papers or wait for an important phone call. What she needed was a guardian angel or, even better, a white knight to come along and whisk her away on his white charger.

And then the telephone rang.

CHAPTER NINE

A Temporary Liberation

Cornelius regarded James and Odile as two of his closest friends and thought he knew them well, but that afternoon they displayed reservoirs of brilliance he had never seen before. He had told them nothing about Katrina other than the fact that she had proved to be far less irritating than he had expected. She had burst in upon them at the restaurant, her darting eyes apparently contained only by the dark shadows that sat beneath them. In their place, he would have assumed she was, at the very least, demented.

When she left them with the same suddenness with which she had arrived, Odile had immediately responded with the practicality that never failed to impress him. 'Cornelius,' she had said, 'your friend is in trouble. We must help. I do not understand. Please explain.'

So Cornelius had explained. He told them that Katrina had only found out on the ferry that the love of her life was now the love of her sister. He told them that she was anxious to demonstrate that she was free of past affections by inventing an attraction for Cornelius. As far as he could gather, he said carefully, Katrina had somehow been compelled to embroider the initial fabrication and pretend that she and Cornelius were very much in love. He told them that in order to save him any embarrassment arising from the deception, she had manufactured a scenario whereby his warring friends were in dire emotional turmoil thus excusing him from having to accept any awkward invitations. Unfortunately, since her sister had seen that there was no evidence of any such turmoil, she was intent on inviting them all over. He told them that it was all very confusing but. . .

'I understand perfectly,' Odile said. 'You and James must go over to their table now. Cornelius, you must try to look passionate. James, you must try to look unhappy. So, go!'

And they had gone. And James had been superb. Later, Cornelius was the first to admit that *he* had been hopeless. He had seen Katrina sitting at the end of the table like an unwanted bottle of cheap wine, and he had been so angry he had found it difficult to even look at the three couples in front of her. But James had been magnificent, he had said everything that needed to be said and he had nudged Cornelius with a whispered, 'Passion!' Cornelius had no idea how he was supposed to show this but he had at least sort of kissed Katrina and had also managed to pat her arm. His final memory of that lunch would be of Katrina, sitting there, bestowing on him a smile of true sweetness, while her awful sister wittered on about nothing.

When he woke the next morning, he found that Katrina was lodged in his brain like an M25 traffic jam, blotting out all other matters of interest. It was clear she was having a ghastly time. Cornelius had visions of bacchanalian orgies going on around her while she pretended to read her biography of Mary Shelley. Of course none of this was anything to do with him. On the other hand, as her supposed lover, he should, at the very least, ring her from time to time.

It was during his second cup of coffee over breakfast that he said abruptly, 'I think I might ring Katrina. I might suggest I take her out for the day. She'll probably say no but it would be nice to ask. Will that be all right with you?'

James shook his head gravely. 'I don't know,' he said. 'I thought we were supposed to need you here in order to prevent domestic discord breaking out.'

'*Que tu es bête*,' Odile said calmly. 'Go to the telephone, Cornelius. Talk to Katrina.'

Which was fine except that Cornelius had no idea what he was going to talk *about*. He did not want her to think his call was inspired by compassion. Cornelius had never liked being an object of pity or sympathy and he was fairly sure that Katrina would feel the same. There was also the possibility that he had misinterpreted her situation. Cornelius was aware that he often *did* misinterpret things. She might even be enjoying the company of her family. He realized he had almost talked himself out of ringing, and when he did press the numbers he decided he would put the phone down if no one answered quickly.

He heard Katrina's voice, slightly breathless and with an appalling accent, enunciate, *'Bonjour?'*

He got as far as saying hello when she interrupted him with an enthusiastic, 'Oh, Cornelius, how lovely to hear you! How *are* you?'

'I'm very well. I wondered if . . . I thought I'd do some sightseeing today and I wondered if you'd care to accompany me?'

'Oh, I would! Cornelius, you are so kind, I would love to come out with you, I would really, *really* love to. Thank you.'

He was both relieved and disconcerted to be the focus of such untrammelled enthusiasm. 'Shall I pick you up in half an hour?' he asked. 'Or is that too soon?'

'It's not too soon at all. I'll be ready and waiting!'

'I'll see you then. Goodbye.' Cornelius put the receiver down. Now all he had to do was decide where he should take her.

*   *   *

He was relieved to see her waiting for him by the side of the road. He had not been looking forward to running the gauntlet of the terrifyingly confident young persons and the equally terrifyingly confident older persons. Katrina stood, clasping her bag in front of her, like a schoolgirl at

110

the bus stop with her satchel. He brought the car to a halt and leant across to open the passenger door.

'Cornelius, this is so kind of you,' Katrina breathed, putting her bag down by her feet and fastening her seat belt. 'All the young have gone off to the Ardeche and you have saved me from having to accompany Rose and Lewis to a restaurant in Montelimar that Rose says is incredibly romantic. So thank you. I feel like I've been liberated. Are you sure your friends don't mind losing you?'

'I felt almost aggrieved,' Cornelius said. 'They didn't mind at all.'

'I did like them! And the way James referred to his disastrous marriage was masterful. Will you tell him how grateful I was?'

'I will. I must say that I had no idea he was such a consummate liar. He and Odile thought you were very nice, by the way.'

'I'm not nice,' Katrina said solemnly. 'I'm not nice at all. Ever since I came here, my head has been full of the most horrible thoughts. I am jealous and bitter and twisted and nasty. And the worst of it is that I know I should be so happy for Rose. She lost her husband of twenty-seven years and I should be so pleased that she's found someone else, and I'm not pleased at all. I'm cross that she didn't tell me before, so I didn't have to waste a precious week's holiday by being fractious and irritable out here, and I can't stand Cam's boyfriend, and . . .' Katrina sighed deeply and pushed back her hair with both her hands. 'If I'm absolutely honest, the person I'm really cross with is *me*. I never learn. I knew the holiday would be a

111

disaster as soon as Rose mentioned it. I should never have agreed to come.'

'I don't see why,' Cornelius said. 'No one could have predicted all this business.'

'That's just it! You don't understand. *I* could have. If it hadn't been Lewis it would have been something else. There's *always* something else where Rose is concerned. I could tell you any number of stories. Like once, she rang and said she was worried about me, I sounded so tired on the phone, what I needed was a complete change of scene. She said she and her family were going to Florence at half-term and would I like to bring Ollie and Susie down for a restful break in the country? She and Roger had a fabulous house in a village near Salisbury and I thought: why not? So off we go, and find Cam there. She hadn't wanted to go to Florence, apparently. Which was fine except that Cam was just sixteen and made Lolita look like Little Bo Peep. Then I find a note from Rose asking me to make fifty fairy cakes that evening, for the Church Festival bring and buy. Then, the next evening, Cam goes out to a party and ends up in Casualty after drinking too much cider. And then the day after that, some builders come to install Rose's new kitchen. Rose told me later she'd booked the holiday to Florence as soon as she knew the builders were coming because she knew she wouldn't be able to abide the mess. I think it was the worst half-term I've ever had.' She put her palms together and shook her head. 'Actually, I think it's better if we don't talk about Rose or any of my other holiday companions at all. But you see why I appreciate your coming to my rescue today. You have no idea how wonderful it is to get away. Where are we going?'

'Quite a long way,' said Cornelius. 'I thought I'd take you up to the Vercors: limestone mountains thirty miles long and twenty miles wide with a huge plateau in the middle. French Resistance camps hid out there during the war. We're driving to a little village called Vassieux. There's rather a sad story attached to it.'

'Wait,' said Katrina. She moved her bag away from her feet and made herself comfortable. 'Tell me.'

So Cornelius did. 'A week after D-Day,' he said, 'all the members of the Underground for miles around were summoned by the Allies and General de Gaulle to join the resident Resistance groups on the plateau. The plan was that they would all rise up against the enemy. Nearly three thousand men turned up. The Allies promised four thousand paratroops, proper weapons and supplies. The idea was that the Allied troops would land on the south coast of France and the Resistance groups in the Vercors would attack the Germans from the rear.'

'And something went wrong?'

'Something went very wrong. The Allies never did land on the south coast and the promised troops and supplies never arrived. As the weeks passed, the situation became dire. Five thousand men were now massed on the plain. Many had no shoes and no weapons. Food was scarce. Once the Germans realized there was to be no invasion, they invaded the Vercors. I don't think the Allies ever intended to land in the south, they wanted the Germans to think they were so they'd take their eye off northern France. Twenty thousand German

113

soldiers besieged and devastated the area. One of the villages they destroyed was Vassieux.'

Katrina grimaced. 'How terrible. Was everyone killed?'

'Some of the Resistance people escaped but not many. One man who got out sent a signal to London. It's a masterpiece of understatement: "Arrested. Tortured. Shot. In good health." People were very brave.'

'It's funny,' Katrina said. 'Here we are driving through all these little towns with people like us who are worrying about mortgages and marriages and what to eat for supper. And sixty-odd years ago, their grandparents were facing death and betrayal on a daily basis.'

'Nothing's changed,' said Cornelius. 'Do you remember all the journalists and historians telling us that the end of the Cold War would bring an end to all conflict? And then think of Rwanda and the Balkans and Darfur and Iraq and Zimbabwe and Burma and Palestine and . . .' He shrugged. 'People haven't stopped doing unspeakable things to each other. In that context, I don't think your irritation with your sister can be described as evil and twisted.'

'On the contrary,' Katrina said, 'everyone knows that in a war people will do things they'd never dream of doing in peacetime. There are always far more nasty people than nice people in that situation. I *am* living in peacetime so I have no excuse.'

Cornelius glanced fleetingly at Katrina. 'I'm of the opinion,' he said, 'that in time of war, you would be one of the nice people.'

They had lunch at a roadside café and ate baguette sandwiches under the watchful eye of an enormous sheepdog. For the first time since she had come to France, Katrina felt in a holiday mood: relaxed, stimulated by her surroundings, conscious that she was enjoying herself and pretty certain that she was going to go on enjoying herself. 'I wish Ollie was here,' she said, shifting her body to one side so her legs could stretch out and feel the sun. 'I wish both my children were here but Ollie, I know, would love coming on this trip today. He's fascinated by the Second World War. Years ago, we were at a school jumble sale and I bought an old video of that TV series called *The World at War*. Ollie adored it all. He's been hooked by the subject ever since. If he were with us now, he'd be bombarding you with questions about the Resistance.'

'He sounds impressive,' Cornelius said.

'He's not particularly brilliant; I mean, he's bright but he's not *that* bright. The thing about Ollie is . . . Well, you know how some people –' Katrina hesitated but restrained herself from naming any of the occupants of her holiday residence—'some young people can make one feel inherently absurd simply because one has wrinkles? Well, Ollie isn't like that. Neither is Susie, actually. They are both enthusiasts. They're not afraid to show their enthusiasms. I think enthusiasm is very attractive, don't you?'

Cornelius was slow to answer and Katrina thought perhaps he hadn't heard her. She was about to repeat herself when he said with great finality, 'It is the very best of qualities.'

Katrina looked at him uncertainly. He seemed to be staring at the tree on the other side of the road but she was pretty sure he was seeing something very different. He looked so *desolate*. Her initial reaction was to burble away about something else but she sipped her drink and waited for him to speak again.

He glanced at her suddenly. 'I'm sorry,' he said, 'I was thinking of an Australian girlfriend I once had. She was very enthusiastic.'

Cornelius might not like telling lies but Katrina had a strong suspicion that he had just told one. She was quite certain that it was not some Australian girlfriend who had caused him to look so unhappy. Nevertheless, she gave an encouraging smile. 'Were you fond of her?'

'I suppose I must have been since I invited her home for Christmas. Or perhaps I only invited her because I didn't want to spend Christmas alone with my mother. Anyway, it turned out to be a bad idea.'

'Why? What happened?'

'All went well until we sat down to watch the Queen's speech on Christmas Day. She insisted we should show respect for Her Majesty by standing up. My mother displayed great presence of mind by inventing rheumatic knees. I stood up out of politeness but by the time the Queen's speech finished, so had my infatuation.'

Katrina nodded. 'It's funny how something quite small can change one's attitude. I went out with a nice boy once and I liked him very much until one day I realized he looked just like a monkey.'

'My Australian girlfriend laughed like an

elephant,' Cornelius said.

'You can't possibly know how elephants laugh,' Katrina said. 'I don't think elephants *can* laugh.'

Cornelius rubbed his chin thoughtfully. 'You may be right,' he said at last. 'But if they *could* laugh, they would sound like my Australian girlfriend.'

*   *   *

The road up the mountain was steep and it curved like a helter-skelter. They pulled into a lay-by near the top and got out and looked down at the tiny little cars at the bottom. 'I feel I'm on the top of the world,' Katrina said. They were *very* high up. She gulped and raised her eyes to the mountain peaks.

'I came here a few years ago with James,' Cornelius said. 'He thought the mountains looked like an army of giants.'

'They do,' Katrina agreed. 'Did he want to paint them?'

'Yes,' said Cornelius. 'Unfortunately, he made them look like the Loch Ness monster on a bad day.'

'I'm sure he's not as bad as you say he is,' said Katrina. She looked up at Cornelius. 'I am having such a good time today. Thank you for bringing me here.'

'It's a pleasure,' he said. He felt a twinge of disquiet and said abruptly, 'Shall we go on?'

At the top, they drove into a long tunnel and when they came out on the other side, the plateau spread out around them, a generous patchwork of varying shades of green, punctuated by the odd occasional hamlet.

117

They arrived at Vassieux soon after. The museum was set apart from the village in a square, rather drab building. Inside, there were tattered uniforms, old tobacco tins, photographs, flags and last letters from young men to their mothers and their girlfriends. The last time Cornelius had been here he had found the place fascinating. This time he found it less easy to look at the photos of young boys in their ill-fitting uniforms and the letters that tried so hard to conceal their fear and their homesickness.

They walked back to the car in silence and it was only when they had driven back past the café where they had had lunch that Katrina said, 'Thank you for taking me to that place.'

'I'm afraid,' said Cornelius, 'that it was a rather depressing visit.'

'It was. There was a boy in one of the photos who looked just like Ollie. It certainly puts into perspective all my silly preoccupations with Lewis and Rose.'

'We all have silly preoccupations,' said Cornelius, 'and most of them aren't silly, they're just normal. It's war that's not normal.'

'I bet you don't have any silly preoccupations.'

Cornelius gave a short laugh. 'In the last few days,' he said, 'I have wasted huge amounts of time wondering whether to send my wife a postcard or not. I spent a whole day worrying that I had a terminal illness after a game with Luc in which I dropped the ball too often. I only stopped worrying after I finally beat him. And then after James told me that I was the least convincing lover he'd ever seen, I started worrying about that.'

'That doesn't count,' Katrina said. 'You were

simply contaminated by my own preoccupations; and anyway, I thought you were a jolly good lover.'

'Thank you,' Cornelius said. 'I shall be sure to tell James what you said. I was wondering . . .' He paused to negotiate a particularly sharp bend in the road. 'Do you have to go straight home? Why don't you come back and say hello properly to James and Odile?'

'After yesterday's pantomime? I don't think so. I'm far too embarrassed.'

'I know they'd like to see you.'

'Well . . .' Katrina hesitated. 'I would like to apologize to them. Perhaps we could just stop off for a few minutes.'

It was soon clear that there was to be no quick getaway. Cornelius had bought the boys a croquet set and James had just finished setting it up when they arrived. Cornelius and Katrina were quickly press-ganged into playing. Cornelius discovered that Katrina was every bit as competitive as Luc, and Luc's delight over his final narrow victory was all the sweeter for Katrina's furious attempts to beat him. Katrina would almost certainly have taken up Luc's challenge to another game had not Odile appeared with bread and juice for the children. She told James and Cornelius to fetch more suitable refreshment for the adults. In the privacy of the kitchen, James told Cornelius that he should bring Katrina over again: high praise indeed from someone who was nearly as antisocial as Cornelius. When they returned to the garden they found the women in intense conversation about the difficulties of growing hibiscus bushes in Britain. It was only when James offered Katrina a second glass of wine that she looked guiltily at her

119

watch and said she should get back to Rose.

By mutual agreement, Cornelius dropped Katrina by the side of the road. When Katrina tried to thank him again, he felt another sharp twinge of discomfort. 'Katrina,' he said, 'please stop being so grateful. I did not take you out as an act of charity. I enjoy your company. I have enjoyed today and if you wish to come out again, you only have to ring.' He gave her a mock salute. 'I am C. C. Hedge and I am at your service.'

'Thank you,' Katrina said. 'What does the second C stand for?'

'I'd rather not talk about it,' said Cornelius. 'My second name is even worse than my first.'

'Actually,' Katrina smiled, 'Cornelius is definitely growing on me.' She hoisted her bag onto her shoulder. 'It has been a fabulous day. You are a good man and I promise I won't take up your kind offer to ring you. You've done more than enough and, besides, if you saw me again you really would have to come in for a drink with Rose. Goodbye and thank you. I'll see you on Saturday with my suitcase packed and I'll be ready as early as you like.' She turned and walked quickly towards the blue gates.

Cornelius reversed into the drive and turned back towards Cleon. She was still convinced he had done her a favour. The truth was that in the entire day there had not once been a moment when he had found her company onerous. He drove back, unable to shake off the uncomfortable feeling that he was guilty of fraudulent behaviour.

*   *   *

120

In the kitchen, Rose was slicing tomatoes and Lewis was chopping mushrooms. Rose looked up and raised her eyebrows. 'So the wanderer returns. I suppose we should be honoured that you're good enough to come back and eat the meal we are cooking for you.'

Katrina put her bag on the table and glanced a little apprehensively at her sister. 'You saw the note I left? I didn't like to disturb you.'

'Your note?' Rose let out a short laugh that was notable for its entire absence of good humour. 'The one that said, "Gone out for day with Cornelius. Have a good time"? Yes, we saw that note.'

'Rose,' Katrina said, 'are you angry with me?'

'Angry? Why should I be angry? I invite you for a holiday and you stay for just one week and you waltz off with your new boyfriend for a whole day. Why should I be angry?'

'I can't imagine,' Katrina said crisply. 'Cornelius rang and invited me to go out sightseeing with him. Given the choice between playing gooseberry with you two and going out on an expedition with Cornelius, it seemed far more sensible to go for the latter. I thought I was doing you a favour.'

'If I may say so,' Rose said, frantically shredding a lettuce, 'that is typical of you. Attack is always the best form of defence for you.'

'I'm not attacking, I'm simply pointing out that I did not think my company would be required in a romantic restaurant in Montelimar. I'm sorry you're upset but I assumed you'd be pleased.'

'Well, excuse me, but I think I know better than you what I want. And I have to say that I think it's rather rude of Cornelius not to come in and say

121

hello. Anyone would think he didn't want to talk to us. Am I really so disagreeable?'

'That is the sort of question,' Lewis said, 'that only a beautiful woman would dare to ask. There's no point in putting the risotto together until the Young get back. Why don't we open a bottle of wine and have a drink?'

'All right,' said Rose. 'I'll go and put a cardigan on.' She went across to Katrina and gave her a light hug. 'I forgive you, darling. It's impossible to be cross when Lewis says such nice things! I won't be a moment.'

Katrina felt very strongly that she had nothing to be forgiven *for*. Rose's lightning changes of mood always irritated her because she herself was incapable of such emotional flexibility and was stuck with feeling cross. She watched mutinously as her sister disappeared through the sitting room, and then went over to the corner cupboard to get some glasses.

Lewis took a bottle of rosé from the fridge. 'Katrina,' he murmured, 'you're looking very disgruntled.'

'I'm *feeling* very disgruntled,' said Katrina.

'It wasn't you Rose was cross with. Sam had told her they'd be back by five and she was worried. Cam rang just before you got in to say they'd be here soon and Rose was cross they hadn't rung earlier.'

'There was no need for her to take it out on me.'

'You're right. Have a glass of wine.'

'And there's no need to smile in that more-in-sorrow-than-in-anger way of yours.'

'I had no idea I was smiling like that. I shall never want to smile again.'

Katrina raised her eyebrows but accepted the proffered glass.

'What shall we drink to?' Lewis mused. 'Friendships renewed?'

Katrina gave him a withering look. 'I shall drink to you and Rose. I can't think of any two people who deserve each other more.'

Lewis grinned and took a sip. 'Did you have a good time today?' he asked. 'Where did you go?'

'We went to the Vercors mountains. We had a great time.'

'I'm glad to hear it.' Lewis pulled out a chair from the table and sat down. 'Your friend Cornelius seems a nice man. He is obviously a man of few words.'

'Only with people he doesn't know.'

Lewis bowed his head. 'You seem to have got to know him remarkably quickly.'

'Yes,' Katrina said, 'I suppose I have.'

'I almost feel jealous.'

Katrina looked at him sharply. 'That's a very stupid thing to say.'

'It was,' Lewis agreed. 'Let's forget I ever said it.'

'That won't be difficult,' Katrina said. 'I make a practice of discounting everything you say.'

'Darlings!' Rose wafted in. 'I'm quite good-humoured again! I need a big glass of wine and then I want to hear about your day, Katty. And I must tell you about our lunch. I think I had the best fish soup in the world!'

*　　　*　　　*

Katrina lay in bed that night, her mind a kaleidoscope of thoughts and pictures. She had

123

promised herself she was not going to think about Lewis and instead she thought back to her conversation with Odile that afternoon. 'Cornelius is happy in your company,' Odile had said. 'He has been sad for so long.'

Katrina felt warmed by Odile's observation and hoped it was true. It was obvious that Cornelius still loved his wife. What was her name? Lucy Lambert? Katrina couldn't imagine why any woman would want to leave Cornelius. She wished she knew him well enough to tell him that.

CHAPTER TEN

Shelley, Chomsky and a Tactless Remark

Cornelius arrived promptly at nine on Saturday morning. Katrina was opening the blue gates before he had even got out of the car. 'Hi!' she said brightly. 'My suitcase is in the kitchen!' It was clear from her constricted smile and resolute cheerfulness that something was wrong.

He followed her into the house. Lewis and Rose were sitting at the table and for a crazy moment, Cornelius felt like a callow youth squaring up to meet the parents.

'Good morning, Cornelius,' Rose said. 'Would you like some coffee?'

It was at that moment that Cornelius realized Rose was wearing a flimsy nightdress that left *absolutely* nothing to the imagination. He swallowed and fixed his eyes on the coffee-maker by the window. 'I think we should get going,' he said.

Lewis stood up and came over to shake Cornelius's hand. He, at least, was wearing clothes. 'I'm sorry we haven't seen more of you,' he said, 'but I'm sure you've been a great help to your friends.'

Cornelius cleared his throat and glanced at Katrina, who responded immediately. 'We must go,' she said. She went over to kiss her sister. 'Goodbye, Rose, thank you for everything. This is a beautiful place.'

'I suppose,' Rose said, 'I should be grateful you've deigned to visit us at all. Heaven knows when we'll see you again.'

'Look,' Katrina said, 'I never meant to upset you. If it really means so much to you, then of course I'll come to your party.'

'And you'll bring Susie and Ollie?'

Katrina looked as if she were trying to digest a particularly hard piece of gristle. 'I'll bring Susie and Ollie.'

'Thank you, Katty!' Rose stood up to embrace her sister and Cornelius quickly looked away. He hoped Rose wouldn't embrace *him*. He cleared his throat again.

'We really *must* go,' Katrina said. 'Goodbye, Lewis.'

'Katrina,' Lewis said, 'am I allowed a kiss?'

Cornelius hoped she'd say no but she offered her cheek for the briefest of moments before saying gaily, 'Say goodbye to the Young for me. Please don't come out.'

Lewis, however, insisted on taking Katrina's case to the car. Cornelius opened the boot and Lewis placed it on top of the other bags. Cornelius and

Katrina got into the car and Lewis went over to Katrina's window which Katrina, after a moment's hesitation, opened.

Lewis bared his teeth at Cornelius. 'Drive safely,' he said, 'you have someone very important in the car with you.' He smiled down at Katrina ready to make some other equally nauseous comment and Cornelius, having turned on the ignition, gave in to an irresistible urge to put his foot on the accelerator.

He didn't say anything to Katrina until he had turned onto the main road, and then murmured a muted apology for the suddenness of their departure. 'We have a long journey,' he said stiffly, 'I thought we'd better get on.'

'Please,' Katrina said, 'don't apologize! I am *so* glad to get away!' Her face was tense and her arms were folded tightly in front of her.

Cornelius grunted sympathetically but said nothing. He found it difficult to understand why someone as intelligent as Katrina should be in love with someone so supremely pleased with himself. On the other hand, he had never understood why some men—men like Lewis—were irresistible to so many women. All Cornelius knew was that if he were a woman and Lewis tried to give him a lingering kiss, he would run for cover immediately.

'Rose and I had a stupid row last night,' Katrina said. 'She's having a party in a few weeks. She wants to *introduce* Lewis to everyone. I said the children and I couldn't come but I didn't have any time to think of a good excuse so I said we were having Amy and her husband to dinner—Amy is one of my partners—and of course Rose got mad and said I see Amy at work every day and why

126

couldn't I change the date and then I said . . . Well, it doesn't matter what I said because now I've agreed to go and the whole thing is a disaster.' She shook her head and then smiled suddenly. 'You've been invited too, by the way.'

'Oh,' said Cornelius. 'Do you want me to . . . ?'

'No, no, I wouldn't dream of making you endure one of Rose's parties. The whole thing is stupid. Let's not talk about it any more. How are James and Odile and the gorgeous Luc and Pierre?'

'Very well. The marriage is still intact.'

'I'm glad to hear it.' Katrina stretched her arms in front of her. 'It's so nice to be going home. I can't wait to see Ollie. And Susie will be back next week.'

'How old is she?' Cornelius asked.

'She's twenty-one. She's just graduated from York University. At the moment she's in Edinburgh with her boyfriend. They're both performing in the Festival.'

'Is the boyfriend nice?'

'Liam? He's lovely. Great fun and never stops talking. I wouldn't care if he wasn't great fun. I'm just glad Susie has a boyfriend.'

'Why?' Cornelius asked sympathetically. 'Is she ugly?'

'Of course she's not ugly! Actually, she's very pretty. She hasn't had a boyfriend in years, that's all. She was very badly hurt when she was sixteen. She met a boy called Ash. He was three years older than her, a friend of Cam and Sam. She met him at one of their birthday parties.'

'Ash? That's an unusual name.'

'I think it's short for Ashley, like in *Gone with the Wind*. Now I come to think about it, the whole

127

thing is a bit like *Gone with the Wind*. You know how Scarlett spends the whole book thinking she's in love with Ashley and only realizes in the last chapter that the man is utterly wet? Well, that's like Susie except she never *did* realize how awful Ash was. She thought he was wonderful and then at a party they kissed and it was all incredibly romantic, and then some friends came up and they got separated and when she finally found him again, he was locked in a passionate embrace with someone else! What do you think of that?'

'Well,' Cornelius said, 'speaking as the devil's advocate, they weren't involved in a relationship at the time and indiscriminate kissing does seem to be something that teenagers do these days.'

'Yes, but they'd been flirting for months. For Susie, that kiss was the culmination of a courtship. And after that he totally *blanked* her. Up until that party, he used to come round to the house quite often. Actually, I never trusted him. He was one of those good-looking boys who think they can get anyone. What do girls see in boys like that?'

A vision of Lewis parading his bronzed chest flashed before Cornelius. 'I can't imagine,' he said with feeling.

'Anyway, as far as Susie was concerned, that was the end of romance. She didn't want to have anything more to do with it. I seriously thought she'd spend the rest of her life stuck in some sterile time warp, mourning the end of her teenage love affair. The first time she brought Liam home I felt like hugging him.'

They had arrived at the motorway. Cornelius stopped by the kiosk and Katrina leant out of the window to collect the toll card. She didn't speak again until Cornelius had successfully negotiated his way onto the fast lane and past two enormous lorries.

'I've noticed something about us,' she said sternly. 'Whenever we're together, I always end up talking about me. We never talk about you.'

Cornelius shifted a little uneasily in his seat. 'Oh, I don't know,' he said.

'I do. You know about my pathetic little affair with Lewis, you know about my family. All I know about you is that you're a wine merchant and you are divorcing your wife.'

'*She* is divorcing *me*,' Cornelius corrected.

'I can't think why,' Katrina said loyally.

'You've never lived with me.'

'Are you so difficult?'

'I suppose I must be.' Cornelius hoped Katrina would change the subject but she remained with her head cocked to one side, her eyes expectant and sympathetic. 'When we married,' he said, 'she used to call me her strong, silent husband. By the time she left me, I think she just thought I was silent.'

A fly appeared from nowhere and made a kamikaze attack on the windscreen. Cornelius opened his window and the insect, after lurching drunkenly in front of the steering wheel, flew out towards the sky. Cornelius closed the window and glanced at Katrina. He suspected she hadn't finished with the subject of his marriage. 'Tell me,' he said; 'why are you so interested in Mary Shelley?'

'It started at school. We had to study Shelley's poetry and I didn't like it very much so of course I felt sorry for his wife and then I discovered she'd

129

had to cope with so much right from the start. Her mother died soon after giving birth to her, so Mary always felt she was responsible for her mother's death. Which she wasn't. What happened was that the doctor came to see her, arrived after she'd given birth and fatally infected her during his examination. He'd come straight from the morgue and hadn't washed his hands. And then there were the children.'

'What children?'

'Mary's children. Shelley and his friends were always complaining about Mary's bad moods. It occurred to none of them that the deaths of three of her four children might have had something to do with the fact that she wasn't always a little sunbeam. What that poor woman had to go through was . . .'

Katrina talked about her with such passion and indignation that it was difficult to remember that Mary had been dead for over a hundred and fifty years. From the way Katrina talked, one might deduce that she was a close friend or relative. Cornelius did not find this odd. He had often felt a far greater affinity with dead people—Arthur Conan Doyle, for example, or Charles Darwin— than he had with his peers.

They stopped at Dijon for lunch. By then, Cornelius had learnt so much about Mary Shelley that he felt he could confidently deliver a lecture on her. They sat by the canal, eating baguettes filled with slabs of cheese and slices of the sweetest tomatoes. 'What I don't understand,' said Cornelius, 'is why Mary is a heroine for you? I mean, I know she wrote *Frankenstein* and was married to a romantic poet who treated her badly but . . .'

'It's what happened *after* the marriage that's interesting,' Katrina said. 'Shelley was a rotten companion. He kept falling in love with stupid women and he couldn't understand why Mary got depressed every time she lost a child, and yet she never stopped loving him. I think that's rather noble. She was only twenty-five when Shelley died yet she never married again.'

'Of course,' Cornelius mused. '*There's* the connection.'

'Where? What are you talking about?'

This happened to Cornelius sometimes, usually when he was particularly interested in something. He would come to a conclusion and then surprise himself, and often his companions, by articulating it. The last time he had done this was at a dinner party given by one of Lucy's acting friends. The rest of the table had embarked on an envious and deeply bitchy discussion about a mutual acquaintance who had recently bought a house on the strength of a sixty-five-second appearance in an advert for furniture polish. Cornelius had become increasingly intrigued by his host's hair, which sprang from his forehead with quite extraordinary exuberance. Cornelius had been wondering if he used curlers to achieve such an effect. Finally, understanding dawned: the man was wearing a toupee! He did not even realize he had voiced this discovery until he saw everyone looking at him. Lucy had been furious and had lectured him all the way home.

'What is?' Katrina asked. 'What is the connection?'

'Nothing,' Cornelius said, sensing danger. 'I was

131

talking randomly.'

'No wonder you hate lying,' Katrina said. 'You're rotten at it. Now tell me what you meant.'

Cornelius fixed his bottle of water with an intense stare. 'Well,' he said, 'Mary went on loving Shelley for the rest of her life even though he'd treated her badly and, in the same way, Lewis still has the power to seriously upset you even though he treated you badly. Just like Shelley.'

'That,' Katrina said hotly, 'is entirely different.'

She didn't, he noticed, say *why* it was different. 'I'm sorry,' he said, 'I was thinking aloud. I didn't mean to say that.' Somehow he had made it worse, he could see he had made it worse. 'I'm sorry,' he tried again. 'My wife always says I need to learn about tact.'

Now she smiled. 'That's all right,' she said. 'Let's change the subject.' She took a swig from her water bottle and wiped her mouth with her hand. 'Tell me about that book you were reading on the boat.'

'The Noam Chomsky?' Cornelius brightened. He felt as if she had pulled him out of quicksand. 'I'll tell you about it in the car. Are you ready to go?'

The rest of the journey passed surprisingly quickly. Cornelius enjoyed talking to Katrina; conversations with her rarely seemed to reach a rational conclusion, they diverged into unexpected areas, picking up unusual nuggets of information along the way. So today, they started by talking about Chomsky's attack on North American policy towards South American countries and then Katrina told him about a film she had loved, called *Missing*. It starred Jack Lemmon and Katrina said it was probably just as informative as Chomsky's book and was almost certainly a lot more gripping. Cornelius responded by asserting that in his experience cinema was the exact opposite of informative. He recalled a truly terrible film he had once, long ago, been dragged to by his sister. Ali McGraw had spent an eternity getting ready to die while looking impossibly radiant with beauty and health and expensive make-up. The film, he said, was thoroughly mendacious and gave its viewers a wholly distorted view of death-bed endings. Katrina told him that some death-bed endings *were* wonderful. 'Do you know what Sir Arthur Conan Doyle's last words were to his wife? "You are wonderful," he said and then he died.'

Cornelius felt particularly stirred by this, not just by the great man's last thoughts but by the fact that Katrina had—quite randomly—referred to a man who happened to be a particular hero of Cornelius.

They had an hour to spare before boarding the ferry and Katrina suggested returning to their pavement café for a light supper. 'We might see that girl and her lover again,' she said. They didn't but that was the only disappointment. This time Cornelius felt no need to disappear. It seemed extraordinary that only a week ago he had sat at this same table with this same woman and with such very different feelings about her.

Harmonious relations were endangered one more time when they were halfway across the Channel and Katrina discovered that Cornelius intended to drive her back to her house. 'I live in Clapham,' he said. 'You're hardly any distance from me. If you think I'm going to abandon you in the middle of the night, you're wrong.' Katrina protested vigorously and only stopped when Cornelius told her that if she persisted in being so tedious he would start talking about Noam Chomsky again.

They arrived outside her house at a little before midnight. Cornelius carried her case to the door and refused her offer of coffee.

'You will at least come to Sunday lunch with us soon?' she asked. 'I'll email you next week. Will you come?'

'Thank you,' Cornelius said. 'I shall enjoy that.'

'Good,' Katrina said. 'And thank you so much. The best bits of my holiday . . . they were all with you. You've been so kind.'

'Not at all.' Cornelius cleared his throat. 'I was thinking . . . Are you sure you wouldn't like me to come to Rose's party with you?'

'Of course not.' Katrina laughed. 'It was bad enough making you go through that silly pretence in France. I have no intention of prolonging your agony. I shall wait a few weeks and then inform Rose that you have definitely dumped me.' She reached up to kiss him on the cheek, said, 'See you soon,' and disappeared into the house.

Cornelius returned to the car. He felt oddly bereft, which was ridiculous. Why should he be upset by the news that he was about to terminate a non-existent relationship? He turned the ignition and drove off, furiously castigating himself. If he had been Lewis, he would have assured her that far from being kind, he had enjoyed helping her out. If he'd been Lewis, he'd have told her that meeting her was the best thing that had happened to him in a very long time. If he'd been Lewis, he'd have told her that he would very much enjoy taking her to Rose's party. Not for the first time in his life, Cornelius wished he wasn't stuck with being Cornelius.

CHAPTER ELEVEN

Respite

Holidays, Katrina decided, were brilliant. Of all the species on the planet, only Man had invented the concept of the Holiday and it was a mark of genius. Was there any mechanism better suited to developing an appreciation of one's domestic environment?

Katrina had been away for only a week and yet here she was, sitting in front of her favourite pub, waiting for her son to bring out the drinks and feeling that of all the places in the world, Greenwich was the very best in which to live. The sun was shining, the sky was blue, the geraniums in the window box across the road provided a vibrant splash of crimson colour.

Ollie emerged from the bar with a bag of peanuts gripped between his teeth and very full glasses in his hands. He set down the drinks and put the nuts in the middle of the table. 'I've ordered food,' he said. 'Tim says he'll bring it out when it's ready.'

Ollie, of course, was the icing on the cake. There could be *nothing* better than to sit in the sunshine and see his cheerful face, a face that was utterly foreign to smirking or smarming or thinking he was beautiful. Unlike Francis, who obviously thought he was God's gift to everyone, Ollie had never been satisfied with his appearance. He thought he had a nose like an aardvark. He didn't. It could almost be described as a Roman nose; almost, since God had taken His eye off the ball for a moment, leaving a slight indentation in the middle. In recompense, he had been supplied with dark, arching eyebrows, eyes set wide apart, great cheekbones and a determined chin. The last two years had seen a transformation. He had lost all his puppy fat, his shoulders had broadened and he had grown at least a foot. Katrina thought he was beautiful.

He sat down opposite her, took a sip of his beer and gave a contented sigh. Ollie was as transparent as a mountain stream. His moods and thoughts rippled across his features like a gentle breeze. It was arguable, of course, that Katrina's view of him was not wholly impartial: nevertheless, after spending seven days with Cam and Sam and their friends, she felt particularly blessed that her son just happened to be the nicest young man she had ever met.

'I'm sorry I wasn't in when you got back,' he said. 'I was playing poker with George and Dan. I thought you weren't getting home until the early hours.'

'I was lucky. The ferry came in on time and Cornelius insisted on giving me a lift all the way home.'

'Cornelius? Is that the man who drove you down to Rose's house? What was he like?'

'Very nice. At first I thought he was going to be rather scary. He's quite imposing to look at, he's very tall and very thin with lots of hair. But he couldn't have been kinder. I'm going to invite him to Sunday lunch soon and then you'll meet him.'

Ollie opened the bag of peanuts and poured what looked like half the contents into his palm. 'And how was Rose? Is she missing Roger a lot?'

Katrina took a sip of her wine. 'No,' she said, 'I don't think she is. She has a boyfriend. He was there.'

Ollie's eyes widened. 'She has a *boyfriend*? That is so *weird*! I can't imagine her with someone new. Do you remember that time Roger bought us all pasties? We didn't like them, so he ate every one? He was so cool. Do you like the new man? Is he like Roger?'

Katrina reached in her bag for her sunglasses. 'No. He's not like Roger at all. He's urbane, confident, dresses well. He's an actor, extremely good-looking. I can't imagine him ever wanting to consume a plate of pasties. He and Rose seem to be very happy.' She helped herself to some peanuts and looked at her son expectantly. 'Now, tell me about you. How's the job?'

'It's mind-numbing. Basically, I'm just there so frustrated customers can vent their spleen on someone.'

'What do you say to them?'

'I take all their details so they think the company will do something. Which it almost certainly won't. It's a terrible job.'

'But?'

'But what?'

Katrina laughed. 'For someone who went to bed at three and got up only an hour ago, you are extraordinarily wide awake and . . . and bouncy. Something has happened!'

Ollie swung his legs round and tucked them

under the table. He folded his arms in front of him and looked earnestly at Katrina. 'There's this girl,' he said. 'I don't want to talk about her, really. I mean, I don't think anything's going to happen, you see, so . . .'

'That's fine,' said Katrina, 'I quite understand.'

'She's called Sophie. She was at Rhiannon's house last week. She has a holiday job at the Tower of London. How cool is that? She's very small but she has a fantastic figure and she has these blue eyes that look straight at you when she talks and she's not silly or giggly but she's not all serious and intense either. I mean, she's really into the environment and she's a supporter of the Green Party but she also does a brilliant karaoke of KT Tunstall. She's pretty amazing, actually . . .'

'But you don't want to talk about her.'

Ollie gave a sheepish grin. 'I know. I can't help it. I really like her but I don't want to mess it up this time so I'm going to play it really cool and be just friendly at first—you know, talk about ice caps and things . . .'

'Since when have you been concerned about ice caps? I couldn't *pay* you to go to that Greenpeace lecture with me last month and that was really brilliant.'

'I'm interested *now*,' Ollie said. 'I am.'

Katrina frowned. 'Why did you mess it up last time?'

'Oh.' Ollie thrust his hands through his hair, which he had allowed to grow since he'd left school; it rather suited him, Katrina thought. 'I met Sophie last year. She's a friend of Hannah who was in that school play with me—about dead people, remember? She came to the after-play party and I thought she was great. The trouble was, I asked George for advice.'

Katrina smiled. George was Ollie's mentor in all things pertaining to the opposite sex, mainly because, as far as Katrina could understand, he had lost his virginity at the age of fifteen to a very drunken twenty-four-year-old.

Ollie took another slug of his beer. 'George said I should go and *engage* her in conversation and *awaken* her interest and then I should offer to walk her home after the party. So I went up to her but I forgot about talking to her first and instead I went straight into the question. Trouble was, I was so nervous I got that wrong too and I ended up asking her if she'd like to take *me* home.'

'What did she say?'

'That was the trouble. She didn't say anything. She just looked at me as if . . . she just looked at me. So this time I am not going to blow it, I am going to play it very cool and I shan't text her for at least three days.'

'Very sensible.' Katrina stopped to smile at the fresh-faced young man who was approaching their table with two plates of chicken and chips. No question, holidays were brilliant.

*   *   *

After lunch, Ollie went off to see friends in the park. Katrina went home with the laudable intention of unpacking her suitcase and cleaning the kitchen floor, which had developed an unpleasantly sticky sheen under Ollie's supervision. But the weather was beautiful and she had another week before she had to go back to work. The unpacking and the floor could wait.

She took a deckchair and the phone and went out into the small garden at the back of the house. In just a short time, the greenery had assumed jungle-like proportions. That too could wait. She sat down and savoured the fact that she had another week of freedom. For a few moments, she closed her eyes, enjoying the sensation of the sun on her face and the sweet sound of a chatty bird in the garden next door. Then, with a sigh of pleasure, she settled down to ring her daughter.

Katrina had never liked the telephone. Her view was that if she couldn't see the person she was talking to, she was unable to tell if her company was welcome or not. Even with Ollie, she felt duty bound to keep her words to a minimum. Susie was the one person in the world whose telephone conversation she could enjoy in the complete confidence that Susie would always want to talk to her.

'Mum!' Susie's voice shot from the phone like a rocket. 'It's *you*! *Hello!* How *are* you?'

Katrina could always tell in the first two seconds how her daughter was. A tired, downward-inflecting, 'Hi, Mum, how are *you*?' presaged clouds and rainfall. There was no middle way with Susie, she was either happy or she was sad, and today she was very, very happy.

'I'm very well,' Katrina said. 'It's good to be home again.'

'Did you have a good time in France? What is Rose's house like? Is Rose still missing Roger terribly? Tell me everything!'

'The house was lovely, huge swimming pool, gorgeous courtyard. Rose was fine. She has a

140

boyfriend. He was there with us.'

There was a brief hiatus while Susie processed the information. 'I thought you said the only reason you were going out there was to stop Rose from feeling lonely?'

'That's what I thought,' Katrina said. 'It turned out I wasn't necessary at all.'

'I'm sorry, Mum, that is so typical of my aunt! You didn't want to go out there in the first place. I can't believe she has a new man already. What's he like?'

'He's an actor,' Katrina said. 'He's called Lewis Maltraver. He used to be a well-known soap-opera star. I met him once when I was arranging a purchase for a TV company. He's . . . he's charming.'

'What's wrong with him?'

'Nothing's wrong with him! He's an attractive man and he and Rose are very happy. I can't say I enjoyed myself hugely, though. He and Rose were all over each other, and Cam and Sam were all over their partners too. Oh, dear . . .' Katrina paused. 'I'm sounding terribly ungrateful.'

'Course you're not. Rose got you there under false pretences. What about the man who was giving you a lift? Was he all right?'

'He was lovely. Rose thinks he looks just like Jarvis Cocker.'

'What do *you* think?'

'I think she's right. He has different hair but otherwise he's very similar. He's tall and thin and he has the same sort of glasses and he often has an expression on his face that makes it difficult to see what he's thinking. He was nice. I enjoyed his company.'

'Is he married?'

'I said I enjoyed his company, Susie, nothing else! He is married but he's getting divorced and I get the feeling he doesn't want to be. His wife's an actress: Lucy Lambert.'

'Never heard of her.'

'Well, that's not surprising given that only one in ten thousand actors are successful.'

'Mum, there is no point in giving me your Acting is a Ruinous Profession lecture because I don't care! Oh, Mum, I am having the best time of my life, I am so happy!'

Katrina smiled and leant back in her chair. 'Tell me,' she said.

So Susie did. She was living in a flat with what sounded like the entire cast of *Hamlet*. For their first performance, only three people came, but it was all right because only one of them walked out in the middle and the other two had cheered at the end. The night before, thirty-four people had come and everyone said Susie's mad scene was incredible.

'And what about Liam?' asked Katrina. 'Is he getting good audiences?'

'Better than us and he's had some fantastic reviews. And, Mum, we've met this really nice girl called Honey. That's not her real name, she won't tell us her real name, she says it's terrible. She was born in Knutsford like Liam, isn't that funny? But she left when she was small and now she's based in London. She's in her last year at drama school and she's had an agent for years. Do you remember that series we used to watch, about a witch and her family? She played the annoying daughter! She's going to come and see me when we get home.

142

You'll like her. And, Mum, can Liam stay the first two weeks in September? He told me to send his love to you. I'll be so sorry to leave Edinburgh! I mean, I'm looking forward to coming home next week but it's all so exciting up here. Life is so good!'

Yes, Katrina thought, when she finally rang off, life was very good. She had two wonderful children, she loved her home and she could look forward to a week of gardening and reading and meeting friends. For the next week, at least, she was going to relax and be happy and she was not going to allow herself to think about Lewis Maltraver at all.

*　　　*　　　*

She almost managed it. She tidied the garden, discovering with delight that the lupins she'd planted the year before had flourished, despite the weeds that had tried so hard to obliterate them. She vacuumed every room in the house, determined to clear it of Omo's excess fur (a thankless task since he was currently moulting for England). She drove down to Sussex and spent a pleasant day with her friend, Alicia, who made exquisite silver jewellery in an old shed in the garden of her equally exquisite Tudor house. Katrina drove back home with her head full of fantasies of relocating to the country. Then she got home, waved to the children from number seven and knew she could never leave Greenwich.

Only the nights were bad. She would fall asleep quite easily but would wake quite suddenly at five and find the same question going round and round

143

in her head: *What am I going to do about Lewis?*

For once, she was happy to go back to work. Perhaps, if she could recover her pre-holiday routine, she could manage to forget her post-holiday preoccupations.

Carol was there before her, eager to fill her in with the events of the last two weeks (one resignation, one birthday, one new client, one very angry old client and a fascinating new training scheme on people skills), and anxious to know if Douglas's boss had been a satisfactory driving companion. Katrina assured her that Cornelius had been both kind and considerate.

'I'm so glad,' Carol said. 'I was sure it would be all right but Douglas says he can be a little odd.'

'He isn't odd at all,' Katrina said irritably. 'I thought he was courteous and considerate. Anyway,' she gave a dismissive smile, 'I must get on.'

She felt a slight pang of guilt, but only a *very* slight pang, when Carol withdrew. Then she turned to her computer and frowned at the long list of emails.

Amy dropped by twenty minutes later. 'Are you free for lunch? I'd love to hear about your holiday.'

'Great. I'll see you at twelve thirty.'

'Fine.' Amy disappeared. She knew as well as any the mysterious way in which work seemed to mushroom during a holiday.

Katrina worked steadily throughout the morning. She answered her emails, spent thirty precious minutes soothing the very angry old client, cold-called one potentially amazing future client and went through two hideously complicated

144

documents. At half past twelve, she pushed back her chair and went off to find Amy.

No one could look less like a probate lawyer than Amy. A stranger might guess her to be an eccentric illustrator of children's books or possibly a much-loved primary school teacher. At a cursory glance she might be mistaken for a little old lady in her small, circular spectacles, her cheerful round face, her white hair parted in the middle and held back in a small bun, her long linen skirt and her broderie anglaise blouse. A closer inspection would take in the lively blue eyes, the merest smattering of wrinkles, the ever-present dimples and the silver elephant earrings.

Amy was indeed an expert on probate but she was certainly not a little old lady. Her hair had gone silver at the age of twenty-four and now she was one year off fifty. For most of her twenties she had been unhappily in love with a man who promised her everything but the babies she yearned for. On her thirtieth birthday, he left her for his secretary, who gave birth to twins six months later. At the age of thirty-five she fell in love with a client, a fifty-three-year-old widower. Over a candle-lit dinner, he asked her to marry him and promised her a football team of children. They went back to his home and were making passionate love when he made an odd little sound, fell on top of her and died. After that, Amy packed away her dreams of babies and of love. Her career in the company flourished and she bought a garden flat that became, in Katrina's eyes at least, the epitome of all that was elegant and serene: sanded floors, pale white walls, discreet lighting, Bose CD player and no TV.

Four years ago, she met an accountant called Eddy who was still smarting from the fact that his now ex-wife had decamped to Berkshire along with their two children and his now ex-best friend. Eddy had an Errol Flynn moustache and a wicked smile to match. Three months later, with a speed that had startled all her colleagues, he and Amy were married and Amy's minimalist flat was suddenly full of Eddy's plasma TV, his vast CD collection, his monster leather armchair and his fifteen cookery books.

Amy was one of the reasons why Katrina enjoyed her job. At least once a week, they had lunch together at the small café five doors from their office. Today, as they sat outside on the pavement, eating linguini salad and drinking iced mineral water, Katrina regarded her friend with warm affection and said, 'It's good to be back.'

Amy twinkled sympathetically. 'Was your holiday *that* bad?'

'Worse,' said Katrina. 'My bedroom was sandwiched between two pairs of young lovers, which meant that I had to listen to their sexual marathons in stereo. Don't laugh, Amy, it wasn't funny. And on top of that, my poor, grieving sister turned out not to be grieving at all and was there with a brand-new man who just happened to be an old boyfriend of mine from years ago.'

'How fascinating,' Amy said, inclining her head to one side while she considered the ramifications of Katrina's statement. 'Since your sister is enamoured of him, I assume he is still attractive.' Amy put her fingertips together. She reminded Katrina of a school teacher considering some arcane, academic problem. 'Was he uncomfortable with you? Were you uncomfortable with *him*? Did your eyes lock when you met? Did you ever read those *Angelique* novels when you were a teenager? I used to love them. Angelique frequently locked eyes with gorgeous French aristocrats and every time she did, three pages on there would be lots of lovely, naughty sex.'

'I didn't have any lovely, naughty sex,' Katrina said regretfully, 'I just heard it.'

'But what was he like with you? Was he pleased to see you?'

Katrina shrugged. 'I don't know. He's an actor. He's good at concealing his feelings.'

'So what did you do?'

'I counted the days till I could come home.'

'I'm not surprised,' Amy said. 'What did Rose think about it? She must have found it rather awkward.'

'Rose never finds anything awkward. Anyway, I didn't tell her. I just said I'd met him once, long ago. Lewis was obviously quite happy to keep her in the dark.'

'How horribly difficult for you.' Amy adjusted her spectacles and took a sip of her water. 'As a matter of interest, had he left you or had you left him?'

'He had, very definitely, left me.'

Amy gave a sympathetic sigh. 'Poor Katrina! What's he like?'

'He's a very good-looking actor. He has that George Clooney quality of looking like he's amused and bemused by all the attention he gets, as if it doesn't really bother him, although really, of course, he loves every moment of it. He has these twinkly eyes and a bedroom smile that he's probably spent years perfecting. Am I sounding horribly bitchy?'

'Yes,' Amy gave a judicious nod. 'But it sounds to me as if you are quite entitled to be. Have I heard of him? Is he successful?'

'He's had his moments. I suppose he is if you consider that most actors spend most of their lives being unemployed. Do you remember *Medical Alert*? He was Dr Rubin.'

'I do remember! It was my mother's favourite programme. Dr Rubin was the handsome one, wasn't he? Is he still just as handsome?'

'Yes, and he knows it. He must spend half his life in the gym because his body is so well toned and his arms are really muscular—'

'I take it you weren't paying him much attention . . .'

'You couldn't help but pay attention. He spent most of the holiday wandering round the place in little black bathing shorts. He and Rose kept going off to make love. Everyone was making love. I read a biography of Mary Shelley. You have no idea how lovely it was to get home and see Ollie again.'

'I can imagine,' Amy said. 'Poor old you. How is the gorgeous Ollie?'

'He got his A Level results a few days ago: two As and a B, so that's all right. And he's fallen in love.'

'Lucky girl. I adore your son. He always makes me feel he's pleased to see me.'

'That's because he *is* pleased to see you.' Katrina had noted the wistful tone in Amy's voice. 'How are you getting on with your stepson? How long has he been with you now?'

'Three weeks.' Amy twirled the linguini onto her

148

fork with careful precision. 'He's very nice. He doesn't say very much to me; he grunts politely, if you know what I mean. It can't be easy for him. He doesn't know many people, the friends he does have are in different parts of London and he obviously finds his job pretty demanding. He watches a lot of television.'

'He's only staying with you for a couple of months, isn't he?'

'That was the original plan. Now his mother's boyfriend has managed to get him a job in this record company near Covent Garden and they've offered to keep him on until he goes travelling in February.'

'Oh,' Katrina said. 'That's quite a long time.'

'I'm sure I'll get used to him,' Amy said doubtfully. 'It's silly. I mean, I always wanted children and now I have one living with me. If you can call an eighteen-year-old a child. The thing is, I realize I don't know anything about eighteen-year-old boys. The only one I know is Ollie and he is lovely. Stephen's far more reserved. There's something else too. Is it just Stephen or do all eighteen-year-old boys have a particularly distinctive aroma about them?'

'Stephen is not alone,' Katrina said. 'I know the smell well: pungent and aromatic.'

'It's certainly very strong. He doesn't seem to shower very often. I splashed out on a Diptyque candle last week—*Foin Coupe*—Cut Straw. When I'm on my own, I get it out and light it. And the spare room—Stephen's room—do you remember my spare room?'

Katrina nodded. She had stayed there one night last year and could recall crisp white Egyptian linen, coffee-coloured silk bedspread, long luxuriant cream curtains.

'Well,' said Amy, 'it looks different now.'

'Yes,' said Katrina, 'I imagine it would do. Do Stephen and Eddy get on?'

'They do. It's lovely to see them together. They go off to horror films and football matches and now Eddy's bought this motorbike—'

'Eddy's bought a *motorbike*?'

'It's a monster, a great big black monster. I'm terrified he'll kill himself with it.' Amy folded her arms. 'I don't know. It all feels so easy when you fall in love with someone. You never think of all the people and history that trail along behind. Eddy's so happy to have Stephen around, which is marvellous, but sometimes now I almost feel like I'm the one who's the visitor. Occasionally, very occasionally, I do marvel at the fact that I married Eddy without a thought. I jumped off the cliff without even wondering if I had a parachute.'

'Well,' Katrina said, 'speaking as someone who gets vertigo at the mere sight of a metaphorical lift, I think you were quite right to get up on that cliff. At least you get to see the view from the top.'

'Yes,' said Amy, 'I do. It's just it's not quite what I thought it would be.'

*   *   *

Cornelius climbed out of his car and reached in the back for the wine and the flowers. He had spent a long time wondering whether to buy the flowers. At the garage, he had picked up first one bouquet and then another. He had almost decided not to buy any but the man behind the till had

150

looked at him with such suspicion that he had been embarrassed and had grabbed the yellow roses.

The door was flung open by a tall, dark-haired teenager with an engaging smile. 'Hi,' the boy said. 'You must be Cornelius. I'm Ollie. Come on in.' He ushered Cornelius into the hall. 'Go on down. I don't know where Mum is. I'll go and find her.'

'Thank you.' Cornelius watched Ollie leap up the stairs, two at a time. Surveying his surroundings, he admired the blue-and-yellow-striped wallpaper and the ancient mirror to the right of the front door. A corner of the frame was slightly chipped and there was a small crack along the edge of the glass. Below the mirror stood a small, narrow table on which sat a couple of recycled envelopes, waiting to be posted. Beyond the mirror was a door and there was another opposite the stairs. To the left of Cornelius there were some stone steps going down to the floor below.

Following Ollie's instructions, Cornelius proceeded down them and found himself in a large airy kitchen that encompassed the entire lower-ground floor. It was clear what Katrina's favourite colours were. The walls were sky blue and at intervals along the central length of the room, three canary-coloured metallic lamps hung like inverted cones from black chains. Two of them illuminated the island unit that stood between the cooker and the dresser and the other presided over the dining area.

Beyond the circular pine table (on which stood two very promising bottles of Merlot), French windows looked out onto a pleasantly scruffy small garden. Cornelius thought of his own cramped and windowless kitchen. This room was clearly the heart of the house. There was an enormous, dark sideboard on one side of the table, almost certainly inherited from elderly relations, Cornelius thought. On top of it were Sunday papers, a flowerpot with a variety of pens and pencils, a framed photo of two small children and a vase with sweet-smelling roses with the palest of pink petals, very different from the spindly specimens he'd bought. On the other side of the table the walls were lined with shelves containing cookery books, an atlas, photograph albums and casserole dishes.

Drawn by tantalizing smells, Cornelius wandered over to the stove. The roast beef sat on top of it like the Crown Jewels. Its pink-coloured flesh and its crisp coating of fat made him remember he was hungry. He allowed himself one last respectful glance and then turned his attention to the notice board on the wall by the fridge.

There was a council leaflet on recycling, a flyer advertising a production of *Hamlet*, two passport-sized photos of Ollie making a funny face and a *Far Side* calendar which almost obliterated a cut-out article intriguingly titled *How To Be Happy: Ten Easy Steps.* Cornelius pushed aside the calendar and began to read. There was *Make a New Friend Every Week* which was, of course, very laudable and about as helpful as exhorting people to Make Lots of Money. *Plant Something and Watch it Grow* was only slightly less demanding. Cornelius had been given a bonsai tree by his sister for his birthday and had dutifully watered it every day. Despite his care, he had watched it die and hoped very much that no one would ever again give him something that needed nurturing. *Take Exercise Every Day* was possibly a good idea, as was

Do Some Voluntary Work for your Community
unless, like Cornelius, one lived in a place that
didn't seem to have a community. *Tell Your Loved
Ones You Love Them* was all very well but if
Cornelius were to ring his sister and tell her he
loved her she would probably catch the first train
to London to see if he had gone mad. *When You
Wake Up in the Morning, Count Your Blessings* . . .
Cornelius blinked and decided that if he ever met
the writer of the article he would dislike him on
sight. At the top of the notice board was another
cut-out article on *How to Tone Your Bottom.*

He was reading about the importance of
clenching one's pelvic muscles when Ollie came
back, followed by Katrina who looked flustered
and sounded breathless. 'Cornelius, I am so sorry.
I got some fat on my shirt and went to change and
then a robin flew into my bedroom and I couldn't
get it out and it nearly dashed its brains out on my
mirror before it flew back into the garden. It is
lovely to see you!'

Cornelius was unsure as to whether he should
kiss her cheek or not. Instead, he held out the wine
and the flowers which, rather to his surprise, he
found he was still holding.

'How very generous,' Katrina said. 'Do you see
the cream jug by the sink? Could you put them in
there for now and I'll have a lovely time arranging
them later.' She tore a piece of foil from the roll
on the island unit and covered the meat. 'I'll leave
it to stand for fifteen minutes and then we can eat.
Susie will be down in a minute. She's on the phone
to her boyfriend. Ollie, get Cornelius a drink.'

There was a difference about her: she had a
confidence that had been absent in France. In her

153

green linen trousers and cream-coloured shirt, she looked, Cornelius thought, like spring. He unwrapped the roses, filled the jug with water and stuck the flowers in it. There were only four of them and they lolled disconsolately against the rim of the jug. He should have bought more. Or he should have bought none at all.

Ollie went to the fridge and took out a bottle. 'If you don't like this,' he said, 'then it's my fault. Mum told me to go and get some good white wine and the man at the off-licence said this was his favourite. Mind you, the man at the off-licence has a poster of Danni Minogue on his wall so I'm not sure I can trust him.'

'It looks very good,' Cornelius assured him.

Katrina took out four glasses from one of the kitchen cupboards and looked a little anxiously at Ollie, who was attacking the cork with more enthusiasm than expertise. 'Ollie . . .' she began and then smiled as a stunning girl, dressed in jeans and a pink vest, came through the doorway. 'This is Susie!' she said proudly.

Cornelius, who had just sat down on one of the three high stools by the island unit, stood up again. Katrina's daughter had slate-coloured eyes and long brown hair that shone like burnished copper. She was also blessed with her mother's flawless complexion. 'Hello,' he said, 'how very nice to meet you.'

The girl took one look at him and burst into tears.

CHAPTER TWELVE

Katrina Has Doubts About Cornelius

Before Cornelius could say anything—not that he could think of anything *to* say—the girl turned on her heels and fled upstairs.

Katrina put down the glasses. 'Ollie,' she said, 'if I'm not back in five minutes, stir the gravy. If I'm not back in ten, baste the potatoes.' She turned to Cornelius. 'I'm so sorry. Make sure Ollie gives you a drink. I won't be long.'

After she had gone, Ollie finally wrested the cork from the bottle and poured some wine into a glass which he gave to Cornelius. 'I hope it's all right,' he said.

Cornelius took a sip and gave an encouraging nod. 'It's very good.'

'That's a relief.' Ollie poured himself a glass and regarded it with a purposeful frown. 'The man at the off-licence said it was very dry.'

'It is,' Cornelius said. 'It's very dry. Just how I like it.'

'Well,' Ollie said, 'we might as well sit down. I'm sure Mum will be back in a minute.' He took his glass over to the table and pulled out a chair.

Cornelius followed him and sat down.

'I'm sorry about Susie.' Ollie scratched his head, directed an anxious glance at the ceiling and sighed. 'She was fine before you came.'

'Oh, dear,' said Cornelius. 'I'm so sorry.'

'I don't mean that you had anything to do with it, I just mean that . . . you know . . . She *was* all right.

155

She got back from Edinburgh two days ago. She was in the Festival there.'

'I see,' said Cornelius.

Ollie began drumming his fingers on the table and then, realizing what he was doing, stopped. 'Have you ever been to Edinburgh?' he asked.

'No,' said Cornelius.

'Neither have I,' Ollie said.

It was clear that Ollie, like Cornelius, was struggling. In the ensuing silence, they could both hear the sounds of Susie's desperate sobs upstairs. Cornelius racked his brains for something to say. 'I went to a concert last week,' he ventured.

'Did you?' Ollie asked with an impressive simulation of interest.

Cornelius nodded. 'Yes. I saw the Zutons. They were very good.'

'You saw the Zutons?' Ollie's face lit up with genuine enthusiasm. 'I *love* the Zutons.'

'So do I. And they are excellent live performers. I felt very *positive* for at least three days afterwards. I tried to recreate their sounds on my guitar but—'

'Do you play the guitar? I want to get a guitar. How long have you been playing? Are you good?'

'I'm afraid I'm rather bad. I bought one six months ago and I've been teaching myself with the help of a book. I've learnt a few chords but it seems to take a long time for my fingers to find the right strings. I shan't give up, though.'

'Of course you won't. I'm just the same. I have a friend who's brilliant and he's taught me a bit. I'm hoping Mum will give me a guitar for Christmas. I'd buy one myself but all my earnings are going towards travel. I'm off to Thailand as soon as I've earned enough money.'

'It's a beautiful country,' said Cornelius. 'I went there last year. And I visited Vietnam. And Laos...'

But Ollie had leapt from his chair and was pulling out the huge atlas from under the pile of photo albums. He put it in front of Cornelius. 'Can you show me where you went?'

Cornelius took another sip of his wine and opened the atlas. He felt the familiar surge of excitement he always experienced when he looked at the strange territorial shapes and the wide expanses of blue.

When Katrina returned, they both jumped guiltily. Katrina made straight for the neglected gravy. 'Luckily for you two,' she said severely, 'it is just about all right. Susie will be down in a second. Ollie, lay the table. Cornelius, would you be able to carve the meat?'

*   *   *

The meal was perfect: soggy Yorkshire pudding, buttered cabbage, thick, aromatic gravy, crisp and crunchy roast potatoes with deceptively fluffy insides. Susie came down when Cornelius was standing over the stove, attacking the joint for the second time. She went straight to him. Her eyes were red-rimmed and puffy. It was evident that, like her mother, she had an amazing capacity for tears.

'I want to apologize,' she said. 'I didn't mean ... I'm so sorry.'

Cornelius, flustered, said, 'Not at all, not at all, it happens all the time.' He caught Katrina's eye and hastily corrected himself. 'I mean, it doesn't

157

happen all the time but it does happen *some* times
. . . Can I give you some beef?'

He noted approvingly that she was as impressive
as her mother. She responded politely and when
she took her seat at the table she listened gravely
to his rather stilted enquiry about her career plans.
She told him that she had always wanted to be an
actress and was already selecting her pieces for
auditions to RADA and LAMDA and Guildhall
and Central School.

'My wife is an actress,' Cornelius said.

'Mum told me. Does she get a lot of work?'

'She hasn't done as well as she'd hoped. The last
play she was in was three years ago. She did a
Terence Rattigan play in Bromley. She does the
odd voice-over. At the moment she does the voice
in the Terrible Tots advert.'

Katrina's mouth twitched. 'I think you mean
Trimble Tots. Though, actually, I think Terrible
Tots sounds much better.'

'Of course. I always get it wrong. Trimble Tots.
It's about nappies that . . . that . . . I'm not sure
what is special about them. I think perhaps they
retain moisture or perhaps they *absorb* moisture,
anyway they do *something* with moisture.'

'I know that advert,' Susie said. '*Trimble Tot
nappies for discerning tots!* Your wife has a lovely
voice.'

Cornelius nodded. 'She does. She's a very good
actress. Everyone says so. She should have been
more successful. It seems very unfair.'

'I'm afraid,' said Katrina, 'that unfairness is the
major characteristic of the acting profession. If
you're born into an acting family, you have no
problem at all however little talent you have. For

most people, rejection and humiliation and poverty are the order of the day . . .'

'You've said all this a thousand times,' Susie said. 'And I don't know why, because you know I don't care. I want to act.'

'You are beautiful,' Cornelius said thoughtfully, 'so you might just make it.' He looked enquiringly at Katrina. 'Do you mind if I have another Yorkshire pudding?'

'You do realize,' said Katrina, as she walked Cornelius to his car, 'that you achieved the impossible? I am *so* glad you came today!'

'I'm sorry,' Cornelius said, 'I don't follow you.'

'Susie wasn't eating a thing. Then you told her she was beautiful and she ate her food. Thank you!'

'I wish I could say I was trying to help. I wasn't trying to cheer her up or compliment her . . .'

'I know. You said it as if it was a simple, obvious fact and that made it all the more gratifying. Cornelius, I . . .' Katrina paused and, for the first time that day, looked uncomfortable. 'I don't want you to think that our family makes a habit of bursting into tears in front of strangers. It isn't something we usually do.'

'I'm sure it isn't,' Cornelius said.

'It was unfortunate timing, that's all. When you arrived, Susie was on the phone to her boyfriend. They'd both made friends with a girl in Edinburgh. Now he's told Susie that he and the girl are rather more than friends. The girl's name,' Katrina added with venom, 'is Honey. She was supposed to be coming to stay.'

'If I were her,' Cornelius said, taking in Katrina's

159

glittering eyes, 'I'd give that a miss.'

'If I were Honey,' Katrina said, 'so would I.' She waited while Cornelius got into his car and wound down his window. 'Thank you again for everything you did in France,' she said, 'and thank you for coming today.'

'I had a very good time,' Cornelius said, 'and I like your children.' He put his key in the ignition and glanced up abruptly. 'I wonder if you would be able to help me out next Saturday? I'm sure you're busy but—'

'I'm not,' said Katrina. 'What can I do?'

'Elizabeth, my mother, is having her eightieth-birthday party. She lives in Kent. She is very fond of my wife and refuses to believe our marriage is over. She keeps ringing Lucy in an effort to get her to come back to me. It occurred to me that if I were to take a female companion with me to her party she might realize that her campaign is fruitless.'

'Well,' said Katrina, 'since I made you become my lover for a week, the least I can do is become your companion for an evening. Of course I'll come. I'd be delighted to help.'

'Thank you. Can I pick you up at seven? Good. Good. Goodbye, then.' Cornelius drove off quickly. What had he *done*? He had told a *lie*! He had no idea whether his mother was still in regular contact with Lucy or not. That he had spoken out of panic was hardly an excuse. He had had the feeling that Katrina was saying goodbye to him and that he would never see her again and out of his mouth, without any thought, had come this fully formed story. For a man who valued honesty beyond all else, he had proved to be remarkably adept at telling a falsehood. But at least he would see Katrina again.

*   *   *

When Katrina came back to the kitchen, she found Ollie consuming another helping of fruit salad. 'Where's Susie?' she asked.

'She's taken the phone up to her room,' Ollie said. 'Your friend was nice. He looks very like—'

'Jarvis Cocker, I know.'

'Except for the hair. Susie reckons he's still in love with his wife.'

'I think Susie's right,' said Katrina. 'It's very sad.'

'I wonder why she left him.' Ollie reached for the cream and added a generous spoonful to his pudding. 'He told me he went to see the Zutons last week.'

'What are the Zutons?'

'Only one of the best groups in England today. I can't believe you haven't heard of them. I play their music all the time. How can you not have heard of them?'

'I can't imagine.' Katrina studied the remains of the meal. 'How very annoying,' she said. 'There is *one* roast potato left.'

'I'll have it,' said Ollie. He watched his mother rummage in the cupboard. 'Cornelius went to Thailand last year *and* he went to Vietnam. I'd like to go there. Shall I show you the route he took?'

'Yes,' said Katrina, transferring the remains of the beef from the carving dish to a plate, 'after we've done the washing-up.'

'What about Susie? She should help too.'

'Susie,' Katrina said firmly, 'is nursing a broken

161

heart. You and I can do it.'

'Great,' said Ollie glumly. He stood up and took his bowl to the dishwasher. 'I just want you to know that if Susie is still nursing a broken heart tomorrow, I'm going on strike.'

*   *   *

On Saturday evening, Katrina gave herself an hour to get ready and spent at least half of it picking out and then discarding various garments. What did one wear to an elderly lady's birthday party? In the end, she wore the same black dress that she wore to everything.

Cornelius arrived punctually at seven. He had obviously made an effort but he still resembled a scarecrow. He wore navy pinstriped trousers that made his legs look even longer than usual. He wore a crumpled but clean white shirt and a navy tie. His curly, springy hair looked as if he had at least tried to brush it.

'I'm all ready,' Katrina assured him. 'Now . . . Have I got my keys? Yes. Have I got . . . No, wait a minute.' She dashed back into the hall and collected her gift. Clutching it carefully, she came out and closed the door behind her. 'I didn't know what to get your mother. I hope she likes orchids. Right! Let's go!'

Cornelius opened the car door for her and then went round to his own side. 'You look very pretty,' he said and switched on the ignition.

Katrina smiled at him. 'You never fail to surprise me,' she said.

'Really?' Cornelius checked his mirror and drove out into the road. 'Why is that?'

'You're not the sort of person to give charming compliments. And I don't mean that in a bad way.'

'The thing is,' Cornelius said, 'it is factually correct that you look pretty, so I thought it was worth saying in case you hadn't noticed.'

'I hadn't,' Katrina said. 'And it's very kind of you to tell me but I think it's an indisputable fact that not everyone would agree with you and that therefore it is a subjective judgement on your part.'

'I wasn't being subjective. I spoke as a disinterested observer.'

Katrina laughed. 'You see, now you've spoilt it by telling me that.'

'Should I tell you that I'm interested?'

Katrina's eyes met his and for a moment Katrina felt nonplussed since Cornelius both looked and sounded as if he genuinely wanted an answer. Almost immediately, she berated herself. What a sad person she was that she could allow one kind sentence to lead her into such an absurd deduction. 'Just remember,' she told him, 'that this evening, that is exactly what you are supposed to be!'

'I will do my best. How are Ollie and Susie?'

'Ollie is *very* well. After talking to you about Thailand and Vietnam, he's full of plans for next year. Susie, on the other hand, is still very subdued. It's horrible, she's lost all her bounce. She cries a lot and keeps trying to work out where she went wrong with Liam. Yesterday she even asked me if I thought she had an irritating voice. I tried to explain that the fact that Liam has fallen for Honey doesn't necessarily mean that Honey is more attractive than she is, but at that age you

163

take rejection so personally.'

'I'm not sure age has anything to do with it,' Cornelius said. 'I think one always takes rejection personally.'

'Yes, but at least *we* know that love is a pretty random emotion and that if someone doesn't love you it doesn't necessarily mean there's anything wrong with you. Look at Edward the Eighth and Mrs Simpson. Most of his friends couldn't see what he saw in her but he thought she was perfect. Love's funny like that, don't you agree?'

'I don't know,' Cornelius said. 'I don't pretend to be an expert.'

'Neither am I but I know enough to think that Liam is an idiot and that there are plenty of men who would probably trample over Honey to get to Susie. I said this all to Susie but she just said that I haven't seen Honey. I must say, the more I hear of her the more I dislike her. She is obviously a vile, conceited liar.'

Cornelius smiled. 'Another disinterested observation?'

'Not at all. I am happy to tell you I subjectively hate the girl. What really gets me is that Susie is just like she was when that horrid boy, Ash, treated her so badly five years ago. What if it takes her another five years to get over Liam? She's starting her job next week so I hope that will distract her a little.'

'What is she going to do?'

'It's just a waitressing job in a fairly seedy hotel. I wish she'd never got the acting bug. I have this fear that she's going to spend an entire year doing a horrible temporary job and then find she hasn't got into drama school. At least she has a friend who is starting at the hotel at the same time and I suppose it will keep her busy.'

'Yes,' said Cornelius. 'And that's the best thing she can do. She should be busy. She should be very busy. She should be so busy that when she goes to bed she falls asleep at once. Keep her on the move.'

'I'm sure you're right.' Katrina cast a sideways glance at Cornelius. She had never heard him speak with such earnest conviction. She presumed he was talking from experience and wondered if he was thinking of his looming divorce. She wished she knew him well enough to offer sympathy. Instead, she put her hands together and said briskly, 'Anyway, tell me about tonight. Do you know who will be there?'

'Yes,' said Cornelius. 'You'll see my sister, Juliet, and her husband, Alec. They live in Sussex. They're the ones who've organized the party for Elizabeth.'

'What are they like? Does Juliet look like you?'

'Fortunately for her, she does not. She has my mother's looks. I think you'll like her. Alec is nice too. He's a typical Scot: he's lived in England for thirty years but retains a thick Scottish accent and gets sentimental on New Year's Eve.'

'Are you and Juliet the only children?'

'Yes. Mother married twice more after my father died and we collected various stepbrothers and stepsisters along the way but none of them stuck.'

'So who else will be there?'

'I hope my nephew and niece are coming but when I spoke to Juliet yesterday she thought it was doubtful. Michael's wife is pregnant and is being sick all the time and apparently Jenny has flu.

Henry and Amanda are coming. They're neighbours. They're both ex-pats and used to live in Kenya. Henry's very fat and looks like a walrus. Amanda has a very racy past, at least she does if half her stories are true. And then there'll be Dennis, who is very dull but loves my mother so she likes to have him around.'

'What happened to your mother's husbands?'

'Husband number two got the sack very quickly. He drank too much. Husband number three died in mysterious circumstances a few years ago. Juliet and I are almost certain he got fatally overheated in a massage parlour. He was always an old lecher. I remember taking Lucy to meet my mother and him after we got engaged. When we were about to leave, he kissed her and put his tongue down her throat. He was the dirtiest of dirty old men.'

'It must have been very difficult for your mother.'

'I don't think,' Cornelius said dismissively, 'that she ever noticed.'

Katrina glanced out of the window. On the other side of the road, a man was walking a particularly lugubrious bloodhound. She turned back to Cornelius. 'You said your mother's friend looks like a walrus. Would that be a disinterested judgement or a simple fact?'

Cornelius smiled. 'Wait and see.'

*   *   *

Cornelius's mother lived in a small village that looked just like one of those locations beloved by Hollywood when shooting films set in England. Cornelius parked outside a cottage at the end of the immaculate high street. The red front door

166

opened directly onto the pavement. Cornelius looked at it for a moment and said without much enthusiasm, 'Here we are.'

Katrina got out of the car, holding her orchid with care. Cornelius opened the boot and pulled out a cardboard box containing six bottles of wine. Katrina approached the door. 'Shall I ring the bell?' she asked and did so after receiving a quick nod from Cornelius. He seemed to be far more nervous about visiting his mother than she was.

The door was opened by an elderly man with a green bow tie, green-and-brown-checked shirt and a pale brown cardigan. 'Cornelius, dear boy,' he said, 'how very nice to see you.' He cast a vague smile in Katrina's direction and Katrina instantly decided that this must be the dull, would-be lover.

She was right. 'Hello, Dennis,' Cornelius said. 'This is Katrina.'

'Delighted to meet you,' Dennis said, with unabashed curiosity. 'Come in.'

The door opened into a large, flag-stoned sitting room with an inglenook at one end and a Victorian cast-iron fireplace at the other. The windows both had window seats, on one of which sat an elderly lady in a long, shimmering kaftan of the palest pink silk. Standing on either side of her stood a generously proportioned matron in a green-and-yellow-striped dress and a red-faced gentleman who did indeed look exactly like a walrus. In the middle of the room, a short, stocky man with a shiny bald head was opening a bottle of champagne while an attractive lady in a grey linen skirt and matching top stood hovering beside him, ready to catch any liquid in her glass.

As the newcomers stepped into the room, there

167

were cries of 'Cornelius!' but the eyes of everyone were fixed not on him but on Katrina.

A moment later all was action. Introductions were made (by Dennis, since Cornelius was busy putting the crate of wine he'd brought underneath the piano) and champagne was poured. Katrina gave her orchid to Elizabeth, who declared that she *adored* orchids and *loved* the fact that it was the exact colour of her kaftan. 'Henry,' she said, giving the orchid to the walrus, 'could you be an angel and put it on the piano for me? Katrina, come and sit by me here. It is so sweet of you to buy me a present.'

Katrina joined Elizabeth on the window seat. 'It's very kind of you to invite me,' she said. She felt increasingly uncomfortable. Unwittingly or not, Cornelius had given her the impression that his mother was cold and possibly remote. This woman with her cheerful eyes, round face and expansive gestures was charming, eminently likeable and clearly intrigued by Katrina's presence.

'I was saying only a little while ago to Amanda— Amanda, didn't I say this earlier?—that I was delighted when Cornelius asked if he could bring you.'

Amanda, whose short white hair sprang back from her forehead with awesome discipline, nodded her head and sat down on a high-backed chair. 'Elizabeth has been *very* excited. In fact, we've all been dying to know what you look like, and I know I shouldn't tell you that but one of the very best things about getting older is that you no longer worry about anything you say!'

Her husband, who had placed the orchid on a pile of sheet music, snorted vigorously. 'I have to say, Amanda, that as long as I have known you, you have *never* given a damn about anything at all. You're about as tactful as a fox in a chicken run.'

'Nonsense, Henry,' Elizabeth said, 'Amanda just tells the truth, that's all. Of course we've been dying to see Katrina but our motives are pure, I assure you. We have been so concerned about poor Cornelius and when I look at you now I begin to hope that at last things might go right for him. Now *do* tell us: how did you meet?'

Katrina glanced desperately at Cornelius who was standing at the other end of the room talking to his sister. She saw him smile at her and felt a surge of irritation. Did he not know that she needed him? 'Well,' she began, 'I suppose—'

Cornelius did know. Cornelius was wonderful for Cornelius had left his sister to come and join her, and with exquisite timing said, 'Do you mind if I interrupt?'

Katrina looked up into his face and smiled gratefully. Never had an interruption been more welcome.

'I'm sorry to break up the conversation,' Cornelius said, 'but my sister is very keen to talk to Katrina.'

Katrina rose with an alacrity that she hoped was not too obvious and joined Juliet, her husband and Dennis, who were all standing by the fireplace.

Alec gave her an amiable grin. 'Cornelius said you needed rescuing. Being grilled by Amanda and Elizabeth is an unnerving experience at the best of times.'

'You are a very wicked man, Alec,' said Dennis. He smiled reassuringly at Katrina. 'Elizabeth and Amanda are both delightful women. And I think

169

you should know, Katrina, and I know Alec will confirm this, that Elizabeth,' he paused to fix Katrina with an intense scrutiny, 'is a wonderful *mother-in-law*.'

'Really?' said Katrina faintly.

'Dennis,' Juliet put a hand on his arm, 'there's a plate of baby sausages on the Aga in the kitchen. Would you be very kind and go and get them? And Alec, I think a few glasses need refilling. Mummy's is totally empty. Will you get another bottle from the fridge?'

'We have our marching orders, Dennis,' Alec said. 'You get the food and I'll see to my wonderful mother-in-law.' He gave a mischievous wink at Katrina and walked off with Dennis.

Juliet's eyes twinkled sympathetically. 'I hope you're not regretting you came,' she said.

'Not at all,' said Katrina. She wondered if Cornelius's sister could read minds.

'Cornelius tells me,' Juliet said, 'that your son wants a guitar for Christmas.'

'Well, yes, he does.'

'I might be able to help. My son used to be a guitarist in a Goth band.'

'What does he do now?'

'He's an accountant. I can give you a guitar along with a whole wardrobe of black clothes, black eyeliner and black hair extensions. The guitar is in very good condition, he got another one a year after we bought it for him and so it's not been used too much.'

'It sounds perfect,' Katrina said. 'I think I'll pass on the hair extensions. You must let me pay you for it . . .'

'We can sort something out. You and Cornelius

170

should come and stay for a weekend with us and you can take a look at it.'

'Yes,' said Katrina a little doubtfully.

'We live in Sussex, in a village called Alfriston, it's not far from Lewes—'

'I love Lewes! I know it well! I have a friend who lives in Chailey. Whenever I stay with her, we always go to Lewes and I spend far too much money. My children used to adore the castle there.'

'Ah, the castle,' Juliet sighed. 'Cornelius has always loved the castle. I remember we used to . . .' She stopped and glanced in the direction of her brother. Cornelius was standing, listening gravely to the walrus. Amanda had joined Elizabeth on the window seat.

'My brother can be very clever occasionally,' Juliet said. 'He has found the perfect way to deflect our mother's curiosity.'

'Why? What has he done?'

'Henry joined a wine-tasting club a year ago. He is convinced he is now the world's greatest expert on wine. So Cornelius asks a wine-related question, the answer to which he knows better than anyone, Henry starts pontificating and Amanda and Elizabeth can't get away quickly enough. All Cornelius has to do is stay awake.'

'Very clever!' agreed Katrina. She wondered why Juliet had changed the subject. She was pretty sure it was deliberate.

*   *   *

At dinner, Katrina sat between Dennis and Alec. Dennis was very sweet and spoke with such care that Katrina had to stop herself from finishing his sentences for him. Alec was far more fun. He was interested to hear that she was a solicitor, having retired from the law himself a few years earlier, and he regaled her with numerous and probably apocryphal stories about judges he had known. Katrina darted occasional glances at Cornelius, who sat between Amanda and Elizabeth and opposite Dennis. She could see that Elizabeth constantly deferred to her son, eager for his opinion, touching his arm with her hand. With each solicitation, Cornelius responded with a slight nod and an expressionless face.

At the end of the meal—Juliet had produced a splendid feast of salmon, couscous, new potatoes, spinach salad and tiny crab cakes, followed by an enormous strawberry pavlova—Dennis tapped the table with his hand.

'If I may be so bold,' he said, standing and surveying the table, 'and speaking as Elizabeth's most fervent admirer, I would like to say a few words about our *birthday girl*! I know I can speak on behalf of Henry and Amanda when I say that the three of us are honoured to be representing your friends tonight—'

'All the others have died,' Henry said.

For a moment, Dennis looked slightly flummoxed by this observation. 'I'm sure that's not true,' he said.

'Oh, it is,' said Elizabeth without any visible sign of distress.

'Well, be that as it may,' Dennis persisted, 'we three *veterans* are proud to be here!' He took a sip of his wine and cleared his throat. 'There are many things I could say about Elizabeth—'

'Keep it clean, Dennis,' Henry chortled.

'Henry,' Amanda said calmly, 'you have a mind like a sewer. Carry on, Dennis.'

'Thank you, Amanda,' Dennis said, pausing only to look slightly reprovingly at Henry. 'There are many things I could say about Elizabeth. I *could* tell you that she is an example to us all. I *could* tell you that she has a lightness of spirit and a generosity of soul that gladdens the heart of all those who know her. I *could* tell you these things—'

'You bloody well have done!' Henry pointed out.

'*However*,' Dennis said, ignoring Henry with visible difficulty, 'I felt that my best course would be to tell you what she means to *me*—'

'Keep it short, Dennis,' Henry called out.

'Shut up, Henry,' said Amanda.

'I have known Elizabeth for twenty-four years,' Dennis said, 'and I think I can safely say that she has enhanced my life. We have spent many an intimate evening—'

'Keep it clean, Dennis!'

'Shut up, Henry.'

'We have spent many an intimate evening playing Scrabble or Racing Demon, and if ever I have been brought down by the state of the world, she is always ready with a merry quip! I well remember once when I voiced my fears about global warming and Elizabeth said, "*Never mind the environment, Dennis, where's my gin and tonic?*"' Dennis chuckled at the recollection. 'She is a very special lady. Now, I know I have spoken for far too long—'

'Too right,' said Henry.

'So without *further ado*, I will pass on the baton

173

to Cornelius who I am quite sure has his own thoughts about this happy occasion!'

There was a burst of enthusiastic applause after which everyone looked expectantly at Cornelius.

Cornelius cleared his throat. 'I don't believe,' he said, 'I can add anything to Dennis's speech.'

There was a momentary hiatus in the proceedings, a collective air of bewildered disappointment and then Juliet rose from her seat with her glass in her hand. 'Quite right,' she said, 'Dennis said everything we could want to say. Will everyone raise their glasses to my beautiful mother? To Elizabeth!'

Katrina wondered if anyone else noticed that Cornelius raised and lowered his glass without actually drinking from it.

*   *   *

'I have to tell you,' Katrina said, as she and Cornelius drove back along the Kentish lanes, 'that I felt extremely uncomfortable when we arrived.'

'You didn't *look* uncomfortable.'

'Well, I was. Everyone seemed to be so pleased to see me. And your mother was so kind. I mean, I know she wants you to get back with your wife so it would have been quite understandable if she loathed me on sight. But she was so nice to me. And now I feel really guilty because everyone seems so excited about our great new romance. I bet you the moment we left, they all started talking about it.'

'Of course they did. They like nothing better than a good gossip. You have made them very happy.'

174

'I feel like an impostor. Don't you feel bad about deceiving your family?'

'I haven't. I told them I wanted to bring a friend of mine to the party. That was true. Can I help it if they leapt to the wrong conclusions?'

Katrina cast a shrewd eye at him. 'You knew very well they'd jump to the wrong conclusions. I had Dennis assuring me that Elizabeth was a wonderful mother-in-law, I had your sister saying that you and I must go and stay with them.'

'That would be nice,' said Cornelius, adjusting his driving mirror.

'No, Cornelius, it would not be nice. There were many times this evening when I simply did not know what to say.'

'I'm sorry,' said Cornelius.

'Well, at least I now know what I put you through in France. The thing is, I didn't expect your family to be so *interested*. They obviously worry about you a great deal. I thought everyone was very nice. And your mother is amazing. She doesn't look anything like an eighty-year-old.'

'You must have your sister's party coming up soon. When is it?'

'I'm dreading it. It's next Saturday. It will be appalling. I'm strongly inclined to insist you come to it.'

'I've told you I'd be happy to do so.'

'You would *hate* it. It would be your idea of *hell*. Seriously, it's kind of you to offer to come but it's not necessary. I've worked out everything. You and I are going to break up, probably in the next few days.'

'Are we? May I know the reason?'

'I think you feel that you are not ready to start a

175

new relationship yet, and so I go to the party, supported by my children, looking sad but resigned.'

'Why don't you let me drive you all to the party and then we can go in and you can look happy and romantic?'

'That's all very well but you'd have to look happy and romantic too.'

'I can be romantic,' Cornelius said confidently.

'Right.' Katrina glanced at him doubtfully. She couldn't imagine him *ever* being romantic.

*　　　*　　　*

It was later, while she was taking off her make-up, that she became aware that the evening had left an unpleasant residue of unease in her mind. She liked Cornelius's family and she had enjoyed the drive back. She was grateful that Cornelius was coming to Rose's party next week but . . . and there was no question about it, there was now a very big 'but' about Cornelius. She remembered what he had said after Dennis's speech. In effect, he had quite deliberately thrown a bucket of cold water on the festivities. His sister had acted quickly and avoided any possible awkwardness but the fact remained that Cornelius had made an extraordinarily mean-spirited response to Dennis's invitation to speak. In fact, throughout the evening, Cornelius had not displayed the slightest warmth to his mother.

Katrina was aware that, owing to the unusual circumstances of their first meeting, Cornelius had progressed within a few hours from being a stranger to being a friend. When anyone queried his character, she felt an instant indignant desire to defend him. Now, for the first time, she realized how little she knew the man and, for the first time, she felt a small chilly stirring of doubt.

CHAPTER THIRTEEN

The House of Broken Hearts

There were times—not many of them, admittedly, but this was definitely one of them—when work provided a positive haven of peace. On Monday, Katrina went to Guildford, took a possible new client out to lunch and explained with huge enthusiasm why she could handle his work better than anyone else. On Tuesday, she listened sympathetically to Carol's diatribe against mendacious estate agents (Carol and her husband were trying to buy a flat), spent two hours sorting out a land dispute between two companies, had lunch with Amy and sympathized with her anxiety about her husband's infatuation with his motorbike and his son's infatuation with a dubious new girlfriend. In the afternoon, she finally finished sorting out the very angry client who, for the first time in months, sounded almost civilized as a result.

So long as Katrina concentrated on work, she needn't dwell on her unsettling thoughts about Cornelius—and why *should* they unsettle her? Cornelius was just a friend after all and possibly not even that. At least thinking about Cornelius was less unsettling than thinking about Lewis. So long as she concentrated on work, she could continue to avoid the problem of Lewis. And as long as she avoided the problem of Lewis she could sleep at night.

On Wednesday evening, Rose rang to announce that she was back from France, she looked fantastic, so did Lewis, and they were both looking forward to seeing her and the children on Saturday.

'Can I bring Cornelius?' Katrina asked.

'Of course you can. So . . .' Rose paused. 'You two are still together?'

Katrina bridled. 'Why wouldn't we be?'

'No reason at all,' Rose said. 'I shall tell Lewis he was wrong.'

'Why? What did he say?'

'He reckoned you two wouldn't last beyond the holiday.'

'I had no idea Lewis was such an expert on relationships. Actually, he couldn't be *more* wrong. Cornelius and I are very happy.'

'I'm so glad,' Rose said. 'We will look forward to seeing all of you on Saturday, then. What fun! And Lewis is *most* insistent that I send you his love!'

That night, Katrina did not sleep well.

*   *   *

On Saturday morning, Katrina came home from the supermarket to find the house still quiet. She put her bags on the kitchen floor and glanced at the clock: half past eleven. Ollie had been out last night but Susie had stayed in, and when Katrina went to bed she had left Susie watching an old black and white horror film, her eyes fixed blankly on the flickering screen. Katrina had been pretty sure that her mind was very much elsewhere.

Katrina sighed and opened the doors into the garden and tried to gain sustenance from the pale pink roses overhanging the small lawn. She wished she could stop feeling like a dog whose fur has been ruffled the wrong way. She sighed again, returned to the kitchen and began to unpack the groceries.

Twenty minutes later, Susie drifted in. She wore her pink towelling dressing gown and her hair was pushed behind her ears, exposing the pallor of her complexion and the shadows under her eyes.

'Hello, there,' Katrina said with determined cheerfulness. 'Do you fancy some coffee? I've just put the kettle on.'

'Thanks.' Susie went to the fridge and took out the carton of orange juice.

Katrina spooned coffee into the cafetière. 'What are you going to wear to Rose's party tonight? I thought I'd wear my black dress.'

'Mum, you've worn that to every party Rose has ever had. Last time, she asked you if you *had* anything else in your wardrobe.'

'There's nothing else that's suitable. I thought about wearing my linen trousers but I haven't anything smart enough to wear with them.'

Susie sat down at the table and pulled the paper towards her. 'You can borrow my red top if you like—the one we bought at Topshop.'

'I can't wear that, I'd look ridiculous. It's far too low and it's far too clingy. There's nothing worse than a middle-aged woman trying to look like her daughter . . .'

'It's better than a middle-aged woman trying to look like her mother. At least, *try* the red top.'

'All right.' Katrina brought the coffee over to the table. 'But you have to promise to be brutally honest if . . .' She stopped as her son shuffled into the room in pyjama bottoms and a once-white T-shirt. 'What time did *you* get to bed this morning?'

Ollie sat down opposite his sister and emptied the contents of the cereal packet into his bowl. 'I don't know,' he said. He sighed and reached for the milk jug.

Katrina put three mugs on the table and sat down. 'Did you have a good time last night?'

'No,' said Ollie. 'I had the worst evening of my life.' He paused dramatically and gave another deep sigh. 'Susie, I now know exactly what you're going through.'

Susie looked up abruptly from the newspaper. '*What* did you say?'

Katrina, noting the nascent outrage in her daughter's voice, tried to deflect the imminent storm. 'Susie and I were just talking about—'

'Last night,' Ollie said in a doom-laden voice, 'was *hell*, last night was evil. Nick asked Sophie out and Sophie said yes. I mean Nick is the biggest sleaze-ball you've ever met, he's a complete prat. I can't understand what she sees in him. I really do feel,' he added, pouring a vast amount of milk onto his Coco Pops, 'as if my heart has been broken.' He stared sadly at his bowl and absently put a very full spoonful of cereal into his mouth.

Susie folded her arms and cast a look of smouldering disgust at her brother. 'I cannot *believe* that you are comparing your stupid crush with my relationship with Liam. I went out with

180

him for five months and I thought he loved me like
I loved him. You haven't even been on a date with
this Sophie girl, you just fancy her—'

Ollie protested indignantly but it was difficult to
understand him since his mouth was congested
with Coco Pops.

'There is *no* comparison, none at all,' Susie
continued, her voice rising a couple of octaves.
'You have *no* idea what I'm going through, you
have no idea at all and if you did, you wouldn't be
able to stuff your face like that.' She pushed back
her chair and stormed out of the kitchen.

Katrina decided to wait a few minutes before
going after her. She poured out coffee for her and
for Ollie and silently passed him his mug.

Ollie was outraged. 'I don't see why Susie thinks
she's the only one in the house who has a right to
be miserable. I *seriously* like Sophie. I mean, I
really, really like her. I can't believe she likes Nick.
He is *horrible*, he is *seriously* horrible. I've never
felt like this before.' He bit his lip, picked up the
cereal packet and shook it. 'Do we have any
more?' he asked.

*   *   *

Given her newly ambivalent attitude to Cornelius,
Katrina had not expected to be so pleased to see
him when he arrived outside her front door.
Perhaps it was not so surprising since her children
were both sunk in gloom. She had tried to brighten
Susie's mood by taking her shopping in the
afternoon. They had found a beautiful summer
frock for her in the sales, which had at last brought
a smile to her face, and in an effort to consolidate

the effect Katrina had promised she'd wear Susie's red top. It was only when she saw Cornelius's face that she remembered her earlier reservations.

'You think I'm mutton dressed as lamb, I can tell,' she said without even bothering to say hello. 'Susie told me to wear this. Is it terrible? Should I change?'

'Definitely not,' said Cornelius. 'You look magnificent.'

'Anyway,' said Katrina, 'there isn't time. If we arrive on time we can leave early. Ollie! Susie! Cornelius is here. We're going.'

Another reason to be grateful to Cornelius: she knew her children would behave in his presence, Ollie would not go on about his broken heart and Susie would not insist that he had no broken heart.

On the journey, she spoke earnestly to the two of them. 'Now listen, Cornelius is doing me a great favour by coming tonight. In return, you must both help me to look after him. If any of Rose's more difficult friends try to monopolize him, go to his rescue.' Katrina swung round and looked at Cornelius. 'I promise you we will get away as soon as we can.'

'Katrina,' Cornelius said, 'I know I'm not the most sociable of people but you really do not have to worry. I am happy to stay as long as you want to.'

'You don't understand,' Katrina said. 'Not one of us wants to stay a minute longer than we have to.'

In the back, Ollie's phone let out an enormous belch, a ring tone that was only marginally less irritating than the ear-splitting police-siren screech emitted by his old one. Ollie answered immediately, 'Hello, George . . . Cool. Cool.'

Katrina turned round again and watched Ollie slip his phone back into his pocket. 'That was a very quick phone call,' she said.

'George and Rob are in town. I agreed to meet them at ten. Do you want to come along, Susie?'

'No,' said Susie baldly and then added more softly, 'Thanks for asking.'

Katrina felt her spirits lift. Susie and Ollie were very close and she always hated the rare occasions on which they fell out. 'I have to say,' she said to no one in particular, 'you all look very nice tonight.' Susie did indeed look stunning in her new dress, Ollie had made an effort with clean trousers and a short-sleeved shirt and even Cornelius, with his hair slightly cropped, looked almost normal in his pale brown trousers and white shirt.

The party was in full swing when they arrived. They could hear the babble of voices from the pavement. Rose opened the door to them; behind her the large sitting room was already more than half full. 'Darlings, how lovely to see you!' she said. 'Susie, you look like you've stepped out of a fairy tale. Ollie, you've grown yet again. Katty, you look very . . . . *dramatic*! Cornelius, doesn't she look dramatic?'

'I think,' said Cornelius, letting his eyes wander round the room before resting on Rose, 'she's the best-looking woman in the room.'

'Really?' said Rose, who was wearing a diaphanous pale blue dress over a navy slip. 'What a *very* sweet thing to say! Now, help yourselves to drinks and circulate, circulate!'

Katrina had meant to stay with Cornelius throughout the evening and she was not sure how they came to be separated. Instead, she found

183

herself talking to various people such as Rose's neighbours from downstairs (very nice), and Cam's boyfriend, Francis (just as irritating in England as he had been in France). None of her conversations were memorable, probably because her mind was always on other people in the room. At one point she saw Lewis chatting to Ollie and Susie. The sight of the three of them together made her muscles clench. Sam came towards her with a bottle and she stuck out her glass and said with too much enthusiasm, 'Can I have a top-up, Sam?'

'Certainly, Aunty Katty,' Sam said, filling her glass to the brim. 'Are you enjoying the party?'

'Your mother's parties,' Katrina said with a brittle smile, 'are always an experience. Will you excuse me a moment?' She tried to make her way towards her children but was hailed by Rose who insisted on introducing her to two of her female friends; they were just as glamorous as Rose and looked less than excited at the prospect of meeting Rose's sister. They soon introduced her to someone else. Katrina felt she was drifting like flotsam, with no control over where she went.

At various times she looked around for Cornelius. Once she saw him standing on the balcony with Ollie. The two of them seemed to be eating their way through a plate of smoked salmon sandwiches. Another time she saw him talking to Susie and Cam. A third time she saw him standing with his back to the wall looking down at a short, orange-haired lady in a black and white dress who gesticulated energetically at him. The lady looked like a bumble bee attacking a flagpole.

She was about to go and rescue him when she heard a soft, 'Katrina?' and turned to face Lewis.

His tanned complexion made his blue eyes appear even more striking than usual. He wore a grey suit with a black T-shirt. He looked terrific.

'Katrina,' he said again, 'you ought to wear red more often. It suits you.'

Katrina finished her glass of wine and smiled. 'I am very aware that it's far too young for me. It belongs to my daughter, she insisted I wear it.'

'Allow me.' Lewis held a half-full bottle of wine in his hand and he took her glass and filled it. 'You never did know how to accept praise. Are you well?'

'Never better.'

'It's nice to see Cornelius here.'

'I gather you didn't think we'd last beyond the holiday.'

'I'm delighted to be proved wrong.'

'Not that it's any of your business.'

'You're right. I don't quite understand why I feel it is.' He stared at her intently. 'I'd like you to have a meal with me soon.'

She wished he wouldn't look at her like that. She responded with rough sarcasm. 'A candle-lit dinner for two, perhaps?'

'If that's what you want. I *was* thinking of lunch. This situation is so extraordinary. I think we should talk about it.'

Katrina took a sip of her wine. 'It's an idea,' she conceded. 'Sometime in the future, it might be a good idea. Now, if you'll excuse me, I must go and rescue Cornelius.'

She turned and left him, only to be stopped by Cam who was anxious to know if she could stay in Greenwich for a night in November. 'We're doing a photo-shoot there. It's going to be at somewhere called the Queen's House. Have you heard of it?'

'Of course. It's a beautiful building. It was built by James the First for his wife and Queen Henrietta Maria lived there for a time too. It has a beautiful spiral staircase that—'

'That's why we're doing it there. My boss wants to drape models over the staircase, and apparently there are some fab colonnades as well. She has this idea of putting ordinary people behind the columns, peeping out at the models. You could be one if you like.'

'An ordinary person? Thank you, Cam. It sounds very tempting. Anyway, it will be lovely to have your company.'

'Good.' Cam looked across at Susie who looked as if she was being subjected to a long monologue by a lanky, acne-ridden teenager. 'I'm trying to persuade Susie to come out with us after the party. She can stay the night with me and Sam. Sam says he'll drop her back tomorrow.'

'Well, that's very sweet of Sam . . .' Katrina paused, her attention diverted by the sight of Lewis in intense conversation with Cornelius. She took another gulp of wine and tried again. 'I think Susie might want to come back with us tonight.'

'Susie!' Cam called and waited while Susie murmured something to the teenager before weaving her way through the guests. 'Susie, you *will* come out with us tonight, won't you? It's so long since we've been out together!'

'Well . . .' said Susie, her eyes flickering fleetingly at her mother.

It would have been easy for Katrina to come to the rescue, she could have used any number of excuses—pressing household tasks, newly remembered morning engagements. Instead, she simply murmured, 'I must go and rescue Cornelius,' and wandered off without saying anything. She knew Susie was sometimes irritated by her cousins' tendency to patronize her, but going out on the town with them had to be better than sitting morosely in front of late-night television.

Katrina made her way across the room towards Cornelius and Lewis. 'I think,' she said to Cornelius, 'it's time we were going.'

'The night's still young,' protested Lewis. 'Don't go.'

'We must,' Katrina said. 'I'm meeting a friend for an early morning walk tomorrow.'

'Rose will be sorry you're leaving so early,' Lewis said. 'And so will I.'

'I'm sure you'll survive.' Katrina took Cornelius's arm. 'We'd better go and say goodbye to my sister.'

*   *   *

As soon as they got into the car, Katrina kicked off her shoes. 'Oh,' she breathed, 'I'm so glad that's over! I shall sleep and sleep and sleep tonight.'

'What about your early morning walk?'

'A lie,' Katrina yawned. 'I have no intention of walking anywhere.' She reached out and touched Cornelius's hand. 'Thank you for coming with me. It was far more bearable with you there.' She sat up as he braked at the traffic lights, and stared at the group of teenage girls crossing the road. 'Look at them,' she mused. 'Endless legs, flattest of midriffs! Lucky girls! There's a cold wind tonight, though. Why do they wear so little?'

'Presumably so they can show off their flat midriffs and endless legs.' The lights changed and Cornelius moved on. 'Did you find the party difficult?'

'Not once I got enough wine down me. In a way, it was even nice to get out. My children are testing my patience at the moment. Susie is still stricken over the end of her relationship with Liam and now Ollie is grieving over a relationship he's never even had. I think our house should be renamed the House of Broken Hearts. I am discovering that my sympathy is definitely finite. Anyway, enough of that! What did you think of the party? Did you hate it?'

'No,' Cornelius said, 'I enjoyed talking to your children.'

'I saw Lewis bear down on you. What did *he* want?'

'He wanted to know about you and me. In the politest manner, of course.'

'What did you tell him?'

'I told him I was far more interested in his relationship with Rose.' One side of Cornelius's mouth twisted slightly. 'I was always a very truthful person before I met you.'

'I'm sure you were. I'm sorry. I ought to be given a *degree* in telling lies. I don't deserve you as a friend. You are *far* better than I am. You always tell the truth. That's the way to live. I used to be a Brownie, you know, and Brown Owl always said: "Tell the truth and stand tall." I've never forgotten that. Oh, dear! Everything is in such a mess at the moment!'

'Is it?' Cornelius asked. 'Why?'

'Oh . . .' Katrina waved her hands in the air.

'Don't pay any attention to me, I've drunk far too much and I always talk rubbish when I drink too much.' She sat back in her seat and stretched her arms. 'Ollie didn't say goodbye to me. Did you see him go?'

'Yes. He said you were talking to a lady with a very dark tan and long blue fingernails. He thought he might get sucked into your conversation if he came to tell you he was off.'

'I wish he *had* got sucked into it. The woman is an old friend of Rose. She has far too much money and far too much time and as far as I could understand she spends every day visit-ing aromatherapists, hypnotherapists and psychotherapists. Mind you, even she was more interesting than that man with the cravat who insisted on telling me how many shares he'd bought this year, how many shares he'd sold and his extremely complex reasons for so doing. Oh, I'm so glad it's over! I drank far too much. Have I said that already?'

'I think you might have mentioned it,' Cornelius said politely.

'Well, I'm sorry but it's true. I shall have to drink loads of water before I go to bed. Do you ever get drunk, Cornelius?'

'Not very often.'

'Have you heard of an American writer called Robert Benchley? He drank too much. Someone once asked him if he realized that drinking was a slow death.'

'What did he say?'

'He said, "So who's in a hurry?"'

Cornelius laughed and Katrina, encouraged by his response, launched into a long and very convoluted anecdote about the first time she drank too much. She only reached the end of it, by which time it had metamorphosed into a very different story, as they drew up outside her house.

'Cornelius,' Katrina said, 'thank you so much for this evening!' She leant forward to kiss his cheek, somehow caught his mouth instead, saw him recoil instantly and as quickly withdrew herself. 'Sorry,' she said, 'I am so sorry . . . I didn't mean . . . I'd better go in and start drinking water. Thank you for the lift. Goodnight.'

She fled from the car without waiting for a reply and went straight to her door. She let herself in, went to the kitchen and threw her bag on the table. She opened the French windows, walked out into her garden, gave a shuddering sigh and raised her flaming cheeks to the stars.

CHAPTER FOURTEEN

A Flurry of Emails and a Phone Call

From: *Katrinalatham@parter.co.uk*
To: *Cornhedge@winemart.co.uk*
Sent: 18 September 23:30

Dear Cornelius,
First, I want to thank you for your company on Saturday evening. I am sure that a gathering with Rose and her friends is not your idea of fun and that your agreeing to come with me was motivated solely by an unselfish wish to

give me support on what you knew would be a difficult occasion for me. Secondly, I would like to apologize to you for abusing our acquaintance by drinking too much and therefore forcing you to drive back with a rambling, incoherent, deeply pathetic individual who must have both bored and disgusted you. I feel embarrassed and ashamed by my improper behaviour. I can only assure you that I shall neither expect nor ask you to take any further part in this ridiculous masquerade in which I forced you, against your better judgement, to participate.

Best wishes,
Katrina

From: *Cornhedge@winemart.co.uk*
To: *Katrinalatham@parter.co.uk*
Sent: 19 September 8:45

Dear Katrina,
I must confess to being rather disappointed by your email. I would agree that improper behaviour with acquaintances and strangers can lead to misunderstandings. I had presumed we were friends rather than acquaintances and, as far as I am concerned, friends are those with whom one can feel free to behave properly or improperly according to circumstance. I very much enjoyed Rose's party. I had a long and delightful conversation with your son and a shorter but no less pleasant one with your daughter. (I am sure she must be an excellent actress, she has such a mobile face, don't you think?) I also had an interesting discussion with

a friend of your nephew who works for the record company behind the Kaiser Chiefs (an excellent band, I think, and I believe your son is also a fan). I feel I should remind you that you did *not* ask me to come to the party, I asked *you* if I could come. I must also confess that I was not motivated by unselfishness or disinterested kindness. I came because I regard you as a friend and I enjoy your company. On our journey back from the party, I did not find you rambling or incoherent or deeply pathetic and if the continuation of the masquerade means that I have more opportunities to spend time in your company, I am only too happy to remain a participant. Finally: how are the broken hearts? A little less broken, I hope. Do let me know.

  Cornelius

From: *Katrinalatham@parter.co.uk*
To: *Cornhedge@winemart.co.uk*
Sent: 20 September 23:00

Dear Cornelius,
You are so good! You are indeed a friend and I only used the word 'acquaintance' because I was not at all sure you would *want* to be my friend after seeing how foolish I could be. I am relieved that that is not so. As far as the masquerade is concerned, I am determined to end it. Despite my undoubted capacity for telling lies, I am not happy with deceit and I felt very uncomfortable at fooling your extremely welcoming family. (Incidentally, I still want to buy your sister's guitar for Ollie and I know how

to get it without causing embarrassment by going to Sussex with you as a couple. If you give me Juliet's email address I can contact her and arrange a time to see her when I visit my friend who lives near her.) Finally, an update on the broken hearts: Ollie is still very sad, which I hate because he is normally so happy and positive about everything. As for Susie, it is all DISASTER and it is ALL MY FAULT. At Rose's house, Cam invited her to go out with them after the party. I knew Susie did not want to go but I encouraged her to do so because I thought it would be good for her to get out. STUPID, STUPID ME! Susie DID go out with Cam and Sam and met a few of their friends, one of whom was ASH! Do you remember me telling you that Susie had a disastrous relationship with a HORRIBLE young man when she was sixteen who behaved APPALLINGLY to her and who broke her heart so brutally that she was scarred for YEARS? Well, Ash is that young man! I should have known this would happen since Susie originally met him while out with her cousins. He's one of their oldest friends. So Susie comes back on Sunday afternoon in the company of Ash who has taken her out to lunch and has apparently been KIND and SYMPATHETIC and UNDERSTANDING. Susie's heart is healing with a speed that I can only describe as alarming. According to Susie, Ash has no designs on her but is proving to be a WONDERFUL friend. Since I am so pleased to see that Susie is no longer drifting round the house like a lonely ghost, I am unable to

remind her that her new saviour is a RAT of the first order. There is nothing KIND or UNDERSTANDING about Ash and I am sufficiently desperate about things that if her unfaithful ex-boyfriend, Liam, turned up at the house tomorrow I would welcome him with open arms. The worst of it is that if I hadn't made her go out with Cam and Sam, she would never have met him—Ash, that is—again. Otherwise, everything is fine.
  Very best wishes,
  Katrina

From: *Cornhedge@winemart.co.uk*
To: *Katrinalatham@parter.co.uk*
Sent: 21 September 11:00

Dear Katrina,
I understand that mothers have an unrivalled capacity to blame themselves for anything that goes wrong in the lives of their daughters but I don't see how you can take responsibility for the re-emergence of Ash in Susie's life. She could, after all, have told her cousins that she did not want to go out with them on Saturday night and she could also have chosen to reject Ash's overtures. Furthermore, if she told you he was only being a friend, then might it not be possible that he is indeed nothing more? Perhaps he has found God or maturity or both or perhaps he is genuinely moved by Susie's grief and wants to make up for his past behaviour. I don't see that you can interfere since Susie is of an age when she needs to make her own decisions. Since you can do

nothing, you might as well stop worrying. You say Susie has recovered her equilibrium. Good. Most human beings spend most of their time being discontented or preoccupied. At Susie's age, I was very professional at being miserable. As far as I can remember, misery is an entirely natural state for most people between the ages of seventeen and twenty-five. At that age, misery can almost be enjoyable. As far as Ollie is concerned, one can only hope that a more perspicacious girl crosses his path very soon so that he can forget about the charms of the one who has inexplicably chosen to see someone else.

Cornelius

PS What were *you* like when you were twenty-one?

From: *Katrinalatham@parter.co.uk*
To: *Cornhedge@winemart.co.uk*
Sent: 22 September 22:30

Thank you for your kind words and you are right, of course. There is no way I can influence the life of my daughter and I have been trying very hard not to say anything at all. Having said that, I am finding it quite difficult to do this. In the same way, if I had been sailing a little boat alongside the *Titanic* when it was going straight for the iceberg, I would have found it difficult to decide to leave the captain to pursue his own plan of action. So while I totally agree that I should let Susie sort things out for herself and let her make her own mistakes, it is very hard to watch her teetering on the edge of making a

195

mistake the size of the universe (or at least an iceberg). In the circumstances I think I've been quite tactful and, personally, I think Susie was unfair last night to tell me that I should try to stop living my life through her. She even told me I had no idea about men and women of her generation and she also said I was an extremely bad judge of men, citing her father as evidence. I have an uneasy feeling that her observations are only too true but, given that I have been making such Herculean attempts not to interfere, they do seem a bit excessive. All I did, by the way, was to warn her to be a little wary about Ash—this after she'd been on the phone to him for forty-five minutes—and to remind her of his behaviour five years earlier. Anyway, I have now decided to be a hundred per cent silent and unconcerned about anything relating to my daughter's well-being. Meanwhile, Ollie continues to be sad about Sophie. He saw her last night with some friends and he says it was very frustrating because he and she get on so well and they both have so much in common. Sophie's mad about music like he is and, even more spookily, wants a guitar for Christmas. (Which reminds me, remember to send me your sister's address.) Ollie says her boyfriend, Nick, is an utter creep and although I have never met him I feel sure that Ollie is right. Hope I haven't bored you with all this, don't bother to answer.

Love,

Katrina

PS At twenty-one, I was completely unacquainted with misery (unlike you: why were you so miserable?). I had met Paul and was madly in love and preparing to get married and live happily ever after. The happily ever after didn't last, of course, and the misery came along later.

PPS I should have listened to your advice about Susie.

From: *Cornhedge@winemart.co.uk*
To: *Katrinalatham@parter.co.uk*
Sent: 23 September 18:10

Actually, Katrina, I feel guilty about attempting to give you advice about Susie. Having never had a daughter I am totally unqualified to pontificate. In your case, I too would have wanted to persuade the *Titanic* captain to change course. I only suggest that you cannot be certain that Ash is indeed an iceberg. He might be just a random snowflake. I enclose an attachment containing my sister's email address and website. She runs a relocation company for people wishing to move to Sussex, if you are interested. I can imagine you at twenty-one and rather wish I had met you then, except that I think you would have found me unbearable. You ask me why I used to be miserable and I suppose that it was easier to be miserable than to be cheerful, and at that age I tended to go for the easier option. I am glad to say that these days misery no longer holds any charms for me.
Cornelius

*　　　*　　　*

Katrina was alone in the house when the phone rang. Susie was out with friends and Ollie had gone over to see Rob to discuss their plans for transglobal exploration. Ollie and Rob had had at least three 'discussion' evenings already and, as far as Katrina knew, the only conclusions made thus far were a joint agreement to exclude Chechyna, Iraq and Siberia from their route.

Katrina had just poured herself a glass of wine and was scrutinizing without enthusiasm the contents of the fridge. The telephone interrupted her attempt to decide between left-over casserole and left-over curry. She lifted the handset from its base, murmured a distracted 'Hello?' and shut the fridge door.

'Katty, darling!' Rose's voice was breathy and urgent. 'I haven't spoken to you since my party. Thanks for your card! How *are* you?' Rose sounded buoyant and enthusiastic. Something had put her in a very good mood.

'I'm very well.' Katrina, armed with phone and wine, walked up to the sitting room, kicked off her shoes and settled herself on the sofa. Rose's phone calls were either very short or very long. The long ones invariably started with a polite query about Katrina's life, which never required more than the simplest of answers.

'And how is Cornelius?'

'Actually,' Katrina said, deciding now was a good time to put an end to the ridiculous charade she had inflicted on him, 'I wanted to talk to you about me and Cornelius.'

'How extraordinary,' exclaimed Rose, 'because that is exactly the reason why I rang you! And

198

before I start, I don't want you to think I've been interfering or trying to mess things up for you because I haven't. My sole concern has been a strong desire to look out for my little sister. So I'm going to be perfectly frank and put my cards on the table—'

Katrina had been glancing idly out of the window, enjoying the tranquil scene of a robin pecking at the lawn. At the sight of Omo streaking across the grass and narrowly failing to slaughter the poor bird, she felt compelled to interrupt Rose. 'Your horrible cat,' she said, 'has just carried out an unprovoked attack on a sweet little robin. My garden was a haven for wildlife before Omo came.'

'He *is* a horrid cat, isn't he?' agreed Rose. 'I never liked him.'

'Neither do I,' said Katrina, settling back on to the sofa.

'I'm sure that's not true,' said Rose comfortably. 'I wish you wouldn't interrupt me . . . What was I saying?'

'You said you wanted to put your cards on the table.'

'Yes, that's right and that's exactly what I'm going to do. Ever since you mentioned the name, it's been running through my head like one of those pop songs you can't stand but you can't stop singing, you know what I mean?'

'No, I have no idea what you mean. If you're referring to Cornelius—'

'No, of course I'm not. A name like Cornelius doesn't run through your head, it bursts straight into it like a question mark. I am talking about Lucy Lambert, of course. As soon as you mentioned her, it rang like a distant bell in my head and it's been getting louder and louder ever since.'

'How very uncomfortable for you.'

'Don't be sarcastic, Katty, it doesn't suit you. Anyway, a few evenings ago I was showing Lewis some of my old photo albums and suddenly there she was, staring at me from the end of the row in front of Miss Drommett!'

'Who is Miss Drommett?'

'She'd gone by the time you came. Miss Drommett was our maths teacher—rather sweet and quite unable to keep control, she used to burst into tears at least once a week. Anyway, then I knew. Lucy Lambert was at school with me! She was in my class!'

'Are you talking about Cornelius's wife?'

'Unless there are two Lucy Lamberts,' Rose said impatiently, 'of course I am. Really, Katty, you're very slow tonight. I have to say I'm not surprised I didn't remember her. We were never close friends. She was rather a drama queen even then. She always got the main parts in school plays and she'd go on and on about how nervous she was, when it was obvious that she simply adored being the centre of attention; and when she got the part of Juliet she took so long to die that the whole audience was almost begging her to shut up and expire so everyone could go home. Anyway, as soon as I saw the photo I said to Lewis that I just had to get in touch with her.'

'I don't see why. If you never liked her.'

'I didn't say I didn't like her. It's simply that we had very little in common. But somehow I felt fate was telling me to seek her out.'

'It wasn't that you were dying of curiosity. . .'

'Well, I admit I was a little interested, who wouldn't be? So, I set to work and I got in touch with Emily Sharp—do you remember Emily? The year you arrived, she was Head Girl. She always wanted to be a missionary.'

'Did she become one?'

'I don't think so. She works for a cosmetics company now, spreading the good news about moisturizers, so I suppose it's not that different. She got in touch last year because she was trying to arrange a school reunion, she's still trying to, I think. I knew that if anyone knew where Lucy was, it would be Emily, and of course I was right. So then I rang Lucy and of course she was *thrilled* to hear me and I suggested we have lunch and so we did!'

'You had lunch with Cornelius's wife?'

'Yes, I did. Today. She's very nice, I liked her. She's actually very pretty in a washed-out, Mia Farrow sort of way: big eyes, trembling mouth, too thin. She has a wonderful voice, very soft and low and I'm sure she must have worked very hard on it because I don't remember her having it at school. We had a lovely chat about the good old days and then I said I thought it might be possible that she was married to my sister's boyfriend—'

'Rose,' Katrina said sternly, 'do you realize you've been completely out of order? Cornelius is a very private person. I'm not at all sure he would be happy with you ferreting about like this.'

'I couldn't agree more—he wouldn't be at all happy, but I don't care. What I do care about is your happiness and if I can stop you making a huge mistake it's worth incurring his anger. You're very sweet and trusting, Katty, which is lovely but I have had a lot of experience where men are concerned and I always thought there was something funny about Cornelius.'

'Rose, I do not want to hear a long list of grievances from an estranged wife, and this whole conversation is making me feel very uncomfortable.'

'Katty, this is important, please shut up and listen. This is something you need to know.' Rose paused dramatically. 'I am going to tell you why Lucy walked out on Cornelius. And I have to tell you that once you've heard, I doubt very much if you'll want to see him any more.'

CHAPTER FIFTEEN

The Red Angel Wins

For many years now, Katrina's brain had harboured two angels, a red one and a white one. Both were ever ready to offer advice and, generally, the latter proved far wiser than the former. When Paul had asked Katrina to marry him, the white angel suggested that a man who had already been engaged three times in the last four years might not be the steadiest of husbands. When Katrina had fallen in love with Lewis, the white angel queried the credibility of a man who refused to be seen outside her house with her. Now, right on cue, the white angel was on hand to help. 'Tell Rose you don't want to hear any more. Tell Rose you have faith in Cornelius. Tell Rose you are happy to wait for Cornelius to tell you about his life in his own time.'

'Rose,' Katrina said, 'how do you know this woman is reliable? She left her husband so she's hardly likely to speak with any sort of impartiality. For all you know, she might have told you a pack of lies.'

'She's not bright enough to tell lies,' Rose said. 'She never was. And besides, she was genuinely upset. You should have seen her cry when she showed me the photo of their son.'

'Cornelius doesn't have any children.'

'I *thought* he told you that!' Rose crowed. 'I told Lucy I thought he told you that! Of course, that just set her off crying again.'

'I can't remember if he *did* tell me that. I just assumed . . . I certainly got the impression that he didn't have any.'

'Katty, what sort of relationship do you have with this man, for heaven's sake? Don't you ever *talk* to each other? How can you not know whether or not your boyfriend has children?'

'I've told you, it wasn't a case of not knowing, it's what I thought. Cornelius doesn't like talking about himself.'

'Well, I can see why! He doesn't like talking about himself because he knew you'd be horrified if you knew what he's really like. Honestly, Katty, I despair of you sometimes! The man had a son. I saw the photo. He was called Leo and he looked just like his father except he had a lovely smile and I don't think your Cornelius even *knows* how to smile.'

'But . . .' Katrina hesitated. 'I don't understand. I wonder why he's never mentioned him.'

'I suggest you ask *him*!' Rose said. 'But I tell you it is an undeniable fact that he had a son called Leo. He would be twenty-three now.'

'Two years older than Susie.' Katrina frowned. 'What do you mean, he *would* be twenty-three?'

'He died,' Rose said. 'He died about fifteen months ago. Cornelius was with him when it happened. They'd all been out to dinner to celebrate Leo's degree results. He'd just heard he'd got a First. The next morning Cornelius and Leo walked down to the florist's to get some flowers for Lucy, it was her birthday or something. They were outside the shop when Leo collapsed and fell. I gather Cornelius tried mouth-to-mouth and then the ambulance people arrived and tried something too, but it was no good. He just died.'

'*Why?* What happened? Was it a heart attack?'

'Lucy said it was something called Sudden Adult Death Syndrome—it's the grown-up equivalent of cot death, apparently, a sort of instantaneous heart failure. It's pretty rare and it was just jolly rotten luck.'

'Yes.' Katrina swallowed. 'I can't imagine how they could bear it.'

'Well, Lucy couldn't,' Rose said flatly. 'She told me that all she could remember of the first few weeks was lying on Leo's bed all day and crying into his pillow. But I'm telling you all this because I feel it's important you know that your dear boyfriend was completely useless. He refused to talk about Leo, he took only a couple of days off work, he didn't even try to comfort poor Lucy. And then, to cap it all, he came home one day and told her he was taking two months off work so they could go and visit the Far East.'

'I don't see why that's such a bad idea. He probably thought it would do them good to get away.'

'Come off it, Katty, it was a *crass* idea. Cornelius knew very well that Leo was planning to go to Vietnam and places. It was the most incredibly tactless thing to suggest, and Lucy was in no state to go anywhere anyway. She says she told him all this and all he said was that he'd go on his own. And he did! Can you imagine that? He left his wife, who was having a complete nervous breakdown, and he buggered off to Thailand or wherever without her! It's unbelievable!'

'He obviously needed to go.'

'We all *need* lots of things, it doesn't mean we can have them! In a proper marriage, each partner will respect the *needs* of the other.'

Rose never failed to amaze Katrina. For a woman who had raised selfishness to an art form, such outrageous self-righteousness, such blatant hypocrisy could only be responded to with speechlessness. If Katrina did respond, she would never stop talking.

'So, anyway,' Rose said, 'he goes away and leaves Lucy entirely on her own, even though he knows very well she might do something dreadful to herself. Her friends, of course, were appalled by his behaviour and Lucy says they saved her. One of them persuaded her to come and join her in some interior-design business and Lucy says it kept her sane. And now she's doing voice-overs and is making good money for the first time in her life. She says she still dreams of proper acting, of course, but Lewis says if you're not Judi Dench or Maggie Smith you don't get a look in if you're a woman and you're over thirty. Anyway, I was telling you about Cornelius. He finally came home after a couple of months and Lucy told him it was over. Can you blame her?'

'I don't know. I can understand why she feels so hurt but—'

'There's no *but*, Katty, the man behaved like a louse and Lucy was quite right to dispatch him.'

'I'm sure she thought she was completely in the right but even you must realize she's not going to have an objective opinion. Can you imagine anything worse than watching your child die? Cornelius must have been in the most terrible state.'

'I'm sure he was. That doesn't excuse the fact that he failed to take any notice of the fact that his *wife* was in a terrible state.'

'Rose,' Katrina said, 'I really don't feel happy talking about this. I feel disloyal. And, anyway, I have to go. I'm cooking supper.'

'All right, but before you go, just remember that your boyfriend not only *looks* peculiar—my friend Anna thought he was just like a stick insect—but he also is a *very peculiar* man. And by the way, he really upset Anna at the party. He can be *so unnecessarily* rude.'

'What did he do?'

'She was trying to draw him out . . . she's terribly good at drawing people out. She asked him what he did and he told her he sold wine, then she told him she drank wine all the time and he told her she should try Alcoholics Anonymous!'

Katrina swallowed a laugh. 'I'm sure he was joking.'

'Anna said he was deadly serious. What did you

want to tell me, by the way?'

'I didn't want to tell you anything.'

'Yes, you did. You said you had something to tell me about you and Cornelius.'

'Oh,' said Katrina, 'I can't remember now. It can't have been very important.'

'Well,' said Rose darkly, 'don't say I didn't warn you.'

Katrina switched off the phone, leant back against the cushions and shut her eyes. She could *see* Cornelius and his son walking purposefully down the road, intent on their mission, talking about . . . what would they be talking about? And then, when it happened, she could imagine all too clearly the bewilderment, the panic and, finally, the terror Cornelius must have felt as he watched his son dying in front of him . . . Oh, it was horrible, horrible!

As a teenager, she had developed a morbid fear of death and had spent many hours trying to come to terms with the fact that her life would end in black oblivion. When she became a mother, her own mortality seemed far less worrying. There were even times when black oblivion seemed rather attractive. Instead, she would sometimes wake in the early hours of the morning and dwell on the dangers that awaited her children: freak bolts of lightning, debilitating illnesses, drunken drivers, fanatical terrorists. Most of the time, she had become adept at censoring such time-eating preoccupations. The death of Cornelius's son was like a dark shadow blotting out the sun, reminding her of the ease with which one's happiness could be destroyed in a single moment of random bad luck.

She heard a key in the lock and voices in the hall and went through immediately.

Susie was there with her friend Tara, both of them talking about the DVD they had seen at a friend's house. 'You must see it, Mum, it's called *Children of Men* and it's brilliant, all about England in the future and there's been some virus and now no one can have children and so there's this crumbling, dying world with no children in it and it's really horrible, and we were going to get a pizza afterwards but we hadn't enough money so we came back here. Have you had supper yet?'

The girls looked like sisters in their waitress uniform of black trousers and white shirts. Tara's dark hair, streaked with red highlights, was plaited while Susie's fell loose about her shoulders. Katrina smiled and said, 'No, I haven't. I shall make us a soufflé. Come and talk to me while I cook.' Katrina led the way to the kitchen. She was overwhelmed with delight at the presence of her happy, beautiful daughter. She poured wine, broke eggs, grated cheese while the girls talked about the scariness of the film and the sex appeal of Clive Owen before reverting to the subject that was currently obsessing them, namely the true awfulness of the hotel they worked for.

'I went up to Jane at lunch,' Tara said, 'and I told her the couple at table ten were complaining very loudly about their steaks. So she told me to replace them with new ones, and then I asked her what to do about table fifteen who were complaining about their chicken pie, and she told me to explain that the chef was new.'

'Is he new?' Katrina asked.

'He's been there for eighteen years,' Susie said.

'He's so gross. He told me this morning he liked his meat tender and then he said—I can't believe he said this—"I bet your meat is tender," and he wriggled his horrid eyebrows at me and flashed his grey old teeth.'

'Yuck!' Tara made a face. 'What did you say?'

'I sort of simpered and said, "Oh, Richard!". I feel rather sorry for him, really. He lives with his mother and I bet he's never had a girlfriend.'

Katrina raised her eyebrows. 'If he says things like that then I'm not surprised.' She heard a loud knock on the door and said cheerfully, 'I'll go!'

Ollie was standing impatiently outside. He couldn't stay, he and Rob were off out to see some friends, he'd left his wallet on the table and . . .

Katrina surprised them both by hugging him tightly. 'I love you, Ollie!' she said.

'Thank you, Mum,' Ollie said politely. 'I love you too.'

*   *   *

Rose's revelation was like a persistent tummy ache. At the most unlikely moments she would be attacked by a twinge of discomfort. She was at a very boring meeting on Tuesday morning when her eyes suddenly filled up, and on Wednesday Carol was telling her about the flat that she and Douglas just *had* to have, when a crystal-clear image of Cornelius in front of a florist's came into her mind and she had to use all her concentration to bring her attention back to Carol.

All in all, it was a relief to meet Amy for their weekly lunch on Thursday. They had a pleasant time dreaming up subversive responses to Andrew

209

Tennyson's latest email. Andrew Tennyson was in the conveyancing department and this year he was organizing the forthcoming bonding weekend in Essex. He had sent out an email asking each partner to prepare an individual party piece with which to entertain their colleagues at the end of the three-course dinner.

'I suppose I could recite a sonnet,' Amy said doubtfully.

'I think you ought to read out loads and loads *and loads* of sonnets,' Katrina said. 'It would be worth it just to see the look of tortured panic on Andrew's face. I think the whole "party piece" idea stinks, to be honest. It's all right for people like Andrew who love standing up and showing off. I shall have nightmares for weeks about it.'

'I had a nightmare last night,' Amy said. 'I dreamt I blew up Eddy's motorbike.'

Katrina laughed. 'That sounds more like a wish-fulfilment dream than a nightmare. On the positive side, it's nice that he's found a new passion.'

'Not if it's going to kill him. He wants me to go and buy some leathers and a helmet. I've told him I can't do it. I told him I had a psychic premonition that something bad was going to happen with that bike.'

'Did you really have a psychic premonition?'

'No. I just didn't want to admit to Stephen and Eddy that the thing terrifies me. I'm sure they both think I'm utterly pathetic. I suspect Stephen can't understand why his father married such a sad old woman.'

'Forty-nine is not old.'

'It is to Stephen. Do you realize his mother is ten

years younger than me? I catch him looking at me sometimes and I know what he's thinking. He's wondering what on earth his father ever saw in me.'

'That is rubbish and, what's worse, it is paranoid rubbish.'

'I was struck by a thought the other day. Four years ago I was the same age Eddy is now and four years ago I was having my own little mid-life crisis, worrying about life passing me by, etcetera, etcetera. Do you remember? I nearly became a Buddhist and then I went to tap-dancing classes instead. And then I met Eddy and fell in love and married him. It occurs to me that Eddy is having *his* mid-life crisis now. Hence the motorbike. And then there's the matter of Stephen's girlfriend. I'm glad he's found someone, but she's so odd. She doesn't really talk, she mumbles and I can never hear what she says so she thinks I'm deaf. And they come in late and cook revolting food and in the morning I see these dirty saucepans with what looks like green cement in the bottom of them . . .'

'Have you said anything to Eddie?'

'No.' Amy shrugged. 'He's so keen for me and Stephen to get on and I don't want to rock the boat. I sort of feel that if I do nothing, the problem might go away. I just wish . . .' She stopped and waved a hand. 'Forget it! I'm being silly!'

'You're never silly. What were you going to say?'

Amy gave a bleak smile. 'It's only that I feel so *old* at the moment. I feel old beside Stephen and Eddy. I wish I didn't, that's all.'

'You're not old. You are mature and wise. Did you read about the latest scientific report to hit the papers? A team at Boston University analysed a group of chimps in Uganda and found that the males vastly preferred the ageing females to the younger ones.'

'I saw that,' Amy said, 'and I also read about the scientists' conclusion, which was that, unlike humans, female chimps are fertile throughout their lives and male chimps go for mature females who will make sensible mothers.'

'Oh,' said Katrina. 'Perhaps . . .'

'No. There's no perhaps. Eddy and I tried but . . . nothing happened and now it can't happen.' Amy moved her plate and put her elbows on the table. 'Right. We've talked quite enough about me. What about *you*? What is happening in your life?'

'Susie was on the phone to Ash last night. Only twenty minutes this time.'

'But they're still just friends?'

'So Susie says. She hardly ever mentions the late, unlamented Liam any more so I should be grateful. I just have this awful feeling of doom whenever she mentions Ash's name, and I know I can't say anything so I feel like I have indigestion the whole time. And poor Ollie is still sad about Sophie. He is definitely smitten. I've been dreading him going off on his travels but now I'm counting the days. At least when he's in Thailand or India or Africa or wherever he decides to go, he'll have lots of new experiences to distract him. I wish I was going away somewhere.'

'You are going somewhere,' Amy pointed out. 'Have you forgotten our exciting night at the Green Ring Hotel in three weeks? You and me and our sexy colleagues bonding like mad over the chicken salad and sausage rolls and all the hilarious party pieces?'

'Oh, hell!' Katrina said. 'I *really* wish I was going away somewhere.'

*   *   *

In bed that night, Katrina's mind was far too active for sleep. What was it Amy had said over lunch? 'If I do nothing the problem might go away.' In Katrina's case, this was not an option. She had had another email from Cornelius, telling her about an upcoming radio programme on the Vercors. Katrina had planned to fire off a reply but found that she could write nothing. As long as she didn't acknowledge her awareness of his tragedy, she knew she could not recapture the ease and informality that characterized her dealings with him. After supper, she had sat down at her desk and, having littered the floor with numerous, ever more convoluted efforts, she had written one final version.

Dear Cornelius,
It appears that your wife and Rose were at school together. They met for lunch recently and Lucy told her about your son, and Rose told me. I just wanted to say how sorry I was.
    Love, Katrina

She didn't hear from him for nearly a week. His email was short.

Thank you for your condolences.
    Cornelius

Condolences: such a cold and formal word. The
213

more Katrina read that sentence, the more it seemed to her that Cornelius had in effect terminated their friendship. Intensely private as he was, he must have judged that she had transgressed the boundary. Like Eve, she had succumbed to temptation and bitten the apple of knowledge. It was absurd to use a word like betrayal in this context—after all, she had simply listened to her sister's account of a conversation with Lucy—but a part of her felt that she deserved to forfeit his confidence. Perhaps it was that sense of guilt that had stopped her from telling Rose that her relationship with Cornelius was over. How ironic that this was now almost certainly true. She had exiled herself from the small circle of his trusted friends. She was not sure why this upset her so much. All she knew was that, for the first time in years, she felt lonely. The bloody red angel had won again.

CHAPTER SIXTEEN

A Disgruntled Ex-Husband and an Angry Sister

Katrina had been planning to ring her ex-husband for a fortnight now. Each day, she had written herself a note saying 'Ring Paul', and it was only when the pile of notes on her desk became too messy to ignore that she picked up the phone one evening.

She didn't ring him very often. Usually, it was to remind him of important dates like the children's birthdays. Invariably, Paul's partner, Clarrie, would answer the phone and would regale Katrina with the latest list of Paul's inadequacies as a father, all of which Katrina would hear with sympathy. Tonight, she got Paul.

'That's weird,' he said. 'It must be telepathy. I was about to ring you.'

'Very weird,' Katrina said. 'Paul, I want to talk to you about—'

'Clarrie's left me.'

'What?'

'Clarrie's left me. Three days ago, she left me.'

'Oh.' Katrina pulled out the chair by her desk and sat down. 'Paul, I'm so sorry.'

'She's broken my heart. You can't imagine how I feel.'

'Well, actually,' Katrina said, 'I can. You probably feel how I felt when *you* left *me*.'

'You don't understand,' Paul said. 'She's taken the children.'

'The *children*?'

'My daughter and my unborn son who is due to emerge into the world very soon, only to find that his father is nowhere to be seen. I can't believe she's done this to me. I mean, I left Rachel to be with her.'

'I seem to remember,' Katrina said, 'that you left Rachel and your son, Caspar, to be with Clarrie. And before that you left Ruth and your sons, Crispin and Bertie, to be with Rachel, and before that you left me and—'

'The point is,' Paul said, 'no one's ever left *me* before. You wouldn't believe the things Clarrie said to me. She's been so cruel and vindictive. I tell you, my eyes have been opened, they really have

215

been opened. At least, I've never been cruel. Do you remember when I told you I was leaving you? Do you remember I bought you a lovely bunch of flowers?'

'You did. That was very nice of you. You also told me I was like a comfortable pair of old slippers. You said Ruth was like a pair of high heels and at your particular stage in life what you needed was high heels.'

'Well,' said Paul, 'there you are. At least that's not cruel.'

'Paul,' Katrina said, 'as a matter of urgent information, I must tell you that no woman wants to be compared to a pair of old slippers.'

'I don't know how the stupid hob works,' Paul said plaintively. 'I keep burning my food. I feel like I'm going mad. I'm not used to being on my own. I'm a wreck, Kat. I look terrible.'

'I'm sorry. Perhaps Clarrie will come home soon.'

'She won't. She said such terrible things.' He gave an incredulous laugh. 'She even told me I was hopeless in bed.'

'Really?'

'I know. Can you believe it?' He paused. 'I'm not hopeless. Am I?'

'No . . . Well . . . No.'

There was another pause. 'That's not exactly the ringing endorsement I was looking for.'

'You're not hopeless,' Katrina soothed. 'Perhaps you're a little *brisk*.'

'Brisk? What do you mean, *brisk*?'

'Brisk can be good,' Katrina said quickly. 'When you don't feel like sex and you want to get it over and done with as quickly as possible, brisk is great.'

'Katrina, you are not helping me here. Are you

216

saying you never enjoyed sex with me?'

'No. Not at all. It's just that sometimes a little *lingering* is nice. Paul, I don't think Clarrie left you because of your sexual technique. I think she probably left you because she felt you weren't giving her much support. Perhaps you should ring her, go and see her . . .'

'No way,' said Paul. 'She left me, remember? I'm not going to crawl to her. I've been thinking a lot lately. I really miss you and Susie and Ollie. You know it's my birthday in three weeks? November the tenth? I'd really like my family about me then.'

'Which one?' Katrina asked. 'You have so many.'

'Don't pretend to be obtuse, Kat, it doesn't suit you. Rachel and Caspar are in Madrid. Ruth won't let Crispin and Bertie near me. As far as I'm concerned, you and Susie and Ollie are my proper family now. Will you come and stay for my birthday?'

'I can't. On November the tenth, I'm going off to a weekend conference in Essex. I'm not sure about the children. I know Cam will be staying here—'

'Who's Cam?'

'Oh, for goodness' sake, Paul, you know who Cam is. She's my sister's daughter and she's helping to organize a fashion shoot in Greenwich that week. I don't suppose she'll mind being on her own for a bit. I'm sure Ollie and Susie will try and get over to you if they can.'

'Will you tell them to ring me? And tell them I really need them right now, tell them I'm right at the edge. By the way, why did you ring me?'

'I can't remember. It can't have been that important.'

'Kat, was I really hopeless in bed?'

217

Katrina sighed. 'No. You were a tiger.'

'Thank you,' Paul said. 'I knew you'd tell the truth in the end.'

*   *   *

Over supper that night, Katrina told Susie and Ollie about their father's misfortune. She was not entirely surprised to find they were less than sympathetic. Susie said they had always wondered how Clarrie could put up with him. Katrina said that was all very well but it didn't alter the fact that Paul was very unhappy and needed their support. 'He wants us to go and stay with him on his birthday. I've got this beastly conference weekend in Essex so *I* can't go. I know it's a pain but it would mean an awful lot to your father if you went. He is so miserable. If you don't go, he'll have his wretched birthday all on his own.'

'If we do go,' Susie pointed out, 'all three of us will have a wretched weekend. The house will be a tip and he'll want me to do all the cooking. And I'll have done a full day's work at the hotel. Can't we go down on the Saturday?'

'But his birthday's on the Friday. He's so looking forward to seeing you. It's only for a weekend.'

Susie gave a theatrical groan. 'My weekends are very precious. If we do go, I'm not getting him a birthday present. I can't afford one and he hasn't given me any for at least two years.'

'Your father won't mind about presents. He'll be happy that you've made the effort to go and see him.' Noting the stony silence that followed this assurance, she thought it best to change the subject. 'Anyway,' she said brightly, 'what are you

218

both doing this weekend? Anything exciting?'

'I'm going to Nick's party,' Ollie said gloomily.

'Won't that be fun?'

'No,' said Ollie, 'it won't.'

'Mum!' Susie admonished. 'How could you forget? Nick is going out with the love of Ollie's life!'

'You may mock,' Ollie said with dignity, 'but actually she is.'

'You might just find,' Katrina said, 'that he isn't. You might go to the party and find there's a beautiful girl waiting for you to sweep her off her feet.'

'Not very likely,' said Susie. 'Ollie doesn't do sweeping, do you Ollie?'

'No,' said Ollie, sighing heavily. 'I'd probably fall over and drop her.'

'If you ask me,' Susie said, rising from her chair and collecting the plates, 'if Sophie prefers Nick to you, she doesn't deserve to be the love of your life. Nick is so pleased with himself. He always has been. I remember him at school. When he was twelve and spotty and half my size, he came up to me at break and asked me to go out with him. I'll never forget his chat-up line: "How'd you like to come out to the games arcade after school and I'll show you a good time?" Yuck! Just promise me, Ollie, you won't spend the whole night staring wistfully at Sophie.'

'I'm not quite that sad,' he said. He got up and went to the fridge. 'Anyone for a yogurt?'

'Yes, please,' said Susie. 'I'll get the spoons.'

Katrina took a banana from the fruit bowl and looked hopefully towards her daughter. 'I thought I'd get a film out on Saturday,' she said. 'I want to

219

see *Little Miss Sunshine*. Amy says it's the best film she's seen in years. What about it, Susie?'

Susie returned to her seat and yawned. 'I'd love to but I'm going to meet Ash in the afternoon. He wants me to help him buy a birthday present for his sister.'

'Oh,' said Katrina, 'that's a pity.'

'A pity I can't watch a film with you or a pity I'm going out with Ash?'

'That's very unfair. I didn't say a thing.'

'You don't have to, Mum, you're *so* transparent! Ash and I are friends. He's nice. Honestly, Mum, if I can forgive him for upsetting me five years ago, isn't it time you did?'

'I just . . .' Katrina paused. 'I just don't want you to get hurt, that's all.'

'I have no intention of getting hurt! Ollie, are you bringing those yogurts over or not?'

'I'm sorry.' Ollie brought them over and sat down. 'I rang Cornelius today,' he said.

His intervention had the desired effect. Katrina lost all interest in Ash and stared at her son. 'Why?' she asked.

'There was nothing to do at work and I was plotting my travel itinerary. I've lost the piece of paper with Cornelius's suggestions on it so I gave him a ring. I asked him to lunch on Sunday.'

'You did what? Really, Ollie, you might have asked me first. I'm sure he has much better things to do with his time. What did he say?'

Ollie dug his spoon into his yogurt. 'That's just what *he* said.'

'You mean he *did* say he had better things to do with his time?'

'No, he said he was sure *you* had better things to
220

do with your time than cook for him. So I said you wanted him to come round.'

'Well, really, Ollie, why did you say that?'

'Because otherwise he wouldn't have agreed to come and I need to talk to him.'

'Do you mean he said he *would* come?'

'Yes. Why wouldn't he? That's all right, isn't it?'

'Yes,' Katrina said, 'that's fine.'

*   *   *

For the rest of the week, Katrina was preoccupied by Ollie's news. She was convinced that Cornelius didn't want to come to lunch. She suspected he only accepted the invitation because he disliked telling lies and had been unable to think of a convincing excuse. Nor was she happy with the fact that he believed she was a prime instigator in the invitation. He had made it quite clear that he disliked her intrusion in his private life and she hated to think that he might think she was too obtuse to make a tactful retreat.

When the doorbell rang on Sunday, she could feel her face go crimson. She was glad that Ollie was on hand to let Cornelius in. As he came down the stairs, she busied herself by checking the roast chicken. At least, she reassured herself, Cornelius could assume that her heightened colour was due to the heat from the oven.

Once again, he had brought flowers and wine and dismissed her embarrassed thanks with an easy, 'Please, Katrina, I am happy to bring them. It is so kind of you to feed me.'

'Mum loves feeding people,' Ollie said.

'Well, I enjoy being fed,' Cornelius responded.

221

He gave Katrina a warm smile. 'It is very good to see you again.'

'Cornelius,' Ollie said, 'I've got the atlas out. Can I show you my latest ideas?'

Cornelius followed Ollie over to the table while Katrina stirred the gravy and steamed the spinach. She was happy, quite ridiculously so. Cornelius had smiled at her and she saw they were still friends. He was not cross with her, he was not cross at all.

Relief made her talkative. Over lunch she flitted from subject to subject. She talked about her love of Greenwich and the Argentinian delicatessen round the corner with its generous black sofa and seductive smell of coffee. She talked about Carol at work and her guilt about the fact that Carol's utterly kind willingness to help irritated her so much. She talked about an article she had read which made the worrying claim that most people under thirty no longer visited a dentist. She was about to give her views on the condition of the welfare state when Cornelius suddenly raised a hand.

'I have something to say,' he said. 'I can't believe I forgot about it.' He turned to Susie. 'The other day I was talking to my wife,' he said, pronouncing the last two words a little self-consciously. 'I told her about your attempt to get into RADA and she was very impressed you'd got through the first few auditions. She rang me yesterday. She has a friend who's involved in a new production. I gather it's a horror film, I think it's called *The Recreation of Henry*—no, that's not it, it's called *The Resurrection of Henry*. It sounds like the usual sort of thing . . . aliens taking over humans. Lucy says there's one scene where the hero visits his dentist and, as he goes in, he smiles at the sweet young dental nurse and she says, "Please come this way." She only has the one line, it's important because she says it in a very unusual manner—you know, a menacing but distant sort of manner so the hero knows that she has been taken over. Anyway, the point is, Lucy has arranged for you to go along to an audition for the part. The audition's next Thursday afternoon in Soho. I don't know if you can get time off work but—'

'Of course I can!' Susie breathed. 'I'd get time off even if I couldn't get time off! Oh, Cornelius, this is so exciting, thank you so much! You are so *good*!'

Cornelius looked a little taken aback by such effusiveness. 'Well, it's only one line and Lucy organized it. I simply told her about you.' He reached into his jacket pocket and pulled out a folded piece of paper. 'I've written down the details and also the line you have to say—'

' "Please come this way." I know, I shall practise and practise it!' Susie leapt up and took the paper from Cornelius. 'Mum, do you mind if I get down? I must make some phone calls. I shall ring Tara first. Cornelius, I am *so* grateful! Please thank your wife!'

'I will,' said Cornelius. 'I'm sure she's only too happy to . . .' But Susie had gone, leaving Ollie free to appropriate the remains of her Bakewell tart.

'Well,' Katrina said. 'Susie will think of nothing else until next Thursday.' She smiled at Cornelius. 'You've made her very happy.'

'She might not get the part,' Cornelius warned.

223

'There are others applying.'

'I think she'll get it,' said Ollie. He gave a significant nod. 'I have a feeling this week that the Latham luck is changing.'

Katrina, knowing what was required of her, said, 'Why do you think that, Ollie?'

'Last night,' Ollie said, 'Sophie and Nick split up. I don't know why. They had a row and Sophie left early.'

'Well, don't get your hopes up,' Katrina said. 'They might be making up as you speak.'

'No, they won't. After she left, Nick got off with Harriet Edwards. Sophie can't bear Harriet Edwards.' He caught sight of the clock and pushed back his chair. 'Mum, I said I'd meet George in town. I've got to go. Cornelius, thanks for all your help. Come and have lunch with us next Sunday! Shouldn't he have lunch with us next Sunday, Mum? Bye now!'

There was a slightly awkward silence after Ollie's departure and then Katrina and Cornelius both spoke at once.

Katrina said, 'Do come to lunch next week!'

Cornelius said, 'I hope you'll let me help with the washing-up.' He smiled and then tried again. 'You must be very irritated by your son's kind habit of asking me to lunch with you. I assure you I don't take it seriously. It's been a lovely afternoon, however. I was *going* to ask if I might take you out to dinner next week.'

Katrina laughed. She could see now that he had been worried she had been bounced into inviting him today. 'Dear Cornelius, you do not have to take me out to dinner. I love having you to lunch and it's perfectly clear the children do too. I do it

224

every week, it's an institution in our house, and one more is no bother at all. Of course you must come next Sunday!'

'Well,' said Cornelius, 'thank you very much.'

'And don't you move from that chair. Susie can help with the clearing-up later. I'll make some coffee.'

'Let me at least clear the table.' Cornelius stood up and began to collect the pudding bowls. 'Have you seen Rose and Lewis lately?'

'No,' said Katrina, 'and I don't want to either.' She filled the kettle and glanced fleetingly at Cornelius. She was glad he had brought up Lewis. It reminded her of his kindness to her, his supportiveness. It was funny how quickly she'd come to regard Cornelius as a good friend. She had missed him. Since he had brought up the subject of Lewis she felt it was all right to bring up Lucy. 'I gather you're on speaking terms with your wife, then?'

'Oh, yes,' said Cornelius. 'It's all much better now. We're going for the two-year separation and consent route: that seems to be the most civilized way of ending a marriage.'

'I'm so glad.' Katrina spooned coffee into the cafetière. 'Did you know that Rose told her you and I were—were an item?'

'Yes,' said Cornelius, 'yes, Lucy told me that.' He carried the bowls over to the island unit and cleared his throat. 'I meant to tell you, the other day I was in the National Portrait Gallery with my niece, Juliet's daughter, Jenny—she's an art historian and is doing her best to educate me—and we saw a portrait of Mary Shelley. She looked like a nice woman, I thought.'

225

'I'd like to see it,' Katrina said. She was sure that Cornelius had indeed meant to tell her this. She was also sure he had brought it up *now*, because he had wanted to change the subject. She and Cornelius might be friends but it was clear that Cornelius was still not prepared to discuss his private life with her.

*   *   *

At work the next day, three new jobs landed on Katrina's desk. They were all potentially lucrative, which was good, and they all needed to be done as soon as possible, which was bad. On top of this, she had an internal memo asking her to deliver a detailed appraisal of Carol's capabilities before the end of the day so that a decision could be made about her future. There was also a meeting with the rest of the commercial team at three to discuss ways of bringing in new clients.

Amy dropped by at twelve and said, 'Any chance of lunch today?'

'Sorry,' Katrina shook her head. 'I've ordered a sandwich. I'm up to my eyes at the moment. Let's have lunch on Wednesday. I should be calmer by then.'

'You're on!' Amy waved and left Katrina to mull over the document in front of her.

Twenty minutes later, her phone went. 'Ms Latham?' It was Rebecca from reception. 'I have your sister here and she wonders if you'd like to meet her for lunch.'

Katrina sighed. 'Will you tell her I'd love to but I have far too much work at the moment. Tell her I'll ring her this evening.'

She heard Rebecca's prim voice relaying the fact that, unfortunately, Ms Latham was too busy for lunch, and then she heard Rose's voice, loud and furious: 'You tell Ms Latham that I won't MOVE from here until she comes down and tells me if she was EVER planning to let me know that MY boyfriend is the father of HER SON?'

There was an appalled silence during which Katrina tried and failed to make her mouth move. At last, she heard Rebecca's voice again. 'Ms Latham, your sister says—'

Katrina stood up. 'I heard,' she said. 'Tell my sister I'm coming down.'

CHAPTER SEVENTEEN

A Difficult Conversation

'*Will* you stop frogmarching me out of the building?' Rose demanded. 'And you're hurting my arm!'

'I don't care,' Katrina hissed, ushering her sister out onto the pavement and resisting the temptation to look back through the glass door to observe Rebecca, who would be still sitting there with her mouth wide open or, even worse, sitting there with the telephone clamped to her ear and her mouth opening and shutting and opening and shutting. She tightened her hold on her sister's arm and marched her purposefully down the street. 'I have spent *years* building up a solid reputation at work and you have just blown it to pieces in two seconds. It will be all round the office in five minutes that I've been involved in God knows what.'

'You *have* been involved in God knows what and . . . Where exactly are we going? We've just passed a perfectly adequate wine bar.'

'We are going to the Embankment Gardens.'

'I don't want to go to the Embankment Gardens, I want to have some lunch.'

'Well, tough. If you think I'm going to sit in an enclosed space while you're in this mood, you are very much mistaken. We will go to the gardens, we will have a conversation and then I will go back to work. How *dare* you make a scene like that in front of Rebecca of all people, flinging ludicrous accusations about—'

'Are you saying none of it's true? Are you saying my boyfriend is *not* the father of your son?'

'No, I am not saying that. I am saying that he was *not* your boyfriend when he *became* the father of my son and . . . How did you find out, anyway?'

'If you'd just slow down a bit, I'll tell you. And you can let go of my arm now. I expect there'll be a huge bruise tomorrow.'

Katrina let go of Rose's arm.

'Thank you.' Rose straightened the sleeve of her jacket. 'If you must know, Lewis and I spent Saturday night with some friends in Surrey. On Sunday afternoon, we visited his mother in Tadworth and—Katty, will you please *slow down*?—in her sitting room there was a large framed photograph of her grandmother. She wore her hair up and the photo was in profile and she was wearing a high-necked dress like Victorians do or did, or do I mean the Edwardians? Anyway, the point is, I was drawn to it like a moth to—what *is* it

228

that moths are drawn to?'

'Flames.'

'Yes, well, I was drawn to it like a moth to a flame. I mean, it was bizarre. There was this lady from some bygone era, sitting in profile, reading her book, or at least she was pretending to read a book, and she was the spitting image of Ollie! She had his nose with the funny little dip in the middle, his eyebrows, his chin . . . It was like looking at Ollie in drag. I thought it was too funny for words and I pointed out the likeness to Lewis and he could see it right away. And then his mother gave us tea that was *cold* and her digestives had *mould* on them—I swear she's as mad as a fruitcake—and Lewis just stopped talking. I had to make all the conversation, which was not easy let me tell you and Lewis kept staring at the photograph and not speaking at all. And then we drove back onto the A217 and the traffic was dreadful and Lewis was as white as a sheet, and by the time we got past Merton he asked me when Ollie was born and I said it was a few months after your horrible husband left you, and he looked . . . he looked so odd. You can say what you like about me but I have always been very sensitive and I knew something was wrong and I kept insisting he tell me, and finally he confessed he had once had a fling with you and . . . Why didn't you *tell* me, Katty? How could you *abuse* my hospitality like that? You were out in France, at my invitation and—'

'I went out to France because you told me your children would be frolicking with their partners and you wanted some company. So I get on the ferry and you text me to tell me you are madly in

229

love and frolicking yourself! What am I supposed to do? Should I arrive at your house and tell you the new love of your life is an ex-lover of mine who happens to be the father of my son? Would *you* do that?'

'Yes,' said Rose.

Katrina sighed. 'Yes,' she agreed. 'You probably would.'

'And another thing,' Rose said, 'why didn't you tell me ages ago? I'm not exactly a prude, I would have understood. If I'd been married to Paul, who is a complete bastard, I'd have been as unfaithful as I could be.'

'I was *not* unfaithful to Paul. I met Lewis two weeks after Paul left me. And then Lewis left me a few weeks after that. In fact, he left me the day after I found I was pregnant. I didn't tell *you* about it for the same reason I didn't tell any of my friends. I had been a fool, I had been humiliated and I didn't feel like broadcasting my humiliation.'

'So you let poor Paul believe he was the father?'

'How come he's suddenly "poor Paul"? I thought you said he was a complete bastard?'

'Even bastards,' Rose said piously, 'deserve to be told the truth.'

'I *did* tell him the truth. He came round one night to collect some stuff and found me in a bit of a state. I told him what happened. He was very kind. He said he'd take responsibility—'

'Excuse me,' said Rose, 'but when has your ex-husband ever taken responsibility for anything? Did he ever contribute a penny to your household after he left you?'

'You know he didn't, but it was still kind of him

to pretend to be Ollie's father. Sometimes I think he's forgotten he *isn't* Ollie's father.'

'Well, that doesn't surprise me. Most of the time Paul seems to forget he's anyone's father. Have you told him about all of this?'

'No. I was going to. I even got as far as ringing him but . . . he's going through a difficult time right now.'

'Paul is the sort of man who spends his life going through difficult times. Oh, thank heavens, we're here and there's a bench by that tree. I have to sit down, Katty, my shoes are killing me, they are not designed for marathons.'

Katrina glanced at her watch. 'Ten minutes,' she said, 'and then I *have* to get back to work.'

Rose fell onto the bench, kicked off her shoes and began rubbing her feet. 'I shall have a hot bath as soon as I get home,' she said. 'Come and sit down!' She waited until her sister joined her and then looked at her enquiringly. 'Were you in love with him?'

'Who?'

'Lewis, of course. Were you in love with him?'

'Yes, I suppose I was.'

'Do you want to talk about it?'

'Not really.'

'Why didn't you tell him you were pregnant?'

'I was going to. I'd made a special supper. Then he told me it was over and it didn't seem . . . appropriate.'

'He's stunned, Katty. You can imagine it; one moment he has no children and the next he finds he's the father of his girlfriend's handsome teenage nephew. You can see why he's stunned.'

'Yes,' said Katrina, 'I can see that.'

231

'He's going to ring you. And he wants to see Ollie.'

'He can't. Not yet. Tell him he can't.'

'Katty, he's his *father*. You're going to have to let him see his son.'

'Not yet. I'll have to speak to Paul first and I'll have to speak to Ollie. Tell him he'll have to wait a bit.'

'All right. I still can't believe you never said anything. You are such a secretive person. Is there anything else I ought to know? Is Susie a love child too? Have you had affairs with anyone else I know?'

'No, of course I haven't and you know very well Susie is Paul's daughter. For goodness' sake—'

'Don't you for goodness' sake me. How do *I* know? You never tell me anything. For all I know, you might be running a brothel down in Greenwich!' Rose burst out laughing. 'If you could see your face!' She stretched her arms above her head. 'It's rather lovely here, isn't it? I love this time of year when all the leaves are the colour of toast—nice toast, if you know what I mean, not burnt toast.' She relaxed her arms and put a hand on Katrina's knee. 'I'll tell you something that will make you feel better.'

Katrina blinked. 'What's that?'

'I've forgiven Lewis for everything.' She gave her sister a benevolent smile. 'And I forgive you too.'

'Thank you,' Katrina said. 'That *does* make me feel better.'

*   *   *

Katrina set a fast and furious pace back to the

232

office. It was only after she had bumped into two people—the first, a charming lady with flyaway hair who accepted Katrina's apology with a generous insistence on sharing the blame for the collision, and the second, an unpleasant man in a grey suit who advised her to get her eyes tested—that she took a hold of herself.

When she arrived at her destination, she went straight upstairs without even a cursory nod at Rebecca. She was going to concentrate on her work, she was going to complete all the tasks she had set herself and she was not going to think about Lewis or Rose or Ollie until she went home.

That afternoon, she wrote a glowing testimonial to Carol that was far more positive than she had meant it to be, owing to the fact that she was only too aware that in her present mood she must resist all attempts to see the worst in anyone. She attended the meeting with her commercial department and, despite her earlier intention to mount a spirited defence of the team's work in the last few months, agreed without demur that higher targets and longer hours were called for. In accordance with this conclusion she spent a couple of hours going through the documents pertaining to one of her new jobs.

Her reward, when she finally walked out onto the street at a quarter past seven, was a crushing headache which was not helped by a noisy argument between two teenagers sitting opposite her on the train going back to Greenwich.

For once she was glad the house was empty when she got home. Susie was doing a late shift at the hotel and, judging by the empty pizza carton on the table, Ollie had eaten and gone out. Katrina

233

drank a glass of water with some paracetamol and took herself to bed. She would have to ring Paul, she would have to talk to Lewis and at some point she would have to talk to Ollie. But not yet. Not yet. She needed advice, she needed to talk to someone, she needed . . . and it suddenly became quite clear . . . she needed to talk to Cornelius.

She rang him before she could have second thoughts. 'Cornelius,' she said. 'I'm sorry to bother you. Are you watching television?'

'No,' Cornelius said, 'and you're not bothering me at all.'

'You're not eating your dinner?'

'No, I was practising my guitar. I am very pleased to be interrupted.'

'Thank you.' Katrina took a deep breath. 'I want to ask your advice about something. I've had some news which might—which *will* be upsetting to members of my family. If I . . . if I sit on it for a while I might be able to think of a way of . . . of making it sound more palatable, but the danger is that then someone else might break the news. You must think this all sounds very mysterious and I'm sorry I can't tell you anything more at the moment . . .'

'You don't need to,' Cornelius said. 'I think the answer is quite clear. If this news is going to come out in the end, you might as well be the one to announce it and you should do it as soon as possible. If you don't, you'll only get more and more upset about the prospect.'

Katrina gave a little sigh and twisted a lock of her hair round her index finger. 'Thank you,' she said at last.

'I hope I've been able to help.'

'You have. I knew you would. Goodnight, Cornelius.'

* * *

As she walked into Parters, Sorenson and Company, Katrina was careful to establish eye contact with Rebecca and give her a serenely smiling, 'Good morning, Rebecca.' In the lift, she initiated a chatty conversation on the likelihood of rain with Amanda from conveyancing and Daniel from litigation. When Carol came to see her at half past nine with a sympathetic, 'How *are* you, Katrina?' she responded with a cheerful response and a pile of papers that would keep the woman from having time to make any more concerned enquiries.

Katrina worked hard throughout the day, responding to anyone who approached her with a steely smile and a significant glance at her watch. She left the office at seven and rang Susie to tell her she would be late home.

'I'll make supper,' Susie said. 'I'll do some pasta.'

'You're wonderful,' Katrina said. 'Is Ollie in tonight?'

'Yes. Why?'

'No reason,' Katrina said. 'I'll see you later.' Perhaps Susie would go out later. Perhaps she would have a chance to talk to Ollie, to pave the way. How *would* she pave the way for the revelation that she, his mother, had lied about his parentage from day one? How would she tell him—and later, Susie—that she had slept with a man who was not their father and that in fact 'their' father was only *Susie's* father? She was their

235

mother, she was the one person in their world they should be able to trust unreservedly.

On the train, possible explanations and justifications rattled round her brain. She picked up an *Evening Standard* lying on the seat opposite her. There was a picture of a well-known footballer and his wife. Above it was the caption, *My Husband's a Liar!*

Katrina put down the paper.

*   *   *

At home, the reason for Susie's readiness to cook was soon apparent. Over the tagliatelle and mushrooms, she announced to her mother and brother that she needed their help. 'I've been working on my audition,' she said, 'and I realize I have to convey two messages. I mean, I know I should appear to look like a sweet, attractive young dental nurse but at the same time I have to invest, "Please come this way," with an undercurrent of menace and a lack of humanity so that the hero is almost certain, but not totally certain, that I am now an alien. I wish I had time to go and do some research—'

'Into aliens?' enquired Ollie. 'Do you know any?'

'Into dental nurses, stupid! If only I had time I'd go to our dentist and ask if I could observe one.'

'That wouldn't work,' Ollie said. 'Cornelius said you're supposed to be an attractive young woman. Mr Duncan's dental nurse is really old.'

'No, she isn't,' Katrina protested. 'She's in her mid-thirties.'

'She is definitely not attractive,' Ollie said. 'And she's at least forty.'

236

'Anyway,' said Susie, 'I haven't got time to go and see Mr Duncan so it doesn't matter. But I do need to get the line right. I reckon there are three possible ways of doing it and I want you to give your opinion on each of them. This is Number One.' She pushed back her chair, stood up, cleared her throat and fixed Ollie with a seductive smoulder. 'Please,' she flicked her hair back, 'come this . . . way.'

Ollie took his plate over to the stove. 'I think that's probably the worst impersonation of a dental nurse I've ever seen,' he said. 'You look like that girl in the advert who keeps flicking her hair back and jumping in puddles because she's so happy to have her own hairspray.'

'I must say,' Katrina said, 'I wouldn't have thought that a dental nurse who's just been taken over by an alien would come on to a patient in that Mae West sort of way. I mean, would aliens even *know* how to behave like Mae West?'

'Who,' Ollie asked, returning to his seat with a full plate of tagliatelle, 'is Mae West?'

'You must have heard of her,' Katrina said. 'She was the great *femme fatale* of the nineteen thirties. She was the one who greeted a man in a film with the words, "Is that a gun in your pocket or are you just pleased to see me?"' She laughed and was aware that her children were looking at her with a mixture of disapproval and surprise. She realized she had committed the heinous sin of revealing that she had some knowledge of sexual activity.

'Anyway,' said Susie, 'this is Number Two.' She fixed her eyes on the French windows. 'Please— come—this—way.'

237

Ollie gave a decisive shake of the head. 'No,' he said. 'You sound like a robot. It's far too obvious.'

'All right,' said Susie. 'This is Number Three.' This time she favoured Ollie with an enchanting smile and said sweetly, 'Please come this way.'

'Better,' Katrina said. 'But I don't think you should smile. I think you should look straight at the patient and speak very seriously. What do you think, Ollie?'

'Well,' said Ollie, 'there's a James Bond film on ITV4 in a few minutes and I'm pretty sure there's a dental nurse in the plot . . .'

*   *   *

Katrina could, of course, confide in Amy but she knew she would not. They had been friends for years, during which time Katrina had had three unhappy love affairs. There had been Harry, who had slept with her for two months before telling her that he had finally decided he was gay. That had been a real humiliation. Had it been her performance in the bedroom that had driven him into the arms of her successor, a muscular bouncer from Nottingham? There had been Thomas, whose possessiveness had been initially flattering and had become gradually constricting. Then, three years ago, she had met William, who had started seeing her after his wife kicked him out and who stopped seeing her after his wife invited him back home again.

Katrina had told Amy about none of these relationships for the same reason that she would not talk about her current crisis concerning Ollie. Katrina had a reputation at work—at least, she thought bitterly, she *had* a reputation until Rose's appalling outburst—for being competent and calm; a woman who managed her life as successfully as she managed her career. Since Katrina believed that her personal life, apart from her children, comprised a series of spectacularly wrong decisions, it was important to her that in the office she could count on the respect of her peers. Cornelius was an exception in that he had witnessed her in meltdown, and she assumed that that was why she had contemplated seeking his advice. Amy was different. Katrina had no wish to reveal the extent of the mess she had brought upon herself.

Consequently, at lunch on Wednesday, when Amy told her with a quizzical eye that rumours were flying round the office, she merely laughed and said, 'I knew they would be. Rebecca's eyes were practically gleaming on Monday. My sister discovered I'd once had a brief fling with Lewis and started acting like I was still having an affair with him. She made all sorts of outrageous accusations and I had to virtually force her to leave the office so I could have a quiet talk to her in the park. She couldn't have picked a worse day either, I had so much work.'

'Has she calmed down now? How did she find out?'

'From Lewis. I should have told her before but it's the sort of thing that gets more difficult to reveal the longer you leave it. How does one drop something like that into the conversation? *Hi, Rose, how are you and Lewis, and by the way, I don't think I ever mentioned he was once a boyfriend of mine* . . . The whole thing is so annoying, I don't even like to talk about it.'

'Well, in that case,' Amy said briskly, 'let's change the subject. Eddy has come up with a brilliant idea for our cabaret piece at the bonding weekend—'

'*Our* cabaret piece? Are we doing it together?'

'Yes, we are! I was ranting to Eddy about the impossible targets our chief executive is setting us and the fact that he expects us all to be perfect legal specimens *and* find the time to rehearse cabaret turns at the same time, and Eddy ran out of the room and came back with his book of favourite film dialogues. You and I are going to perform the final scene from *Some Like It Hot*—you know, the one where Jack Lemmon in drag tries to tell his millionaire admirer that he cannot marry him, and finally whips off his wig and tells him he's a man, and the millionaire shrugs that nobody's perfect.'

'Brilliant!' said Katrina. 'And you can introduce it by delivering a little lecture about the dangers of chasing impossible targets!'

'I thought you could do that. Why don't we drive up together? I'll collect you and we can practise on the journey.'

'Great,' said Katrina, 'but let *me* collect *you*. I enjoy driving.' Katrina had been a passenger in Amy's car before. Amy had never once stirred from the slow lane. It was no surprise that she didn't like Eddy's motorbike.

*   *   *

At home that evening, Susie was out, doing an extra shift to make up for her absence the following afternoon. Having ascertained that Ollie

240

was staying in, Katrina decided that tonight she would try to broach the subject of Lewis.

She surprised Ollie by opening a bottle of wine. 'It's been a hard day at work,' she said, 'I need a reward.' She told him to pour two glasses while she served up the cauliflower cheese. Over dinner, Ollie chatted about the tedium of his job, Katrina told him about Amy's suggestion for their cabaret piece, and all the time she felt her heart beating faster and faster. Finally, she sat back and said—as if she had just thought about it, as if she had not rehearsed every word in her mind on the journey home, 'Ollie, it's so interesting, watching you and Susie growing up. It makes me remember my own youth and all the mistakes I made . . .'

'Actually, Mum,' Ollie said earnestly, pushing away his plate and leaning forward, 'I want to talk to you about that.'

Katrina blinked. 'You want to talk to me about my youth?'

'Yes. When you were young, did you ever go out with a boy who'd been like . . . like, you know, like a *friend*?'

Katrina sighed and realized they were talking about Sophie. 'I did,' she said, 'when I was seventeen. He was a good friend too, but I think I always secretly fancied him. We were dancing at a youth club party one evening and a smoochy number came on and suddenly it was all very romantic. He was called Paul.'

'Paul?' Ollie sounded disappointed. 'It was Dad?'

He's not your dad, actually. Actually, Ollie, your dad is . . . 'No, it was another Paul. We went out for two weeks and then he said he didn't want to risk losing our friendship by being romantically

241

involved. It turned out he'd got this crush on his sister's French penfriend.'

'Did you stay friends with him?'

'No, I don't think I ever said more than two words to him after that.'

The phone rang and they both jumped. 'I'll get it,' Ollie said.

Katrina poured herself another glass of wine and heard her son say, 'Really? Great! Great! Thanks, George, I'll be there in five minutes.' He put down the phone and smiled at Katrina. 'I've got to go, Mum. George has sighted Sophie in the Rat and Fiddle. I'll see you later!'

Katrina heard the front door slam and felt her heartbeat return to normal. She wasn't sure whether she was glad or sorry that Ollie had been called away. She smiled grimly. She was glad because she was a coward. She was glad even though she knew that until she sorted this whole mess out she would not get a decent night's sleep.

The phone rang again and Katrina picked up the handset. She heard a voice say, 'Hello, Katrina,' and felt her heart start up its crazy dance again.

'Hello, Lewis,' she said.

CHAPTER EIGHTEEN

Re-enter Lewis

From: *Katrinalatham@parter.co.uk*
To: *Cornhedge@winemart.co.uk*
Sent: 19 October 21:15

Dear Cornelius,
I am very sorry but something has come up and I won't be able to give you lunch on Sunday. I have to go out. I am consequently in the doghouse with my children who are not only annoyed that their mother will not be cooking the only good meal of the week but are also sad to be missing you. I suspect Ollie wanted to bore you with yet more location possibilities for his big adventure and Susie wanted to tell you about her audition. She's pretty sure she didn't get the part, she says there was a girl there who was a combination of Gwyneth Paltrow, Julia Roberts and Katie Holmes, none of whom I suspect you have heard of. The audition was held in some fusty old building in Soho and Susie loved every minute of it. She said there were about ten other girls, including the super-beautiful one, and when it was her turn she had to perform in front of a panel of the casting director and two young men who kept looking at their phones. She was given a white coat to wear and she had to say her line five times, each occasion in a different way. This was easy for Susie who has been regaling Ollie and me

all week with well over a thousand different permutations of 'Please come this way.' I am sure that if anyone ever says those words to me, I will have an immediate Pavlovian response and run screaming in the opposite direction. Susie was told she would hear next week and I'll let you know what happens. Sorry again about Sunday.
  Love, K

From: *Cornhedge@winemart.co.uk*
To: *Katrinalatham@parter.co.uk*
Sent: 20 October 9:06

Dear Katrina,
I am sorry I won't be seeing you on Sunday but I confess to a slight feeling of relief since I felt that your son had press-ganged you into inviting me. Do tell Ollie I am happy to give him advice without the lure of an invitation to Sunday lunch. He can ring me at any time. I am glad Susie enjoyed her audition and I shall keep my fingers crossed for her. I have heard of Julia Roberts and Gwyneth Paltrow but not Katie Holmes. Should I have done?
  Yours,
  Cornelius

*   *   *

Katrina woke at five on Saturday morning and tried, without success, to return to unconsciousness. Eventually, she gave up trying and reached for her book. She was reading *Atonement* by Ian McEwan and she had been enjoying it. Now, however, after frowning through a couple of chapters, she returned it to her bedside table. Perhaps this was not the best time to read a novel about the destructive ramifications of one person's lie. Damn Lewis, she thought, damn Rose, damn everyone.

After she got up, she put on an old Pulp CD— Jarvis Cocker's 'Common People' had to be the best record of all time—and got to work, cleaning every area of the kitchen. She only stopped when Susie came in, yawning repeatedly and complaining that she *really* didn't feel like working today. Over breakfast they—or rather Susie—went over the different ways in which she might have said her precious line of dialogue, and whether the smile that passed between members of the panel when she gave Interpretation Number Three was a good or a bad sign.

After Susie had gone, Katrina went out into the garden with her secateurs and ruthlessly pruned the tall, gangling buddleia in the back flowerbed. When she'd finished, it resembled a Bruce Willis haircut. The buddleia seemed to stare at her with gentle reproach. It had needed cutting back, she told herself; it was ridiculous to allow an untidy shrub to make her feel like an evil Delilah to its sad Samson. Nevertheless, she had lost the urge to attack anything else and she returned to the house.

She was beginning to feel seriously exasperated with herself. Her weekends were so precious and normally she loved being able to potter about her domestic domain. She never, ever, felt bored or listless. Yet, now, she stood in the middle of her kitchen, unable to summon much enthusiasm for anything and unsure what to do. She wished she could be like Ollie, who possessed an enviable ability to sleep until midday.

This was unbearable! Cornelius was right. She had to speak out as soon as possible. She would go and buy a nice lunch for the two of them and then she would come home, wake Ollie and sit by his bed and tell him the circumstances of his birth in a calm and matter-of-fact manner. She grabbed her handbag, ran up to the front door and walked briskly towards the delicatessen.

She splashed out on half a dozen slices of prosciutto and a large piece of ricotta cheese and returned home, practising her forthcoming exposition. 'Ollie,' she would say gently, 'wake up, I have something to tell you.' That wouldn't work, Ollie always took at least half an hour to wake up properly. She would make him a cup of tea, leave him to reach full consciousness and then return. She would sit down beside him, take his hand and everything would be all right.

Except it wasn't. When she got home, she could hear Ollie in the shower upstairs and when he finally came down, he told her he had to rush as he was taking Sophie out to London Zoo for the day as part of his being-a-good-friend-who-will-become-more campaign. It was obvious that now was not the time to deliver traumatic news.

At lunch, Katrina ate her prosciutto and ricotta in solitude, with only Radio 4's *Any Questions* for company. The last question put to the panel was a query about the most valuable quality in today's society. One of the panel chose honesty.

It was at that point that Katrina lost her appetite. She was suddenly aware of another presence in the room and turned to face Omo, who was treating her to one of his unblinking stares. Anything would be better than spending the afternoon with Omo. Katrina cleared away her meal, pocketed her house keys, walked out of the house and set off for the park.

Greenwich Park, in Katrina's biased opinion, was the best of London's parks. Not only did it possess undulating slopes and majestic trees, it also boasted the best view in the capital, and it was to this that Katrina made her way. She walked fast and furious and finally arrived at the top of the hill near the famous Observatory. She sank onto the grass and looked down at the elegant old buildings that flanked the dazzling white Queen's House. Cam's beauty people were right: it would form a perfect backdrop for a fashion shoot. Behind it was the river and beyond that the shimmering skyscrapers of Canary Wharf, on either side of which, like doodles on the skyline, were scattered hundreds of cranes, evidence of London's seemingly unstoppable expansion. The panorama never failed to inspire Katrina and even now it gave her a little spark of optimism, a belief that somehow things would work themselves out.

At the bottom of the hill, a teenage girl and a small boy were throwing a ball to each other, backwards and forwards, backwards and forwards. Every now and then, the boy would stop to make a squawk like a chicken and the girl would put her hands on her hips and wait, with impressive resignation, for him to continue.

Katrina lay back on the grass and let herself go over Lewis's phone call on Wednesday. It had been an unsettling conversation. He had been composed and dignified but very determined. He *had* to see her as soon as possible. He suggested a small Italian restaurant in Denmark Street. He said he was sure she would like it. Was it possible that after all these years he remembered she had once voiced a liking for Italian food? It was far more likely that since he liked it, he assumed she would too. She had been on the point of asking if Rose was coming when he told her that Rose had decided not to join them since she felt it was a private matter between the two of them. 'Also,' Lewis admitted, 'she has a better offer. An old friend has invited her to lunch at the Ivy and Rose would miss her grandma's funeral for an offer to eat out at the Ivy.' Katrina nobly refrained from informing him that Rose had indeed missed her grandma's funeral two years ago, in order to go to a friend's party in Paris.

Katrina had not wanted to go out on a Sunday—it was the only day she could be sure of seeing both her children, and she didn't like letting Cornelius down—but Lewis had been insistent. He was rehearsing all week and he had promised to attend some function with Rose on Saturday. There was another reason why Katrina was less than happy about waiting till Sunday to see him. She knew that until she met Lewis, every waking moment would be spent obsessing about what he was going to say to her and what she was going to say to him.

Cornelius was right. Life was far simpler if one always told the truth. She wished Cornelius were here now. If he were to appear on the brow of the hill, she would beckon him over and she would tell him everything about Lewis and Ollie, and he would say something sensible in his dry, succinct manner and somehow she would feel better. On the other hand, of course, he might look at her with distaste and ask her how she could have saddled Ollie with an incompetent fake father when he could have known his real one, who was clearly over the moon about his newly discovered son. At the moment, she could think of no rational justification or even explanation for her conduct. And if *she* couldn't, how the hell would Ollie or Lewis?

Later, back at home, prompted by her conscience, which had elbowed everything else out of the way and settled centre-stage in her brain, she rang Paul. Within a few minutes, she wished she hadn't. Paul was in the throes of self-pity. He'd lost half a stone, he told Katrina; he had a strong suspicion that he was clinically depressed and he'd had a terrible stomach ache for at least twenty-four hours. When Katrina told him, hesitantly, about Lewis, he exploded. What right did a man like that have to swan into Katrina's life and demand his paternal rights when it had been Paul who had shouldered those responsibilities for the last sixteen years and it had been Paul who had cherished the boy as if he were his own? Katrina felt it prudent not to remind him that Ollie was, in fact, eighteen, nor did she suggest that 'cherishing' was perhaps an odd word to apply to occasional phone calls and even more occasional visits. Instead, she assured him that Ollie's view of Paul would not be affected by the arrival of Lewis. (She was pretty sure *this* was true.) Mollified, Paul proceeded to promulgate his latest theory about his life, which was that he and Katrina would have been far happier if he had never left home. Katrina, who didn't think anything of the sort, resorted to clichés and made soothing noises about water under bridges. Paul suggested he came up and spent the evening with her, at which point she forgot her recent decision to tell the truth at all times and invented a pressing engagement. Which was true in a way, she thought afterwards, because she did have a pressing engagement with *Gigi* on TCM.

*   *   *

She woke late the next morning and lay back against her pillows, enjoying the pale sun easing its way between the leaves of the horse chestnut tree in the next-door garden. She glanced at her radio clock. Three hours to go. She got out of bed, put on her dressing gown and went downstairs, stooping to collect the Sunday paper from the door mat.

In the kitchen there was a smell of stale beer and tobacco but the place was tidy. She opened the bin, fished out a collection of beer cans and two bottles of what had been extremely cheap white wine and transferred them to the recycling bin.

She made some coffee and, yawning, wondered who the children had been entertaining late last night. Had Ollie spent the evening as well as the day with Sophie? Had he succeeded in providing her with a shoulder to cry on? And what about Susie? 'I am not going to worry about Susie,' she thought. 'Not today.' She took the paper and her mug of coffee to the table and was soon absorbed in an extremely interesting article. The writer suggested that all prime ministers who stayed in office for more than five years went mad. It cited

Margaret Thatcher and Tony Blair as evidence and made a pretty persuasive case.

At last, having checked that she still had two hours before she had to leave, Katrina went upstairs. She emerged from the bathroom forty-five minutes later with the feeling that she had taken her hair, skin and teeth to the dry-cleaner's. As she went to her wardrobe, she pulled out the item which had made her conscience act like a diva deprived of her orchestra. On Friday lunchtime, despite an appalling workload, she had gone shopping. The result was a pinkish-grey dress of deceptive simplicity that fitted her like a glove and gave her hips that even Kate Moss (all right, not Kate Moss, but certainly Meryl Streep) would be envious of.

Katrina justified the expense by telling herself that she needed to be confident while confronting Lewis. Her conscience remained unimpressed by this excuse and continued to throw a tantrum.

At twenty to twelve, she studied herself in the mirror and went downstairs for a final coffee. Susie was sitting at the table and did not look up from her perusal of the film reviews. 'Did you have a good time yesterday evening?' Katrina asked.

'Great, thanks.'

'I thought I heard you with some friends last night,' Katrina continued carelessly. 'Was there anyone I know?'

'Just friends.' Perhaps Susie was aware of her mother's disappointment with this limited response because she glanced up and immediately whistled. 'Mum, you look wonderful! That's a new dress, isn't it?'

'This?' Katrina said, looking at the garment as if

she'd only just noticed she was wearing it. 'Yes, it is quite.'

'Well, it's fabulous! *Who* did you say you were having lunch with?'

'Just an old friend,' Katrina said, feeling her face blush and wishing she could be as cool as her daughter. She threw her coffee down the sink and said quickly, 'I must go or I'll be late. Help yourselves to anything in the fridge for lunch. I know you'll find some prosciutto and some cheese and if you want to cook something . . .'

'Mum, we'll be fine,' said Susie. 'Have a good time.'

Was Susie being sarcastic? Of course she wasn't. Katrina let herself out of the front door and told herself to stop feeling paranoid.

*　　　*　　　*

She arrived at the restaurant far too early and took herself off for a walk round Soho. When she returned, she was relieved to find that Lewis was waiting for her and had already acquired wine and olives. He didn't see her so she was able to appreciate how good-looking he was in his dark grey jacket and black T-shirt. He had to be the only man over forty who could still look good in a T-shirt.

She walked over to their table and Lewis looked up and fixed her with his blue eyes. 'Wow,' he said, 'you look amazing.'

'Really?' Katrina raised her eyebrows. 'I must say—'

'Just for once,' Lewis said, 'allow me to pay you a compliment without throwing it back in my face.'

He poured her a glass of wine. 'I think we should make a toast,' he said. 'To our son.'

Katrina paused and raised her glass. 'To Ollie,' she said. She wished he would stop looking at her. He was making it extremely hard for her to remember all those carefully crafted sentences she had composed on the train.

'Do you know something?' Lewis said. 'I wish I could have a word with my thirty-something self. If I could, I would warn him that he would be crazy to leave you. I'd tell him that he'd be throwing away a chance of lasting happiness.'

Katrina gave an involuntary laugh. 'That wouldn't work,' she said, 'because *I'd* be telling my twenty-five-year-old self that she should take one look at you and turn on her heels.'

'I would hope,' Lewis said, 'that my thirty-something self might be able to prove that he did possess some redeeming features.'

Katrina wrenched her eyes from his with difficulty and drank a supportive gulp of wine. 'That would be difficult,' she said. 'As soon as you realized I had a child you couldn't get out of my house fast enough. I should have remembered that.'

'I came back, though.'

'Yes, after you'd made up a story that anyone else would have seen through at once. In fact, the only reason I didn't see through it was because I'd mixed you up with Dr Rubin, and I knew Dr Rubin would *never* have behaved so . . . so *caddishly*. I still can't believe I swallowed it, though . . . *I'm afraid I can't be seen in public with any women other than my co-star* . . . I have to say it's a brilliant way of getting a woman to cook for you all the time.'

253

'I was a bastard,' Lewis said. 'But you should still have told me you were pregnant.'

Katrina raised her chin. 'I *was* going to tell you. You probably don't remember the last dinner I cooked for you. I spent a fortune on it. I was about to tell you I was pregnant when you told me you didn't want to see me any more. Somehow, it didn't seem a good idea to say anything after that.'

'Were you *ever* going to tell me?'

'As a matter of fact, I was. Within minutes of Ollie's birth, I decided that you had a right to know. He was such a beautiful baby! Then Paul came to visit me, he brought grapes and a paper. After he'd gone I picked up the paper and saw a photo of you and Sister Green holding hands at the wedding of your co-star. It was only then that I realized your whole stupid story about keeping your private life secret was just that: stupid. Whatever happened to Sister Green, by the way?'

'I married her.'

'How nice for you.'

'Not very. She left me five years later.'

'I'm sorry.'

'You needn't be. I wasn't a very good husband.' He smiled. 'Shall we study the menu?'

Katrina, in her present state, was quite unable to choose anything. In the end, she said she'd have what Lewis had.

As soon as the waiter had left with their order, Lewis leant forward. 'What kills me,' he said, 'is that all these years I've had a son growing up just a few miles away from my home. I've missed *so much*! You should have told me.'

Katrina took a hefty slug of wine. 'Lewis,' she said, 'tell me honestly: if I'd told you at the end of

254

that dinner I cooked for us, after you told me that your career left you no time to take on any responsibilities, if I'd told you I had just discovered I was pregnant by you, would you *truly* have said you were thrilled by the news?'

Lewis opened his mouth and shut it again and shook his head. 'Truly,' he agreed, 'I wouldn't. But it doesn't alter the fact that I'm finding it very difficult to accept that you kept my son's existence secret from me.'

There was a large lump in Katrina's throat which she removed with a further swig of wine. 'In our very brief relationship,' she said, 'if you can describe what we had as a relationship, you made it painfully clear that anything to do with children terrified you. It was therefore pretty obvious that if you knew you were a father you would be devastated. Once Paul knew I didn't want any money from him, he was happy to take responsibility for Ollie's paternity. Nevertheless, every time I saw you on television, I agonized about my decision not to tell you. I have *never* felt comfortable about the decision I took. So you may have spent the last eighteen years not knowing your son existed but I have spent the last eighteen years worrying about what I had done and what I should do. When I was on that boat to France and Rose texted me that you were going to be there, I felt like . . .' She stopped and shook her head.

'Tell me. You felt what?'

'I felt as if Nemesis had finally tracked me down. I didn't know what to do. I was in a terrible state.'

'You met Cornelius on the boat, didn't you?'

'Yes. He was wonderful.'

Lewis refilled her glass. 'How *is* Cornelius?'

'He's very well.' She sniffed. 'So don't lecture me about keeping silent all these years, because everything you said and did indicated that you were the last person in the world to want to be the father of my baby, and I've had to live with the consequences for a hell of a lot longer than you have.' Her eyes were brimming with tears and she took another slug of wine. Thank God she hadn't driven here.

'Katrina,' Lewis said, 'please don't cry.' He leant forward and kissed her very gently on the mouth.

'For God's sake!' Katrina exploded. 'What was that for?'

Lewis gave an apologetic smile. 'I can't bear to see women cry. I wanted you to stop crying.'

'You succeeded. Don't do it again.'

Perhaps it was just as well that the waiter arrived at that moment with their first course: bruschetta and artichokes, liberally sprinkled with Parmesan and mint and oozing olive oil. Lewis ordered a bottle of Chianti and Katrina concentrated on the plate in front of her.

'Katrina,' Lewis said, 'I can't say I'm not sad about missing Ollie's childhood but I am absolutely not trying to suggest you were wrong in any way to keep his existence from me. In any case, I'm not interested in recriminations. I am anxious to see my son, that's all.'

'You've seen him already,' Katrina said, wilfully misunderstanding him.

'I have. I keep thinking back to Rose's party. I remember telling her what a good-looking nephew she had. Don't you find it *extraordinary* that we should all meet up like this?'

'Yes,' said Katrina.

'No, you don't. Why don't you?'

'I always had the feeling that you'd turn up again one of these days.'

'Did you?' Lewis asked softly.

'Yes. And I don't mean it like you think I do.'

'You have no idea what I'm thinking.'

'Yes, I do. I can see exactly what you're thinking. You imagine me spending my life wistfully clinging to the hope that one day I'd see your bronzed and muscular body once more.'

'Do you really think I have a bronzed and muscular body?'

'Shut up, Lewis. For your information, what I *meant* was that I always felt that one day you'd turn up and find out the truth. That's *all* I meant, so stop looking as if you know you're irresistible, because you're jolly well not.'

'I can understand your anger,' Lewis said. 'I hate to think I caused you so much pain. I hate to think I ruined your life.'

'You didn't ruin my life. You were one of the best things that ever happened to me.'

'Really?' Lewis murmured.

'Of course. I can't imagine my life without Ollie.'

'That's very generous of you.' Lewis leant forward, 'Look here—'

'Tell me,' Katrina said, 'what are you working on at the moment?'

'Katrina . . .' Lewis paused, gave a light shrug and began to talk about the director who had already asked every female member of the cast to sleep with him, and about his own success in extending his part to a second episode. It was only after they finished the lamb and were enjoying what remained of the wine that Lewis returned to his major preoccupation.

'Look,' he said, 'I know this is difficult for you but I want to see Ollie. I want to see him soon. I want to see him this week.'

Katrina bit her lip. 'You have to let me tell him about it all first. It's difficult. How do I tell him that the man he's called Dad all his life is not his dad, and that his aunt's boyfriend *is*?'

'You just *tell* him,' Lewis said. 'If you can't do it, I'll be happy to do so.'

'No! I'll do it, I'll do it soon.'

'I don't want to put pressure on you but—'

'Yes, you do!'

'Yes, I do. I'm going mad here. I can't sleep, I can't think, I can't concentrate on anything until I've seen him. Ollie is my son. *I have a son!* Let me come round one evening this week . . .'

'No!' Katrina exclaimed. 'Don't do that. I'll tell him. I'll tell him tomorrow and I'll get him to ring you.'

Lewis reached into his jacket pocket and pulled out a notebook. He tore out a piece of paper, scribbled a number and passed it to Katrina. 'That's my mobile number. If I haven't heard from either of you by the end of the week, I'll ring you.'

'But there's no pressure.'

Lewis grinned. 'None at all.'

Katrina gave a reluctant smile. She had been determined to go on the offensive, to be in charge, to insist she would do things in her own time. It was impossible to resist his charm. It might have been easier if she hadn't drunk so much of the very good Chianti.

'I wish,' Lewis said, 'you hadn't aged so well.'

Katrina frowned. 'I *beg* your pardon?'

258

'I look at you,' Lewis said. 'I want to have a rational conversation about Ollie and how I go about creating a relationship with him, and there you sit, looking like a Christmas present that is just waiting to be unwrapped and . . . it's confusing.'

Katrina opened her mouth and shut it again. At that moment she knew she would like nothing more on earth than to be unwrapped by Lewis. She swallowed and took another sip of her Chianti. 'Tell me,' she said, 'how is Rose?'

CHAPTER NINETEEN

Reverberations

Charm, Katrina thought as she sat in the train watching a grossly fat schoolboy in the seat opposite her exploring his right nostril with his index finger, was an elusive quality. People who had charm—people like Lewis—were past masters at making those around them feel special; they had excellent eye-contact skills, were amusing, and were often self-deprecating in the way that only those with true confidence can be.

What she should remember—she wished the boy would stop doing that, he was now attacking his left nostril, and oh, yuck, he had struck gold, or rather green, and was brandishing it in front of him—what she should remember was that charm was not a characteristic that often survived close acquaintance. After all, Cary Grant was probably the most charming man of the twentieth century and he had had nearly as many wives as Henry

VIII. And then there was Serge Gainsbourg, who was possibly the second most charming man of the twentieth century but who proved so difficult to live with that even Jane Birkin, who adored him, had felt compelled to leave him.

There was no question that charm was an overrated quality. It was true that Lewis knew better than anyone just what to do to make a woman feel desirable; it was true that he himself remained outstandingly desirable. It was also true that as the boyfriend of Katrina's sister, he should not have flirted so outrageously with Katrina, particularly since he was trying to persuade her that he was unable to think about anyone else except his newly discovered son.

Nevertheless, she thought, as she stepped from the train, she must talk to Ollie as soon as possible. She was quite convinced that the dull headache currently afflicting her was caused by her anxiety about this. It certainly had nothing to do with the fact that she had drunk a little too much at lunch yesterday.

At one, Katrina was studying her computer screen, chewing thoughtfully on a mozzarella baguette, when Susie rang to say she would not be back for supper. Katrina told her to have a good time and rang off, her heart beating fast. The coast was clear, tonight should be the night. But how could she ensure that Ollie would not go out? How could she keep him at home with her? Illumination dawned and she rang Ollie at once. 'Hi,' she said, 'I thought we might have a takeaway this evening.'

*   *   *

Ollie sat with a glass of beer in front of him. Katrina had an equally large glass of water. Her tension headache had disappeared in the early afternoon despite the fact that the tension hadn't. Between them there was a plethora of cartons containing onion bhaji, chicken tikka, vegetable kurma, prawn rogan josh, mushroom biryani and spicy poppadoms.

Katrina waited until they were well into the meal before finally clearing her throat. 'Ollie,' she said, 'I want to talk to you. I want to talk to you about Lewis.'

'Lewis?' Ollie said. 'Rose's boyfriend, Lewis?'

'Yes,' said Katrina. 'I don't think I've told you this but I met him many years ago, long before Rose did. In fact, I met him . . . nine months before you were born.'

'Did you?' Ollie took a poppadom and dipped it into his vegetable kurma. 'That is weird. Mind you, it's not as weird as Hannah's parents. They were at nursery school together and Hannah's dad can remember hating Hannah's mum, and then they met again twenty years later and Hannah's dad thought she was wonderful and couldn't believe it when—'

'Yes, that's very weird,' Katrina said. 'It's funny how these things happen. I can remember exactly the day I met Lewis. Paul had just left me. I was organizing the purchase of a building by a TV company and while I was being shown round the place, I met Lewis. He was busy rehearsing. In those days, he was quite famous. He was a star of a soap opera called *Medical Alert* and everyone watched it. I mean, it was as popular as *EastEnders*

261

or *Coronation Street* is now. Anyway, I met him and we . . . we started seeing each other.'

'Did you?' Ollie actually took his eyes off his food. 'So Lewis is your ex-boyfriend?'

'Yes,' said Katrina, 'I suppose he is.'

'That really is weird! Why didn't you tell me before? When you went to France did you recognize each other? What did you say to Rose? Did she mind?'

'I didn't tell her. I found it all a little embarrassing.'

'Poor you. No wonder you didn't like your holiday. Can you pass the chicken tikka?'

Katrina passed the chicken tikka. 'Yes,' she continued doggedly, 'it wasn't an easy time. You see, in the days when I was . . . seeing Lewis, I was very, very smitten by him and then . . . *nine months later* . . . you were born.'

'Cool,' said Ollie. 'Were you and Lewis still seeing each other then?'

'No, we only went out for a few weeks. Lewis felt he couldn't sustain both a career and a relationship, so he decided to end our relationship.'

'Poor old Mum. So are you going to tell Rose?'

'Am I going to tell Rose what?'

'That you used to see Lewis.'

'I *have* told Rose. I've told her something else too.'

Ollie nodded encouragingly.

'The thing is . . . as I've just said . . . I was with Lewis for just a few weeks and then . . . *nine months later* . . . you were born.'

Ollie nodded. 'Do you want that last poppadom?'

'No, no, I don't.' Katrina tried to remember what

she was about to say. 'The thing is, Ollie, what I'm trying to tell you is—'

'Poor old Mum,' Ollie said again. 'You must have been very miserable when I was born.'

'Well, yes . . . no. No, of course I wasn't, you were the most beautiful baby, but that's not the point . . . The thing I'm trying to tell you . . . and it's something I should have told you long ago, and I did *always* mean to tell you at some point . . . The thing I'm trying to tell you,' Katrina took a deep breath, 'the point I'm trying to make, Ollie, is that you are not actually Paul's son.' Katrina braced herself. 'In fact, your real father . . . your biological father . . . is Lewis.'

Ollie put down his poppadom and gawped at her. 'What did you say?'

Katrina looked at her son and saw the dawn of understanding in his eyes. 'You are the result . . . the biological result . . . of my relationship with Lewis. I should have told you before. Ollie, I am so sorry. If you knew how often I have thought about telling you . . . I never told Lewis about you because I didn't think he'd want to know. But he does know now and he is very upset that I didn't tell him.'

'Lewis is my *father*?'

'Yes, he is.'

'I don't understand. Why couldn't you tell me before?'

Katrina's throat felt raspingly dry. She raised her glass to her lips and drank deeply. 'I know this will seem stupid to you, but things were different then. I didn't want people to know that I'd had a short and obviously failed relationship so soon after Paul had left me. Paul was happy to claim you as his son

263

and it seemed the easy thing to do. I felt I'd acted like an idiot, and I know it all sounds ridiculously prim and self-indulgent and—'

'So Dad isn't my dad?'

'Well, no . . .'

'Phew,' said Ollie. 'Well, that's a relief.'

'A relief?' Katrina looked at him for a moment and then burst into near hysterical laughter. 'Of all the reactions I imagined, I have to tell you this one didn't come close!'

'Be honest, Mum, would you want Dad . . . I mean, Paul . . . as a father? Is he still Susie's father?'

'Well, of course he is.'

'Poor old Susie!' Ollie's eyes narrowed in thought. 'Hey! Does this mean I don't have to go to Croydon on Dad's birthday?'

'Of course it doesn't. Paul loves you. He regards you as his son. Of course you must go.'

'Damn.' Ollie went over to the fridge and collected a second beer. 'So when did you tell Rose and Lewis all this? That must have been crazy!'

'It was,' Katrina said with a heartfelt sigh, 'but I didn't actually tell them. They found out. Rose went with Lewis to see his mother and on the wall there was a framed photo of his grandmother or his great-grandmother, I can't remember which. Rose says you are the spitting image of her.'

Ollie frowned. 'I look like his *grandmother*? Yuck!'

'Anyway, then, of course, I had to tell them everything. Lewis is desperate to see you.'

'Is he?' Ollie looked less than excited by the prospect.

'You must see that he is!'

'Yes, but it's going to be really awkward. I hardly know him! I've only met him once and that was at Rose's party. I wouldn't know what to say.'

The phone rang and Katrina pushed back her chair and went to answer it.

'Katrina, it's Lewis. I had to ring . . .'

'I've just told Ollie,' Katrina said.

'Oh, God. Can I speak to him?'

'Hang on.' Katrina went over to Ollie. 'It's your father,' she said.

'Which one?' Ollie hissed.

'Lewis,' Katrina murmured. 'It's Lewis.'

She wondered whether she should go but decided that if Ollie wanted privacy, he could always take the phone somewhere else. She took the cartons of food, along with Ollie's plate, to the stove and put them in the bottom of the Aga to keep them warm, trying not to look as if she was straining to follow her son's conversation.

'Yes,' Ollie said. 'Yes, it is . . . Yes, I am . . . Yes . . . I don't know, really . . . Yes, it's in Fulham . . . Yes, all right . . . Yes . . . Bye, then.' Ollie passed the phone back to Katrina and made straight for the stove.

'Hello, Lewis,' Katrina said.

'Katrina, I love you! You are a wonderful woman. Thank you for giving me your son!'

'Well, I haven't *given* him to you—'

'He's meeting me after he finishes work tomorrow. I'll take him out for an early supper. I'll speak to you soon. Thank you!'

Katrina put the phone back on its base and looked at Ollie. 'I hear you're meeting him for a meal tomorrow. He sounds very happy.'

Ollie—back at the table, tucking into second

helpings—said glumly, 'I hope he doesn't want to hug me.'

*   *   *

In the circumstances, perhaps, the row was inevitable. Susie came back from work the next day in a foul mood. The film people had said they'd let her know by Monday. They had obviously chosen the Katie Holmes/Julia Roberts/Gwyneth Paltrow girl and they hadn't even bothered to ring her. Also, she'd had a miserable day at the hotel, receiving an unfair dressing-down from a guest for the fact that there was a grub embedded in his salad and a further dressing-down from the manager for not noticing said grub in time.

Katrina came back from work in a foul mood because she was on tenterhooks about Ollie's meeting with Lewis. Also, she'd had a miserable day at the office having received an unfair dressing-down from a client who was furious because someone else in Katrina's department had failed to send him absolutely vital documents.

Had Katrina not been so tired and preoccupied, she would have noticed that Susie's conversational tone was unusually clipped and humourless. As it was, she commiserated with her daughter about the appalling bad manners of people who forgot to make phone calls when they had said they'd make phone calls. And then she served up the sausage casserole and tried to suggest in as tactful a way as possible that now might be the time for Susie to reconsider her future. Later, of course, she realized that there was *nothing* tactful about choosing this particular evening to deliver such a lecture.

'The trouble with all these casting people,' she said, 'is that they can choose from literally thousands of people. They can be as rude as they like because they know how powerful they are.'

'Mum, you don't *know* any casting people. How can you possibly know what they think?'

'I've read the statistics. Everyone wants to be famous these days, everyone wants to act. You are a very good actress. You're extremely talented—'

She should have stopped there. Perhaps she would have stopped there if Susie hadn't rolled her eyes and said, 'You so don't believe that! You've never had any faith in me. You have always been waiting for me to fail!'

'Now that is not true. If you'd got into drama school first time around—'

'Oh, right, so I didn't get into drama school so therefore I should give up straight away and get a proper job, a really boring job like you have—'

'My job isn't boring and I just think that you've left university with a good degree and you could be doing any number of things and instead you work in a crummy hotel in the very slim hope that you might get into drama school next year. It seems to me—'

'I know what it seems to you. It seems to you I should give up at the first hurdle and do something, anything as long as it isn't the one thing I feel passionate about! You may be happy to have a boring life but I'm not. Ash says that—'

'Oh, Ash says . . . What on earth does Ash know about anything?'

'A lot more than you do, as it happens. I can't

believe you are so vile about Ash. You haven't seen him for years—'

'If I don't know anything about Ash, it's not my fault. You're so secretive about him. I have no idea whether he's a friend or a boyfriend—'

'I cannot *believe*,' Susie exploded, 'that you are accusing *me* of being secretive. That just makes me want to *laugh*.' Susie let out a sound that was not even an approximation of a laugh. 'Ollie rang me tonight when he was on his way to meet Lewis. Did you *really* think he wouldn't tell me what you told him? He's not like you. He doesn't keep secrets. So don't tell me that I never tell you anything, because you never tell *us* anything and you'd have clung on to your sordid little secret if it hadn't been forced out of you!'

'That's not fair,' Katrina stammered. 'You don't know the facts—'

'No, of course I don't know the facts because you've done your best to make sure we don't know them! Or at least that *I* don't know them! Were you ever going to tell me?'

'Susie, I'm so sorry, I didn't think—'

'Well, that's quite obvious because if you did think you might have realized I had as much right as Ollie to know whether we share the same father or not! I suppose if Rose hadn't started seeing Lewis you'd never have told us anything! You are such a *hypocrite* and if there's one thing I know it's that I don't want to ever be like *you*. I'm going out!'

Katrina did not stir from her seat. She heard Susie run upstairs and a few moments later she heard the front door slam. This isn't fair, she told herself, none of this is fair. She began to cry and made no effort to staunch the tears because there was no one to see her except for bloody Omo, who had stalked into the kitchen and positioned himself in front of the door. Katrina continued to cry because she couldn't help thinking that everything Susie had thrown at her had been more or less true. Her affair with Lewis *had* been sordid, the chances were that she might *never* have told Ollie the truth and at this moment it did indeed seem sensible that Susie should want to avoid living a life even remotely like her mother's.

A good bath with a liberal dose of bath oil, the creators of which promised all sorts of subsequent sensual excitements, helped assuage the damage wrought by Katrina's weeping fit. She went to bed with Susie's latest magazine and was disturbed from an in-depth analysis of celebrity cellulite by a knock at the door.

Katrina said, 'Come in,' and braced herself for whichever of her children came through the door.

'Mum,' Ollie said, 'sorry to bother you . . .'

'Don't be silly, come and talk to me.'

Ollie came and sat down beside her. 'I ate supper *hours* ago and there's some sausage stuff in the fridge. Are you keeping it for tomorrow or . . . ?'

'Go ahead. Finish it up. There's some left-over rice in a blue bowl which you can microwave. But Ollie, tell me, how did it go with Lewis?'

'Oh,' said Ollie, in a tone that suggested he'd already forgotten his momentous meeting, 'it was all right. We went to Pizza Express and I had a margherita with extra salami and—'

'Ollie, I don't care what you ate. Did you get on? What did you talk about? Was it difficult?'

'A little bit at first but he was nice. He didn't try

to hug me or anything.'

Katrina's mouth twitched but she said gravely, 'I'm glad to hear it.'

'He wanted to know if I liked acting and I said it was weird that Susie wasn't his daughter because she was the actress in the family. I think he thought that was pretty weird too.'

Katrina smiled. 'I can see that he might.'

'I liked him. He wants me to meet his mother sometime and I said I would.' Ollie stood up. 'I'd better go. Rob's downstairs. If you're sure we can eat it all, I'll let him have some sausage stuff too.'

'Fine. Is Susie downstairs or is she still out?'

'I haven't seen her. Night, Mum.'

Her son was amazing. She had spent years worrying about this terrible secret and the psychological effect it would have on him. Unless he was concealing great inner turmoil, which would be very unlike Ollie since one of the wonders of Ollie was that he could never conceal anything, he was far less concerned by the discovery of his true father than he had been by the discovery some weeks ago that Katrina had thrown away the denim trousers that had had more holes than material. He genuinely didn't seem to mind that his mother had lied to him. Katrina wished she could say the same about her daughter.

*　　　*　　　*

Susie rang Katrina the following afternoon. 'Mum, can't stop, my tea break is over, but had to tell you. I've got the part! Bet you can't believe it!'

'Oh, Susie,' Katrina breathed, 'I am so pleased! Darling, I am so—'

270

'I know, me too! Gotta go! Bye now!'

*   *   *

Katrina left work early that day. She stopped off at the supermarket when she got back to Greenwich. She bought champagne, salmon fillets, spinach, avocados and a chocolate gateau. Her mobile rang just as she'd struggled home with her bulging bags and put them on the kitchen table.

'Mum? Don't worry about supper for Ollie and me. We're staying in town, we're going to celebrate with friends. See you tomorrow!'

Katrina switched off her phone and tried to swallow the aching disappointment she felt. It was no more than she deserved. She was pretty sure that Ash would be one of the 'friends' and she had made it impossible for Susie to bring him home. And as far as Susie was concerned, her mother had never shown any support for her acting ambitions and was therefore hardly entitled to share in the celebration.

Katrina swallowed again and reached for the notepad. She tore a piece of paper from it and started to write.

Darling Susie,
Hope you had a great evening. If you're not working tomorrow night, can we celebrate here? Please feel free to invite Ash. I am very proud of you.
All love,
Mum

She attached it to the fridge with some Blu-tack. She began to empty the supermarket bags. She put the avocados in the fruit bowl and the salmon fillets and the spinach in the fridge. It was only when she took out the champagne that she started to cry.

CHAPTER TWENTY

Lewis Surprises Katrina

From: *Katrinalatham@parter.co.uk*
To: *Cornhedge@winemart.co.uk*
Sent: 25 October 21:30

Dear Cornelius,
Susie WILL be a dental nurse! She got the part! She and Ollie are out celebrating this evening. Susie is a little distant with me at present. That's my fault: I have failed to hide my antipathy towards her choice of career and her choice of boyfriend. I am determined to be more positive now and have suggested that the terrible Ash comes to dinner tomorrow night, so you can think of me plastering a fake smile to my face and pretending I don't think he's lower than pond life. Will you please thank your wife for providing Susie with such an exciting opportunity? Tell her that Susie is over the moon.
   Love,
   Katrina

From: *Katrinalatham@parter.co.uk*
To: *jul@homefind.co.uk*
Sent: 25 October 21:45

Dear Juliet,
I am coming to Sussex the weekend after next to stay with a good friend in Chailey. Are you still interested in selling your son's guitar? If so, I hope it might be convenient for me to pop in and look at it on the Saturday or Sunday. If neither of these days is convenient, don't hesitate to let me know.
All best,
Katrina

From: *Cornhedge@winemart.co.uk*
To: *Katrinalatham@parter.co.uk*
Sent: 26 October 10:55

I have passed on your message to Lucy and she is delighted Susie has got the part. Please pass on our congratulations. Do you remember me telling you about my friend who had an affinity with robins? He is also a folk singer in his spare time and is performing at a pub in Greenwich in two weeks' time: Friday, 10 November. Would you care to accompany me? I hope your meal with Ash is satisfactory,
Cornelius

From: *Katrinalatham@parter.co.uk*
To: *Cornhedge@winemart.co.uk*
Sent: 26 October 21:30
I would love to have met your robin friend but I
have a tedious work do I have to attend. Can
you come to lunch this Sunday? I know Susie
and Ollie would love to see you and I'm busy
the next two weekends. The evening with Ash
was not satisfactory since Ash couldn't come.
Susie didn't even bother to make up an excuse
for him. I suppose I am not surprised. If I were
Ash I would not jump at the prospect of
spending an evening with a grumpy and
glowering gorgon. I do hope you can come on
Sunday. I feel unaccountably gloomy at the
moment and your company would lift my spirits.
　Love,
　Katrina

　　　　　　　*　　　.　*　　　　　*

In fact, Katrina knew exactly why she felt gloomy.
She was gloomy because Susie was barely speaking
to her and, try as she might, Katrina was unable to
kid herself that her daughter's coolness was due to
anything other than the recent revelation about
Lewis. Katrina was also gloomy because she was
meeting Rose for a drink after work on Friday. As
if by instinct, Rose had rung her just as she was
about to give a very important presentation and
Katrina had agreed to her suggestion in the
knowledge that if she didn't agree Rose would just
continue talking until she *did* agree.
　Katrina arrived to find Rose sitting at a table

with two glasses and a bottle of Chablis, which suggested that she intended the meeting to be a long one. Rose looked stunning in a simple grey jersey dress. Katrina felt correspondingly frumpy in her black trouser suit.

Clearly, Rose thought so too. 'Katty, you look so tired,' she cried. 'Let me pour you a nice big drink and you can relax. How *are* you?'

'I've been better,' Katrina admitted. 'I've had a frustrating day at work—'

'Don't talk to me about frustration!' Rose exclaimed. 'I spent two hours twiddling my thumbs at home this morning waiting for my new sofa to arrive and then I finally got a call to say their van had broken down and they would not be coming till next week, and then this afternoon I went to the hairdresser and Jon cut at least an inch too much off my hair. See? What do you think?'

Katrina studied Rose's glossy auburn locks and said, quite truthfully, that Rose looked wonderful, adding a little sourly that she wished *she* had time to spend an afternoon at the hairdresser.

'You should make time,' Rose said. 'Your hair does look a little *limp* at the moment.' She smiled and raised her glass. 'Here's to you, Katty! I want to tell you I feel no bitterness or resentment towards you. I admitted to Lewis last night that I felt a little sad because I wished *I* could be the mother of his child, and do you know what he said?'

'No,' said Katrina, feeling pretty sure that whatever it was she wouldn't like it much. She wished Rose would keep her voice down. The young woman sitting at the next table was trying too hard to look as if she wasn't listening.

'He said if it hadn't been for me, he would never have known he *had* a child and then he said that Ollie was my nephew and therefore was more or less my child anyway. He said we have the same smile! I've never noticed that!'

Neither had Katrina who did not trust herself to speak and applied herself to her wine instead.

'He's so happy, Katty. He says he and Ollie have the most extraordinary rapport. Lewis is so good with young people. We saw Susie and Ash last week . . . Did Susie tell you?'

The young woman at the next table stood up and called out, 'Mum!' to an elegant woman in a dress like Rose's.

Katrina watched the two women embrace. 'No,' she said, 'I don't think she did.'

'I've known him since he was tiny. He's such a nice boy. He and Sam are terrific mates and his parents are my dearest friends. We always used to use their house as a base when we visited London. Now we live here, we see them all the time. And I have to tell you, Ash and Susie make a lovely couple. Which reminds me: I've invited Susie and Ollie, and Ash of course, to lunch on Sunday.'

'But I've invited Cornelius!' Katrina protested.

'Have you?' Rose narrowed her eyes thoughtfully. 'Do you know, I think that's rather serendipitous! Lewis said I must invite you too, so of course I was going to but, actually, given the circumstances, your presence might be a little tricky. I am sure that Ollie will find it far easier to relax with his father if you're not there. It is such a bizarre situation. Cam and Sam find it absolutely fascinating.'

'Do they?' Katrina finished her glass and poured

276

herself some more wine.

'Of course they do. I was talking to my friend Dinah, and she said I was being amazingly magnanimous about it all, but I told her that it seems to have made me and Lewis closer than ever. And Ted, her husband, said—'

'I don't want to know what her husband said. I suppose I should be grateful you haven't made an announcement about it in *The Times*. As far as Sunday is concerned, I'm not sure that Susie and Ollie can come. Cornelius was looking forward to seeing them.'

'Well, they've already accepted, and anyway it gives you and Cornelius the chance to have a lovely, intimate meal together.'

'That's all very well but—'

'Katty, I hate to say this, but I think you need to guard against being a tiny bit *proprietorial* about Ollie. I can see why you're jealous, it's quite understandable. Ollie has just discovered he has a glamorous new father—'

'As opposed to his un-glamorous old mother.'

'You wouldn't be quite so un-glamorous if only you'd get a proper haircut! You've had Ollie to yourself all his life, you have to learn to share him. And of course that shouldn't be too difficult for you *now*.'

'Why now, particularly?'

'Well, after all,' said Rose, 'it's not as if you're on your own any more. You have Cornelius!'

'Right,' said Katrina. 'I have Cornelius.'

*   *   *

On Sunday morning, Ollie kissed his mother

goodbye, sent Cornelius his regards and set off for the bus stop. Perhaps it was just as well that Susie had stayed the night with Sam and Cam, a euphemism, Katrina was sure, for staying the night with Ash. Susie would have noticed at once that the fridge did not seem well prepared for a Sunday lunch with Cornelius.

Cornelius was not coming to lunch. Katrina had looked at her emails before going to bed on Friday night and had found a disappointingly brief message from him to say that he was otherwise engaged on that day. She did not tell Ollie this because she would then have no excuse not to attend the jolly family party with Rose and Lewis.

So now here she was on her own, with a perfect opportunity to work out how to repair her relationship with her daughter. In the past she had fantasized about a time when she would be able to tell her children about Lewis. She had imagined them all embracing one another; she had imagined how wonderful it would be to unburden herself of the secret she had carried for so long.

Well, now she had revealed her secret and the effect had been like a stone thrown into a muddy pool, stirring up great dollops of guilt and recriminations and darkening her relationship with Susie. Both her children were drawing ever closer to Rose and Lewis and would probably end up adopting them both as preferred parental figures, leaving Katrina to moulder away in Greenwich on her own.

A loud mew alerted her to Omo's presence in the room. Katrina glared at him. 'I am not being sorry for myself,' she said. 'I am taking a cold and dispassionate look at my situation.' She bit her lip and shook her head. There had been many times when she had felt despondent about her life. This was the first time she had been reduced to explaining herself to her cat.

*   *   *

Ollie rang at five to tell his mother not to worry about supper for him or Susie since they had only just sat down to lunch. Katrina could hear lots of noise and laughter in the background and Ollie sounded relaxed and happy.

In the evening Katrina looked at her emails and found one from Juliet inviting her to lunch next Saturday and giving her some details about the guitar. It was the last sentence that transfixed Katrina. 'Cornelius came down for lunch today and told us you two were no longer seeing each other. Alec and I are so very sorry . . .' Katrina sat and looked at the screen without moving. Finally, she roused herself and sent a reply accepting the invitation. She switched off the computer and went into the kitchen to make a cup of tea. She wondered why she felt so desolate at being dumped by a non-existent boyfriend.

*   *   *

At midday on Wednesday, Katrina received a call from an unusually coy-sounding Rebecca in reception to say that a Lewis Maltraver was downstairs and would like to take her out to lunch.

'I'll come down,' Katrina said. She was pleased she was wearing her blue skirt and long-sleeved white T-shirt today, and immediately she was cross

279

with herself for wanting to look good for him.

In the lobby, Rebecca was twirling her necklace round her fingers and laughing. Katrina had never heard her laugh before.

'Ah, Katrina,' Lewis said. 'I asked Rebecca here to ring the prettiest solicitor in the office and she called you immediately.'

'You had to give me quite a few clues, actually,' Rebecca smiled. Katrina had never seen Rebecca's teeth before.

'I have loads of work,' Katrina said uncertainly, 'I was going to have a sandwich.'

'Forget that,' said Lewis, 'I'm taking you out. I have no rehearsals today so I thought—'

'Oh,' Rebecca breathed, 'are you an actor? I thought I recognized you! Are you rehearsing something interesting?'

'I think it might be,' Lewis said modestly. 'It's a serial for BBC2. It's called *Sins of the Fathers*. I'm playing the father.'

'Oh!' Rebecca leant forward. 'How terribly exciting!'

'I do hope you'll watch it. I would be fascinated to know what you think of it.'

'I'm sure you would be,' Katrina said. 'Perhaps you can come back some time next year and ask Rebecca for her opinion. Now, I think we should be going—' She gave a brisk nod to Rebecca, put her arm through Lewis's and propelled him from the building. 'Honestly,' she muttered, 'you are the most shameless flirt . . . "I would be *fascinated* to know what you think of it" . . . You are so *blatant*. Where are we going? I can't be too long.'

'I thought,' said Lewis, 'I'd take you to Gordon's Wine Bar.'

'Oh,' said Katrina.

'Is that all right? You look surprised.'

'No. That's fine.' It was stupid to be so impressed by Lewis's choice of venue for their meal. It was, after all, only a few minutes' walk from her office. Situated on the edge of the Embankment Gardens, it was purportedly the oldest wine bar in London. Its walls were covered in historical newspaper cuttings and photos of past celebrities. Entering the candle-lit cellar, in which one ate on rickety tables set against mottled brown walls, was like stepping back in time. It happened to be Katrina's most favourite place in the world and the fact that Lewis had chosen it meant, she told herself sternly, nothing at all.

'So,' she said, 'why have you no rehearsals today?'

'Until a few days ago,' Lewis said, 'I thought my part was finished. I died last Thursday. However –' he paused and smiled broadly—'the powers that be seem to like what I've done and have decided to resurrect me.'

Katrina laughed. 'Don't tell me. They're going to do a Bobby Ewing and make the whole thing a dream so that you never really died at all.'

'Really, Katrina, this is a serious production! No, they've decided to do a couple of episodes in flashback. They want to show me engaging in various sinful incidents—'

'Which no doubt involve intimate scenes with sundry nubile young actresses?'

'It's hard work,' sighed Lewis, 'but someone has to do it.'

A stunning woman with long hair and a short skirt walked past them. Katrina noticed that the woman's eyes settled on Lewis for a moment. She also noticed that Lewis's eyes had settled on the woman. 'So what have you been doing this morning?' Katrina asked. 'Have you been getting into character, feeling your way into the part, making yourself think lecherous thoughts about any young girl who comes your way?'

'Actually,' said Lewis, 'I've been to the Velasquez exhibition at the National Gallery.' He glanced at Katrina and grinned. 'Don't look so surprised. I'm not quite the philistine you obviously think I am.'

'Really? I stand corrected. What did you think of the exhibition?'

'Superb. His paintings are so real, they instantly connect you with the past, you can imagine *meeting* these people, and his technique is incredible. You see a glass of wine and the liquid is translucent, I don't know how he does it. There's a portrait of Philip the Fourth of Spain—he was Velasquez's benefactor—and I kept going back to it. The King pops up in quite a few of the pictures but this is the only one of him when he was old. Apparently, his wife and his son had recently died and the eyes show such weariness and loneliness that . . . Well, it's strangely affecting.'

Katrina stared at Lewis. First, he had chosen her favourite wine bar and now he was displaying a sensitivity that she had never seen before. She was beginning to think she had been decidedly reckless in agreeing to have lunch with him. 'I wish I could see it,' she said. 'Poor Philip the Fourth.'

'Oh, he was all right in the end,' Lewis said. 'He married his niece and had some more children.'

'Oh,' said Katrina and she decided to stop feeling sorry for the Spanish king. On reflection, she

282

didn't think she'd waste time worrying about Lewis's sensitivity either.

They had arrived at the wine bar. They had a brief contretemps over the choice of beverage with Katrina saying she had to keep a clear head for the afternoon's work and Lewis insisting she had to help him celebrate his extended employment. Katrina shrugged and allowed him to buy a bottle of Rioja from the landlord who asked them to give him their food order. Lewis chose poached salmon and salad, which made Katrina blink since that was also what she wanted.

As a result, Katrina felt that she did actually need a restorative glass of alcohol. They went through to the cellar and sat at a table with the candlelight flickering on Lewis's face, revealing the fact that Lewis's eyes were directed solely at her.

Katrina took a sip of her wine and tried to take command of the situation. 'So,' she said, 'what is this all about? Why are you taking me out to lunch?'

'That,' Lewis said, 'is a very silly question. Any man would want to take you out to lunch. I wanted to see you and I thought I'd surprise you.'

'I don't like surprises.'

'Nonsense. Surprises are very good for the mind. They keep the brain flexible.'

'My brain's quite flexible enough, thank you very much.' She glanced at him suspiciously. 'Why are you grinning like that? It's very annoying.'

'You look so funny when you're cross. I know exactly what you must have looked like when you were a little girl. I am so glad you are back in my life. You enrich it.'

Lewis was a professional charmer, Katrina told

herself, just remember that. 'I have *not* come back into your life,' she said. 'You seem to have come back into mine.'

'And as a result I've found our son. Isn't that extraordinary? We have a son! You should be so proud of him. He has such energy and enthusiasm and honesty. I think I'd love him even if he weren't my son. It's funny: those two words, *my son*, they make me feel so . . .' He bit his lip and blinked furiously.

Startled, Katrina hesitated before replying. She had been so preoccupied with her own feelings, she had never considered how traumatic this whole business must be for him. 'In my defence,' she said slowly, 'all those years ago, I knew that you lost interest in me the moment Susie came into my bedroom.'

'That's not true. I admit I was taken aback—'

'You were happy to have sex with me so long as you didn't have to have a proper relationship. And supposing—just supposing—I'd come and sought you out when you were in the throes of your romance with Nurse whatever-her-name—supposing I'd told you I'd just had your baby—can you honestly say you'd have welcomed me with open arms?'

'I don't know. I suppose I wouldn't. I was such an idiot then.' He reached for her hand. 'I wish you had come to lunch on Sunday with your children. We missed you.'

Katrina knew she should remove her hand but it seemed churlish to and it had been a long time since her hand had been held by anyone. 'I'm sure you didn't,' she said. 'I'd have been the spectre at the feast.'

'You have to face them all sometime. The first time will be awkward, the second time will be easier and the third time everyone will have forgotten all about it.'

Katrina gave a short laugh. 'You don't know my family.'

'I'm beginning to.' He released her hand and reached out to touch her face. 'I must have been mad to walk out on you.'

'Lewis—'

'It's still there, isn't it? That chemistry between us? And don't tell me you're in love with Cornelius because I don't believe it. I know a little about chemistry and there is not a drop of it between you. But you and me—'

'Lewis, stop this. You're supposed to be in love with my sister.'

'I am,' he said. 'I'm in love with both of you.'

Fortunately for Katrina, she was spared the need to make a response by the arrival of their meal. She used the interruption to collect herself and to decide that the best policy was to ignore his last remark. She tucked into the salmon, commented on its excellence, and asked Lewis if he knew that both Samuel Pepys and Rudyard Kipling had lived in the house above the cellar. Lewis said he had no idea. Katrina told him she had once learnt by heart Kipling's poem 'If' simply because she had loved it so much.

'Can you still remember it?' Lewis asked, topping up their glasses.

'No,' Katrina said, 'I wish I could.'

'It's always been a favourite of mine,' Lewis said. He put down his knife and fork, put his hands in his lap and proceeded to recite it.

Lewis was an actor so it was no surprise that he could bring such an air of depth and understanding to the famous words of advice from a father to his son. For once, however, Katrina did not doubt his sincerity. They were both silent when he finished.

'Excuse me,' a voice said, its upward inflection denoting either an Australian accent or a long acquaintance with *Neighbours*. A well-built young woman was smiling at both of them and holding out a mobile phone. 'Would one of you mind taking a photo of me and my friend? This place is so Dickensian, isn't it? We want to take a picture for the family back home.'

'I'd be delighted,' Lewis said. He stood up and waited for the woman to settle herself beside her female companion. Lewis told them to smile and the women giggled and gave rather self-conscious grins.

When Lewis returned, he said. 'Well?'

'Well what?'

'Aren't you going to tell me more of the history of this place?'

Katrina bridled. 'Are you telling me you aren't interested?'

'On the contrary. I must confess, however, that I'm rather more curious as to what you think about my problem.'

Katrina swallowed. 'What problem is that?'

'You and Rose. I'm in love with both of you.'

Katrina gripped her glass. 'I'm afraid,' she said lightly, 'I have no solution for you.'

'I have,' Lewis said.

'Really?' Katrina raised an eyebrow. 'How tantalizing!'

'I hope you'll think so. Do you remember that couple from downstairs? They've been very kind to Rose. I think you met them at her party.'

'Yes, I did. I liked them.'

'They're moving. They are putting their flat on the market.'

'Rose will miss them.'

'Katrina, do you not understand? It came to me this morning: why don't you buy the place? Sell up, leave Greenwich and move into their flat? It has three bedrooms, plenty of room for you and Ollie and Susie.'

'I'm sorry,' Katrina said, 'I'm being very dense but . . . are you suggesting Rose and I *share* you?'

'Don't say anything now. Just promise me you'll think about it.' He glanced at her plate. 'Aren't you going to eat the rest of your meal? I thought you liked it.'

'I do,' Katrina said, 'but I seem to have lost my appetite.'

'Katrina,' Lewis said, 'it could work, you know.'

Katrina looked about her. The Australian girls were looking at the photos on their mobiles and giggling. Behind them, a couple were murmuring endearments to each other. Katrina turned her attention back to Lewis. 'Do you know something?' she said. 'You are a *most* peculiar man and you have *most* peculiar ideas. I'm quite sure Kipling wouldn't approve of you.'

'I don't care about Kipling,' Lewis said. 'I'm far more interested in Katrina.'

CHAPTER TWENTY-ONE

Lunch in Sussex

On Saturday morning, Katrina packed her overnight bag and drove away from Greenwich. It was a perfect autumn day with a hazy, melting sun leaking gentle rays of light across the blue sky.

As Katrina sped towards Sussex, she reflected that she had never in her life been so glad to leave her children behind. Ollie, of course, was being wonderfully relaxed about everything and Katrina knew it was absurdly irrational on her part to wish that he would display at least a little more agitation about the news that his father was a virtual stranger. Nevertheless, if she were absolutely honest—and heaven knew, it was high time she *was* a little more honest—it was irritating, extremely irritating, to find that Ollie was far more concerned about the lack of progress in his pursuit of Sophie than about the duplicity of his mother. If Katrina had known he would be so unconcerned, she would have told him a long time ago and saved herself years of guilt and angst. And meanwhile Susie, who, she told herself a little too forcefully, had *no* reason to feel aggrieved, could barely speak to her mother without revealing her hurt and sense of betrayal. But then, of course, Katrina admitted to herself forlornly, Susie *did* have reason to be aggrieved. Susie, who had always been so open about her thoughts and her feelings, had discovered that her mother was a liar, and with every clipped exchange she showed that she had shut the door and bolted it fast, locking Katrina out of her life. It was, very definitely, a good time to get away.

Alfriston was a picture-book perfect village on the edge of the South Downs. Katrina drove slowly through the main street, noticing with delight the big, beamed pub, the tiny shops and the thatched-roof cottages. Following Juliet's directions, she drove on towards Seaford and turned off up a long, narrow track. It was only now that she remembered she was supposed to be Cornelius's ex-girlfriend. She was wondering whether she should say anything about him, when she reached the end of the track and stopped in front of an old gate beyond which was a field and open country. It was the house on her right that made her gasp with pleasure.

The salmon-painted mill sat on the top of the hill like an inverted ice-cream cone. A discreet L-shaped extension had been attached to its rear and in the front a sprawling lawn rolled down the hill. It was the most gorgeous place Katrina had ever seen.

She parked the car, got out and stretched her arms, breathing in the cool, fresh, unpolluted air. She had a sudden impulse to climb over the gate and stride across the hills but all such thoughts were stopped by a welcoming 'Katrina, how nice to see you!'

Alec was wearing baggy brown cords and a pale yellow polo shirt under a ribbed navy-blue sweater. He was flanked on either side by two golden Labradors with waving tails that synchronized perfectly.

Katrina walked towards him. 'This place is

amazing,' she told him. 'And you're so lucky to have the Downs right on your doorstep. I'd love to explore them. They look so inviting!'

'If you're up to it,' Alec said, 'we could go for a quick walk now. Rollo and Folly here are desperate for exercise. Juliet prepared lunch this morning but she's had to visit a friend in hospital in Lewes and won't be back for another half-hour. Or would you rather have a drink and put your feet up?'

'I would *love* a walk!'

'Good! Do you hear, boys? Walkies!'

Both dogs responded with feverish excitement and yelps of delight. As Alec opened the gate, they careered across the field like drunken missiles, following first one smell then another. Katrina, who had originally wondered whether she should dress up for Cornelius's relations, was glad she had chosen her trousers and her sensible shoes.

Alec was an agreeable companion, amiable and relaxed, with an obvious love of the countryside in which he lived. Katrina felt a million miles away from the traumas and the turmoil of the last few weeks and she bestowed a grateful smile on her host. 'I am having a lovely time! I'm so glad I'm here!'

'It's good to see you,' Alec said. 'I must tell you that we were all so sorry to hear that you and Cornelius have fallen out.'

'So am I,' Katrina said, and even as she said it, she wondered why it was that she felt she was telling the truth.

'Elizabeth is heartbroken! She thought you were perfect for her son!'

'I thought she was great fun,' Katrina said. She

hesitated. 'When we went to his mother's birthday party, I couldn't help noticing that Cornelius was a little distant towards her. It seemed rather sad.'

One of the Labradors bounded up towards Alec and he bent down to throw a stick for him. 'One of Juliet's most treasured possessions,' he said, 'is a letter Cornelius wrote to her two weeks after she'd started university. He must have been about eleven then. It was very short: "Dear Juliet, I hope you are enjoying university. I wish you were still at home. Yours sincerely, C.C. Hedge."' He laughed. 'Cornelius is not an easy man to get to know.'

'That,' Katrina said, 'is the understatement of the year.'

'I first met him when he was twelve and I still don't understand him. He was thirteen when his father killed himself.'

'Killed himself?' Katrina repeated. 'His father killed himself?'

Alec nodded. 'I liked his father. Peter was an interesting man, passionate about poetry and wine. He always said he'd have liked to have been a wine merchant. It's a pity he never lived to see his son go into that world. He was a stockbroker, a very good one, I imagine, since he made a lot of money. He adored his children and they adored him. When we were at university, Juliet was always talking about him.'

'Why did he kill himself?'

'He was a manic depressive. They don't call it that now, do they? What *do* they call it? Something to do with spectacles . . .'

'Bi-polar?'

'That's it. That's what he was. He had a difficult relationship with Elizabeth. She was very pretty,

291

used to flattery and attention, neither of which Peter was particularly adept at providing. When it happened, we were far away. Juliet and I were students at Keele University. Juliet always says that Elizabeth felt left out of the closeness that existed between her husband and her son. Cornelius has never talked about any of this. To her credit, Elizabeth told us what happened and, despite what you might think, it would be wrong to paint her as the villain of the piece.'

'I don't understand.'

'Elizabeth has always had a rather *flexible* attitude towards reality.'

'That's just what Cornelius told me.'

'Cornelius knew that better than most. Sometimes, she says things for effect; sometimes, she says things she would like to be true. It's not so much that she means to tell lies, it's simply that she gets carried away by the moment. I gather that on this particular occasion she had a violent row with Peter in front of Cornelius and told him that Cornelius was not his son.'

Now the second Labrador returned and Alec rooted around for another stick. Katrina gazed out at the sloping hills. In the distance she could see the sea, twinkling like a treasure trove. She swallowed and said, 'What a terrible thing to do! Was it a lie?'

'Of course it was. It was a stupid lie. Cornelius was the spitting image of his father. Had Peter been even halfway rational he would have known it was ridiculous. But Peter was not a rational man at the time. That night he took himself off to the garage and hanged himself. Cornelius found him in the morning.'

'Oh, my God,' Katrina whispered, 'poor Cornelius.'

'Yes,' said Alec, 'and poor Elizabeth. She fell apart, begged Cornelius to forgive her, told him she'd never meant to say that, it had just come out and of course it wasn't true, and then she had hysterics. It must have been ghastly. And Cornelius didn't say anything. He never said anything. It was impossible to know what he thought. I'm telling you this because it explains why he doesn't display the . . . kindness . . . you might expect him to show towards his mother.' He sighed again. 'I'm sorry. This is not a good subject for a beautiful autumnal morning. Juliet would be very cross with me. Let's go home and have some lunch.'

'Yes,' said Katrina. She took one last look at the sparkling water on the horizon and then turned her back on it.

*   *   *

Inside, the mill was every bit as impressive as it was outside. The hall was dominated by a huge brass gong which had been very effective, Alec said, at waking Michael and Jenny when they were teenagers. On the right, Katrina had a glimpse of a circular, elegant sitting room. She followed Alec through the doorway on the left into the more recent extension, a large open-plan area. She noted a dark, round, burnished-oak table with six leather-upholstered chairs and, beyond them, a television, two armchairs and a big sofa covered in an old rug ('For the dogs,' Alec said with a grimace).

293

Finally, there was the kitchen and it was there they found Juliet, cutting up chives and listening to Nina Simone on the CD player. She smiled when she saw Katrina and went over to kiss her cheek, apologizing for being late, explaining about her sick friend, expressing pleasure at seeing Katrina and announcing that lunch was ready.

It proved to be a cornucopia of mouth-watering tastes and glowing colours. The chives had been prepared for the main dish, a combination of smoked trout, horseradish, potatoes, onions and soured cream. There was also a carrot and coriander salad, a dish of French beans and a plate of gorgeous, crumbling ciabatta. As if all this wasn't enough, Juliet had produced a large platter of oozing Brie, creamy Gorgonzola and a slab of mature Cheddar.

Katrina, initially disconcerted by the trouble which her hostess had taken, soon relaxed. It was pleasant to witness the gentle ribbing between the husband and wife, the affectionate reprimands with which Juliet tried to check her partner's more outrageous pronouncements. Today, Alec was exercised by a variety of gripes: the deteriorating quality of news programmes, the lamentable state of the NHS, the total incoherence of flat-pack-furniture assembly instructions and, last but not least, the inhumanity of local councils. This final target was prompted by the fact that a disabled friend had been fined two hundred pounds after his disabled sticker had inadvertently fallen from his car window. Having explained the situation to his council, he had received a letter assuring him that nothing could be done and reminding him to pay the fine within nine days. Alec became so incensed while reciting this tale that he roused his dogs, which padded over to him and wagged their tails supportively.

It was a long and leisurely meal and only after coffee did Katrina realize how late it was. Juliet caught her anxious glance at the clock and suggested they go upstairs to look at the guitar.

The spare room, pleasingly circular, was part of the original mill. Its windows opened out onto the garden below and the walls were painted a dusky pink. Katrina took in the big brass bed and the bookcase with an entire shelf devoted to the books of Agatha Christie. However, it was the framed photo on top of the chest of drawers that interested her most. She went over and picked it up. Cornelius beamed out at her. He was wearing a grey lounge suit and held a glass of champagne. On his left was a smart young man with short dark hair and a wide grin. On the right of Cornelius there was another young man, with a shy smile, an aquiline nose and hair that looked every bit as undisciplined as that of the man beside him.

Katrina looked enquiringly at Juliet. 'Is that Cornelius's son?' she asked.

'You know about Leo?' Juliet looked surprised.

'Yes. It must have been terrible.'

Juliet came over and nodded. 'It was a nightmare. It was so sudden and Leo had never been ill in his life. My two adored him, especially Jenny. We used to visit the castle at Lewes when he was small and he loved it and would run around shrieking with delight. Jenny was five years older than him and she would run along behind him, terrified he'd fall down the hill! That photo was taken at Michael's wedding.'

'They all look so happy.'

'They were. It's hard to believe that less than two years later, Leo was dead.' Juliet smiled. 'He was a lovely boy, so curious, so eager to find out everything there was to know. He had all sorts of plans. He was a great one for setting himself targets. He was determined to go to the Far East before he was twenty-five, South America before he was thirty, the Arctic—or was it the Antarctic?—before he was thirty-five . . .'

'Did he and Cornelius get on well?'

'Oh, yes. They had what I'd call a healthily combative relationship. Leo thought Cornelius was appallingly apathetic about politics and the environment. Cornelius thought Leo was a philistine about classical music and kept trying to interest him in Mahler and Bach. They enjoyed arguing with each other. They always enjoyed arguing with each other. I remember one Christmas when Leo was still at primary school and we all watched *Star Wars*, and twenty-four hours later he and Cornelius were still debating the rival merits of Luke Skywalker and Han Solo. There are still times now when I can't believe Leo isn't alive.'

'When I heard about it,' Katrina confessed, 'my first reaction was one of utter selfishness. I thought of my own children, I thought how I would feel if either of them went, and I felt so grateful I had them.'

'I know. I think that's quite natural. What can be worse than losing one's child? That's why Cornelius and Lucy split up. They were happy for a long time. Lucy was a tower of strength in the early days when Cornelius was building up his wine

296

business and Cornelius was so proud of Lucy's acting talent. We were all surprised by their separation. The trouble was, they both mourned their son in different ways. Lucy thought Cornelius was cold and uncaring, Cornelius thought she was wallowing in her grief and it embarrassed him. Even today, Cornelius can't bear to talk about Leo. It's a terrible business. They've both been so unhappy.' She looked directly at Katrina. 'I'm sorry things didn't work out between you and my brother. I really thought you might make him happy again.'

Katrina flushed. 'Well,' she began, 'I don't think ... I mean, I know—'

'I'm sorry,' Juliet said quickly, 'I really didn't mean to bring this up. Now, let me show you our guitar!'

It was clear that Juliet was as eager as Katrina to change the subject. For the next fifteen minutes, the two women threw themselves into a bout of hard bargaining with Katrina demanding she pay more and Juliet insisting she wanted far less. Eventually, Katrina refused to buy the instrument unless Juliet took seventy-five pounds for it, and a settlement was reached.

Downstairs, Alec was asleep in an armchair with his faithful hounds, also sleeping, sprawled across their sofa. When Katrina finally said goodbye, she left with the knowledge that in different circumstances she would have wanted to keep in touch with them. As she drove towards Chailey, she kept thinking of that photo. She had never seen Cornelius smile like that. Perhaps he would never do so again.

It was good to arrive at Alicia's beautiful home

and find that her friend's only pressing preoccupation was the litter of six puppies that had been born to Alicia's dog three days earlier.

*   *   *

The revelation came to Katrina as she drove back to Greenwich the following afternoon. Something Juliet had said kept bothering her, hooking itself in her mind like a jumper snagged by a bramble. Leo and Cornelius used to argue about music and the father tried to interest the son in Mahler and Bach. It didn't make sense. Cornelius liked the Zutons and the Arctic Monkeys. There was something else that wasn't right. Juliet had said Cornelius wasn't interested in politics. That couldn't be right either. Cornelius, after all, had been gripped by that book by Noam Chomsky; he had been fascinated by the parallels between Ancient Rome and the United States. None of this added up.

It was only when Katrina joined the M25 and narrowly missed being crushed by a vast black lorry that she suddenly understood. Cornelius had *not* been interested in contemporary music, he had *not* been interested in history or politics and he had probably *not* been interested in the Far East. It was Leo, not Cornelius, who had been interested in all these things. But when Leo died, Cornelius had picked up his baton and embraced the concerns of his son. He had behaved in the same way with his father. Hadn't Alec said that Cornelius's father would have liked to become a wine merchant? Surely it was no coincidence that Cornelius had chosen to go into that very same profession?

It was so obvious. Those who said he was a cold fish who didn't know how to mourn the deaths of his loved ones could not be more mistaken. What Cornelius had done with both his father and his son was to live their lives within his own. Every day that Cornelius lived, he made choices that ensured that the legacies of Leo and his father continued. Cornelius wasn't odd or peculiar or eccentric, Katrina thought: Cornelius was amazing.

CHAPTER TWENTY-TWO

Some Like It Hot

From: *Katrinalatham@parter.co.uk*
To: *Cornhedge@winemart.co.uk*
Sent: 06 November 22:10

Dear Cornelius, I had lunch with your sister and her husband yesterday. (Do you remember I wanted to buy your nephew's guitar for Ollie's Christmas present?) I like Alec and Juliet so much and do hope we shall meet again sometime. They both expressed regret at your news about our 'break-up'. I know it is absurd to be upset about the end of a fictitious relationship but I confess I feel a little bereft! Time to get back to the real world, Katrina! Hope you are well.
  Love, Katrina

The following week was horrendously busy and the

tranquil landscape of the Sussex Downs soon seemed a million miles away. The bonding weekend was starting on Friday which meant that five days' work had to be fitted into four, on top of which all the partners were supposed to set down their detailed ideas for the Dynamic Development Seminar on the Friday afternoon. Thus far, Katrina had failed to draft any details, largely owing to the fact that she had as yet formulated no ideas and had never felt less dynamic. Telephone messages from Lewis and Paul and Rose went unanswered while the one person from whom Katrina did want to hear was conspicuous by his silence.

At home, the mood in the house remained sombre. Ollie was preoccupied by the fact that his campaign to win Sophie's friendship had worked only too well, rendering it impossible for him to change gear and become Mr Sex on Legs. Susie was sullen about going to Croydon at the weekend, particularly since this was also the week of Cam's photo-shoot in Greenwich and Cam had suggested Susie join her and her colleagues on the Friday evening. Ollie had tried to lighten Susie's mood by pointing out that he had far more reason to be cross about going to Croydon, since he was not even related to Paul. Susie responded by shooting a venomous look at her brother and her mother and shouting that it wouldn't surprise her if Paul wasn't *her* real father either. Katrina then lost her temper with Susie, Susie lost her temper with Katrina, and Ollie—very sensibly—retired to his bedroom. Full civil war was only prevented by a timely call from Cam to confirm that she was arriving on Thursday evening and to ask if Susie would be an angel and come out with her and the photographer that night so he could use her as a stand-in model while he tried different shots of the Queen's House. Susie was more than happy to do this and for a few glorious minutes almost forgot she was angry with her mother.

Katrina stayed at the office until eight on Thursday evening but at least she had finished all her allotted tasks and had even managed to cobble together some admittedly woolly ideas for the seminar the next day. At home, she put a pizza in the oven, poured herself a large glass of wine and joined Ollie in front of a TV drama about a psychopathic misogynist at loose in Berkshire. After the second murder, she passed what remained of her pizza to an ever-ravenous Ollie and after the fourth she decided to check her emails (still no word from Cornelius), and then went upstairs to pack her bag.

Susie and Cam came in just as Katrina was going to bed. Cam kissed her aunt and told her the photographer had fallen for Susie. Susie told Cam she was talking complete rubbish but she had the glow of a woman who knows she is admired. She said goodnight to her mother, which was good, but failed to make eye contact with her, which was depressing. Cam thanked Katrina for letting her stay and told her she and Susie and Ollie were about to watch a brilliant film on television about a perverted plastic surgeon wreaking revenge on sundry ex-girlfriends. Katrina had time only to tell Cam to feed Omo the following night and to help herself to any food from the freezer or fridge.

It was good to be in the car with Amy the next morning, driving up the A12, conferring good-humouredly about their forthcoming cabaret spot, rehearsing the last lines of *Some Like It Hot*. Originally, Amy had been going to dress as a man but they had decided it would be more fun to confuse their audience by sticking to their natural genders and dressing as glamorously as possible. At the climactic moment, Katrina, playing the Jack Lemmon part, would confess not that she was a man but that she was a solicitor, at which point, Amy, playing the millionaire, would conclude with the final famous line, 'Nobody's perfect.' It wasn't so very funny but by the time they had turned off the A12, both women were convinced they would be the stars of the evening.

For once, the organizers had excelled themselves. The hotel was surrounded by large gardens with weeping willows, a lily-covered pond and manicured lawns. Amy and Katrina shared a twin-bedded room with a gleaming en-suite bathroom and an enticing minibar. They unpacked their evening clothes and put them on hangers before joining their colleagues in the seminar room for sandwiches and bottled water.

Three hours later the women returned to their room, their enthusiasm sapped by a tedious and unnecessary speech from Richard Carter in probate, and a long and acrimonious debate on the role of mentors in the firm between Angela Cartwright and Jason Evans in litigation. Since everyone knew that the two protagonists had recently terminated a year-old affair, no one had wanted to risk stumbling into the crossfire by intervening and it was only when someone's mobile went off that the chairman felt able to bring the proceedings to a halt.

A long swim in the hotel pool followed by a soak in the jacuzzi proved an effective restorative. Katrina and Amy now felt ready to enjoy the evening. They spent an indecently long period of time getting ready for the dinner and at half past six stood in front of the wardrobe mirrors, grinning at their reflections.

'Do you think we've overdone it?' Amy asked. 'You don't think we have too much make-up on?'

'Nonsense,' Katrina said firmly. 'We are glamorous, gorgeous women!'

Amy did not look convinced. She stepped backwards and tilted her head to one side. 'Actually,' she said, 'if we don't let anyone get too close, we don't look that bad.'

'Of course we don't!' said Katrina. She sat down on her bed, swung her legs onto the duvet and leant back against the pillows. 'I really wasn't looking forward to this weekend but I am definitely acquiring a taste for luxury. Wasn't that jacuzzi lovely?'

'Wonderful,' said Amy. 'But it's the swimming pool I love. Remind me in the morning that I want to do thirty lengths before breakfast. When you think about it, life's pretty good, isn't it?'

And that was when the telephone rang.

*   *   *

Within twenty minutes, they were on the road back to London.

'We're going against the traffic,' Katrina said. 'That's good.' She glanced across at Amy and noted the tense rigidity of her face and body, her back ramrod straight, her hands clenched together on her lap. Katrina bit her lip and concentrated on overtaking the van in front of her. 'We'll soon be there,' she said. 'I promise you, we'll soon be there.'

'Stupid, stupid, stupid!' Amy muttered. 'That stupid motorbike! I *knew* something would happen! I *said* something would happen! Didn't I always say something would happen?' She thrust her fingers through her hair, forgetting the fact that a short time earlier she had twirled it into a bun with a handful of hair pins, which now scatted about her like confetti. 'He's going to die! So *stupid*!'

'Amy, stop it! You don't know that. You don't know that at all. You said yourself you could hardly understand what Stephen was saying. The poor boy is almost certainly hysterical and almost certainly doesn't have a clue what is really going on. There's no point torturing yourself and imagining the worst unless . . . until—'

'Until I find out for myself. I know. Oh, God.' Amy began to rub the sides of her face with her hands.

Katrina was tempted to accelerate further but was aware of traffic cameras taking photos. God knew what a photo of her and Amy would look like: two middle-aged women in party frocks and too much make-up, careering down the A12 like a latter-day Thelma and Louise.

'You shouldn't have come with me,' Amy said. 'There was no need. I could have got a taxi back to London. You should have stayed.'

'And done the cabaret on my own? No, thank you!'

'Stephen was crying. He thinks his father is going

to die, I could tell.'

'Stephen is in a state of shock. He's young and he's frightened. He doesn't know what he's saying. Was he on the bike when the accident happened?'

'I don't know. He couldn't speak for long, some nurses were seeing him, so I suppose he was, but I don't know. He said Eddy was trying to avoid a cat. Can you believe it? I can't believe it.' Amy gave a strangulated sob.

'Breathe deeply,' Katrina said. 'Sit back in your seat and concentrate on breathing deeply.'

Amy took a couple of breaths. 'I should never have married him,' she said. 'This is all my fault.'

'Amy! How is any of this your fault?'

'He's younger than me. He married an older woman and he yearned for excitement. It's my fault.'

'You're right,' Katrina said. 'And while you're about it, I think it's time you took responsibility for all that's happened in Darfur and Iraq and Palestine and Chechnya and New Orleans, and you might as well wonder why you weren't able to stop General Pinochet murdering all those people in Chile . . .'

'I'm serious.'

'I know you are and it's really scary. I always thought you were an intelligent woman.'

'Katrina!'

'Don't you Katrina me! I've never heard anything so ridiculous. If you want to blame someone, blame the cat. I can't believe you're so stupid!'

Amy sniffed. 'I *am* stupid. I wish I was like you. I wish I had a calm, ordered dignified life—'

'Really? Now that *is* stupid. That is very, very stupid. You have no idea. If you only knew.'

Katrina gave a short laugh. 'Remind me to tell you sometime why that is so stupid!'

Amy stared out of her window for a few moments and sniffed before turning back to Katrina. 'If I only knew what?'

Katrina shook her head. 'It doesn't matter.'

'Yes, it does. Tell me. I need to be distracted. Please distract me. Make me feel good about myself. Tell me you make mistakes, like me.'

'Oh,' Katrina sighed, 'I make mistakes, I make planet-sized mistakes. My daughter is currently not talking to me because she has just found out that I have been lying to her for most of her life.'

'What do you mean?'

'Ollie and Susie have different fathers. Do you remember me telling you that Rose was going out with an old boyfriend of mine?'

'The actor in *Medical Alert*? Don't tell me he's Ollie's father?'

'I met him just after Paul left me. I fell in love, Lewis did not, and the result was Ollie.'

'Katrina! You never said a thing!'

'Of course I didn't. I was thoroughly ashamed. It wasn't calm, it wasn't ordered and it certainly wasn't dignified. And by the way, since then, I've had three very undignified and completely disordered and totally disastrous affairs. So don't start wishing you were like me because you'd be a . . . Oh, hell!' Katrina lowered her indicator and turned abruptly into the middle lane in order to let a madman in a blood-red Ferrari overtake her.

A merry tune rose up from the depths of Amy's bag and she plunged her hand in to extract it. 'Stephen! Yes! . . . What? . . . Stephen, please slow down, I don't understand . . . Yes . . . Right . . . Oh,

God! . . . No, it's all right, I'm fine . . . I know, I wish I were too . . . I'll be with you as soon as I possibly can . . . Don't worry, I know where it is . . . That's fine . . . Good . . . I'll see you soon. Bye for now.'

Katrina swallowed, raised the indicator and swerved back into the fast lane.

'The doctor's spoken to him,' Amy said. 'He thinks Eddy's going to be all right. He's not unconscious any more. Stephen said something about a scan.'

'Oh, Amy!'

'Stephen said he wished I was with him. I said I wished I were too.'

'You will be soon.'

Amy's phone began to chirp again. 'Stephen? . . . What? . . . Thanks for telling me . . . All right . . . I'll see you soon. Now drink that cup of tea. Bye now.'

Amy put the phone back in her bag. 'He wanted me to know,' she said in a shaky voice, 'that Eddy wanted *me* to know that he doesn't want to ride motorbikes any more.'

*   *   *

Katrina stopped off on her way home and bought a cheese sandwich, which she wolfed down in the garage forecourt. Pausing only to throw the empty carton in the bin, she climbed back into the car and caught sight of her reflection in the driving mirror. Now she understood why the attendant had regarded her with such suspicion. Her eye make-up was smudged, giving her the appearance of a weary panda. He probably thought she was some desperate, over-the-hill lady of the night. The thought made her smile.

Yawning, she drove out onto the street. She felt as if she could sleep for ever. The frantic drive to the hospital had exhausted her. She would never forget the sight of Amy, holding up her turquoise frock, dashing into the hospital with her glasses halfway down her nose, her white hair flying in all directions. Katrina had spent about twenty minutes trying to find a place to park, then she had rushed to the hospital to be met by a tall, gangly boy, deathly white, with an arm in a sling and a bruise on his face that was proving nicely, like an uncooked loaf. Amy was with Eddy, he told her. Eddy was conscious and he was going to be all right. He had offered to get her a coffee from the vending machine but Katrina could see that the poor lad was almost asleep and she said she needed to get home. He had surprised her by hugging her and they had both had tears in their eyes when she left.

As she drove through Deptford, it began to rain. She yawned again and braked abruptly as a wide-shouldered man in a red T-shirt and black leather trousers ran crazily across the road. Katrina straightened her back, gripped the steering wheel and drove cautiously the rest of the way.

Taking her bags from the car, she walked up to her door and unlocked it. The hall light was on and Katrina's eyes were drawn to a large bouquet of flowers on the table below the mirror; they were enclosed in pink cellophane and jammed inexpertly into a jug. She picked up the card lying on top of a particularly lurid yellow chrysanthemum and began to read it.

A giggle from the sitting room made her stiffen. Susie! Susie was in there with Ash, Susie had not gone to Croydon. Furious, Katrina marched through the open door into the sitting room. She noted the muted light provided by the small lamp on the piano, switched on the main light and then stopped, dumbstruck. She had forgotten that Cam was staying, but it wasn't the sight of Cam that made her freeze. Cam was wearing a slinky little number that made her look like a far more convincing lady of the night than Katrina.

Katrina cleared her throat and Cam instantly disentangled herself from her companion, pulled an errant shoulder strap back into place and stood up.

'Good evening, Cam,' Katrina said in a voice as cold as ice, 'Would you mind leaving Lewis and me alone for a little while? I want to talk to him.'

Cam opened her mouth to speak, looked at her aunt, raised her eyebrows and walked silently out of the room.

'Katrina,' Lewis said, rising with some difficulty from the sofa, 'I don't know what you think's been going on—'

Katrina folded her arms. 'Oh, I think you do. At least Cam still had her dress on.'

'You are jumping to conclusions—'

'Conclusions are staring me in the face. I come home late in the evening, I find a room in virtual darkness and there on the sofa I see my twenty-four-year-old niece, dressed to kill, up close and personal with her mother's boyfriend . . .'

The sound of the doorbell made them both jump. 'I won't be a minute,' Katrina said. 'You stay right there.'

She went to the hall, realized her party shoes were killing her and kicked them off. She pushed her hair back, straightened her shoulders and opened the front door.

Cornelius stood in the doorway, a tartan scarf round his neck, the faded black jacket with the too-short sleeves making him look more than ever like a scarecrow.

'Cornelius!' she stammered. 'What are *you* doing here?'

'I know it's very late,' he said, 'but I was driving past and I saw you had lights on and I thought you might still be up. I hope you don't mind . . .'

'No,' said Katrina faintly, 'it's just that at this precise moment—'

Behind her, she heard Lewis say, 'Hello, Cornelius.'

Katrina turned and hissed, 'Will you *please* go back to the sitting room?' She tried desperately to recover her composure. 'I'm afraid, Cornelius, this isn't a very suitable time.'

'No,' said Cornelius, 'I can see that it isn't. I think, no, I *know,* that I would rather not see you any more. Goodbye, Katrina.'

The words were all the worse for being spoken in a tone of polite and measured consideration. Katrina swallowed and tried to speak but nothing would come out. She felt as if she were taking part in a play or a film. It certainly didn't feel like real life. Perhaps this really was a nightmare. She watched Cornelius stride down the path, climb into his car and drive out of her life.

CHAPTER TWENTY-THREE

Some Like It Very Hot

Behind her, Lewis said, 'What a very peculiar man!'

Katrina turned on him. 'Don't you *dare* say anything about Cornelius! You know *nothing* about him!'

'Perhaps,' Lewis suggested, 'I should go.'

'Yes, I'm sure you'd love to, but before you do, I want an explanation.' She took hold of his sleeve and pulled him back into the sitting room. 'Do sit down,' she said. 'You might want to do up the buttons on your shirt.'

Lewis did up his buttons. 'Katrina, I am telling the truth here—'

'Given our romantic history, I am sure you will understand that I might need some convincing of that. By the way, is that your jacket on the piano stool?'

Lewis picked up his jacket and put it on. 'Katrina—'

'And if there are any other bits of your clothing scattered around, please take them too.'

Lewis sighed. 'Katrina, are you going to let me explain what happened?'

Katrina sat down on the piano stool. 'Go ahead.'

'Thank you.' Lewis sat down on the sofa, rubbed his face with his hands and took a deep intake of breath. 'Right. This is the truth. Cam rang me on Wednesday. She told me she was going to be here on Friday evening and needed to talk to me. She

311

said she'd give me supper. She refused to say what was worrying her over the phone and she didn't want Rose to know. She sounded upset. I was curious and I suppose I was a little pleased that she felt she could confide in me. So I came here tonight, we had supper and she told me she was tired of Francis and depressed because she could never meet a man she could really like. After supper, she suggested we move to the sitting room and that's when everything went wrong. Suddenly, Cam is telling me how attractive she finds me and she's stroking my thigh . . . I mean, it's a terrible situation—'

'It sounds like absolute hell for you.'

'You can mock all you like but I am the victim in this. *Cam* was trying to seduce *me*.'

'That must be a novel experience for you.'

'It happens to be true. You have every right to be sceptical but I swear I did not come here in order to seduce Rose's daughter. The whole situation is extremely awkward.'

'You didn't look very awkward when I came in, Lewis. You looked very comfortable.'

'Well, I wasn't. I was thinking on my feet.'

'It looked to me as if you were thinking with an entirely different part of the anatomy. I don't know. Perhaps you're right, perhaps if I'd come in three seconds later, I'd have found you giving Cam a moving talk about the depth of your love for her mother. Perhaps you'd better go home, Lewis, because right now you're making me feel very sick.'

'If you don't believe what I say, ask Cam. Ask her to deny that she was coming on to me. I have no idea why. Perhaps she has a thing about older men,

312

perhaps she's jealous of her mother. I'm not in the wrong here.'

'I will talk to Cam. Now, I really do think you should go. It's been a long day and I'm very tired. Just go home.'

'What are you going to do?'

'Don't worry. I won't say anything to Rose. Now go.'

'All right.' Lewis stood up. 'Can we talk soon? When we're both calmer and less tired? This is all so silly.'

'I do agree with you.' Katrina walked past him into the hall and opened the front door. 'Goodnight, Lewis.'

He came up to her and hesitated for a moment. 'I know I'm bad, Katrina. But I'm not that bad, I promise you.' He gave Katrina a sad little smile, turned up the collar of his jacket and walked quickly down the path.

Katrina shut the door and murmured, 'Liar!' under her breath. She heard the clatter of pans coming from the kitchen and went down to find Cam washing up.

'Leave that,' Katrina said. 'I'm making tea. Do you want some?'

Cam dried her hands with a tea towel. 'Thanks. And there's some Chardonnay in the fridge if you want alcohol.'

'Tea will do very nicely.' Katrina put the kettle on and reached for the tea bags.

Cam sat down on one of the high stools. 'I'm sorry about all this,' she said. 'I thought you weren't coming back till tomorrow.'

'Evidently.'

'What did Lewis tell you?'

313

'He said you were trying to seduce him.'

'I didn't have to try very hard. Why did you come back early?'

'A colleague's husband was hurt in a motorcycle crash. I drove her back to London.'

'Is her husband going to be all right?'

'I think so.'

Cam kept her eyes fixed steadily on Katrina. 'I'm not in love with Lewis.'

'I didn't think you were.'

'I quite fancy him, though. Don't you?'

Katrina's mouth twitched. 'I don't find him as attractive as I used to.'

Cam raised a defiant chin. 'When I realized I'd have the house to myself, I rang Lewis. It seemed too good an opportunity to miss. I couldn't ask him round to my flat. Sam's always around.'

'I see.'

'No, you don't. You won't understand. You're so different. I'll tell you, though. I've been planning it for ages. What's funny is that it seems pretty silly now, really. I only wanted revenge.'

'Revenge? Revenge against whom?'

'Against my mother, of course.'

'I often think,' Katrina said, 'that you and Sam are the only people your mother has ever loved. Why on earth would you want revenge?'

Cam pushed back her hair and made a face. 'I don't quite mean revenge, that's a little excessive. I just wanted to get my own back, tit for tat, that sort of thing. All very juvenile, I know. Poor Aunty Katty! You look so tired!'

'I am tired. I am also confused. What on earth could your mother have done to warrant your behaviour tonight?'

314

'Quite a lot, actually. When I was seventeen, I started seeing someone. I liked him. I liked him very much. He was our gardener and Mum didn't approve. Then I told her I didn't want to go to university. She thought it was because of Sean but it wasn't. She decided the relationship had to stop and so she stopped it.'

'What did she do? Did she sack him?'

'No,' Cam said. 'She slept with him.'

Katrina, in the process of pouring boiling water into two mugs, looked up at her niece in surprise and then swore as she realized one mug was now overflowing.

Cam gave a faint smile. 'I told you, you wouldn't understand. You don't do things like that.'

'How do you *know* Rose slept with him? Did she tell you?'

'That wouldn't have been nearly dramatic enough. Her timing was impeccable. I came back from school, heard some sounds, walked into Mum's bedroom and found them under the duvet. Poor Sean leapt out of bed like he'd been electrocuted. It was total pandemonium. I was screaming at him and he was desperately trying to find his boxer shorts and there was Mum lying back against her pillows looking like she'd just swallowed heaven knows what.' Cam raised her eyebrows. 'She probably *had* just swallowed—'

'Cam!'

Cam smiled. 'I'm sorry, Aunty Katty.'

'I wish you wouldn't call me that, you have no idea how much I hate it. Katrina will be fine.'

For the first time that evening, Cam looked taken aback. 'I'm sorry,' she said, 'I didn't realize.'

'Well, you do now.' Katrina handed Cam her tea.

'What happened to you and Sean after you found him with Rose?'

'Nothing happened to me and Sean. I took great care to make sure I never saw him again. So Mother was very successful.'

'Cam, I'm not trying to defend Rose here, but she . . . well, she's always been one for finding *original* solutions to problems. In her own peculiar way, she probably thought she was doing the right thing for you.'

'Oh, I know. She told me. I'm sure she thought she was being a dutiful mother. I also know she fancied Sean like mad.' She smiled. 'Poor Aunty Katty—sorry, Katrina—you're trying so hard not to look shocked.'

'I *am* shocked, you're right. But I also know that Rose loves you very much and I know she must have persuaded herself that it was the right thing to do. And also, Cam, do you really want to spoil her relationship with Lewis? She loves him.'

'Yeah, but it doesn't stop her bonking Uncle Teddy, though.'

Katrina blinked. 'Who's Uncle Teddy?'

'He's an old family friend. He's an old, *rich*, family friend. Sometimes he takes her out to lunch, and they get together every few months for a weekend of sex and sin and shopping. They've been at it for years.'

'Cam, how do you *know* all this?'

'After the Sean business, I snooped around a bit. I nearly told Dad. I'm glad I didn't.'

'So am I.'

'It's funny,' Cam said, 'I feel a lot better now. I don't want to have sex with Lewis any more. The thing is, I'm pretty sure he *would* have succumbed

316

to my wicked wiles.'

'So am I,' said Katrina grimly.

'So now,' Cam said brightly, 'I don't need to do it.' She smiled at Katrina. 'You won't say anything to Mum, will you? I suppose I don't actually want to muck things up between her and Lewis.'

'I won't say a thing,' Katrina said. 'I've thought for a long time that she and Lewis are made for each other.'

'Me too.' Cam yawned and stretched her arms. 'I think I'll go to bed.'

'I think that's an excellent idea,' Katrina said. 'By the way, when did those flowers in the hall arrive?'

Cam yawned again. 'Your neighbour brought them round. She said a florist arrived with them in the morning and she took them in for you. Do you have a secret admirer?'

'Alas, no,' Katrina said. 'Can you sleep in tomorrow?'

'Unfortunately not. We have another photo-shoot to do.' Cam came round and kissed her aunt on the cheek. 'Goodnight, Aunty— Goodnight, Katrina.' She picked up her tea. 'Did I hear Cornelius come round earlier?'

'Yes,' Katrina said. 'He couldn't stay long.'

'He's a wine merchant, isn't he? Where is he based?'

'I believe he's in Dulwich. Goodnight, Cam.'

'Are you coming to bed? You look exhausted.'

'It's been a long evening. I'll be up in a minute.'

Katrina waited until Cam had left the room and then she gave a long sigh. She remembered the cold contempt in Cornelius's eyes and bit her lip. She put the milk in the fridge, finished her tea and switched out the lights. In the hall, she picked up

317

the card and read it again. 'I want my slippers back xxx' It was typical of Paul that he had managed to send the most irritating romantic message of all time. It was, even for him, particularly crass given that she had only recently lambasted his old description of her. She went through to the sitting room, dropped the card in the bin, switched out the lights and went upstairs to bed.

From: *Katrinalatham@parter.co.uk*
To: *Cornhedge@winemart.co.uk*
Sent: 12 November 9:28

Dear Cornelius,
I am sorry you left so abruptly on Friday and while I, of course, respect your wish to terminate our acquaintance, I would just like to clarify what must have seemed like a compromising situation in which I was betraying my sister with Lewis Maltraver. Earlier that evening I was at a business dinner do in Essex—hence my evening attire—but I had to leave early to drive a colleague back to London to see her sick husband. When I came home I found Lewis there with a member of my family and then you arrived and I assume you instantly concluded I was behaving badly. I confess I am a little hurt that you think I could behave so shabbily, but nevertheless . . .

Katrina stopped and screwed up her forehead in concentration. She felt almost relieved when the phone interrupted her attempts to express her sense of injustice. For a moment she hoped it might be Cornelius but it was Ollie, wanting to check that Katrina would be at home in the afternoon. Both he and Susie had left their house keys behind. Katrina assured him she would indeed be at home and told him to ring when they arrived in Greenwich and she would have tea ready for them.

She put down the phone and looked at her half-finished email. Then she sighed and pressed the Cancel button. There was no point in humiliating herself by writing a pleading message to Cornelius. Even if he accepted her explanation—and reading it back to herself she could see how implausible it sounded—he was clearly disgusted with the entire miasma of deceit that seemed to follow her everywhere she went these days. The fact that he was so quick to see the worst showed what he really thought of her. Her relationship with him—such as it was—was over. It was time to turn her attention towards her children.

Thus it was that when her children returned, they were ushered into the kitchen to find home-made scones—and Susie's favourite, carrot cake *with* icing—waiting for them on the table. Katrina knew that Susie knew that it was a blatant attempt to curry favour but it did at least engender a weary smile from her and a heartfelt, 'I am *so* hungry!' from Ollie.

'Sit down and tuck in,' Katrina said, filling the teapot with boiling water. 'How was Paul?'

Susie threw her bag on the floor and took off her jacket. 'It was just as I said it would be. The house was a tip. I spent most of Saturday cleaning it. And Dad is *so* sorry for himself. He kept telling us he's a man who can't live without a woman. He said he sent you some flowers.'

'He did,' Katrina said. 'They arrived with a rather cryptic message.'

Susie nodded. 'I think he's planning to come and live here.'

'You're joking.'

Ollie, who was ladling what looked like half the contents of the jam jar onto his scone, nodded sagely. 'I'm sure he is. He mentioned the Irish stew you used to make, three times. He hates living on his own. He can't even make a piece of toast without burning it. Susie made us cheese on toast for lunch today and he acted like she'd made the best meal he'd ever had. He even asked her how she made it.'

'Oh, dear,' Katrina said. 'Poor Paul.'

Susie gave a theatrical shudder. 'That's what Dad kept saying: "Poor Paul!" And then he'd follow that up with an I'm-being-very-brave smile. He makes it very difficult to feel sorry for him because he feels so very sorry for himself. And he's mean. He ordered a takeaway last night and I swear he only ordered enough for two people. By ten we were all starving again and had to eat some cereal.'

'Yeah, Mum,' Ollie said without rancour, 'and meanwhile you were eating a three-course meal at a posh hotel.'

'Actually,' Katrina said, 'I wasn't. For your information, my supper last night consisted of sardines on toast and a seriously past its sell-by-date yogurt.'

Ollie reached for another scone. 'Why? Was the trip cancelled?'

'Not at all. We spent Friday there and in the evening we were getting ready for our wonderful three-course meal. And then Amy's stepson rang

320

to say that Eddy had crashed his motorbike and was about to die.'

'Oh, my God!' Susie exclaimed. 'Poor Amy! What did she do?'

'I drove her back to London and we went straight to the hospital. Basically, Stephen had panicked. Eddy's going to be fine. He has a broken collarbone and lots of bruises, and his bike is going to the scrapyard. I spoke to Amy this morning. She says the funny thing is that she and Eddy were planning to attend a special screening of *Easy Rider* tomorrow evening.'

'That reminds me,' Ollie said. 'Don't make me supper tomorrow. I'm going to the cinema with Sophie.'

'Really?' Katrina smiled. 'Do I take it the campaign is working at last?'

'Not yet,' Ollie said. 'I keep waiting for the right moment.'

'A nice romantic film will do the trick,' Katrina said. 'What are you going to see?'

'The Al Gore documentary,' Ollie said gloomily, '*An Inconvenient Truth.*'

'Oh,' said Katrina. 'I suppose a contemplation of the end of the planet might help produce a sense of romantic urgency.' She passed the carrot cake to Susie. 'Will you be in tomorrow? I could get us some nice steak, if you like.'

'Don't bother,' Susie said coolly. 'I'll be out.'

'Fine,' said Katrina. She might have known it would take more than a carrot cake, even if it did have icing, to make Susie forgive her.

*   *   *

The phone was ringing when Katrina came back from work on Monday. She flew into the study, picked up the receiver and uttered a breathless, 'Hello?'

'Katrina, it's Paul. How are you?'

'Well, I'm very well.'

'Good. Did you get my flowers?'

Katrina pulled out the chair from under her desk and sat down. 'Yes, I did. They are lovely, very colourful . . .'

'Good. Katrina, there is no easy way to say this—'

'In that case,' said Katrina with desperate energy, 'I wouldn't say anything. It was sweet of you to be so generous. Now—'

'Katrina, Clarrie's decided to come home!'

'Oh!' Katrina kicked off her shoes. 'Oh, Paul, I'm so glad!'

'That's very generous of you. You might have been thinking that . . . But, of course, I owe it to the children. You must see that I'm doing the right thing here, don't you?'

'Of course I do,' Katrina said warmly. 'And I hope you'll be very happy.'

'I must say,' Paul said, 'you're taking this very well. But, after all, you're used to being on your own . . . I want you to know that I am and always shall be very fond of you.'

'Thank you, Paul,' Katrina said gravely.

'Not at all, not at all. It was very nice to see Susie and Ollie over the weekend. I had a good talk to Ollie. He assured me his feelings for me are quite unchanged.'

'I'm sure that's true.'

'Yeah, I feel pretty confident about Ollie. Tell him and Susie I'm all right now, will you?'

322

'I certainly will, Paul. Thanks for ringing. Goodbye now.' Katrina put down the phone and rolled her eyes. Trust Paul to assume she was gagging to have him back. Absolutely typical. She stared at the computer but resisted the temptation to turn it on. She had checked her emails before leaving the office and there was nothing from Cornelius. There *would* be nothing from Cornelius.

She went through to the hall and hung up her coat. Omo wandered out from the sitting room and stared at her. 'What exciting things are we going to do tonight, Omo?' Katrina said. Omo looked at her with distaste and Katrina sighed. She went down to the kitchen and opened the fridge. 'I know,' Katrina told Omo, 'I'm going to have a glass of wine and then I'll feed you and then I'll feed me.'

Omo looked unamused, as well he might.

The telephone rang and Katrina closed the fridge door and went to answer it.

'Katty, darling, it's your big sister! How are you?'

'I'm very well.'

'That's wonderful! Cam says she had such a nice time with you. She told me about your poor friend. Is her husband going to live?'

'Yes, he is.'

'I'm so glad! Listen, I want you and Cornelius to come to supper on Saturday. What do you say?'

Katrina leant against the sink and pushed her hair back. 'I'm afraid,' she said carefully, 'that we can't. Cornelius and I have decided to stop seeing each other.'

'No! Why? When did you decide this?'

'This weekend, as it happens.'

'How frightfully annoying! We've got Roger's cousin and his wife coming and they're deadly dull and they'll want to talk about poor Roger, which won't be much fun for poor Lewis. I can't think of anyone else I could inflict them on. Why have you broken up? I thought you were very happy together. Oh, my God, Katty, please tell me you're not still holding a candle for Lewis?'

'Of course I'm not! It's simply that . . . Well, Cornelius is a very private person, very reserved. It's not easy to have a relationship with someone like that . . . I know so little about him.'

'Katty, darling, will you allow a big sister who's been around a bit to give you some advice?'

'Well, actually—'

'It is always risky starting relationships at our age. A man over forty is always going to have secrets he'd rather you didn't know about.'

'I know and I understand that. But Cornelius is particularly reserved and—'

'Well, really, Katty, talk about the pot calling the kettle black!'

Katrina frowned. 'What do you mean?'

'You must be about the most buttoned-up person I know, for goodness' sake! You never tell anyone anything!'

'That's not true!'

'It most certainly is! Far be it from me to bring up a delicate subject but you never breathed a word about Lewis to anyone. You didn't even tell Lewis's *son* about Lewis! You never ever *do* breathe a word about your private life! It wouldn't surprise me if you had a galaxy of secret lovers hidden away under the floorboards!'

'Rose,' Katrina said, 'this is so unfair—'

'No, it isn't. If you want to tell me you've split up with Cornelius because he's so odd-looking or because he has no charm or manners or because he has no dress sense or because he's boring, I'd agree with you one hundred per cent, I'd be with you every step of the way. But don't tell me you've split up with him because he's *reserved* because I bet you, you know more about him than he knows about you!'

'That's not true,' said Katrina, 'and this conversation is very silly. I was merely trying to explain why we can't come to dinner on Saturday.'

'Damn! I suppose you could come on your own.'

'I'm afraid I'm busy that night.'

'Why? What are you doing?'

'I'm going on a speed-dating evening.'

'Oh, very funny. Well, if you can't come I'll have to try someone else. Bye now.'

Katrina put the receiver down and put a hand to her flushed cheeks. Then she went to the fridge and took out the bottle of wine.

Over supper—biscuits and cheese (Rose had ruined her appetite), and another glass of wine—Katrina tried to reason her way out of her depression. It was absurd, it was surreal to be so upset about breaking up with a boyfriend who had never been a boyfriend. Come to think of it, it was pretty sad to use such terminology in relation to a man who hadn't been a boy for as long as she hadn't been a girl. Lately, she seemed to spend far too much time mourning the death of a relationship that had never even existed. It was a measure of how pathetic her life had become. It was time to take herself in order and stop being so silly.

Katrina reached for the paper and turned to the political comments page. There was a long article about famous political alliances: Winston Churchill and Lloyd George, Iain Macleod and Edward Heath, Margaret Thatcher and Keith Joseph, Tony Blair and Gordon Brown . . . The last two made her smile: that was another great friendship that had never been a great friendship. She turned the page and read a piece about the advantages and disadvantages of faith schools and then an obituary of a woman professor who had been sustained by her long and happy marriage.

Katrina stood up, cleared away the remains of her supper and went upstairs.

It was an hour later, when she was sitting in bed reading a new book—a biography of Mrs Jordan, mistress of the future William IV and mother of his thirteen children, who was cruelly dumped by him just before he became king—that Katrina started to cry.

It was horrible. She couldn't stop. Great rending sobs that seemed to uproot her insides kept issuing from her, one after the other and when she remembered that the last time she had cried like this had been on the ferry with Cornelius, she cried even more. She got out of bed, collected a box of tissues from her dressing table and climbed back under her duvet. She tried breathing deeply but still the tears came. She only stopped when she was surprised by a knock at her door.

It was Susie, who took one look at her mother and rushed to her side, embracing her fiercely. 'Mum!' she said. 'Mum, don't cry!'

In the presence of such sympathy from a daughter who had been so cruelly wronged,

Katrina started crying all over again, finally managing to gasp, 'I'm sorry I'm such a bad mother!'

Now Susie started crying too and in no time tissues were littering the duvet like snowflakes. Mother and daughter hugged each other and then Katrina blew her nose and said, 'I'm sorry . . . I'm being stupid . . . I'm fine now.'

'Oh, Mum,' said Susie, 'I've been so unhappy!'

'I know,' Katrina nodded her head violently. 'So have I!'

'It's just . . .' Susie paused and bit her lip. 'I've always told you everything and then I find out that Ollie and I have different fathers and his father's Lewis and you never said *anything* and it made me feel like our whole relationship was based on a *lie* and you weren't the person I thought you were at all and you didn't even bother about telling me! It was like . . . like you didn't care about me.'

'Listen, Susie.' Katrina took her daughter's hand and stared at her earnestly. 'The reason why I didn't say anything—why I've *never* said anything—is because I felt so ashamed. Think about it. Your father walks out on me and within weeks I've fallen for a smooth-talking actor who's only interested in a bit of fun and has no intention of having a proper relationship with me. And then, all these years later, he turns up again and this time he's properly in love with my glamorous sister who's never had any trouble getting people to love her. I should have told you, I know I should have told you, but I didn't want you to see me as this poor, plain woman who can never live up to her sister. I know *now* it was wrong not to tell you and I wish to God I had done, and I can't bear you

327

thinking our relationship isn't important to me when it's one of the few things in my life I've been really proud of and . . .' Katrina stopped and groped for yet another tissue.

'Oh, Mum!' Susie pressed her mother's hand. 'And you're not poor and plain! And you *can* keep a man! Ollie and I know about Cornelius. Cam told us ages ago. And we really like him.'

Katrina bit her lip. 'Susie,' she said, 'I have one last confession to make. Cornelius and I do not . . . we aren't . . . There *is* no romance between us. There never has been.'

'But Cam says—'

'When I met Cornelius on the ferry, I had just received a text from Rose. It told me that she had a new lover who was in France with her and his name was Lewis Maltraver. I was upset. I couldn't bear the thought of Rose and Lewis being deliriously soppy together and feeling sorry for me. So . . . so I asked Cornelius if we could pretend we had fallen for each other. Cornelius wasn't very happy about it but he agreed to go along with it. There was . . . There *is* no relationship.'

'But . . .' Susie frowned. 'You seem so good together and it's obvious that Cornelius likes you.'

'He's been very kind.'

'But he came to Rose's party and he's been over to lunch . . . He does like you!'

'He likes you and Ollie,' Katrina said, 'and he felt sorry for me. So,' Katrina raised a watery smile, 'there you are! And meanwhile I've been so involved with all my problems I didn't even notice what was happening to you. I know I've been pig-headed and prejudiced about Ash. Please tell him he is wholly welcome in this house. I take it you are in love with him?'

'I'm not sure,' said Susie. 'After what happened with Liam, I've decided it's best to be a little more . . .'

'Circumspect? Cautious? Careful?'

'All those!' Susie gave Katrina a quick hug and stood up. 'I must go to bed. I have an audition with RADA in the afternoon and I need to go over my words.'

'Oh, Susie, you never told me!'

'I know. I'm sorry. They're letting me jump the first audition stage as I got so far last time. I'm really nervous.'

'I promise to keep my fingers crossed for you. Are you doing the same pieces you did last year?'

'No, I'm doing something from *As You Like It* and then a piece from an Alan Ayckbourn. Ash is taking me out afterwards.'

'Will you ring and let me know how it goes?'

'Of course. But it's going to be weeks before they let me know if I've got through to the next round.' Susie went to the door and paused. 'I'm glad we're friends again. I hate that I made you cry.'

'I love you, Susie.'

'I love you too. No more crying. Goodnight.'

Susie went out and shut the bedroom door softly behind her. Katrina switched off her light, gave a long sigh and drew the duvet up to her chin. Definitely no more crying. She felt as if she had cried enough for a lifetime. It was a relief to have told Susie everything. She had pulled herself out of the sticky mire of deceit into which she had fallen and was once again on firm land. She shut her eyes.

Five seconds later, she opened them again. She

had *not* pulled herself out of the mire. She had *not* told Susie everything. Worse, she had let Susie think she was crying about Susie when in fact she had been crying about . . . She was not even going to think about the person she had been crying about because if she *did* think about that person . . . Katrina rolled over onto her front and buried her face in her pillow.

CHAPTER TWENTY-FOUR

Improved Relations

An unexpected consequence of Cornelius's entanglement with Katrina had been a renewal of communications with his wife. She rang him in September and he was rather taken aback when he heard her voice. He hadn't spoken to her for at least six months.

'Cornelius,' she said. 'How are you?'

Cornelius was so surprised, he had to sit down. 'I'm well,' he said and then, when she didn't speak, he added, 'How are *you*?'

'I'm well. I'm very well.' There was a pause and then a hurried, 'I'm feeling a little *guilty*, actually. An old friend rang me out of the blue and suggested lunch and she told me you were going out with her sister . . . which I'm very happy about.'

Cornelius had no idea what she was talking about and was about to tell her so when he remembered Katrina. He should, of course, tell Lucy that he was *not* 'going out' with Katrina but he had a strong sense that such a denial would be disloyal to

330

Katrina. On the other hand, he also felt that he was being disloyal to Lucy by not telling her the truth. He compromised by saying nothing at all.

'The thing is,' Lucy said, 'I was always a bit in awe of Margaret—'

'I'm sorry,' said Cornelius, 'but who is Margaret?'

'She's changed her name now, I don't know why. She's called Rose these days. At school she was always so popular and confident. I suppose I was flattered that she'd got in touch with me. And she's great fun. You met her, of course, in France.'

'I did,' said Cornelius. 'And I agree with you. She is certainly confident.'

'Anyway, she took me to a very expensive restaurant and we had some lovely wine and I probably drank too much, particularly since it was in the middle of the day, and we got talking about you, and I think I may have given her the impression . . . I think it's possible I might have sounded rather cross and resentful when speaking about you and I felt bad afterwards, but Margaret—I mean, Rose—was so understanding and sympathetic, and you know how it is when . . . Well, you probably don't know, Cornelius, but most normal people find sympathy is a little like chocolate or tobacco: once you get a taste of it, you want some more, and, if I'm absolutely honest, it was very nice talking to someone who wanted to *listen* to how I felt . . .'

Lucy's voice, initially so crestfallen, had risen to a pugnacious crescendo and Cornelius said quickly, 'Lucy, I quite understand. I don't mind what you said. I'm sure I deserved everything you said about me.'

'Well, I must say,' said Lucy, her voice reverting

331

to its previous softness, 'I think you *do* but I don't want you to think I was trying to . . . to sabotage your new relationship by speaking out of turn.'

'Of course I don't.'

'It's just . . . Well, it was nice to talk to someone about . . . about Leo.'

She waited for him to respond and Cornelius wanted to respond, he really did, and he could tell by the careful manner in which she had voiced that last word, that she wanted him to say something and that, if he did, everything that had gone wrong between them might begin to go right. But he couldn't, he couldn't say anything, and so he was silent.

Lucy gave a little sigh and then she said brightly, 'So! Are you going to tell me anything about her?'

'Who?' asked Cornelius.

'Your new lady, of course! Really, Cornelius, you are so obtuse sometimes!'

'Oh. Well,' Cornelius said cautiously, 'it's early days, you know.'

'You're hopeless,' Lucy said, but she sounded quite good-humoured. 'You always were. I've never been able to work out whether it's because you don't like talking about personal relationships, particularly *your* personal relationships, or whether it's because you don't actually find them very interesting.'

'I'm sorry,' Cornelius said. 'I'm a dull sort of person, I'm afraid.'

'No,' said Lucy, 'you're infuriating but you aren't dull. I wish you'd come back to the house sometime and let me cook you a meal. You won't, though, will you?'

'Ah, well, I don't know . . .'

'I do. I wish I could do *something* for you. It doesn't seem right that I'm living in our lovely house in Wimbledon while you're holed up in a grotty little hovel in Clapham.'

'Clapham is a perfectly decent place and it is not a hovel, it is a flat—'

'It's a *hovel*. Michael told me.'

'Michael?'

'Your nephew Michael, who helped you move in? I still do talk to your family, you know. Michael says your place is hideous and depressing.'

Cornelius looked round at his sitting room/dining room and tried to see it through the eyes of Michael and Lucy. They would not approve of the grey linoleum or the threadbare orange rug that lay across it like an ineffective toupee. Neither would they like the white plastic table on which he ate his meals or the mottled green chair on which he was currently sitting.

'I'm happy here,' he said firmly.

'I wish I could help you in some way. I'm feeling guilty again.'

'Well,' Cornelius said slowly, 'perhaps you *could* do something. Katrina has a daughter, a lovely girl who is dead set on being an actress. She's waitressing while trying to get into drama school. It occurs to me that you might have some contacts . . . I don't know how these things work . . .'

'My contacts aren't what they were,' Lucy said, 'but I'll certainly see what I can do. I'll ring you if anything comes up.'

'Thank you,' Cornelius said.

'Are we friends, Cornelius? We are friends, aren't we?'

'We are very good friends,' Cornelius assured

333

her.

'Goodbye, then,' Lucy said and rang off before Cornelius could say goodbye back to her.

He stared at the rug for a few minutes. He was trying to work out why he felt no shame in deceiving her about Katrina. It dawned on him that he didn't actually feel he *had* deceived her. He did feel—he very strongly felt—that he was indeed 'going out' with Katrina, the only slight area of difficulty being that Katrina was unaware of this state of affairs. He sighed, picked up his guitar, arranged his fingers with care and began practising the first few bars of Del Shannon's 'Runaway'.

*   *   *

Two weeks later, Lucy rang again. 'Cornelius! You owe me big time! I've got an audition for your girlfriend's daughter! It's for a tiny part in a new sci-fi film. They want a nice young girl to play a dental nurse who gets taken over by aliens. If you're interested, I can email you the details.'

'I am *very* interested,' Cornelius said. 'You are a very kind woman.'

'I'm glad to be of help. Tell her not to get too excited. There will be dozens of other would-be dental nurses. How are things going with Katrina?'

'Oh, well, you know,' Cornelius shifted uneasily in his chair. 'It's—'

'It's early days, I know! Cornelius, let's meet for lunch. I'll treat you. What are you doing on the twenty-first?'

'Nothing, but I assure you, you don't have to treat me.'

'I want to. I've just received a very nice cheque

for my loo advert. We can go to the Japanese restaurant in Wimbledon. And I promise I won't interrogate you about Katrina.'

Cornelius smiled. 'Can I have that in writing?'

When he finally came off the phone, Cornelius felt an unaccustomed lightness of spirit. For months he had been haunted by his last meeting with Lucy and the recurring image of her face crumpling while he had stood there unable to say anything to comfort her. Who would have thought that they had just had a protracted, cheerful and affectionate conversation together? It was a minor miracle.

When he arrived at the restaurant, Lucy was waiting for him. She was looking particularly lovely today. Her blonde hair seemed to float around her and she was wearing a dress that seemed to be similarly insubstantial and ethereal. She reminded him of one of those dandelion clocks he used to blow to smithereens. Not that he wanted to blow Lucy to smithereens.

'You look marvellous,' he said.

'So do you,' Lucy said, 'though I wish you'd get rid of that old jacket, it's falling apart.'

'I like my old jacket, it's comfortable.'

'It looks like you slept in it. Would you like some wine? I know you hate waiting ages for your food so I came here especially early. I've ordered the Maki Yuki special: deep-fried sushi of eel and snapper.'

Cornelius poured out the wine and studied the label. 'Lucy, this is expensive.'

'It's on me. You wouldn't believe how much money I'm making from one little advert *and* I've now been offered another one for disinfectant.'

335

'Disinfectant,' he murmured. 'Well done.'

'I've never earned so much for doing so little. That's one of the things I want to talk to you about.'

'What? The money you're making?'

'Sort of. I've done a lot of thinking since our last phone call and I feel—I do really feel—I'm ready to sell the house now.'

'Lucy,' Cornelius said, 'there's no need. I told you—as far as I'm concerned, you can stay there for ever if that's what you want.'

'I know. And I thought . . . I thought that's what I did want. But now . . . I think now it's healthier if I move on. I don't need that big house and I . . . I feel . . .' She pushed back her hair. 'I know you don't like talking about the past but . . .'

Cornelius felt the old panic forcing its way up to his throat. He managed to say, 'No . . . I would rather we didn't.'

'I was only going to say that I realize now I don't need . . . I don't need to be surrounded by . . . by what we used to have. So I have arranged for estate agents to come round on Monday. And when we've sold the house, perhaps you will move out of your revolting hovel and get yourself a proper place.'

'I've said all this before: the house belongs to you.'

'It belongs to both of us. As for the furniture—'

'I don't want anything. I don't want *anything* from the house.'

'All right. That's fine. But when I sell it, we share the proceeds. I won't argue about this so let's not say any more about it.' She smiled. 'I saw Margaret yesterday.'

'Who's Margaret?'

'Oh, really, Cornelius, do you listen to anything I say? Margaret is Rose!'

'Oh, yes. It's very confusing. Why on earth did she change her name?'

'You've asked me that before. I've no idea. Anyway, she was in a terrible state.'

'Was she?' Cornelius took a sip of his wine. It was very good. 'I imagine Rose gets into a terrible state quite often.'

Lucy laughed. 'That's not entirely fair. If I found out that my boyfriend was the father of my sister's son, I think I'd be upset too.'

Cornelius had been checking out the meal on the next-door table. Now, he directed his entire concentration on his wife. 'I'm sorry,' he said, 'but can you repeat what you just said? I don't understand.'

'Oh, lord!' Lucy bit her lip. 'I assumed you would . . . I'm sorry. Forget I said anything.'

'I can't. Are you telling me Lewis is Ollie's father?'

'Cornelius, I'm so sorry. It didn't occur to me that Katrina wouldn't have told you. I promise I'd never have . . . Are you very upset?'

Cornelius nodded. 'Yes. I'm pretty sure I am. If you could meet Ollie . . . You would like him very much. I can't understand how he can be the son of Lewis. I suppose he's a very good argument for the nurture over nature debate.'

'It doesn't worry you that Katrina has said nothing to you about this?'

'I think she did try to,' Cornelius said, 'in a rather oblique sort of way. But, no, it doesn't worry me. Why on earth *should* she tell me?'

'Well, if you're not worried, I suppose it doesn't matter, but . . .' Lucy began and then stopped as the waiter arrived. 'Here's our food!'

Cornelius said nothing as the food was served. He stared at his shoe and frowned.

Lucy waited until the waiter had left them and then asked, 'What are you thinking about?'

Cornelius sighed. 'I was trying to imagine myself as a woman,' he said. 'And I was wondering what I would feel if Lewis made advances to me, and I honestly think he would leave me cold.'

Lucy smiled. 'Oh, Cornelius,' she said, 'I do miss you sometimes!'

'Thank you,' said Cornelius. 'I don't see what's so funny, though.'

'Cornelius, if you were a woman, there is still no way Lewis Maltraver would ever want to chat you up!'

'I'm sure he wouldn't but, if he *did*, I would most definitely repel his advances.'

'I'm glad to hear that but I don't think it's ever going to be something you have to worry about.'

'Did *you* ever come across Lewis?'

'Years ago I met him at a party. He was mildly flirtatious.'

'Did you find him attractive?'

'I suppose so, but I wasn't interested. I was madly in love with someone else.'

'Really? Who was that?'

'Funnily enough, it was you.'

'Oh,' said Cornelius, trying not to look pleased.

'I do remember he had a wonderful way of making me feel as if I were the only woman in the world he wanted to talk to.'

'I have to say,' Cornelius said, 'speaking as

someone who is totally unprejudiced, I find him a rather loathsome creep. The funny thing is, Ollie doesn't look anything like him.'

'That's what Margaret—I mean, Rose—said. Apparently, Lewis took her down to Surrey to meet his mother and there was a picture of his great-grandmother, and Rose said she took one look at her and guessed the truth. Of course she was stunned and then it all came out that Lewis and Katrina had once had a short-lived liaison. And so Rose marched round to confront Katrina . . .'

'Poor Katrina.'

'Well, yes, but I think you should have some sympathy for Rose. Why didn't Katrina tell her what had happened?'

'Why should she? It was nothing to do with Rose.'

'It's nothing to do with Rose that her nephew turns out to be the son of her boyfriend? I know your aversion to gossip, Cornelius, but there is a difference between gossip and profound truths.'

'There is nothing profound about Lewis,' Cornelius said grimly.

'Well, we're not going to agree about this so let's change the subject. How's your sushi?'

'It's very good.' He fixed her with a careful scrutiny. 'You really are looking very well.'

'I'm feeling well.' She eyed him intently. 'I have a boyfriend.'

Cornelius strove for an appropriate response. 'Well!' he said and then, sensing disappointment, elaborated a little. 'Well, well!'

'Do you want to know what he's like?'

'I certainly do.'

'He's younger than me. He's seven years younger. And he's not really a boyfriend yet. He asked me out a month ago and I said no, and then I thought about him a little more and I thought: why not? So I rang him and we went out to dinner.'

'Where did you go?'

'A little Persian café near Marble Arch. He's nice. Of course it's . . .'

'Early days? I hope it works out for you.'

'Do you?' Lucy asked. 'You don't mind at all?'

Cornelius put his head to one side and considered. 'I don't mind,' he said.

Lucy gave a rather tight smile. 'Good.'

'Perhaps,' Cornelius corrected himself, 'I mind a little.'

'Cornelius,' Lucy said, 'you're a rotten liar.'

*   *   *

A few days later, Cornelius got an email from Katrina to say that Susie had won the part of the dental nurse. This was good news but the tone of the email was flat and low-key and he wondered if she was still pining for Lewis. He wished he had the confidence to drive round and see her. He enjoyed the Sunday lunches with her and her children but the thought of being a sort of Uncle Cornelius figure was somewhat depressing. Yet again, Cornelius wished he possessed even a little of Lewis's expertise. Before his marriage, any relationships he had had with women had seemed to happen almost by chance. He needed advice from someone who knew about women.

Of all his friends, Edward was not the most

obviously suited for this role. True, he had been married for thirty years now, but it had to be said that it was not the sort of marriage to provoke many envious sighs. Miranda was a serious lady who had written a number of books on sexual dysfunction and was a counsellor specializing in sexual problems. According to Edward, she kept a notebook in which she awarded her husband marks every time he displayed courtesy or sensitivity. Every time he chalked up twenty points, Miranda allowed him to have sex with her. As a result, Edward was invariably courteous and sensitive. Unfortunately, Miranda subtracted marks every time he left an unnecessary light on or brought mud into the house or displayed behaviour that was disrespectful to the domestic environment. Since Edward was not blessed with a great memory, moments of sexual bliss were frustratingly infrequent.

On the other hand, Edward had a secondary career as a folk singer of deeply romantic love songs. His voice could melt even the hardest heart. So when Edward rang to tell him he had a forthcoming engagement in a pub in Greenwich, Cornelius decided to confide in him.

'Edward,' he said, 'I've made friends with a lady called Katrina.'

'Katrina? That's a good, strong name.'

'That's what I think,' Cornelius said, encouraged by his friend's perspicacity. 'The thing is, we've become good friends. I've met her children. They're both exceptional.'

'Have you met her husband?'

'She doesn't *have* a husband, she's divorced. I've been to Sunday lunch with her twice.'

341

'Is she a good cook?'

'She is a fantastic cook but that's irrelevant.'

'You only say that,' Edward said sadly, 'because you have never been married to a woman who can't cook.'

'The point is,' Cornelius said, 'I need to know how I can move from the good-friend level to the . . . to the more-than-good-friend level.'

'Oh,' said Edward, 'that's easy.'

'Is it?'

'Invite her to my folk evening. Every time I sing, "You Are the Key to My Door" people fall in love.'

Edward spoke with such conviction that, despite himself, Cornelius was impressed. As soon as he put the phone down, he fired off an email to Katrina.

Katrina replied that she had to go to a work do that night. Instead she invited him to yet another Sunday lunch. It was painfully clear that Katrina had no interest in exploring any other levels. In time, he thought, he would learn to be happy with just her friendship. For the time being he was relieved that he could genuinely turn down her invitation since his sister had already invited him down to her house in Sussex. To be exact, she had invited him and Katrina, but Cornelius, aware of her discomfort at his mother's party, had not even thought of passing on the invitation.

Cornelius had only been in his sister's house for one hour when Juliet said for the third time that she was so sorry Katrina couldn't come with him. Cornelius decided to speak out and bring to an end any further speculation about his mythical love life. He told Juliet and Alec that he and

Katrina were no longer seeing each other and that he would rather not talk about it. Not for the first time he was grateful to his brother-in-law, who interrupted Juliet's immediate enquiry for more information with a long and very funny story about their neighbour's attempts to sabotage their son's latest relationship with a soft-porn actress.

For the next week, he was moderately successful in putting her out of his mind. His big mistake was to go to Edward's folk evening. He sat beside Edward's son, Jasper, a nice young man with strong political views. Tonight, however, Jasper had brought along his new girlfriend and had eyes only for her. As she had eyes only for Jasper, conversation with them was difficult. And then, when Edward sang 'You Are the Key to My Door' Cornelius felt such a longing for Katrina that he could concentrate on nothing else. The fact that he was just a few minutes away from Katrina's house was too tempting. Surely she'd be back from her work meeting by now. As soon as he could, he made his excuses and left. He had to see her, he had to at least try to explain what he felt.

It was only when he stopped the car outside her house that the thought occurred to him that it was a little late for a visit. Still, there were lights on and what he wished to say would not take long.

He walked up the path, took a deep breath and rang the doorbell. What exactly *was* he going to say? He felt as if his vocal chords had set in concrete. Then, suddenly, the door was opened and there stood Katrina. She looked different but he couldn't work out why.

'Cornelius,' she said. 'What are you doing here?'

She didn't look particularly pleased to see him.

Cornelius swallowed and squared his shoulders. 'I know it's very late,' he said, 'but I was driving past and I saw your lights on and I thought you might still be up. I hope you don't mind . . .'

Katrina looked as if she *did* mind. She said, 'No, it's just that at this precise momen—'

And then Lewis sauntered into the hall from the sitting room, looking as if he owned the place. 'Hello, Cornelius,' he said. Most of the buttons on his shirt were undone and he had a smirk on his face that made Cornelius itch to hit him.

Katrina had no shoes on. She was wearing her black party dress and what he now realized was an intimidating amount of rather smudged eye make-up. There were flowers in the hall and when she turned to Lewis and told him to go back to the sitting room, Cornelius glanced at the note perched on top of the bouquet: 'I want my slippers back xxx'

Katrina turned back to Cornelius. Her face had gone pink and she sounded acutely embarrassed as she said, 'I'm afraid, Cornelius, this isn't a very suitable time.'

'No,' said Cornelius, 'I can see that it isn't. I think, no, I *know* that I would rather not see you any more. Goodbye, Katrina.'

He turned on his heels, walked away from her as fast as he could and climbed into his car. As he drove away, he put on the windscreen wipers and it was a few seconds before he realized it was his eyes not his screen that needed wiping.

CHAPTER TWENTY-FIVE

An Unexpected Visitor

It was not the end of the world. A few months earlier he had not even known of Katrina's existence. He had been fine. He would be fine. All right, at the moment he felt as if Katrina had shone a torch on his world, revealing for the first time the dank and empty cave in which he lived. Once the memory of that light faded—and fade it would—he would readjust, learn to see again in the dark. He would be fine. He knew what he had to do. It was very simple: live one day at a time, concentrate on simple objectives until everything was settled once more.

It was not easy. He had agreed to meet his niece at Tate Modern on Saturday. He was early and wandered around the rooms, and every picture he looked at seemed to connect him to Katrina. The Bonnard painting with its jolly pink-chequered tablecloth reminded him of Katrina's own warm and welcoming kitchen. A Picasso painting of flowers recalled the roses on her sideboard. The Rothko canvases with their vast, uncompromising slabs of colour seemed to echo uncannily his state of mind. One particular painting, a dark-red rectangle, was a perfect representation of his jealousy of Lewis. He remembered the note on the flowers in Katrina's hall. He could imagine Lewis leaning forward seductively to lend Katrina his slippers. Knowing Lewis, they would probably be shiny black slip-ons. Cornelius gritted his teeth and strode out onto the balcony. He gazed out at the Thames and forced the slipper image from his mind, only for it to be instantly replaced by a memory of the drive back from Rose's party and his barely controlled urge to take her in his arms and kiss her.

It was all right. It would be all right.

On Tuesday he was working in his office when his secretary came in and said his niece wished to see him. 'Tell her to come through,' Cornelius said, mildly curious as to the reason for her visit.

When the door opened again, Cornelius looked up and frowned. Instead of Jenny, there was a blonde young woman in a short black skirt, shiny black ankle boots and a shocking-pink jacket. He tried to remember where he had seen her before.

'I *am* a niece,' the girl assured him, 'it's just that I'm Katrina's niece. I wasn't sure you'd let me in if I told you who I was. And then as soon as I said it, I thought that you might not even *have* a niece. I take it you do have one?'

'Yes,' said Cornelius. He remembered her now. She was Rose's daughter.

'Can I sit down?' Cam pulled up a chair without waiting for his response. 'It took ages to find you. No one in Dulwich seems to have heard of you. I can't imagine how you sell any wine.'

Cornelius glanced very deliberately at his watch. 'Most of our customers are hotels and restaurants.'

'Really?' Cam crossed her legs. 'I'll come straight to the point. I've come to see you about Katrina.'

Cornelius stiffened. 'I'm afraid I'm a little busy at the moment. In fact, I'm extremely busy. So I really don't have time to—'

'I won't be very long. My mother rang her last

night and Katrina said you and she had stopped seeing each other. I wanted to tell you, you're making a big mistake.'

Cornelius straightened his back. 'I don't wish to be rude but—'

'Yes, you do,' Cam said. 'You'd like to be very rude. You think it's nothing to do with me, but you're wrong. I'm the reason why you walked out on my aunt.'

'I assure you that—'

'I was there,' Cam said baldly. 'I was in the kitchen. I heard everything.'

Cornelius gave her a startled glance and leant forward. 'I'm sorry, I don't quite follow you. You were in the house on Friday evening? I don't understand.'

'I don't expect you do. If you *had* understood, you wouldn't have stormed out of the house like that. You thought Aunty Katty—God, I must stop calling her that!—you thought Katrina was about to embark on a night of passion with Lewis Maltraver.'

Cornelius couldn't speak. He picked up the red pencil on top of his in-tray, gripped it fiercely and nodded at the girl.

'Actually,' she said, 'you were almost right apart from one small detail. Katrina had only come in a couple of minutes before you. I was the one who was about to set sail with Lewis.'

Cornelius stared at her blankly. He was listening to her with obsessive concentration but nothing she said made any sense.

'It's not something I'm proud of,' Cam said. She tossed her hair back from her face. Her tone was calm and conversational and she seemed to be entirely unconcerned by what she was telling him. 'My mother had behaved badly to me and I wanted to get my own back. It was silly, but there you are. We're all silly sometimes, aren't we? I was staying at Katrina's for a couple of nights. We were doing a fashion shoot in Greenwich. I had the house to myself. Katrina was staying the night in Essex on some working weekend jaunt and my cousins had gone to see their father in Croydon. It seemed a good opportunity . . .'

Cornelius was still bewildered. 'A good opportunity for what?'

'A good opportunity for seduction. I wanted to seduce Lewis.' Her mouth twitched slightly. 'There! I've shocked you, haven't I?'

'No,' said Cornelius, 'I'm finding it a little difficult to follow, that's all . . . You set out to seduce Lewis?'

'Yes, and I would have done too if Katrina hadn't come back.'

'I don't doubt that for a moment.'

Cam gave a faint smile. 'That's what Katrina said! The trouble is she *did* come back.'

Cornelius cleared his throat. 'Would you mind telling me why?'

'One of her work friends had a husband who died or something . . . No, he didn't die but he was rushed to hospital, and so she and Katrina left the hotel and Katrina drove her back to London to the hospital and then she came on to Greenwich and found Lewis and me in the sitting room. Katrina was furious with both of us.'

'Was she?' Cornelius smiled faintly and gripped the edge of the table with his hands, fearing that, if he didn't hold on to it, he would jump up and

348

embrace this charming young girl who, with a few words, had shot down the dark cloud of despair that had so recently engulfed him. 'That must have been awkward for you,' he said.

'It wasn't the best moment of my life,' she agreed. 'Poor Lewis was *so* embarrassed. I felt quite sorry for him. Katrina told me she wanted to talk to him, so I went off to the kitchen. I've never seen my aunt look like that before. She actually quite scared me. I heard you come and I heard you leave and then I heard Lewis leave and then Katrina came into the kitchen and we drank some tea and talked about me and Mum and Lewis.'

'I see,' said Cornelius.

'I hope you do. Knowing my aunt, she's unlikely to come over here herself and explain to you what really happened and I don't want to be responsible for wrecking her love life. That's why I'm here. Katrina is different from my mother and me. We're not very nice people. Katrina is. I'd have thought you'd have understood that.' She stood up. 'If I were you, I'd get over there quick and start grovelling.'

Cornelius pushed back his chair. He walked over to Cam and held out his hand. 'Thank you *very* much for coming to see me. It was good of you to take the time and the trouble. I don't agree with you on one matter. I think you *are* a very nice person.'

Cam's face went a little pink and she suddenly looked a lot younger. 'Thank you,' she said. 'I hope you sort everything out.' She shook his hand and walked out of the room.

Cornelius stood for a few moments and then pushed his hands through his hair. 'Oh, my God,' he said aloud, 'what have I done?'

* * *

At half past six, Cornelius strode up the path to Katrina's house. He carried a very good bottle of wine with him. As he pressed the bell, he cursed himself for his ineptitude. He should have brought flowers.

Ollie answered the door and gave him a welcoming grin. 'Hi, Cornelius, I didn't know you were coming round. I'm going to see the Zutons next week. Have you bought a ticket?'

'No,' said Cornelius. 'No, I haven't.'

'I've only just got in myself. Come on in. I'm making a cup of tea. Do you want one?'

'No. Thank you.' Cornelius followed Ollie down to the kitchen. How odd to think that only a few days ago he had stood in Tate Modern thinking about this room, and here he was, in it again. It seemed a lifetime since he had last been here.

'Mum won't be long,' Ollie said. 'She's usually back by now.'

Cornelius put his bottle on the table and sat down. 'How is she?'

'She was in a terrible mood this morning. She said she had a headache.'

'I'm sorry to hear that.' Cornelius watched Ollie fish a tea bag from his mug. 'How are *you*?' he asked.

Ollie gave a despondent shrug. 'I'm all right.'

'You don't sound all right.'

Ollie poured a little milk into his mug. 'I'm really keen on this girl. Did I tell you about her? She's called Sophie. And we're very good friends but it's impossible to tell her that I really like her, and we keep seeing each other and *nothing happens*. I think I'm just going to stop seeing her. It's a bit depressing.'

'May I offer you some advice?'

'Feel free.'

'Tell her what you feel. Nothing will happen unless you tell her. Ring her. Tell her you want to take her out to dinner. Be direct. Be honest. Be brave. *That* is what you should do.'

Ollie looked slightly taken aback by Cornelius's enthusiasm. 'Do you think so?' he asked uncertainly. 'It could be really embarrassing.'

'Sometimes,' Cornelius said, as much to himself as to Ollie, 'you have to risk embarrassment. Look at Galileo or Darwin or Copernicus. Do you think they'd have ever changed the world if they'd worried about looking stupid?'

'That's true,' agreed Ollie. 'And there's Newton. I bet he had to put up with loads of jokes about apples falling on his head when he discovered gravity.'

'I don't know that he did,' Cornelius mused. 'All his peers knew he was incredibly clever. His own professor at Cambridge resigned his chair when Newton was only twenty-seven and insisted he should have it in his place.'

'I wonder if Newton had problems with women,' Ollie said gloomily.

'I rather think . . .' began Cornelius and promptly forgot what it was he did think because he heard the sound of the front door being opened.

'Mum!' Ollie called. 'We're in the kitchen!'

A few seconds later, there she was and when she saw Cornelius she went bright red and just said,

'Oh!'

His face felt like it was on fire. He stood up and said, 'Hello.'

Ollie took a package from his mother's hand. 'You've bought a new book,' he said. He pulled it out of its bag and turned it over. 'Noam Chomsky! Sophie likes Noam Chomsky!'

For a moment, Katrina's eyes met those of Cornelius and then she turned back to Ollie and said carelessly, 'I needed something to read.'

Ollie put the book down. 'I'll be back in a moment,' he said, 'I want to make a phone call. The kettle's just boiled if you want a cup of tea.' He went to the door and smiled at Cornelius. 'Wish me luck!'

'I'm sure you don't need it.'

Katrina, having taken off her jacket, had been paying great attention to folding it neatly. Now she put it on one of the stools before looking enquiringly at Cornelius. 'What's that all about?' she asked. 'Why does Ollie need luck?'

'He's going to ring Sophie, I think.'

'He's always ringing Sophie.' Katrina went to the fridge. 'I need something stronger than tea,' she said. She pulled out a bottle of white wine and said, 'There are glasses over there.'

Cornelius got the glasses and watched her open the wine. She poured out their drinks and took up her glass. 'I must say that I'm a little surprised to see you,' she said. 'I seem to remember you said you never wanted to see me again.'

Cornelius stood at the other end of the island from her. 'I wish I could tell you,' he said carefully, 'that I worked out on my own how stupid . . . and . . . offensive I have been. In fact, I've had help.

Your niece visited me this afternoon.'

'Cam?' Katrina gave him a startled glance. 'Cam came to see you?'

'Yes. She wanted me to know about her plan to—er—seduce Lewis, and your own subsequent intervention. She thought I might have got the wrong idea.'

'And did you?'

'Katrina, I know better than most people how strong your feelings are for Lewis. On the boat—'

'Cornelius, I did not weep copiously on the boat because I was madly in love with Lewis. The reason I was crying . . . There's something you don't know—'

Cornelius waved an impatient hand. 'You mean about Ollie being Lewis's son. I know all that.'

'What? *How* do you know that? Did Ollie tell you?'

'No. Rose told Lucy. Lucy told me.'

'I see. You never said anything.'

'Of course I didn't. It was none of my business.'

'Oh.' Katrina was silent for a moment. 'I wish you *had* said something. I so wanted to talk to you about it. I've spent too many years regretting the fact that I lied about Ollie's father. I always thought I'd get found out in the end. When I got that text on the boat, I felt like everything was falling apart. I wasn't jealous about Rose being with Lewis . . . No, that's not quite true. I *was* jealous, I was jealous that she'd found an attractive man to love her.' She gave a short laugh. 'I don't know why I'm telling you all this. As you so rightly said, none of this is any of your business.'

Cornelius cleared his throat. Take a risk, Cornelius, remember what you said to Ollie.

353

Remember Darwin and all those others. 'Katrina,' he said, 'I've been jealous as hell of Lewis.'

'*Jealous?*' The word shot out of her mouth and before Cornelius could work out if she was shocked or disgusted or just surprised or even sympathetic, Ollie rushed in and seized Cornelius's hands in his.

'It worked! You were right! You are brilliant! I said to her, "Look, Sophie, I'm fed up with being a friend to you and I can't do this any longer. I want to be more than friends and it's driving me crazy," and then I couldn't think of anything else to say, and then . . . Do you know what she said?'

Cornelius dragged his eyes away from Katrina. 'I have no idea.'

'She said, "You took your time!" Can you imagine? So then I said, "Wait there. I'm coming over and I'm taking you out to dinner!" and she said, "Good," and then she rang off! Can you believe it? I'm going to put on a clean shirt, I'll be back in a minute!'

'Take as long as you like,' Cornelius said. '*Please* take as long as you like.'

Ollie waved and disappeared up the stairs, singing, 'All You Need is Love'.

'Well,' Cornelius said, 'that's nice.'

'That's very nice,' Katrina said. 'Cornelius, what was it you said just now?'

Cornelius felt slightly sick. 'I'm not sure I have the nerve to say it again.'

Katrina glanced up at him. 'I wish you would.'

'I said I've been jealous as hell of Lewis.'

Katrina gave a small sigh. 'You *did* say that! I can't believe you said that!' She put down her glass. 'When your sister emailed me and told me you'd announced the end of our "relationship", I thought you didn't want to be friends with me any more.'

'I didn't,' Cornelius said. 'At the risk of imitating your son, I was fed up with being your friend. I think I've loved you ever since I watched you struggling with that terrible tongue we ate in France.'

Katrina's eyes were shiny with tears. She bit her lip. 'I've been so unhappy since Friday. I thought you despised me.'

Cornelius put down his glass and went over to her. 'Katrina,' he said, 'I'm mad about you.' He lowered his head, raised her chin with his hand and kissed her. And then, because it was so wonderful, he kissed her again.

'Do you know something?' Katrina murmured. 'I do wish Lewis was here!'

Cornelius stared at her aghast. 'Why?'

'He said he could sense we had no sexual chemistry. What do you think?'

For an answer, Cornelius kissed her again and would have happily gone on doing so for ever if Katrina hadn't broken away and exclaimed, 'Oh, dear, this is terrible!'

'I'm sorry,' Cornelius said. 'I thought—'

'You don't understand! Susie was so hurt when she discovered I'd not told the truth about Ollie and Lewis. I've virtually promised I will always tell her the truth from now on. I told her there was no romance between you and me . . . And now . . . here we are . . . and she'll think I've been telling whoppers all over again!'

'No problem,' said Cornelius. He felt at this moment as if he could solve every problem in the

355

world. 'You can tell her the whole truth and nothing but the truth. You can tell her I came over here and proclaimed my love for you and that I persuaded you to give me a chance.'

'That's no good,' Katrina said vehemently. 'I have to . . .' She stopped as Ollie flew into the kitchen again, with his unbuttoned shirt flapping around him.

'I need some advice,' he said, doing up his shirt buttons and apparently oblivious to the fact that Cornelius had his arms round his mother. 'I'm going round to Sophie's now. I have twenty-two pounds. Where can I take her out for a romantic dinner for not more than twenty-two pounds?'

Cornelius reached into his jacket pocket and pulled out his wallet. He extracted eight ten-pound notes and gave them to Ollie. 'Be my guest,' he said. 'Take her anywhere. Go anywhere. I'm trying to tell your mother I love her.'

'Oh,' said Ollie. He gave them both a broad grin. 'I thought you'd done that ages ago. Are you *sure* I can have all this? It's an awful lot of money . . .'

'Ollie,' said Cornelius, 'if you don't go now, I might take it back.'

'I'm going!' promised Ollie. 'Thanks a lot! Have a good evening!'

Katrina waited until she heard the front door slam and then looked at Cornelius severely. 'You gave him far too much money.'

'It was worth it. Why can't you tell Susie what I said? It's the truth.'

'No, it isn't. That's the trouble.'

'It isn't?'

'No,' said Katrina. She reached up to stroke his face with her hand. 'You didn't have to persuade me to give you a chance. That's the whole point. You didn't have to persuade me at all. I love you, Cornelius, I absolutely love you.'

Cornelius was glad that the telephone rang at that precise moment. To be the recipient of such life-transforming information was almost too much to bear.

Katrina murmured, 'Damn,' and picked up the handset. 'Susie!' she said. 'How funny—I was just talking about you! . . . What? . . . Oh, wow, that's amazing! . . . Will you tell Ash I am truly, truly grateful? . . . Darling, that's the most wonderful early Christmas present, thank you! . . . What? . . . Yes, that's a good idea, I will ask him. He's here now, as it happens. In fact, I wanted to tell you . . . What? . . . Oh, all right, I'll speak to you later. Be sure to tell Ash . . . Fine . . . Goodbye now!'

She put the phone down and looked at Cornelius with shining eyes. 'That was Susie,' she said. 'And you'll never guess! Ash has got hold of two tickets to a Jarvis Cocker concert at the Roundhouse in Camden on December the sixteenth!'

'Jarvis Cocker?' Cornelius queried.

Katrina laughed. 'Don't tell me that a man who knows all about the Zutons has never heard of Jarvis Cocker! He is the greatest singer and songwriter in the world! And Ash has got two tickets and he and Susie are giving them to me! And do you know what Susie suggested? She said I ought to ask you to come with me. Will you?'

Cornelius took her hand. It seemed to him she had never looked so beautiful. 'I'd go to anything with you,' he said, 'anything at all.'

'You'll like Jarvis Cocker,' Katrina said. 'Jarvis Cocker is gorgeous.'

'I *have* heard of him,' Cornelius said.

'I should jolly well think so.'

'I've seen photos of him. I wouldn't say he's gorgeous.' Cornelius felt a twinge of jealousy. 'I would say he looks rather peculiar.'

Katrina laughed. 'You do realize,' she said, 'that you look just like him?'

'No, I don't!' Cornelius said. 'Do I?'

'You're better-looking.' Katrina said. She put her arms round his waist and looked up into his eyes and as Cornelius bent to kiss her again he knew that for the first time in what seemed like for ever, he was quite happy, in fact he was *very* happy, in fact he was *completely* happy to be Cornelius Coriolanus Hedge.